# SURVIVING
# ICE

## ALSO BY K.A. TUCKER

# SURVIVING ICE

## A Novel

## K.A. TUCKER

**ATRIA** PAPERBACK

NEW YORK   LONDON   TORONTO   SYDNEY   NEW DELHI

**ATRIA** PAPERBACK
An Imprint of Simon & Schuster, Inc.
1230 Avenue of the Americas
New York, NY 10020

First Atria Paperback edition October 2015

**ATRIA** PAPERBACK and colophon are trademarks of Simon & Schuster, Inc.

For information about special discounts for bulk purchases, please contact Simon & Schuster Special Sales at 1-866-506-1949 or business@simonandschuster.com.

The Simon & Schuster Speakers Bureau can bring authors to your live event. For more information or to book an event, contact the Simon & Schuster Speakers Bureau at 1-866-248-3049 or visit our website at www.simonspeakers.com.

Cover design by Anna Dorfman
Cover photographs © Felix Hug/The Image Bank/Getty Images (woman), Terry W. Ryder/Shutterstock (building), Anna Maltseva/Shutterstock (tattoos)

Manufactured in the United States of America

10  9  8  7  6  5  4  3

Library of Congress Cataloging-in-Publication Data

Tucker, K. A. (Kathleen A.).
  Surviving ice : a novel / K.A. Tucker. — First Atria Paperback edition.
    pages ; cm
  I. Title.
  PR9199.4.T834S87 2015
  813'.6—dc23

                              2015030790

ISBN 978-1-4767-7425-1
ISBN 978-1-4767-7427-5 (ebook)

*To Lia and Sadie*

Ice is beautiful and enticing;
cold and hard and uncompromising.

# ONE

# IVY

Ned pauses to stretch his neck and roll his right shoulder once . . . twice . . . before lifting the needle to his customer's arm again, humming along with Willie Nelson's twang, a staple in Black Rabbit for as long as I can remember. After all these years, the aging country singer still holds a special spot in my uncle's heart. He even sports the matching gray braids and red bandanna to prove it.

"You're getting too old for the big pieces," I joke, pulling my foot up onto the counter, where my ass is already parked, to tighten the laces of my boot. I finished my last appointment an hour ago and could have left. *Should* have left, since the CLOSED sign hanging from a hook on the door is dissuading any potential walk-ins. But every once in a while I like to just sit here and watch my mentor work—his hefty frame hunkered down in that same creaky plastic-molded chair. It brings me back to my nine-year-old self, in pigtails and scuffed Mary Janes, trailing my older cousin to the shop so I could draw BIC pen tattoos on burly bikers while they waited for the real thing. It's within these dingy black walls that I discovered my life's passion, all before I turned ten. Not many people can say they've made that discovery, at any age.

"Too old, my ass," he grunts. "Make yourself useful and grab me my damn dinner."

I slide off the counter with a smirk, hitting the button on a cash register that belongs in a museum so I can grab a twenty. "Foot-long again?" The sub shop two blocks away gets at minimum fifty percent of Ned's weekly food budget.

"Don't forget the jalapeños."

"The ones that almost put you in the hospital last time?" At fifty-eight, my uncle still eats like he's in his twenties, even though his body is showing signs of revolt, his thickening midsection and aging digestive system begging for more exercise and less fatty and spicy food.

"I let the girl apprentice here when she was eighteen, and then she abandoned me as soon as she got her license. I let the girl come back six years later to work out of here without paying a fee to the house. I let the girl sleep under my roof without paying rent . . ." he mutters to no one in particular but loud enough for everyone to hear. "If I wanted grief about my life choices, I woulda gotten hitched again." There's a long pause, and then he throws a wink over his shoulder at me, to confirm that he's joking. That he loves his niece and her smart-ass mouth and her acidic personality, and he's ecstatic that she decided to come back to San Francisco and work alongside him again. He'd never take a dime of rent money from me, even if I tried to pay.

And I *have* tried. At two months, when the wanderlust bug hadn't bitten me yet and I realized that I'd be staying longer than my usual four months. At four months, when I was afraid I was wearing out my welcome and started talking about finding an apartment to rent, and Ned threatened to kick my ass out of Black Rabbit if I did. At six months, when I left five hundred bucks cash on his dresser and came home to a note and the money pinned to my bedroom door with a steak knife, telling me never to bring up the subject of rent ever again. Except he put it in more colorful language.

I've been here for seven months now, and for the first time in I don't know how long, I'm feeling no itch to leave. Between working alongside Ned six days a week, hanging out with Dakota, an old friend from high school who moved here from Sisters, Oregon, about a year ago, and hitting the streets at night with a crew of guys who are as into decorating walls as I am, I'm loving San Francisco. This time around, at least.

"I'll be back." I turn to leave.

Dylan, the guy sitting in the chair with arms as thick as tree trunks, clears his throat rather obnoxiously. This is his fifth session this month. One of those bulky arms is nearly all covered in Ned's elaborate ink.

I roll my eyes. He's clocked four hours in that chair tonight, the first half of them spent muttering in an irritatingly croaky voice about how expensive it is to eat organic. I was ready to stuff a cloth into his mouth at around the two-hour mark just to shut him up. I really don't want to give him a reason to speak again. "Did you want me to grab you something?" I ask, not hiding the reluctance from my voice.

"Eight-piece sashimi dinner. Extra wasabi," he says without so much as a "please," his eyes glued to the matte-black ceiling above. It doesn't take a genius to figure out that this guy showed up here flying high as a kite. Ned doesn't care if his clients are high or tipsy, as long as they don't stumble in and they circle "no" to being intoxicated on the client paperwork, he figures it's their ass, should something go wrong. I'm guessing this guy has been smoking weed. He's too calm to be strung out.

"Try again, and make sure it ends with the word 'sub.'" I'm not going the extra three blocks to the sushi place. I'm nobody's fucking errand girl.

Tree Trunks dips his head to level me with a flat gaze before focusing on Ned's brow, furrowed in concentration. "You gonna let her talk to your customers like that?"

"You got an issue, you take it up with her. And good luck, because that girl can handle herself like no one I've ever met," Ned mutters, never one to coddle anybody, even a customer paying well over a grand. He's been running this shop for thirty years "the right way," and he's not about to change for "a bunch of lily-whites ruining a classic culture." His words, not mine.

The guy eyes the full length of me—from the shaved sides

of my hair and my black tank top and leggings, to my full sleeve of colorful ink, which unsettles some people but shouldn't faze him, seeing as he's getting his own done—down to my Doc Martens, and decides against whatever he was going to say, though that pinched expression never leaves his face. "Chicken club sub. Grilled. No oil or mayo."

I could be a real bitch and demand a "please," but I let it go. "Back in ten," I call over my shoulder, heading down the narrow hallway to the back door, grabbing my tattoo case on the way, knowing that if I don't toss it in the trunk of my car now, I'll probably forget it later.

"Watch how that new kid over there makes my sandwich. He doesn't know a tomato from his own asshole!" Ned's shout catches me just before the door clicks shut.

I step out into the crisp evening with my jacket dangling from one arm, and inhale the clean, cool air.

And smile.

I finally know what home feels like.

■ ■ ■

I let myself in through the back of Black Rabbit with my key exactly twenty-two minutes later with two subs: one with double peppers, one with breaded, deep-fried chicken, extra mayo and a splash of oil.

Ned was right; I had to give the dumbass behind the counter step-by-step instructions, going so far as to point out the vat of jalapeño peppers directly under his nose. He won't survive a week before Ned revolts. Just the threat of losing Ned's business will probably get the guy canned.

I'm going to tell my uncle that I think the dumbass is cute, and I'm going to date him. I smile, thinking about how Ned might react to that. I haven't had a chance to parade a boyfriend through here for his guaranteed disapproval yet. In the seven months I've been here, I haven't found one guy in San Francisco that even *I* approve of. That's been the only downfall of this city, so far, and I'm really ready to get out of this dry spell.

Tossing my purse onto the old metal desk that serves as a catchall for mail, office supplies, the archaic security-monitoring system, and anything else that might land there on our way through, I reach for the cowbell hanging against the wall. A gag gift that Ned's kept for years, even though the sound of it makes him wince and curse. I use it to irritate the shit out of him every chance I get.

A shout freezes my hand.

"Quit playing fucking games, old man!"

I hold my breath and try to listen, but the rush of blood flooding my veins and ears suddenly makes it hard to concentrate.

"Don't know what the hell you're talkin' about," Ned grits out, and his voice squeezes my chest, because I can tell that he's in pain. That odd, muted sound of knuckles hitting flesh followed by a groan pulls a gasp from me, and I immediately purse my lips and dart back and out of sight, panicked. Was that loud enough to be heard?

Whoever is up front obviously didn't hear me come in. Ned always jokes that I have the natural graces of a cat burglar, silent and stealthy even when I'm not intending to be.

An aluminum baseball bat leans against the wall next to the cowbell. If I were stupid, I'd grab it and run out front kamikaze-style. But Ned is two-hundred and twenty-five pounds of hardened man, Tree Trunks is even bigger, and someone has gotten the upper hand on both of them. I can only imagine how fast they'd have a hundred-and-ten-pound female subdued, even one that kicks and claws like a rabid wolverine. I don't even know how many guys are out there.

*The security camera.*

I dive for the old thirteen-inch tube monitor sitting on the desk and hit the Power button, desperate to get a glimpse of what's happening out front.

But only gray static appears. They must have busted the camera lens.

I do the only smart thing I can think of. I fumble for my cell phone, my fingers shaking as I dial 911. Hoping my whispers don't carry as I beg for police backup for a robbery in progress. *Can I get to safety?* the dispatcher asks. *I'm not leaving Ned,* I snap. *Stay on the line,* the woman responds. *We're sending help.*

The *ding* of the cash register sounds, and I hazard a peek around the corner and down the long hall, past the private room, and to the open-concept space at the front where Ned does as much of his work as he can. A hulkish man in dark cargo pants and a black turtleneck, with a black balaclava pulled up over his brow, hovers over the register, emptying it of cash with his left hand.

In his right, he grips a gun.

I squeeze my phone—pressed against my ear—tighter.

Beyond him, the window and front door are covered, the shades pulled to block anyone's view inside. They weren't like that when I left. I'm sure the front door is now locked, too, though it's too far to see from here.

"I've always wondered what it feels like to be on the giving end of a tattoo gun," a man with a deep voice and a Chicago accent says, and it's not the same guy I see standing at the register, which means there are at least two of them. Where the hell is Tree Trunks, anyway? Is he in on this? I haven't heard his croaky voice. "I just step on this pedal, right?" The buzz of the tattoo machine fills the shop, followed closely by a series of grunts.

Somehow, I know that it's Ned making those sounds.

"Hurry!" I hiss into my phone, tears streaming down my cheeks, torn between the urge to run out there and pure fear.

The guy who was at the cash register is now searching front desk drawers. He glances behind him. "You know, you're a sick bastard, Mario."

*Mario.* I have a name.

"My ex used to say that to me." A sinister chuckle sends shivers down my back. God, what are they doing to Ned? He has ink in a dozen different places. I did a design for him along the web of his finger when I got here seven months ago and he barely flinched then. "Go and see what you can find in the back."

The back.

*I'm* in the back.

I duck behind the wall, my heart hammering in my chest as heavy footfalls approach down the hallway toward me. The back door is right there, and yet it's not an option because it's in his line of sight and he has a gun.

I have nowhere to run.

"Shhh!" I hiss into the phone, hoping the dispatcher will understand me, will stay quiet so I don't have to hang up on her. I dive under the metal desk, tugging the chair in as far as I can, until my body is contorted around its legs and my entire left side is crammed against the wall. I thank God that I'm dressed in all black and hope it's enough, that he won't spot my bare skin. The female dispatcher hides with me under here, my phone pressed against my chest, smothering any sound she might make. She's my only connection to the outside world—and perhaps the last person I'll ever speak to—and she can surely hear my heartbeat.

Polished black combat boots appear around the corner. They stop for five seconds, and I feel each one of those in my throat.

And then those shoes swivel and stalk toward me.

I can barely focus through my fear anymore, sure that I'm about to find myself looking down the barrel of a gun. *Where are the police?* They should be here by now. We're not far from Daly City, hands down the worst area of San Francisco, where cruisers circle the streets like crows over a ripe cherry tree.

Around me, boxes topple and papers shuffle, and I pray to whoever watches down from above that this guy doesn't decide to check beneath the desk.

"Found something!" he shouts. It's followed by a snort and a low mutter of, "People still use these fucking things?"

I know what he's found. The VHS player that records the feed from the camera in the front on a continuous loop. Ned's never been one to keep up with technology trends and, instead, swears by what he knows.

Sirens wail in the distance. They're so faint at first that I think I'm imagining them.

"Fuck! Did you trip an alarm?" That angry voice—Mario—out front yells, and I allow myself a shaky breath of relief because he's heard them, too, so they must be real. *Only a few more seconds and we'll be safe.*

Ned's laugh—deep and throaty—carries all the way back. Good. Whatever that guy just did to him, Ned's still capable of laughing. Tough bastard.

"Come on! We can't get caught here," the guy above me shouts. He starts fussing with the VCR, first pressing, then slamming the Open button. I know that's what he's doing because she's a temperamental bitch and I've done the exact same thing once or twice when Ned's asked me to change a tape over. "Fuck it," he mumbles, and he begins to tug at the cables plugged in beneath the desk. He's taking the entire machine. He wants whatever video proof might be on there, I guess.

And if he reaches down to unplug the cord, he's going to find more than just a power strip.

I yank the plug out of the socket for him and hold my breath.

The sirens grow louder, three distinct wails now. "Come on!" His boots shift away from the desk. Footfalls pound down the hallway, and the guy named Mario appears, also in polished black combat boots. I can see him only from the waist down, but it's enough to see him peeling a black glove off.

A splatter of blood coats his wrist.

"Who the fuck called the cops? I could have gotten him to talk. I just needed more time." I guess he was obviously expecting to work Ned over at a leisurely pace. I ruined that for them, at least.

They barrel out the back door.

I'm still frozen, unsure if it's over or not.

"Hello? Hello?" A muted voice calls out, over and over again, and I finally remember the dispatcher pressed against my chest.

"They're gone," I whisper into the air, my voice hoarse.

And then I snap out of it.

I drop the phone and scramble out from under the desk, dashing for the door, my shaking hands snapping the dead bolt shut before those two can decide that it's better to hole up in here. The dispatcher calls to me from beneath the desk. "They're gone, out the back!" I yell, hoping she can hear me. I struggle to catch my breath and my balance, staggering down the hall toward the front of the shop, using the walls to keep me upright. I'm drenched in sweat, the relief so overwhelming. "Ned!" I've never been so happy to have the police coming for me. "They're gone!" I round the corner. "It's going to be—"

My words cut off with the sight of Ned's slumped, still body, a puddle of blood soaking into the wood grain floor beneath him.

# TWO

# SEBASTIAN

It's just a regular ringtone. For me, though, it's the wail of a war siren, and I'm immediately alert. There is only one person who has this number, and I didn't expect him to use it again so soon.

The tile is cool against my bare feet as I roll out of bed. I collect the phone from the nightstand with one fluid movement, unhindered by sheets or the morning sluggishness that an average person might face. Stepping through the propped-open patio doors and onto the balcony, I answer with a low, curt "Yeah." The sky is just beginning to lighten over the quiet bay. Dozens of boats sit moored below, their passengers lulled into deep sleep by the ocean air and rhythmic waves. I'm high enough up that I'm not likely to offend anyone with my lack of clothing, especially at this hour. Not that I'm truly concerned by it.

"Ice."

The code name is a sharp contrast to the warm breeze skating across my bare skin. My adrenaline begins to spike, all the same. Hearing it means that I will be forced to leave this haven soon. Sooner than I had hoped.

"How is recovery going?"

I instinctively peer down at the angry red scar on the outside of my thigh, where a bullet drilled into my flesh and muscle just three weeks ago, outside of Kabul. I nearly bled out before I made it to the doc. He patched me up on a makeshift operating table, buried deep in a maze of rooms, and charged me a hefty price. "Like new," I lie.

"Good." Bentley's voice is rich and smooth, a welcome sound in a sea of strangers. "Where are you now?"

I peer out over the beautiful vista of crystal blue water and whitewashed stone buildings, the volcanic rock cliffs in the distance, reluctant to divulge my location. I sank a good chunk of my last payout on renting this one-bedroom villa for the month. It's my private sanctuary, where I can revel in anonymity and peace for a while, before finding somewhere else to drift to.

Bentley has never asked before. But he also has the technical capabilities to trace this call. If he really wants to find out, then he will. In fact, the second I picked up, he probably already had his answer. "Where do I need to be?" I say instead.

"San Francisco."

I hesitate, caught off guard. My assignments are all in the Middle East, Africa, and Asia. Never on homeland soil. This doesn't make sense. But I also know not to question him, especially over the phone. "Give me four days." My rent here is paid up for another three *weeks*.

"I need you here in two."

"Then call someone else." I say it, knowing he won't. Bentley has plenty of highly trained resources at his disposal. If he's calling me, it's because he can't call anyone else. He needs me.

"Fine. Four days. We can discuss more at my place."

Again, I'm taken aback. Never before have I met directly with Bentley when being handed an assignment. But something is different about this one, I'm sensing. Something in his voice tells me that it's more urgent than usual. "I'll contact you with arrival particulars." I don't wait for his answer before I hang up. Our calls are never very long or detail heavy. Just enough for me to know that I'm about to get my hands dirty again, all for the greater good.

A soft meow catches my ear. The resident tabby cat—a whore who hops from one villa to the next, sharing her affections without discrimination—struts across the thick balcony wall to me, her tail curling in the air as she approaches. I stroke the soft patch of fur beneath her chin and listen to her purr while I begin to mentally prepare myself for my return to California.

It's been almost five years since I last stepped foot on American soil. Soil that once brought me purpose, love, and determination. Then pain, weakness.

Disgrace.

What will it bring me now?

My hand drops from the cat's chin, deciding I've given her more than enough. She leans forward, head-butts my arm—allowing me a chance to reconsider, to show her the kind of love that I am no longer capable of—before giving up and scuttling away.

With a sigh and one last glance over the peaceful blue waters, I flick the cigarette butt that sits mashed up on the railing and venture back inside to where an olive-skinned Grecian beauty is sprawled across my bed. She's the smoker, and an unexpected outcome of last night, while I enjoyed a quiet solo meal by the water. A curvy, sensual woman, much like the tabby cat, stalking in to impose herself on my life. Except her affections weren't as easily dismissed, wearing away at my defenses over the hours with throaty laughs and wandering fingertips.

Manipulating my loneliness.

I rarely succumb to it, but last night, I did.

I also must have had too many glasses of that pricey Limnio, because I don't usually end up in my own bed with a prostitute.

I slide a hand back and forth over the smooth skin of her hip until she stirs with a small groan. Eyes as blue as the Aegean Sea below us flutter open to meet mine. Her plump natural lips—that were wrapped around my cock with such expertise last night—curl into a smile. "Good morning, American," she purrs in her thick accent, reaching for me. "You want more, don't you?"

Had I not just received that call from Bentley, I probably would have taken her again. But minutes within getting news of my next assignment, my mind is already shifting focus, shutting down my weak human urges, preparing the rest of me for what is to come.

I quash her efforts for a repeat by filling her groping fingers with her crimson dress. "You can let yourself out."

"But . . . last night was . . ." She stumbles over her own surprise. "Will I see you again?"

There's no use pretending that either of us is something we're not, that we will be more to each other than we were for a few paid hours last night. So I don't bother answering, leaving her on my bed to head to the bathroom, feeling her anger blazing into my back.

"You will pay me!" she suddenly demands.

That catches me off guard and I stop to face her again, to search for the joke in her words. "I already paid you, last night." She was quite adamant that she got her cash before her dress came off. I haven't forgotten. I didn't have *that* much to drink.

The bed creaks as she climbs from it, her naked curves swaying with her naturally seductive strut toward me. "That was my fee for two hours. For the whole night, you will pay me five hundred euro."

I burst out in a rare fit of laughter. "You want me to pay you because you fell asleep next to me?"

Fire dances in her eyes as she glares at me, waiting expectantly.

I simply turn my back on her, locking the bathroom door behind me, shaking my head. I pay for whores so I can get what I want without a hassle. *This* is a hassle.

I soak under the hot water a few minutes longer than my usual seven, wanting to give her adequate time to figure out she can't swindle me, collect her scattered belongings, get dressed, and leave with some semblance of dignity. Mainly, so I don't have to talk to her again.

Honestly, I don't know if she'll leave. She'd probably steal my shit while I'm in here, if I had anything in plain sight worth stealing. This place is a mausoleum, though—empty white walls and sparse furnishings, void of all personality, perfect for renting out. She could take my wallet, with no remaining cash in it, no credit cards, and a false driver's license, if she *really* wants to. My passports and valuables are all locked in a safety-deposit box at the city bank. My other IDs and my gun are in a safe, and I assume cracking safes isn't where her talents lie.

I continue with my morning ritual, taking my time to oil and lather my face before I begin carving the dark stubble from my cheeks with a straight razor. It's the best tool for a well-defined strip of hair along my jaw, the beginnings of a beard that I like to keep short. A suitable everyday disguise, without going overboard.

Giving my body a good dry, I wrap the towel around my waist and open the door. It's been twenty minutes. I assume she has given up by now.

My peripheral vision catches the glint of a blade as it approaches my throat from the right. If I weren't me—with quick reflexes and well-honed combat skills and a steely demeanor—I would have panicked, giving the heavyset man she let into my villa a chance to maim me, perhaps kill me. But because I am who I am—*what* I am—I'm already moving to respond, my blood surging through my veins, my heart rate picking up with excitement.

Deftly grabbing hold of his meaty wrist, I twist until he yelps and is forced to release his grip on the handle, all while the whore stands in the doorway, her face trying to suppress her fright, her arms roped around that impressive rack in a hug. I retrieve the ten-inch chef's knife that one of them must have plucked from my kitchen and set it on my dresser, beyond easy reach.

I'm guessing this isn't the way they expected it to go.

"Who are you?" Besides a three-hundred-pound bastard with an obnoxious layer of chains tangled in the forest of chest hair protruding from a half-unbuttoned shirt.

He answers with a swinging arm, forcing me to duck and throw him face-first against the wall. He rolls his face to the side, smearing blood across the pristine white walls.

And now I'm irritated, because I'll have to clean up that mess. "Let's try that again. Who the fuck are you?" I already know who he is. Her pimp, who must have been sleeping in his car nearby, waiting for her call to see if this scam worked and I paid up, or if he'd need to come and put muscle behind it to intimidate me.

When he doesn't answer, I tug on his arm. If I pull on it any tighter behind his back, his shoulder is going to pop out of its socket.

"You pay Alena for whole night," he forces out in broken English, his face contorted in pain.

That's right. That's her name. "I don't owe Alena anything. We made no agreements for the entire night and I didn't ask her to stay," I simply say.

"You had all night. Pay!" he insists, though it's lacking any conviction. I wonder how much of a cut he's getting. On an island of about fifteen thousand residents, you'd think there'd be no use for this racket. Then again, Santorini sees upward of half a million tourists each year, so there's probably a lot of suckers.

I'm sure she does damn well, especially if letting her gorilla-size boss in when her mark turns his back to extort money is her MO.

I'm well within my rights to refuse, and well within my ability to break a dozen bones in this asshole's body before tossing him to the curb, but right now I just want them to get the fuck out. I release my grip and the guy's body sags with relief. "And here I thought it was true love," I mumble, fishing a twenty from my dress pants that lay rumpled on the floor where they fell last night. Nowhere near the three hundred extra she's claiming. "This is all you're getting out of me."

She scoffs at the single bill. "I could scream," she hisses with defiance, the remnants of her crimson lipstick making her lips look touched with blood. Fire and fear smolder in her eyes as they trail over my naked chest, over the towel hanging low on my hips.

"Or you could take this money that we didn't agree to, walk out that door, and pretend we never met. Which option do you think would be smarter?"

She doesn't answer. She *must* be able to hear the unnatural calm in my voice, the lack of panic or worry. She *must* sense that I'm not her average score. I'd like to give her that much credit, at least.

"This scam of yours isn't really smart, *Alena.*" I take three steps to hover within inches of her face. "You never know what kind of man you will end up trying to dupe." Her pimp is behind me but I've long been trained to be acutely aware of a threat's movements, even when out of sight. So I'm ready for his last-ditch effort to save his reputation when he lunges at me. A quick shift and elbow to his solar plexus and fist to his nose—my eyes never leaving Alena's—stops him abruptly. "And you never know what that man might be capable of." *I promise you, Alena, it's a lot more than even I ever dreamt of.*

She shrinks back now, terror etched across her face.

It's too bad, really. More and more, I've been thinking that I need a home base, after years of simply drifting. Santorini might be the place for me. I would have been a great regular for her. "Get the fuck out of here and don't come back."

Her pimp spouts off a couple of words in Greek to her around his own pain. She snatches the bill from my fingertips and darts out of my apartment with him, slamming the door so hard that it rattles the wall, the dresser, and the knife lying atop it, causing it to slide off. It lands, blade-down, an inch from my left pinky toe.

I start to chuckle.

# THREE

# IVY

"He never changed even a bit, did he?" Ian swings his foot at the trash can. Not hard. Just enough to shift it.

I quietly watch my cousin from my perch on the front desk as he takes in his dad's shop—the dusty collectibles, the grungy black-and-red decor, the wall-to-wall mirrors—for the first time in fourteen years. I was able to get crime scene cleaners in the same day that the police finished collecting evidence, which was a twenty-nine-hour process. It's not like anyone's in a rush to get the business back up and running. But the idea of Ian seeing the dark red stain where his father bled out was not something I could stomach, even if they were estranged. By the time Ian stepped off the plane from Dublin, you'd never know that a double homicide had taken place in here.

All the same, Black Rabbit feels eerily empty. Void of life. I guess that makes sense, since it lost its heart.

"He was Ned, right to the end." Never warm and cuddly, never someone who changed himself to try to please others. He always knew who he was, and for that, he earned the respect of many people.

Including me.

But had Ned been someone else—someone who groveled, begged, who offered his attackers anything and everything he could—would they have spared his life? That question has been haunting me for six days now.

"Where did you find him?" Ian asks quietly.

I point to the leather chair that was still occupied by Dylan Royce—aka Tree Trunks—when I left for subs that night. At some point, the two men with guns must have dragged him out of the chair and forced Ned into it, using the extension cord plugged into the floor fan to secure him. The police haven't revealed anything about the other guy, but since I never heard his nasally voice during the few minutes that I was hiding in the back, I'm guessing he was already dead when I arrived.

Then again, I also never heard the gunshot that gave Ned a quick and painless end to his ordeal.

At first I didn't believe that the hole in his forehead was from a bullet wound. The police say they must have been using a silencer. That makes sense, when I think about the length of the handgun that I saw. But who comes with silencers, unless they're planning to kill instead of simply scare? These guys came prepared, and they knew what they were doing, hiding their faces behind masks and their fingerprints inside gloves, and smashing the camera trained on the front. They even took the VCR to ensure there was no video evidence of their entrance.

In some ways, I'm relieved that they did that. While I want the assholes who did this caught, I don't ever want to have to sit in a courtroom and give testimony while a video of how "Mario" tested his skills with the tattoo machine against Ned's left eyelid is played for a jury.

Ian chews the inside of his mouth. That's one of a few signs that his father's death has affected him emotionally. He hasn't shed a single tear from what I've seen. Neither have I, though—and I'm devastated—so I guess crying is not a good indicator of pain.

But where Ned and I were close, Ian hasn't spoken to his father in years, after he and his mom, my aunt Jun, walked in on Ned in the back room giving a female customer more than just a tattoo. When they divorced, Jun and Ian moved to San Diego, where he lived until he started college in Dublin. He's been living in Ireland for eleven years now. So long that his voice carries a faint Irish brogue.

"I can't believe he included me in his will," he finally mutters, kicking the trash can again, this time denting it.

"Of course he did. You're his son. He loved you." It's true, they hadn't talked since Ian's high school graduation day, but Ned never stopped loving Ian in his own way. I saw it, through the occasional questions that Ned would slip into a conversation, pumping me for information about Ian; and the times I'd catch Ned trolling Ian's social media pages online after I taught him how to navigate this "goddamn computer-age world."

Ned still kept the picture on his nightstand of seven-year-old Ian standing in front of the shop. When I was living in Dublin, I tried talking to Ian about it, hoping to convince him to pick up the phone and make amends with his father, to try and find the good in him. Unfortunately, for all that Ian inherited from his mother—which is most of his phlegmatic personality—he did get Ned's stubbornness.

Ian's head bows, his brow furrowed deep. He saw that picture, too, and now he needs to come to terms with the fact that he will never get the chance to know his father as an adult. "He shouldn't have. I don't feel like I deserve a penny of it."

"Come on, Ian. You were *everything* to him."

Black eyes settle on me, full of regret. "You're the one who came back here. You're the one who bothered staying in touch with him all these years." It's something that has caused Ian and me to have our ups and downs. He thought I was taking sides—the wrong side.

I never saw it that way, though. I was only ten when it happened, too young to really grasp what was going on. After Jun and Ian moved away, I asked Ned why. He said that sometimes people make horrible, stupid mistakes and sometimes other people can't forgive them for it.

I told Ned I forgave him, and that was that.

Ian's thirty now—five years old than me—so we were never especially close growing up, and had even less of a reason to stay in touch after he moved away. It wasn't until I was finishing high school that we reconnected over email and our love of art. Sharing the same passions helps us understand each other. Very few people truly get me. My parents and brothers sure don't. Ned was one. Ian is the other.

I shrug. "I guess that's why he included me, too." Not only am I inheriting half of Ned's estate, he named me executor. What the fuck was he thinking? Me? Dealing with lawyers and real estate agents? It's a sizable inheritance, with this shop and a small three-bedroom house in Ingleside. The house has got a hefty mortgage to go along with it, and it's seen much better days, but it will fetch an easy seven hundred, as is.

"What the hell are we going to do with this place, Ivy?" He shakes his head, punching buttons until the cash register pops open to reveal an empty drawer.

Just like that guy did only days ago.

I squeeze my eyes shut and shiver at the memory. It's one of a few that keep replaying in my head at odd times throughout the day and night, with no warning. The ding of the register, the buzzing of Ned's tattoo machine. The cool metal desk against my skin as I hid.

The blood splatter on that guy's wrist.

The cops blame my fuzzy memory on shock. They say I may remember more with time.

But a part of me hopes I don't.

"Black Rabbit's got a great reputation, a loyal clientele. It makes decent money. And we'll make enough from the sale of the house to pay off the mortgage on the building." After a messy and expensive run-in with the IRS back in the '90s, Ned learned how to keep proper files and pay his taxes and bills on time. Ian and I were able to get a good understanding of the business affairs in one evening of going through the files. We know that he borrowed a hundred thousand against the building—that was previously paid off—only a month ago. But what that money went to, neither of us has any idea. It sure as hell wasn't upgrades. And Ned's bank account is bone dry, which we discovered when making funeral arrangements. It makes no sense, given how well he did here. He didn't employ anyone besides me, and he didn't pay me an hourly salary, because he let me take home all my earnings, without any chair rental fees.

Ned *did* like to gamble, but it was always low-key betting—day trips to the racetracks, poker nights, some online stuff—so if he was into someone for a hundred K, I'd be surprised.

But there's also no sign of that money, which makes me wonder.

"I can't run this place from Dublin and I'm not abandoning my own shop to keep it going," Ian says.

"You'd make more money here, though . . ." The Fine Needle, Ian's shop in Dublin, is great—small and full of character. But it'll never compete against a well-established business in San Francisco when you're weighing dollar bills. I know that argument is pointless, though. I knew before the words even left my mouth. Ian is about political movements and the environment. He's about books and learning and experiencing life. He's never been about money.

"And I'd get to deal with Ned's amazing clientele, right?" He snorts. "You heard the cops. This is probably tied to one of them. I really don't want to end up like that."

"They're reaching for the easiest answer because they can't find another one." A good third of Ned's customer base are bikers and, while most of them are just that—guys who ride motorcycles— Ned also found himself catering to Devil's Iron, the one percent who do more than simply "ride bikes." The cops are having a field day right now, going through potential motives and enemies. They have no other explanation for why two masked men would show up here, empty the register—which had maybe a grand sitting in it—and murder him and a customer.

Ian snorts. "Besides, I'm guessing there won't be too many rednecks and bikers coming in here to get their work done by a California Roll."

"They might, if the California Roll is Ned's son." I smile, despite the derogatory name. I heard it plenty growing up in San Fran, before my family decided they wanted me as far away from my uncle's bad influence as possible. Ian and I are both children of interracial couples. Ned was as white as white can get—born and raised in New Mexico before moving to California and charming a Chinese-American girl named Jun—my dad's sister—with his bad boy ways at a local grocery store.

The result of Jun and Ned's union is a skinny, nonathletic version of Brandon Lee.

I, on the other hand, am a Spanish-Chinese mix. My mother was raised outside Madrid. She met my dad while attending college on a Spanish exchange program. I was actually born in Spain, which technically makes me something other than a Chinese American, but kids are stupid.

"Or Ned's niece." Ian meets my dark eyes with ones of his own. "This place means way more to you than it does me. What if we keep it and you manage it?"

A rare bark of laughter escapes me. Me, manage a shop in San Francisco?

"I was being serious," he mutters.

My gaze shifts involuntarily over to the chair and that prickly ball that keeps lodging itself in my throat when I let myself acknowledge that Ned is gone forever appears once again. "I can't," I whisper hoarsely.

His face softens. "You haven't said much about that night. I'm sure it was traumatic. Are you going to be okay?"

Everyone—Ian, Jun, my parents, local shop owners, regular customers—seems more concerned about how I am than about what happened to Ned and who killed him. None of them knows exactly what I saw. And none of them ever will if I can help it, because no one needs to hear those gory details. "I'll be fine. You know me."

"Yeah, I do. Tough as nails . . . on the outside." His heavy dark brow furrows with concern. "I would have shat my pants. Were you scared?"

"Terrified . . ." And still am, for so many reasons beyond the obvious. Terrified to think what could have happened had I not gone for subs, had the sandwich guy known a tomato from his asshole and made the sandwiches in half the time, had I not been so quiet slipping through the back door.

Perhaps me being there could have saved Ned, somehow. Perhaps me running to the front instead of hiding in the back could have saved him. Maybe I made the wrong choice by crawling under the desk like a mouse. I have so many lingering what-ifs, all of them feeding that guilty burn that now festers deep in my core.

But talking about my guilt means facing it, and I don't have the strength to do that. "So, I guess we should sell it, then."

He sighs. "All the equipment is already set up." As much as he isn't about the money, he's also not an idiot. "If we could freshen it up a bit, someone may be willing to pay good money for it." He pauses. "But . . . I really can't take care of all that." I feel his gaze settle on me, and I keep mine glued to the deep grooves in the wood floor.

Because I know where this conversation is heading.

Ian just started his PhD two months ago. He'll be the most highly educated tattoo artist the world has ever seen in another few years, but that means he can't stay here to handle things. He has all kinds of commitments back in Dublin.

His little cousin, Ivy Lee, is the queen of *not* making commitments. She's free as a bird. Only this bird had plans to leave here and pack up all her clothes and belongings today, so she could hit the road as early as tomorrow.

"I need you here, Ivy."

I groan out loud, but that doesn't stop him.

"This place is packed with useless shit. The walls haven't been painted since he opened thirty years ago. We could make a good chunk off it, just by cleaning and painting it. You know, turn it into something from this decade."

I shoot him a look that says "don't ask me to do this" because I just want to leave and put this all behind me while I'm still numb.

He folds his arms over his chest. "You owe me, and you *know* that you owe me."

Dammit. I *do* owe Ian. He gave me a job and a couch to sleep on for four months last year, when I booked a one-way ticket to Dublin. I needed a change, and I gave him two weeks' notice to accommodate my needs. He rolled with it.

"And you *are* the executor, after all."

I take a deep breath, taking in Black Rabbit's interior. *Really* taking it in. This was Ned's passion, his life. But the place itself is a dump. Anyone walking in off the street is going to lowball us, and that would be almost as offensive to Ned as selling it in the first place. "Maybe someone would pay for the name, too. You know, keep it alive. That wouldn't be so bad."

"It shouldn't take too long." Ian rights the trash can. "A week to empty it out, tops."

I snort. Thirty years of Ned's memories are in here. Thirty years that I can't just toss in the trash.

Ian ignores me. "Another week for the painters. It could be ready to go on the market in a few weeks. Staying for a few weeks isn't that bad. Especially when you have nowhere that you need to be."

I don't say anything, prompting him to continue.

"And you know, maybe we could look at fixing up the house a bit. Paint it, too. I was looking at real estate in the area, and we could get another fifty off that place with some paint and a good clean. Or we could keep it as an investment property and rent it out. A lot of people in that neighborhood rent to students from the college."

"And you're going to manage all that from Dublin?"

He clamps his mouth shut.

"I like how I've gone from staying in San Francisco for a few extra weeks to taking care of a house for months and beyond, in a matter of seconds." This is not an organic conversation. Ian has been trying to convince me to plant some roots and act more responsible. He clearly had this conversation planned. Everything he's suggesting means having legal ties and responsibilities to San Francisco. Funny thing is, a week ago I was entertaining the thought of putting down roots.

Now none of that sounds at all appealing to me.

"We have to sell that house fast or it'll go into foreclosure. Unless you can afford that mortgage and taxes, and all the utilities. I know I can't." It would eat my savings up in two months.

"Yeah. You're right. I'm sorry." He heaves a sigh. "I'm a complete jerk for leaving you with all this."

"I'll manage," I mutter, though I don't know how.

"Look, if you don't want to stay in San Francisco after it's all said and done, you can come back to Dublin. I miss having you there."

"Even though I stole all your good clients because I'm that much better than you are?" I've always been good at using sarcasm and humor to steer conversations away from serious topics.

He chuckles, and the sound squeezes my heart because his laugh sounds like Ned's laugh. "Something like that. Seriously, come."

"Okay. I'll think about it." Though I'm not sure I want the drama of my last trip to Ireland. I'm definitely going somewhere. If it's not Dublin, it'll be somewhere else.

It's obvious that it was Ned who made San Francisco feel like home, because now that he's gone, I just want to get the hell away.

# FOUR

# SEBASTIAN

I spot my driver immediately—a stocky man with cropped gray hair, wearing a boxy black suit and holding a sign that reads CAL ENTERPRISES. An innocuous business name that'll vanish from anyone's memory two seconds after seeing it.

"Gregory White?"

I nod once. That's the name on the passport I'm traveling with today. Almost as innocuous as CAL Enterprises. As are my blue jeans, white T-shirt, and unmarked baseball cap.

"Any checked baggage, sir?"

"No." I sling my carry-on over my shoulder. I never bring enough to check luggage when I'm on a business trip, no matter how long. It slows me down when I need to be moving quickly and discreetly.

The man leads me out to a plain black town car with tinted windows. Nothing over the top. Again, ideal when you're a person who needs to slip in and out of a city unnoticed.

I'm that person, most days of my life.

■ ■ ■

"How long have you been out?" Steve—the driver—asks, his shrewd eyes stealing a glance at me in the rearview mirror before settling on the stone house as we crest the hill. It's designed to look like a Tuscan castle. From what I've seen in my travels, the architects built a commendable replica.

"Awhile." I leave it at that, affixing my attention to the hills and valleys of Napa Valley grapevines ahead. It's not too shocking that this ex-Marine senses my links to the military. Even though I've traded in my crew cut for something longer, more stylish, and I've shed my standard gear for civilian clothes, there's something identifiable in all of us, especially the ones who've deployed, who've pulled triggers that stopped heartbeats. Our movements, our demeanor, the way certain sounds grip our attention, the way we can never truly relax. We all deal with it in different ways. We all let go in different ways.

But most of us never let go all the way.

"Did you and Mr. Bentley serve together in Afghanistan?"

Bentley obviously trusts this guy, to send him to the airport to collect me, to risk the two of us sitting in a car for the ninety-five-minute drive to his Napa vineyard, also his home. But Bentley also trusts me to keep our continued relationship under wraps—which makes the idea of bringing me right to his doorstep all the more strange. This is obviously highly classified. Or personal. Or both.

"No."

That's a lie, and thankfully the end to the questions, as the car snakes up the long driveway, the house growing proportionately until it looms over us. Bentley is already waiting at the heavy wood doors when the brakes squeak to a stop. The sight of his broad smile sparks a wave of nostalgia that I hadn't expected. It's been more than five years since I last saw him, our communication limited to brief conversations on burner phones and wire transfers to offshore accounts.

"It's good to see you." He clasps hands with me the moment I step out of the car, pulling me into a friendly hug. "How was your flight?"

"Long. My secretary will invoice you shortly."

His deep chuckle rattles in my chest just like it did ten years ago, when I was an eighteen-year-old newly enlisted SEAL and he was a thirty-two-year-old officer. He's in his early forties now. Once a trim and powerful man, time and wealth have obviously taken their toll on him, his muscles softer, his movements more relaxed.

Still, I wouldn't want to piss him off.

"Come inside."

The interior of Bentley's estate is as ritzy as the outside. "Overcompensating for something?" I murmur casually, trailing him through a small courtyard within, shaded by high walls all around and decorated with flowers and shrubs and patio furniture.

His chuckle sounds again, even louder now that it echoes through the halls. "Eleanor would say that, but that's because I divorced her before I made my first million."

And he's made many since as the founder of Alliance, a private security company that provides elite protection services to companies and governments, including our own. The contracts are worth tens of millions each—sometimes more—and rife with global media attention, with claims of everything from corruption to undue aggression against civilians in war-torn countries. Bentley pushes on, though, succeeding by continually sticking with his good intentions. Keeping people safe is a motto he lives and breathes every day, and America is a country he loves. He draws no lines when it comes to doing what needs to be done for the greater good. Things that our own government doesn't want to get its hands dirty dealing with.

That's why sometimes he needs me.

We go through another door and pass several staff members in various uniforms who smile and nod but otherwise remain part of the backdrop. "Have you been back to California since—"

"No."

He nods but he doesn't press it any further, reaching for the willowy, pale blonde who rounds the corner. She looks exactly like her pictures in the newspapers and magazines, the Finnish wife of an influential U.S. Navy SEAL officer turned businessman, who likes to dress in white to match her hair and throw cocktail parties.

"This is Tuuli."

Her cheekbones protrude with a bold smile, her deep-set

chestnut eyes flashing with interest as they size me up. "It's nice to meet you, Mr. . . ." she probes, her English perfect, trace amounts of her origin detectable. She's been in California for only four years, when Bentley married and imported her, so I'm guessing she's had the help of a linguistics trainer.

"White," Bentley answers for me, not giving me a chance to use my real name. He obviously wants to keep his beautiful wife in the dark where I'm concerned.

If she senses any deception, it doesn't show. "Well, I hope you'll be staying with us, Mr. White? I can have a room made up for you."

"I need to get back to San Francisco tonight. But thank you." As nice as a few nights watching California put its vines to bed for the winter would be, I have big plans for a hole-in-the-wall motel that accepts cash payments and asks no questions.

Leaning in to plant a kiss on her cheek, Bentley murmurs, "I'll come find you when we're done."

She looks at the diamond-encrusted watch that decorates her slender wrist. "Don't forget that we have that dinner tonight, right?"

"I'll be in my suit and waiting by the door at six p.m. sharp," he promises before continuing on, forcing me to trail, Tuuli's curious gaze on me as I pass. I wonder exactly how much he keeps from her. I wonder if she'd be looking at me like that—and inviting me to sleep under her roof—if she knew the kinds of things I've done for her husband.

Maybe. Obscene wealth has a way of making people view the dark side of reality differently.

Bentley leads me into his office—a grandiose room with vaulted ceilings and Persian rugs and even an American flag in the corner—and gestures to a chair with a perfect view through the French doors of a balcony and, beyond that, hundreds of rolling acres of vineyard.

"How do you cope with such poor work conditions?"

He smirks. "Not exactly the Aegean Sea, but it's a decent view." Of course he traced our call.

He settles against a hefty walnut desk in the center of the

room, resting his arms on his chest. "How have you been, Sebastian? It's been a while."

It *has* been a while, both since I saw him and since someone has called me by my real name. Sometimes it feels like just yesterday that I was squatting behind blown-out walls with this man—my team's leader—doing nothing but waiting. To live, to die, we were never sure what the long hours would bring. It was during those times that our friendship grew, that our mutual trust solidified.

A lot has happened since then. Things that cannot be forgotten.

Things that have left permanent scars.

"Fine." I roll my eyes over the shelves, artfully decorated with books and vases and record albums. Bentley always was a sucker for a good record. My attention zeros in on the gold SEAL trident resting in a glass case. It's identical to the one stored in my safety-deposit box in Zurich.

He sighs, stooping down to access a false panel in one of the bookcases and opening it to uncover a safe. "Still a man of few words, I see."

"Always the ones you need, though."

He nods, more to himself. "Yes, that too." Spinning the dial with deft accuracy, he pops open the door and pulls out a silver briefcase. It's the kind of case I normally open at the start of an assignment, locked by a combination and waiting for me in a secure location, left by one of a few highly trusted Alliance employees who won't ask questions and have no information to share. "We have a situation in San Francisco that needs sorting out. A search and recovery, and potential target elimination."

It has always been so easy to talk to Bentley. We speak the same language.

He sets the case on the coffee table in front of me and pops the latches. I don't even need to look to know that there's a Beretta Px4 inside. It's my model of choice, what I'm most comfortable with, and Bentley always ensures I have one. Next to it is a suppressor, a Gerber multi-tool, a fixed-blade knife, and a new burner phone.

Beneath is a folded copy of the *San Francisco Chronicle* and an un-marked tan folder.

I don't make a move for the folder just yet.

"There was a . . . complication recently," Bentley begins, choosing his words carefully. I never get all the details, but I always get enough to do my job proficiently. "It involves an ex-employee of Alliance, giving explicit details about an assignment in Afghanistan."

"What kind of assignment exactly?"

"Intelligence collection. Marine Corps captured an insurgent and allowed my guys to question him. It was highly successful, leading us to the capture of Adeeb Al-Naseer."

A terrorist on the most-wanted list who bombed an office building in Seattle, killing almost a thousand people.

There's only one reason that I could understand the U.S. forces handing him over, and it's that they wanted to keep their hands clean of what needed to be done to make him talk. "But the general public doesn't need to know the details behind the interrogation," I surmise.

"I'm sure you've been following the news. You know how much heat Alliance has been under lately. The media has cost me millions in contacts, which are smaller and harder to get as it is. The war glory days are over. And if these lies that Royce was spewing get out . . . the Pentagon will hang someone for this, just to appease voters. It'll be Alliance, and that isn't good for anyone."

I nod. Average Americans, driving along in their Chevrolets, filling their stomachs with burgers and their heads with Hollywood's latest heist or action movie, have no fucking clue what it's like to be in enemy territory, fighting a war to make sure it's never brought to American soil again. Half of them are even arguing the need for the war over there to begin with.

So when a journalist latches onto bullshit propaganda about U.S. military and guys like Alliance's contract workers doing unsavory things and blasts it out into the media, all those lefty liberals start screaming. While they enjoy their breakfast coffee under the blanket of safety we've given them. And then our government responds, because it has to. In the end, Bentley will suffer.

Just the thought of that makes me grit my teeth with anger.

"His name was Dylan Royce. He was let go four months ago for performance-related and drug dependency issues. Basically, he was a shit disturber, with a developing taste for violent behavior. We gave him a heavy severance package in exchange for a signed confidentiality agreement. Turns out he didn't think that gag order applied in a tattoo shop. He ran his mouth off to a fucking tattoo artist and the entire conversation was recorded on the store's surveillance system."

"What kinds of things were said?"

"Bullshit. All of it. All kinds of false accusations. But it won't matter if the media gets hold of it," Bentley mutters. "The tattoo shop owner actually called Alliance's 800 number—pulled it off our website, I assume—and told the operator that he had damaging information on Alliance that *I* would want to know about. She didn't know what to do so she put him through to my operatives director's voice mail, where he then left a message threatening to send the video to a journalist."

I see where this is going. "How much was he asking for in exchange?"

"Six hundred and fifty-five thousand."

"That's . . . specific. Why not an even million?"

Bentley snorts. "Who knows. My operatives director called him back and asked for proof, so the guy texted him a short clip of a video, taken by a phone, of a monitor—some crappy little security monitor, it looks like. My guy bought us four days by agreeing to an exchange. Told the shop owner that we needed that time to round up that much cash."

I snort. I doubt Bentley would have an issue filling a duffel bag in an afternoon.

"That's when my operatives director briefed me. I couldn't risk that video floating around for four days so I briefed and dispatched a team within two hours to recover the video from the shop owner

and eliminate both of them from future risk of talking. *Quietly.*
Royce sure as hell couldn't be trusted anymore, gag order or not."

Eliminate.

Kill.

I trust Bentley's decision making, so if he thinks the guys had
to go, then they had to go. "What happened?"

"*That* major clusterfuck happened." He nods toward the newspaper. "Two dead bodies, surrounded by a media and police circus
and a missing videotape. Had they used their heads and followed
orders explicitly . . ." Bentley shakes his head. "My guys were supposed to take out Royce somewhere quiet first and then get to the
shop at closing to seize the tape. But they decided to improvise,
seeing as Royce was at the shop getting work done. A 'two birds
with one stone' robbery cover-up."

I reach for the newspaper, unfolding it to scan the front
page: a double homicide at a dive tattoo shop in Mission District
called Black Rabbit. The inset shows two faces—one, a Caucasian
ex-Marine named Dylan Royce, whom you could easily identify
on the street as such with his bulky size and brush cut; the other, a
Willie Nelson wannabe named Ned nearing his sixties, who doesn't
look like he'd be capable of serious risk to anyone. Then again, I've
watched hundred-pound women produce bombs from beneath
their burkas as they charge a U.S. Humvee, ready to blow everyone
up. I don't underestimate anyone anymore.

But this Royce guy . . . "It says he had a Medal of Honor?"

"Yup. An outstanding soldier, which is why we hired him. He
went downhill, though. It started with Vicodin. He turned into a
real troublemaker after that." Bentley shakes his head.

*What a waste.* "And this Ned guy. Why not just pay him off?"
While I don't ever question Bentley, I'm curious about this. Blackmail is shitty, but it's not an automatic death sentence. At least, not
in my book.

"For the same reason we don't negotiate with terrorists, son."
Bentley's tone is sharper. He's always supported a strong stance on
that. "Guys like that, who jump on the chance to make money off

of horrible things they're not supposed to know about anyways—
they can't be trusted, even after you pay them off. He'd probably
pocket the money and then turn around and bury me by sending
a copy of the video in. Or he'd come back for more. The guy had
all kinds of unsavory connections. We can't risk that shit. I'm not
having my entire life brought down by some fucking tattoo artist
looking to cash in." He sighs. "So now you know why you're here. I
need you to find that recording."

"I would definitely have handled this differently." Namely, I
would have had the video in hand before I pulled the trigger. But
I also wouldn't have pulled the trigger without Bentley's say-so.
"Who are these guys you sent in?"

"They're two guys who worked closely with Royce in Afghanistan. I didn't want to get anyone else outside this issue involved, and
I figured they have a vested interest. One of them, though, is a bit
of a loose cannon. Effective as hell at his job overseas, but . . ." He
shakes his head, his lips pursed with regret. "I should have waited
for you."

I'm surprised he made that kind of mistake. Bentley's the kind
of guy who has three defense plans spinning before a problem has
a chance to rear its ugly head. It's his job to always have control of
whatever situation he finds himself in. It's how he's made his for-
tune. It's why the CIA taps his shoulder when it needs a problem
solved "under the radar."

He heaves a sigh. "If this video gets into the hands of the
media, they'll blow apart what we're doing over there. It will cause
irreparable damage to Alliance as a whole. And we've made so
much good progress. So I think you can see why I need you here.
It's delicate. And it needs to be handled swiftly."

I nod. Everyone talks, eventually. Everyone except me.

So Bentley needs me to get answers out of a corpse, it would
seem. "What exactly am I looking for? A jump drive? A microchip?"

Bentley pops open a cigar box on his desk and pulls out two
Bolivars, rolling them between his palms. "VHS tape. This shop
owner used an archaic system for his surveillance."

A fucking dinosaur in the world of recording mediums. "How many copies are there?"

"Just the one now, I believe. We found the video file of the recording on the shop owner Ned Marshall's phone. Nothing came up on Royce's phone. I'm guessing he had no clue this was happening."

One day, I'd love to sit back and watch Bentley's computer whizzes at work, digging up all this data, seeing what they can find and how fast. But that's all interesting-to-know information, and I prefer to keep curiosity at bay and work on a need-to-know level. "What's the official story?" Obviously the cops are going to be crawling all over a double homicide.

"Marshall has been linked to local motorcycle clubs for years, doing all their ink. SFPD assumes it's either a random robbery or tied to one of this guy's associations, so they're sniffing over there. Royce will likely be written off as unfortunate collateral damage."

"That's good." Having to watch my shadow for police always complicates things. "Has anyone searched their houses yet?"

"Royce moved back in with his mother after splitting with his girlfriend recently. He's still in boxes. We slipped in and lifted his computer, to see if he was shooting his mouth off to anyone else. My guess is he felt the need to unload his resentment with Alliance on someone and figured the old man wouldn't give two shits about what he had to say. Which means we need to focus on the tattoo artist if we want to find that tape. His house, the shop, anywhere it may be hidden. And you're the only one I trust to get the job done right."

My gaze flickers to the silver mark peeking out above his shirt collar, a glimpse of a time when his life was in my hands. Literally. When that bullet pierced Bentley's artery, I was sure he would be gone in minutes, but I jammed my thumb into it to stem the blood flow anyway, keeping him alive long enough to drag him to safety and medical attention.

That bullet led to his retirement from the navy.

Ned's house will be my first stop. It's the most obvious one. "And we know it's not in the shop?"

"Nothing came up in the police report. You'll need to check it out, but keep it low-key. That place is too hot now, after what happened."

I nod. "You said search and recovery, with potential target elimination. You've got two dead here. Who's the third?" "Potential" means it may end up being straight search and recovery. I find the video, I hand it over, I get out. That's not bad. It was my specialty, once upon a time. Low risk of being shot or stabbed, which is always nice. This means there's a chance that I could be back to drinking my coffee and watching the cruise ships port in Santorini within days.

"A young woman by the name of Ivy Lee."

I struggle to keep my expression even, suppressing ugly memories that threaten to rise as he strolls over to hand a cigar to me. I don't want him to see that the past still affects me. Bentley needs to know that I am fine and that I can do what needs to be done. "Who is she to them?"

"She's Ned Marshall's niece and the only family member still in contact with him. They were close—lived together, worked together. Like two peas in a pod. Could have been his daughter." He snips the end of his cigar off with a cutter. "She was hiding in the shop when the team went in to question and dispatch. She was able to give information to the police. A name and a description of one guy's accent; a profile sketch of the other one, which the media circulated. Thankfully, there haven't been any bites. It's a fairly generic sketch."

"Did she say anything about a video?"

He shakes his head. "Not a word."

Which means she could be withholding information that she fears will get her killed.

I feel unease sliding down my back. I've been taking assignments from Bentley for almost five years, and all of them have been for middle-aged male targets and guaranteed threats. This will be the first female target, and we don't even know if she truly is dangerous. I don't like uncertainty when it comes to my job.

Setting the newspaper to the side, I flip open the tan folder. A petite, exotic girl with a full sleeve of tattoos and blue streaks in her black hair looks out at me, her piercing glare making me wonder if she might have seen the candid photo of her being snapped. She's obviously part Asian, but her features are softer and fuller, suggesting a mix with something else.

I slide the end of the cigar into my mouth, reveling in the fresh grassy taste of the paper against my tongue, as I study her face. "What do we know about her?"

He tosses the cutters to me. "She never stays in one place for too long, she makes a lot of cash deposits and has several thousand in savings—a lot for someone her age and in her profession. She associates with dubious people. Bikers, street thugs. Even some dissident Irish Republicans when she was living in Dublin. She's no innocent schoolgirl."

Give Bentley twenty-four hours and he'll have a dossier on anyone.

"We have to assume that she was in on it until we know otherwise, that her uncle involved her at some point, and gave her the videotape to hide."

"And she *needs* to be eliminated?"

"I need to know *all* potential risks are eliminated."

"That sounds like a collateral damage kill, Bentley, and you know I won't do that." My job is all about precision, and if I'm doing it right, there is no collateral damage. "Maybe she has it and doesn't know it."

Bentley pauses to stick his cigar into his mouth and light it. "You're thinking Beijing, aren't you?"

"Yeah." Two years ago, I was hunting down an American-born terrorist who stole a highly communicable virus from the CDC with intentions of selling it to extremists in North Korea. It took some blood and sweat, but he finally admitted to smuggling the tiny vial through American airport customs on his five-year-old daughter and then hiding it inside one of her dolls for the flight to Beijing, where he would await buyer contact.

News of the missing virus never made it beyond the walls of the CDC, buried to avoid pandemonium and public scrutiny; and whichever high-ranking CIA member tapped Bentley's shoulder for help ensured that there would never be a paper trail to the U.S. government when the thief's battered body washed up along the shore.

"Well, if that's the case, she's going to find out soon. She called a real estate agent about putting the place on the market within the next couple of weeks. She'll have to clean it out to sell it, and if she finds a hidden videotape in there, she'll sure as hell play it."

Will it mean anything to her? Will she care?

Bentley draws several long pulls off the cigar to get it going, all the while watching me with a knowing gaze.

The copy of her driver's license says she just turned twenty-five a few weeks ago. "Well, it's definitely not hiding in one of her dolls," I mutter quietly.

Bentley barks with laughter. "She looks like the type of girl who used to light dolls on fire instead."

There's definitely an edge to her, her heavy boots zagged with fluorescent pink laces, balancing out the plaid schoolgirl skirt that barely covers her ass. A skull stretches across her shirt, drawn in pink jewels, the California sun reflecting off them.

I wonder if it's just a look, if her tongue and mind are as sharp.

"I need this handled right, Sebastian, and you're the only one I trust," he says between puffs, the rich, aromatic smoke fighting for my attention.

It's the second time he's said that.

"I'll eliminate a known threat without question. You know that." I settle my gaze on Bentley, who watches me intently. "But I won't end an innocent life."

He pauses and smiles, and there's a hint of sympathy there. "I'm not asking you to. If she doesn't know about the tape, then keep it that way. Find it and bring it to me, and she and the world can go on believing that those other two were random, unfortunate deaths."

"That means I can't question her openly," I warn him. A few hours of questioning always gets me the answers I need. "This will take longer."

He sighs. "Yes, I realize that. But if she has any knowledge of this . . ." He tips his head back and releases a ring of smoke. It holds its shape for a few seconds before dispersing into the air above our heads. "We need to ensure that she doesn't have a chance to talk about it to anyone. Ever. Make it clean and quick and low-key. Coincidental."

Low-key. Coincidental.

A car careening off a road. A body found underwater, tangled in the weeds. A used needle laced with heroin. Something that is tragic but doesn't raise suspicions, especially given that her beloved uncle was murdered so recently.

The way Bentley's talking about it, it's like he's already decided that she is a liability and needs to be gone. But I also know that he's not sure, and that puts doubt in my mind. I never pull the trigger when there is doubt.

I study her severe scowl again. Even with it, there is a unique beauty in her face. She's not on the run, which makes me think Bentley is wrong and she doesn't know anything about what her uncle was up to. That, or her uncle's murder didn't scare her enough. But what if her uncle dragged her into something against her will? What if she knows something she can't simply unknow? Does she still deserve that kind of "low-key, coincidental" end?

It's not my call. It's Bentley's. I have a job to do, and I leave the questions of morality to my commanding officer, knowing he'll make the difficult calls. I'm quite happy letting him do that.

I scan her information more closely. "She's from Oregon?"

"That's her parents' address. She lived there from fifteen to eighteen, and has landed back there a few times for brief stints, but mainly she's been on the move, with no fixed address, crashing with friends and family. She came to San Francisco seven months ago. Before that she was in Thailand for a month. Before that, with family in Madrid for a few months. Before that, Ireland. She has American and EU citizenship. She's been searching out flights to New York, and Singapore, and even Australia on her phone this week. Looks like she's going to be on the move again, so you need to get in there fast."

If only the general public knew how easy it was to collect information on them. There are pages and pages of personal details in this folder: bank records showing a steady income and decent savings, which tells me she works hard and spends smartly; cell phone bills with mostly text messages, which tells me she doesn't like idle chitchat; a credit card statement with a zero balance and nothing but concert tickets, clothes, and ink supplies tells me her interests are simple. Flight receipts that tell me she's almost as mobile as I am, never in one place for too long. There isn't much Bentley can't get in the way of research, but I like to do my own recon anyway.

"I'll pay double the normal rate, because this is more involved than normal. The first half has already been wired." Bentley smiles. "If anyone can get information out of a young woman, I'm guessing it's you."

I ignore him. After what happened with the Grecian hooker, I'm not eager to jump into bed with anyone again, anytime soon. Especially someone whose life I may be ending soon. Not even *my* psyche can handle that. "I need a car."

"Steve will get you one."

"No GPS, no traceable plates, nondescript."

"You know that I run one of the biggest private security companies in the world, right?"

I can't help the smirk. "And yet you need me." Committing Ivy Lee's important details to memory and my phone camera screen—I definitely won't need a picture to identify her on the street—I make my way over to the fireplace. Opening the grille, I take a moment to light my Bolivar, and then I hold the flame to the corner of the folder, until it ignites.

I watch evidence turn to ash as I savor the cigar's mild blend of spicy fruitcake and chocolate, wondering if she's an innocent associate or a guilty accomplice.

"Why did you bring me to your home for this?"

"I figured you missed me." Bentley laughs when I shoot him a questioning look. "Honestly . . . What you do is invaluable to this country and its millions of people, and I know that you give it a hundred and fifty percent. You could have just as easily slipped away into oblivion after discharge."

I smirk. "Haven't I, though?" There are no medals or commendations for a successful assignment. No words of encouragement or pats on the shoulder. What I'm doing, no one will ever know about it. No one will ever talk about it. In many ways, I am a ghost.

"My point is that this life can't be easy. I wanted to see how you were doing, Sebastian."

He wants to see if my head is still screwed on straight. If my self-imposed isolation has taken its toll yet. The funny thing is, I don't mind it. Because the alternative—a life without meaningful purpose, living day to day with disgrace still hanging over me—is not one I ever want to live. I can't tell Bentley that my life is a dream because that would be a lie, but I can say that I'm still grateful that he's given it to me. "Thank you for continuing to trust me."

"It's not hard. You've proven yourself over and over again." He pauses. "Do you plan on seeing your parents while you're here?"

My parents. I still think about them on occasion, and I get the odd update from Bentley, because I asked him to keep an eye on them for me. They still live in the same small bungalow that I grew up in. I'm sure my father still flies the same American flag over the porch, a symbol of the country and his own illustrious career in the navy, although his had such a different outcome from his son's. "No. Not likely."

Bentley frowns. I guess that's not the answer he wanted. "Every time I reach out to you, you're in a different place." He puffs on his cigar. "Have you thought of settling in one location, finding yourself a woman to give you some stability?"

"So I can lie to her every day?"

"She doesn't need to know every detail. There is plenty that Tuuli is happy not to know about."

I flick the last of the papers into the hearth. "I find women when I need them."

"I'm not talking about whores. I'm talking about making a real life for yourself, with a wife. Maybe even some kids."

"You itching for grandkids?" It was a running joke while we served together, that Bentley spoke and treated me more like a son than my own father did. In a way, he's filled that role after my father all but abandoned it.

"I'm serious, Sebastian." And his voice says as much.

A wife and kids. I stopped picturing myself with a wife seven years ago, when my fiancée, Sharon, stood me up at the altar. Turns out it was a smart move on her part, because we never would have lasted. I'm not husband material, not anymore, anyway. And kids?

I've never felt the urge to procreate, and after all the violence that I've seen and committed, I'm even less inclined to bring an innocent child into this world and its problems.

"If the right woman turns up, maybe I will." I don't even try to sound convincing.

Bentley sighs and I sense that he's given up on that conversation. "Just move fast on this assignment. That tape is out there somewhere, and it needs to be found now. Today. Yesterday, in fact. If it comes to it, keep it quiet and clean. But make it fast." His deep frown tells me this video is worrying him. Royce must have accused these other guys of using some highly unpleasant interrogation methods. Things that are divulged by a Medal of Honor recipient will hold sway in the court of public opinion, even if they're not true. The media will release it and the American people will grab pitchforks and light flames.

And burn everything Bentley has worked so hard to accomplish.

I nod, hearing the directive loud and clear, checking the safety on the gun before tucking it into my boot. "I'll call you as soon as I know something."

# FIVE

# IVY

I glare at the last rusted bolt, my face damp with sweat, the socket wrench dangling from my aching hand. Black Rabbit has been open for thirty years and this leather chair has seen every last sinful day of it, stationed in the center of the worn wood floor like some sort of monument. I bugged Ned endlessly to replace it with a more modern design, but he refused.

Now I know why.

Because it is stuck to the fucking floor and is *never* going to move.

Ian left this morning, on a plane for Dublin via New York City, leaving me with some cash for a painter and the freedom to do whatever I want with this place. He's already lost almost a week's worth of business with the Fine Needle being closed and, while he's not driven by money, he needs to pay his bills. Plus he has also missed a week of the political science doctoral program he just started.

I understand why he left and I made sure to offer him a wave when the cab pulled out of the driveway, even though inside my head I was screaming at him to stay.

Not to leave me here to deal with this alone.

We called a real estate agent yesterday afternoon, for both the shop and the house. The woman's name is Becca. She sounds like she knows what she's doing. We also contacted a lawyer, to get the ball rolling on the estate settlement. I think Ian's secretly hoping that I'll change my mind and decide to stay in San Francisco to run Black Rabbit. That emptying the shop of Ned and giving it a fresh look will suddenly inspire me to make it my own. I don't see that happening. I've already got a place to stay in New York lined up with friends, if I want. Or maybe I'll head to Seattle.

But what *is* going to happen before I leave is this chair is going into a goddamn Dumpster so no one ever sits in it again. Whoever buys this shop will just have to get a new one.

I look down at myself, at my tight, torn—on purpose—jeans and my Ruckus Apparel T-shirt, smeared with dust and God knows what else, and chastise myself for not dressing more appropriately. Not that my clothing choice is going to give me the rusted-bolt-twisting superpowers that I need right now anyway.

I drop to my knees, the wood grain rough against my exposed skin, and I grit my teeth as I throw my full weight—which isn't nearly enough—against the wrench's handle. It doesn't move, not a fraction of an inch.

It hasn't my last five tries either. This time, though, I actually lose my balance and tumble over flat on my back. "Fuck!" I yell, whipping the wrench across the floor to clatter noisily in a corner. I pull myself up and lean back against the chair and close my eyes, tears of frustration threatening to spill.

Of course someone chooses that moment to knock on the glass pane in the door.

The sudden sound makes me jump. Most sudden sounds have been making me jump lately.

"Closed!" I holler. I'm in no mood to deal with anyone and kick myself for not shutting the steel grate. I can't bring myself to pull the shades, though. It makes Black Rabbit too dark, too isolated.

Too much like that night.

"Ned was halfway done with my sleeve," a guy's muffled voice answers from outside.

"Well, then I guess you're only going to have half a sleeve."

"Come on, Ivy . . ." he pleads in a whiny voice.

With an irritated sigh, I open one eye and take in the burly man pressed against the glass, watching me. "I don't know you." Ned worked a lot of strange hours, though, especially in the mornings. It's quite possible this guy sat in this chair for five hours before I ever stepped in here.

Or maybe he isn't a client of Ned's and he's here to hurt me because I gave the police information about "Mario." It's a worry that lodged in the back of my mind a few days after the initial shock wore off. What if I saw something I wasn't supposed to see? What if someone thinks I know something that I don't? I certainly don't have any valuable intel. The police thanked me for my help with the information I provided—a first name and shiny black combat boots, and a mediocre description of the cash register man's profile that hasn't resulted in any leads through the media so far. There's a good chance that Ned's murder will go unsolved. Detective Fields was considerate enough to spell that out to Ian and me when we asked.

The bushy blond beard covering the man's face doesn't hide his broad smile. "You mean to tell me you don't remember the scrawny kid who'd come in here with toy race cars, wanting to play?"

That *does* sound familiar. I frown. "Bobby?" Son of Moe, one of Ned's biker customers? This guy looks nothing like that scrawny kid. He could easily pass for thirty, even though I remember him being younger than me.

"In the flesh."

*Holy shit.* I completely forgot about him. "You heard what happened, right?" I can't see how he didn't. It was all over the local news, and his dad was at the funeral, along with a dozen other bikers. Maybe he was there, too. I didn't pay much attention to faces.

A solemn look touches his eyes when he nods. "Come on. Open up."

Reluctantly, I climb to my feet and make my way over to unlock the door. Bobby has to duck to step through the doorway, his heavy boots making the floorboards creak. He's more than double my size, and I don't doubt there's also muscle under all that leather and thick layer of fat. If I hadn't spent so much time with guys like this, I'd be nervous standing in here alone with him now.

But I see the Harley parked outside and the official death's hand insignia on his leather vest that marks him as a member of Devil's Iron, and I'm just plain mad. "The cops said that what happened to Ned may have had something to do with you and your guys. Is that true?" I stare him right in the eye, willing myself to see the truth—or lie—for what it is. Ned was no saint, I know that. I know of a couple instances where some booze and cartons of cigarettes "fell off the back of a truck" and into the hands of guys like Bobby. Ned helped sell some of the inventory through here, to his regulars. People he trusted.

And that's just what I know about. I have no idea what I *don't* know about.

"Me?" Bobby's hands press against his chest. He looks taken aback.

I nod toward his vest. *"You."*

He's shaking his head even before the words come out. "No, ma'am. We had nothing to do with what happened in here." His soft blue eyes roam the shop. "Though trust me, the pigs have been poking around the clubhouse, trying to provoke the guys plenty."

"What have you heard on the street?" It's a ballsy question, assuming that a biker gang that despises law enforcement would offer information that might help in an official investigation, but it's worth a shot.

Bobby shakes his head. "All quiet on our front, so far. What do you know?"

I'm not supposed to say anything . . . "Two guys, one named Mario. One with dark hair, muscular, midthirties. That's all I know."

He dips his head. "All right. I'll ask around, and I promise you, if I catch wind of something I'll pass it along."

He's buttering me up, I can just feel it. "And in return you want . . ."

With a sheepish grin, he holds out a thick arm—the same

circumference as my thigh—to show me the detailed outline of a zombie bride with playful eyes and long lashes covering his biceps. Crisp, clean lines. Sordid humor. Definitely Ned's work. "Ned always said you were a close second to him. I'd love it if you could finish this for me." He peers at me with puppy-dog eyes you wouldn't expect from a guy with his affiliations.

Ned would hate knowing that a subpar artist—basically anyone else—added ink to his work, and even though he's six feet under, I owe it to him to finish it. Still . . . "I'll think about it," I finally mutter, blowing a strand of long hair that fell across my face off. "But not today. I'm busy."

"I can see that." He nods at the chair. "You gettin' rid of it?"

"Yup."

"Why? Ned loved that chair."

*And he died in that chair.* I restrain myself from being that blunt. "It just needs to go."

Bobby's heavy boots clomp across the floor to rescue the wrench from the corner where I threw it. Dropping his massive frame to one knee, he attempts to unfasten the bolt but quits soon after. "It's seized. You're going to need a torch for that."

"Fabulous. Because I have one just lying around."

"I could bring one by and help you out. Say . . . tomorrow, around three?" His eyes flicker to his arm and then to me, and I see the trade-off for his help. He's good, I'll give him that much. I want to say no, but I also don't know anyone else who owns a torch.

I really do need his help.

"Fine." I can't believe I'm actually agreeing to finish that tattoo *here.* I don't even know that I have it in me to do that. I should tell him to meet me anywhere but here: in a garage or bar or back alley or his biker gang clubhouse.

"I'll be here at three." His grin falls quickly. "Ned was a good friend to all of us. We had some great laughs down at the clubhouse on game night."

Game night is a fancy way of saying poker Wednesdays, where Ned would more times than not lose his shirt to a biker. He hadn't been down there in a few weeks, though. Said it was costing him too much lately.

Things are starting to make sense to me. "Was he into it for money with someone over there?"

"Eh." Bobby shrugs noncommittally, and I'm not entirely sure what that answer means.

"Is that a yes or a no?"

"Nothin' major from what I know." He rests a hand on the back of the leather chair. "You know, I always hoped Ned would be here to do my son's one day, too. When I have a son, of course. I don't have one yet." His gaze drifts down my front, stalling over my chest. "I need to find a good woman first."

*Look elsewhere for that good woman, buddy.* The loyalty to my uncle is charming, though, in a weird way. "Well, maybe your non-existent son will still get his done in Black Rabbit. We'll see who buys this place."

"It won't be the same, though." He shrugs. "Unless you'll still be here?"

"Nope. Not a chance." I heave a sigh and, hoping Bobby takes the hint, begin carefully picking away at a photo montage on the wall—dozens of pictures of Ned at different stages of his life, from clean-shaven to handlebar mustache, stuck to the drywall with tape so old it's peeling paint away with it.

"See ya tomorrow, Ivy." The bell above the door jangles as Bobby leaves.

And the silence that returns now is somehow more unnerving than before.

I quietly sort and toss and pack, shifting around the chair, my irritation with that single bolt growing with each moment until I find myself standing there, glaring at it once again. Tomorrow just isn't soon enough.

I get down on my knees again and, holding my breath, throw my full weight into the bolt, just as the door creaks open. "We're closed!" I yell, whipping my head around, my anger at myself for not locking it launched.

A man I've never seen before stands motionless in front of me, amusement in his eyes as he stares. Nothing else about him betrays his thoughts, though. His stance is still and relaxed, his angular face perfectly composed.

My heart begins to race with unease.

"I'd like some work done." His voice is deep, almost gravelly, his tone even and calm.

I climb to my feet, because I don't like anyone towering over me. And because his piercing eyes unsettle me. Unlike the two-hundred-and-fifty-pound biker who just left, this guy makes me nervous. The wrench is still in my fist, and I grip it tightly now. "I'm not working today."

"Tomorrow."

"I'm not working tomorrow either."

The corner of his mouth twitches as we face off against each other. "When will you be working again, then?"

He's patient. It's annoying. But he also seems very interested in this tattoo, which makes it less likely that he's here to hurt me. I relax my grip on the wrench. "I won't be. Not here, anyway. Black Rabbit is closed for good, or at least until it opens under new ownership."

He pauses, his shrewd gaze weighing so heavily on me that I finally have to look away from him. I feel like a sophomore year science class dissection—the unfortunate amphibian donated in the name of education. "That's a shame."

Either he's not from around here or he hasn't read the news. Or he's one of those sickos who gets a kick out of crime scenes. "It is." What's really a shame is that this guy didn't come a few weeks ago, because I gladly would have agreed to mark his entire body with my hands then.

On first-glance impression, he actually reminds me of Jesse Welles, the love of my teenage life, though I'd never admit that to anyone. This guy's eyes are lighter—a cool chocolate rather than near-black—but they have that same intensity; a similar smirk sits atop his full lips. He, too, has dark hair coating his hard, masculine jaw; it's just sculpted to a perfect short beard. He's taller and broader than Jesse. Harder looking, not just by a few years of age but as if by life itself. That's a little concerning, given the kind of life that Jesse Welles has already lived.

But there's something distinctly different about this guy, too. I can't quite place it, but I can feel it. Something slightly "off." Or maybe it's just this place that's making everything in my life feel off—after all, my mind is still in a haze over Ned's death. The last thing I should be thinking about right now is this guy or Jesse or getting laid.

He takes slow, even steps around me, circling the chair, his hands resting in his pockets. "What if I offer to pay you double your rate?"

I frown. I've never had anyone offer to pay more. If anything, they're haggling to lower my hourly charge. Is he an idiot? "Do you know what my rate is?"

His lips twist into a pucker, as if he's thinking about it. "It can't be too much."

I eye him up and down. He's wearing nondescript black hiking boots, a black T-shirt, and plain blue jeans. Not Wranglers but not custom-made. He looks good in them, but I think that has more to do with his impressive build than choice in fashion. "What if I said it was five hundred an hour?"

"Then I'd say that I heard you were really good at what you do."

"You mean kick-ass, right?" To some people, I sound arrogant. But in this business, you have to exude confidence. People are allowing you to take a needle filled with permanent ink to their bodies. They're not going to feel safe with an insecure artist. That's something Ned taught me. He also said that you have to walk the talk, because you won't fool a person more than once and this business is all about referral—except for the odd moron who walks into a shop and flashes his skin without ever so much as looking at a portfolio. It's rare, but it happens.

Thankfully, I can walk the talk. I *am* that good.

"Who'd you hear that from?" I ask.

"A friend named Mike."

I've traveled all over the world and inked hundreds of people. I've worked on at least five Mikes, Michaels, or Micks. Names mean little. "What'd I do for him?"

"A skull," he answers without missing a beat.

Great. Just as useless. I've done at least a dozen skulls. So common.

His upper lip twitches ever so slightly. "Do you normally interrogate potential customers like this?"

"No," I admit. I'm not exactly sure why I'm doing it now. Looking for reasons not to trust this guy, a valid excuse to turn him away, perhaps.

"Then do my reasons for being willing to pay more really matter?" Again, that arrogant little smirk.

In another time, that may have held sway. I've always had a weakness for strong but quiet masculinity. "No, they don't. Because Black Rabbit is closed and I have a ton of cleaning up to do to get the place ready for selling." I can't help my voice from cracking with emotion now. I've managed to keep down so far. If I can just get through this, maybe it'll fade without ever truly surfacing.

He nods toward the chair. "What are you doing with that?"

"Throwing it in the Dumpster, if I can ever get this bolt off."

"Why?"

I'm tired of being questioned about this stupid chair. "Because someone was murdered in it."

Most normal people would flinch at an answer like that, or press with more specific questions. Not this guy. He simply leans over to reach into the toolbox on the floor for another wrench.

"Don't bother. I need a torch," I mutter as he crouches down, the cuffs of his jeans hiking up to show more of his boots.

He ignores me, latching the end onto the bolt. The muscles in his arms and shoulders cord as he works on it, his body rocking back and forth several times until the bolt gives way and begins to rise from the ground, flecks of orange rust dusting the floor.

"That worked?" I exclaim in shock, relief filling my chest.

Bobby was wrong. Or he just tricked me into agreeing to finish his ink for him. Either way, I'm going to call the beefy biker on it—who must have at least fifty pounds and three inches on this guy—when he shows up here tomorrow.

"Use a six-point wrench next time. Better grip," the guy says, standing up smoothly. All of his movements seem fluid. "Do you want help bringing it outside?"

"No. I'll do it myself." He's being too nice to me, and I don't have the energy to be nice back.

A flash of surprise skitters across his face—a momentary lapse of his carefully guarded expression perhaps. "How?" His eyes drift over my limbs, toned but slender.

I know I'm small. I've always been small. When I was young, I was tiny. Thank God for that growth spurt at fourteen or I might have snapped one day and turned homicidal, after a lifetime of people telling me what I can't do because of my size. My teachers, my friends, their parents. Even my own parents worried about me more than they did my brothers. They still do. It's a double-edged sword with them, though. Not only am I small, I'm also a girl. Aka fragile. Weak.

I've spent my entire life proving to them—and everyone—that I'm not a weak little girl. That's probably why I've become so independent. If I don't ask for help, then in my head I'm proving them all wrong. I can't have people seeing me in that light, especially in this profession.

Granted, as I stand next to this tattoo chair that probably weighs as much as I do and I probably *am* physically too weak to drag down the hall, I know that I should accept his help. Too bad I'm also stubborn.

"It's not your problem." I level his unreadable gaze with one of my own, that I know without seeing a reflection isn't pleasant. My friend Amber tells me often enough to wipe it off.

It doesn't seem to faze him. He folds his thick arms over his chest. Waiting for me to ask for help, which I'm not going to do, because then I'd owe him and I hate owing people.

The guy isn't wavering, and this showdown is becoming more and more uncomfortable as each second passes. Finally I break free of his gaze. "If you don't mind, now. I'm going to be here all night as it is."

He tears a sheet of paper towel from the roll and wipes the wrench before setting it back in the box. He wipes his hands next. Again, so graceful. Turning on his heels, he begins walking toward the door, offering a low "You're welcome."

"Wait . . ." I heave a sigh, rolling my eyes.

He stops, turns. Settles that stone-cold gaze like he's expecting something.

Fuck, I already do owe him. I really hate owing people! And somehow I've gone from no customers to two in a matter of thirty minutes. Though, as I study his face—a nose that should be too long and narrow but on his angular face not so; a too-perfect dark trim beard, as if he shaped it with a straight razor or something—I decide there could be worse things than owing a man who looks like him. "Come by on Thursday and we'll talk. Maybe I can do your ink then."

"I'll think about it." He turns and strolls out the front door, leaving me staring at his back in wonder. What was that supposed to be? A hissy fit?

"Whatever," I grumble, locking the dead bolt on the door to avoid any more surprise customers. Holding my breath, I pull the shades down. I dismiss the guy from my thoughts and shift back to my task. This fucking chair that, thanks to the mystery man, can now go into the Dumpster.

I put all of my weight into it as I push.

It doesn't even budge.

# SIX

# SEBASTIAN

With my keys in the ignition, I pause once to get another look at the old storefront signage, at the playful eyes staring down at me, and smile. They belong on a puppy or kitten, not on a feral fanged jackrabbit. Kind of like the exotic girl with the razor-sharp attitude inside. Though her eyes aren't necessarily playful. Soft, yes. Veiled behind a tough act, but I saw the vulnerability there. The need to appear strong when she doesn't really feel it inside.

She *is* strong, I'll give her that. Her uncle was murdered a week ago and she's not sitting in there, crying about it. She's set her grief aside to do what needs to be done, and that's a quality not everyone possesses. She's doing it on her own, too, I presume, because I don't see anyone around to help her.

But she's definitely not unaffected by what's happened. I could see it in the dark bags under her eyes, as if she hasn't slept in days. I saw it in the way she reacted to me entering the shop, her tiny fist curled around the wrench, ready to defend herself if she needed to.

I knew about her two-hundred-dollar-an-hour rate before stepping inside, thanks to a quick website search. That, along with an impressive portfolio of work, confirmed to me that I have nothing to worry about if I were forced to have her hold a needle to my flesh. But for now that's not necessary because I got what I needed.

Information.

She's going to be busy here for a good few hours, which means her house is waiting for me.

I feel the pull, though, to go back and just drag that chair out for her, despite her attitude. She's too arrogant or suspicious or plain fucking mule-headed to accept help when she clearly needed it, stretching her tiny body—that I could snap in two in a heartbeat—to her full five-foot-two stature in defiance, even as I towered over her. She clearly wants it out for emotional reasons, to try to unsee whatever she witnessed that led to her uncle's murder. I want to tell her that it's pointless. She'll never be able to shed those memories.

But I'm not here to be her shrink or her confidant.

And if she knows anything about this videotape, then I'm about to become her worst nightmare.

■  ■  ■

Ingleside hasn't changed much in the years since I've driven through here. The houses are all still small, square, and crammed together, and lining some of the steepest hills in San Francisco with a rainbow of colors—everything from muted gray to Pepto-Bismol pink. Bars cover the first-floor windows of the seedy corner stores and the houses, telling me that the area's issues with burglary haven't abated.

I leave my car a full block down from Ned Marshall's address and walk the rest of the way, keeping my baseball cap pulled down over my face. Of the few people I pass, the majority are Asian. That's a plus. Most prosecutors consider them unreliable witnesses when it comes to identifying Caucasian suspects. Not that I expect to get caught.

I spot the number up ahead and turn to climb the steep steps like I belong here, at this house on the corner with decorative white grates to protect it from invaders. I prefer window entry, but it would require scaling the walls to the second story here, leaving me exposed. So I'm left with going through the front door.

The gate lock takes me ten seconds to pick, allowing me into the small, secluded entranceway, littered with old running shoes and a can of sand filled with cigarette butts. A flawed and idiotic set up in home design. You're just giving people like me cover while they spend the extra time to pick your dead bolt and get into your house. Of course, a dead bolt isn't child's play. It would cause issues for a local thug looking to lift a TV or cash, but it's not going to stop a guy like me, who was picking locks for fun long before I had any real reason to.

I'm inside in another thirty seconds, securing the door quietly behind me. I stop to listen for creaks and voices, the cold metal of my Beretta pressed against my leg, ready to be pulled out of my boot if necessary. I'm ninety-five percent certain that no one else is here. The guy who jumped into an airport taxi this morning with a suitcase was clearly leaving, and there were no signs of anyone else here after the girl left for the shop.

Ned Marshall was an avowed bachelor, that much is obvious. A few mismatched chairs are scattered throughout the living room, a four-person glass-and-brass table with tall-backed white kitchen chairs—the ones from the eighties, with the trademark blue, green, and pink patterned cushions—fill the dining room. My parents had those when I was growing up.

The walls are a faded mint green, probably painted by the previous owner, or maybe an ex-wife, and empty save for a few Zeppelin and Willie Nelson posters. In my initial scan, I see nothing of value, other than the fifty-inch flat-screen hanging on the wall and the corner cabinet of liquor bottles.

But there may be something of worth within these walls. Something that will destroy all the good work that Alliance has done if it gets into the wrong hands.

I slip on my gloves and begin my search.

■ ■ ■

This is what happens when you put a bullet in a guy's head before you get the fucking information that you need out of him.

I wipe the sheen of sweat off my forehead with my forearm,

my frustration settling uncomfortably on my nerves. I've searched under every piece of furniture, in and behind every drawer. I even crawled through the narrow attic.

There's no videotape.

If it's not in this bedroom, then it's not in this house.

I check my watch, keenly aware of the time and how long I've been here. Hours. It's six now. I'm guessing that the girl doesn't often come home to eat, given that a look inside the fridge revealed nothing but soda cans and ketchup. Still, I've mapped my escape route. The window in the back bedroom, which lets out above a small shed in the prison-cell-size concrete backyard, will work if I need it.

Strolling over to the unmade mattress that sits on the carpet, I crouch down to lift red lace panties lying haphazardly on top. This is obviously the girl's room. It feels like it would be her room. Chaotic. Clothes are scattered all over the floor, overflowing from the open suitcase that lies there. That's probably been sitting there since she landed in San Francisco seven months ago.

With only a two-drawer chest and a small closet for her clothes, she could use the lack of storage space as an excuse. With a recent death in her family, she could use the excuse of being in mourning. But my five-minute read of her today told me she's the type that just doesn't give a shit about order on any given day.

I, on the other hand, thrive on order.

I begin searching the usual spots—furniture, mattress, vents—and when that turns up nothing, I move on to the nightstand. Sliding open the drawer, I find no videotape. What I do find is an open box of condoms and a pink vibrator. I'm going to assume that the condoms mean she doesn't hate men, though today's encounter would suggest otherwise. Bentley's report said nothing about a boyfriend, and if there were even a hint of a boyfriend, it would have been in that report. A twenty-five-year-old girl who keeps a box of condoms in her nightstand is definitely responsible and possibly promiscuous. Or at least she isn't opposed to spontaneous sex. She's not keeping these in her dresser for when she meets "the right guy." Women who do that hide their stash in the bottom of their dresser drawer until the guy is actually in the picture.

I reach down and pick up the long, smooth pink vibrator that lies next to the condoms, rolling it in my gloved hand. A tube of lubricant is also in the drawer, and it's half used, telling me that this toy isn't collecting dust, and that this unfriendly girl likes to get off.

She's a bit scrawny for my taste. I like my women with some meat on them. Tits that bounce and hips to grab. Still, invading her most private things right now is stirring my blood.

I set the toy back in the drawer and push it shut, quietly chastising myself. I never have trouble focusing on my task. That's why Bentley trusts me. This must be because my targets have always been middle-aged men with vile reputations.

I move on to a collection of mostly black and purple clothes, rifling first through the mess on the floor and then in the drawers that house her collection of bras and panties. Surprisingly, I find a lot of pink-and-white lace and silk. A feminine contradiction to her edgy exterior.

A well-used sketchbook rests on the floor next to my foot, distracting me from her intimates. I pick it up and begin flipping through. Each page is filled with portraits of various faces, everything from little girls to weathered old men. The detail is impressive, but I guess I shouldn't be surprised. I already knew she was a talented artist.

I know I won't find any tapes in this room, and yet I'm not ready to leave. There could be something of use here. Something that helps me understand her and where she might have hidden it. Or where her uncle might have hidden it for her to find.

A bottle of perfume sits on the counter. I wonder if it's the same intoxicating scent my nose caught in Black Rabbit earlier today. I've been trained to rely heavily on *all* of my senses, so I tend to process my surroundings differently than a civilian would. The way a specific door hinge squeaks or a person's footfall scrapes against the floor, the scent of a cologne that may help identify a person who was in a room just moments ago, the taste of a smoke in the air—it's how I've survived this long.

Pulling my gloves off so as not to get any of the perfume on the leather, I pick up the bottle and spray a small stream into the air. The girlish mix of almonds and coconut permeates the room, and I close my eyes, reveling in its femininity for a few long moments while I clear my thoughts.

A cell phone rings from somewhere in the house.

My eyes fly open.

"Hey . . . I thought you'd be over the ocean by now," says a female voice.

She's in the fucking house.

She's in the fucking house and I didn't hear her come in because I was too distracted by her art and perfume.

This complicates things.

"Dude, that sucks, but at least they got you onto another plane . . . right . . ."

A creak sounds, and I know that it's on the third step because I noticed it when I climbed up earlier.

She's on her way upstairs, and that means my escape route is no longer an option.

Setting the perfume bottle down carefully, I grab my gloves and dive for the only hiding place available, my adrenaline spiking.

SEVEN

# IVY

"Text me when you land over there, 'kay?"

"Did you get far with the shop today?" Ian asks through a yawn. He must be exhausted. Sitting at JFK for almost three hours because of plane issues—after already flying across the country—has to suck.

"A dent. I called that painter but I'm waiting for him to get back to me. Any specific color you want me to tell him to use?"

"You pick. I trust you."

I roll my eyes.

"Thanks, Ivy, for doing this. I know I've left you alone to handle all of this at the worst time."

*That's right, you have!* the bitter little voice in the back of my head screams. I keep it at bay, though, mainly because I don't know why I'm hearing it now. I've never minded being alone. I've preferred it, actually. Only now alone feels very different. It's not thrilling and liberating. It's scary and overwhelming.

"Being busy is good for me right now," I say instead. That's probably true as well. "Safe flight." I hang up and toss my phone onto the mattress with a deep yawn. I had every intention of working on the shop into the night so I could maybe be done with it, but I hit a wall around six and was ready to curl up into a ball in the back room.

I'm guessing it's because I haven't really slept in a week and it's finally catching up to me. The first night—the night that Ned died—I didn't even walk through the front door downstairs until seven the next morning. I didn't sleep the rest of that day, either, and drifted off only when Ian arrived on the doorstep. Every night since then I've found myself staring out the window for hours, until I finally drift off from sheer exhaustion, only to wake up in a cold sweat and with a knot in my stomach a few hours later.

I glance at my alarm clock. It's almost seven. If I go to bed now, I'm afraid I'll be lying awake and restless in bed by midnight. I stretch deeply and glance around the perpetual mess that is my room. I guess I could kill time by putting away my clothes.

My least favorite thing to do, next to folding laundry. But I may as well start the process. Once the shop is in order for sale, the house will be next, and no real estate agent will agree to put this place up looking like it does right now.

Scooping up the items that I know are dirty, I half stagger over to the hamper sitting next to my chest of drawers. A wave of my perfume hits me and I automatically inhale. It was a birthday present that came in the mail from my friend Amber a few weeks ago. I stole enough squirts from her bottle when I saw her last to flag that it might be something I would like. I must have put too much on earlier, if it still lingers in the air now. That or my senses are overloaded from exhaustion.

A basket full of freshly washed, now-wrinkled clothes sits next to my bed. I dump everything onto my mattress and fish out the long black dress with deep slits up the sides that I wear often. This I definitely want to hang in my closet for when I'm not elbow-deep in packing.

I head for the narrow slatted door ahead, turning the dress right-side out on my way.

My cell phone rings, stopping me in my tracks.

I'm relieved, happy to abandon my half-assed efforts to tidy and have an excuse to dive onto my mattress again. When I see who's calling, I'm even happier. "Hey, you."

"Hey. How are you holding up?"

A few years ago, if someone told me that Amber Welles and I would become good friends, I'd have laughed in their face. She'd been my enemy since sophomore year of high school, though she had no idea, and it turns out I didn't really have a good reason for hating her. But I didn't know that until last summer, when a night of Jameson whiskey, unbridled words, and an Irish bartender revealed the former rodeo queen's vulnerabilities, I guess. It allowed me to confront all the ways I thought she had wronged me but hadn't. It also forced me to confront all of my insecurities.

It was a chance to hit the Reset button, and I'm glad I took it.

"I'm okay," I say through a yawn, growing more tired by the second. I lie back and hit Speakerphone before setting my phone on my chest.

"I'm so sorry I couldn't make it to the funeral."

It's the third time she's apologized. "Seriously, I would never expect you to cancel your trip to Dublin for my uncle's funeral. I sure as hell wouldn't cancel my trip anywhere for your uncle's funeral." That sounds awful now that I've said it out loud. But she knows what I mean.

"Still . . ." Silence hangs between us.

"How was your latest reunion?"

I can hear the smile in her voice. "Amazing. And also terrible. It's getting harder and harder to come home."

I knew this long-term relationship arrangement would not work for Amber. "You should just stay over there. I don't know why you'd want to come back."

"Because I have family here, Ivy!" she exclaims, exasperated. Amber is a daddy's girl, through and through. "Just like *you* do, by the way."

"Right. I do, don't I?" I say dryly. A mom and dad and two younger brothers, whom I love very much but don't feel related to. "I just saw my parents a few days ago, for the funeral. They came down and stayed with my aunt Jun at a hotel for two nights. It was long enough." My dad glared at my sleeve of tattoos with disappointment. I've sabotaged any chances for a decent job and respectable husband, he told me. My mom didn't say much of anything at all, having already given up on her daughter. Her focus is now on her two boys—Jin, the nineteen-year-old, who's on his way to med school in another two years, and my twenty-one-year-old brother Bo, who also has Spanish citizenship and was just added to the roster of their national soccer team. "You know, the more I think about it, I wonder if Ned and my mom had a secret affair and I was the result." I frown. "But I guess that wouldn't explain the whole Chinese thing. Maybe I'm just Ned's child, and I have no mother. I just appeared one day."

"Oh my God, Ivy. When did you sleep last?"

"It's been a while," I admit.

"Maybe you should think about coming home for a while."

My mom said the exact same thing at the funeral. I hadn't expected them to show up, to be honest, but they didn't necessarily come to pay respects to Ned—they had no respects for him. But Jun and Ian were here, and they wanted to support them, and me, I guess. "Sisters was never my home." It was just another place that I stayed for a while.

"Portland then, at least? It's only a few hours away."

I sigh. "I know you can't survive without me, but I'm not moving back."

Amber's soft laughter carries through my bedroom, bringing with it much-needed life. "So . . . where to next?"

She has learned about my wayward tendencies by now, although it baffles her that I'm happier not having permanent roots, while she thrives on those roots. She's clearly trying to relate to me by asking this question, but still, I'm tired of answering it. "I don't know. I have friends in New York. I think I'll go squat over there for a while. Pick up some work."

"And what's the plan for the house and the shop?"

"I was at the shop all day, cleaning it out so it can get painted. It's going to take a while, though, seeing as I'm on my own."

She sighs. "I tried to get a few days off so I could come down and help you, but I think I've already pissed my boss off with my crazy schedule and constant traveling."

"Don't worry. I get it."

"What about Dakota? Can she help?"

I snort. "Honestly, I'll be faster working on my own than with Dakota there to distract me with her musings about spirits and auras and the meaning of life." We'd probably just end up smoking a joint and staring at the wall for the afternoon. "I'm managing on my own just fine. Though I had to get help loosening a seized bolt today, from this guy who came in for a tattoo."

"That was nice of him to help. What'd you end up doing on him?"

"Nothing. I refused to do his tattoo," I mutter.

"Ivy . . ." Amber's got the whole motherly reproachful tone down pat already. Her future kids are screwed.

"I know." The guilt over being a complete bitch to him still lingers. "And he was *really* hot, too."

"Let me guess—J.Crew and Calvin Klein?"

"Levi's and Hanes, actually." Amber's making fun of the fact that I wear tats and leather and shave the sides of my head, and yet I go after guys who look like they belong in a chain store catalog. She's right and I can't explain it.

"So Miss Picky actually found a guy she deems 'really hot' and she turned down the chance to tattoo him and then, I'm sure, sleep with him?" Amber mocks. "I think that's a first."

I smile. "It's *definitely* a first."

"What did he look like?"

"Kind of like your brother, actually."

"Ugh. Gross. And where did he want his tattoo?"

"Doesn't matter. I would have made him strip either way," I admit with a smirk.

Amber laughs. "And then you'd have had your way with him and sent him packing."

"What can I say? My affections are fierce but short-lived."

"I still don't know how we became friends."

"Neither do I, honestly." We are as opposite as opposite gets. Amber thrives on long-term commitment. I'm pretty sure that her little "Irish fling" was the most spontaneous, wild thing she's ever done, and ever will do—and now they're in a full-fledged, long-distance relationship. Meanwhile, the longest commitment I ever made was to a guy named Jet, when I was twenty-two and living in Portland. He was a professional rodeo guy. I don't even like rodeo guys. But I dated him for three whole weeks, mainly because we didn't do much talking during that time.

"We just haven't found you the right guy yet."

"Good luck finding me someone who holds my interest for more than a night or two."

"He's got to be out there. And when you find him, you're going to call me and, for once, I'll be the one who gets to tell you to stop talking about a guy so much." I roll my eyes at the cheesy romantic notion. I don't see that ever happening.

"Seriously, how long has it been since you've dated anyone?"

"Dated" is *so* the wrong word for any of my hookups and Amber knows that, but I don't correct her. "Since last summer, in Dublin."

"Oh my God. Wait, does that mean you haven't slept with anyone since—"

"Yup." I admit grudgingly. "The longest dry spell of my short life since high school." As much as I was an outcast in high school, as soon as I got out, I never had trouble attracting guys. Apparently everyone wants to fuck a badass Asian girl at least once.

Unfortunately for them, this badass Asian girl is not an easy score unless she wants to be.

"Maybe you should come back to Dublin then. I know he'd love to see you."

I hum noncommittally. "Grinning Irishmen aren't my type." He actually *did* make me laugh, though I rarely let him see it.

"So . . . Once the store is cleaned out? What are you going to do?" she pushes, back to the serious side of things.

"Once the legal stuff is sorted out, we're going to sell it. Ian can't run it and I don't want to. We also need to get rid of this house and its giant mortgage as soon as we can. Then I'm ghosting."

"Seriously? You know you could run that shop. Isn't that what you've always talked about?"

It's my dream for an older, tamer version of myself. A quiet little shop with character, a steady clientele. "Yeah, but I never wanted it at the expense of my uncle's life."

She sighs. "I know . . . I'm sorry. It's horrible to talk about it like that. But maybe you shouldn't sell so quickly. Can you afford to sit on it for a few months?"

I scowl at the dirty ceiling above. It's the first time I've actually lain in bed in daylight and bothered to look. Now I see that it's in desperate need of paint, as much as every other room in this house. "Did Ian call and ask you to convince me to stay?"

"Ian doesn't have my number, Ivy. Unless you gave it to him."

I roll my eyes. As smart as Amber is, sometimes she doesn't get my jokes. "The shop has a hundred K mortgage on it. Plus, I don't want to stay. It's just not the same here anymore. Everything about San Francisco changed when Ned died. The shop is haunted. This house is big and empty and eerie and . . ." I shudder. "Sometimes I feel like I'm being watched. It's just . . ." I work at my laces, unfastening them so I can kick off my boots. "I agreed to finish someone's tattoo for him tomorrow afternoon and I don't want to do it. I don't even know if I can do it."

"I'd hate to be that person."

"Ain't that the truth," I mumble, unfastening my jeans. I slide them over my hips and kick until they fall from my feet.

"It sounds like you're done for the day. You should get some sleep," Amber chides. "I'm sure you haven't been doing much of that either."

My pillow feels so soft and welcoming beneath my head. "That's the best idea you've had in forever."

She laughs. "Yeah. Okay. Call me anytime. Or text. If I don't answer, it means I'm working or sleeping. Because that's all I'll be doing for the foreseeable future."

"Night. And . . ." I hesitate, because saying anything that may hint at feelings has always been hard for me. "Thanks for calling."

"Of course, Ivy. Now sleep. Nurse's orders."

I press End with a nostalgic smile. Those few weeks with Amber in Dublin were some of the best I'd had in a long time, and I now consider her one of my best friends. Clearly, that says something about me and my ability to make—and keep—friends. Speaking of which . . . I scroll through my texts, squinting to read the words through my bleary eyes. One from Dakota, who's checking to see if I'm still coming over for our usual Wednesday night dinner at her place. As much as I could probably use the semblance of something familiar, dinner is never dinner with just Dakota. It's with her and an array of very unusual people, some whom she may know well, or not at all.

I'll have to call her, but not tonight because that's an hour-long conversation about nothing. I like Dakota a lot, but the girl tends to go off on weed-induced tangents that I don't have patience for.

There's another message from Fez, the pizza delivery guy from down the street from Black Rabbit whom I've befriended over the months.

*The cuts 2nite?*

That sparks my interest. As exhausted as I am, my body is thrumming with tension. I could probably use a night out, to release some of this pent-up anxiety. And if I fall asleep now—which I'm about to—I'll be wide awake by two at the very latest, twiddling my thumbs and needing to get the hell out of this eerie house.

I hit Dial, because the last time I tired-texted, auto-correct somehow turned my errors into a sexual proposition, and Fez definitely doesn't interest me in that way, even if I know he's secretly in love with me and would screw me in a heartbeat, given the chance.

"Hey, Bae."

I roll my eyes. At thirty-five, Fez speaks in slang, clichés, and short form. Not just Bay Area slang either. He's like a mishmash of all the latest slang running through social media, along with oldies that no one uses anymore. I blame it all on YouTube and his attempt at being world famous by videotaping hours of himself every week and posting it online. It's all he talks about. I think it's his way of feeling better about the fact that he still lives with his parents and works at their pizza shop.

Half the time I can't understand what the hell he's saying. The other half, I don't want to know what he's saying. "What time are you going?"

"Sundown."

"Where exactly?" "The cuts"—what he refers to as the rougher part of the Mission District, is a six-block stretch of city, going from Ninth to Fifteenth.

"The ol' depot. You down?"

"Yeah. I'm just going to grab a few hours of sleep, but I'll be there. Wait for me."

"Fo sho. Gonna be epic!"

"See you later." I hang up before he can say anything else. I'm too tired to deal with him right now. Plugging my phone into the charger by my nightstand, I briefly consider just passing out, but I run hot when I sleep, and I always regret it when I wake up sweaty and uncomfortable. Forcing my tired body to a sitting position, I grasp the hem of my shirt and peel it over my head and toss it toward the hamper. I miss. Oh well. Something new to add to the pile.

I wriggle out of my bra and panties, kicking them to the floor. I'm most comfortable sleeping naked. I don't even bother brushing my teeth or washing my face, or pulling the curtains closed so it's not so bright in here. I simply climb back into my bed, pull the sheet up and over my head, and close my eyes.

Expecting sleep to find me.

Waiting for it.

Wondering why, if my body wants to shut down, can't my mind just let me rest?

It's the same thing, night after night. It takes forever for me to push the guilt and anger and hurt aside long enough to give my mind and heart some peace so I can drift off.

And here, I thought tonight would be different.

I kick off my sheet with frustration and roll out of bed, going straight for my sketchbook and charcoal pencil. Even with blurry eyes, it's been my therapy for these times, distracting my inner thoughts, lulling my distress.

Flipping to the back, I stare at the profile sketch of the cash register man. The one that the sketch artist did was all wrong. I kept telling him it was all wrong, and he kept asking me to tell him what to change. Problem was, I couldn't put my finger on it.

Me, whose skill with recalling and drawing faces is probably better than any police sketch artist.

I've tried sketching his face myself the last couple of nights, to see if that makes a difference. So far, it hasn't. I can't figure out why it's wrong. I just know it is. Trying again tonight is only going to frustrate me.

I flip to a fresh page.

I met three people today. A confused delivery guy with the wrong address; Bobby, the enormous teddy bear biker who swindled a tattoo out of me; and the mystery guy, whom I likely won't ever see again.

His is the face I want to see on my page tonight, even if it ends up being an indistinct version of it. Settling back on my bed on my stomach, the cool air from the open window skating across my bare skin, I begin with long, even strokes of my pencil to capture that hard jaw, using the side to shade in the chiseled contours. Even with the dark beard, I could see them. Next I focus on his eyes. The charcoal makes them more menacing. I like that about this medium. It intensifies emotion.

My pencil flies as I unload my memory of his face, which is more sharp and detailed than I had expected. When I'm finished, I find myself staring at a portrait of an extremely handsome man— the first one I've met in San Francisco—whom I turned away today. A man who exuded strength and confidence and something I can't put my finger on. A man who stepped in and helped me without my asking for it, but when I needed it. When I *hated* that I needed it.

Clearly I was not thinking straight today. I could have locked the door and sent him to the back room, and spent hours with him, my hands on his flesh—which I can already tell is hard and sculpted—and my mind on something other than my grief and stress.

I wonder if he'd be interested in a girl who looks like me. With my luck, he's more into a girl like Amber. Everyone wants an Amber. Even *I've* considered an Amber once or twice, when I was drunk and horny and wondering if maybe I've been confused about liking penis all along, and perhaps that's why I've felt no drive to seek out a real relationship.

But I'm not confused at all. I like men, and I definitely would have made myself available for this one had my world not been turned upside down only a week ago.

It's been so long since I've had sex, since I've felt that release.

Getting one last long, good look at the face in front of me, I toss the book to the floor beside me.

And reach into my nightstand drawer, hoping the brief distraction will help my mind settle into sleep.

# EIGHT

# SEBASTIAN

Patience and control are necessary assets in my line of work.

Thank Christ I have both, especially now, as I hold my breath and all movement, afraid to make a sound that will announce my presence.

My assignment was nearly blown tonight. Pure adrenaline coursed through my veins as I watched the girl approach through the slats in the door of this cramped, cluttered closet, waiting for the moment that she caught the glint of my eyes on her. Her hand reached for the handle, and I instinctively ran a series of counter-measures that involved rope and gags and scare tactics through my mind. Things that Bentley wouldn't want me doing just yet.

Things that, frankly, I have no interest in doing to her at all.

But her phone rang and she abandoned her task, and I was saved. Only for a short time, though, because then she stripped down to skin while I spied like a pervert, my gaze glued to her form beneath that sheet, then to her form lying above the sheet, as she worked on something in her sketchbook, the last of the day's sunlight streaming in through the window to give me the most uninhibited view.

And now . . .

I hadn't expected such soft, round curves on her tiny frame, but they are there, in the form of a small but tight ass that I got a good glimpse of when she leaned over for her sketchbook, and tits that stand up so well, they could be fake, but I can tell they're not. She hid her assets well beneath that loose-fitting shirt today.

I'm doing my best to control my breathing, even as hers quickens into soft pants, and her hand begins moving more furtively, and her legs fall apart until each knee is resting against the mattress. My fingers tingle with anticipation, because I had that bubble-gum-pink wand in my hand earlier, and now she has it against herself—in herself—and it's like my hand is right there with it. Almost.

Is she thinking about me right now? I heard everything she said; I'm guessing I'm the "hot guy" she turned away today, whom she would have made strip. That makes me smile, because there was nothing about our encounter that would suggest she'd ever give me the time of day. It sounds, though, like she doesn't give many guys the time of day. Or at least not a lot of time. I'll have to be careful about how I approach her. I don't want her getting bored with me before I've gotten what I need.

This, I can say for sure, has never happened to me. I'm letting my mind wander as I wait, her body tempting a weaker side that I have learned to suppress until now. That has frankly never threatened to sway me during an assignment, where I hunt threats and criminals, vile human beings that the world is better off without.

I do not hunt young, attractive—albeit sharp-tongued—women who pleasure themselves in bed in front of me, who cause me to entertain thoughts of slipping out of this closet and *not* leaving this house. Of walking over to her bed. Of her opening her eyes and reaching for me. Of my stripping and climbing onto her, tossing that wand to the side and finishing her off with my hands, or my mouth.

Or the dick that's pressing hard against my zipper.

But I know that reality will not match fantasy, and that is not my purpose here, so I force down my urges and chastise my dick for even veering in that direction. And yet I still don't look away when she closes her eyes and opens her mouth and arches her back and moans out a release, even though I know that would be the respectable thing to do.

I just fucking can't.

She simply lies there for a few minutes, those tits swelling with her deep breaths, until she calms down. Then, groping the mattress near her thighs, as if she has expended her last ounce of energy, she pulls the sheet up and over her body.

Ten minutes later, she is as still as a corpse, her breathing shallow and slow.

Easing the door open so slowly that it can't sound a creak, I edge out of her bedroom, down the stairs, and out the front door, ensuring that I lock the dead bolt on the way.

* * *

Her boots stomp on each step as she drags herself down the steep front stairs to the Honda parked out front, a tall coffee travel mug gripped in one hand, a black case dangling from the other, oversize black glasses covering half her face. Reluctant to be awake, I'm guessing, even though she logged in at least twelve hours of sleep last night.

I know because I've been sitting in the backseat of my car and watching that upstairs front window since midnight, waiting for her to leave, like she told someone on the phone that she would. But the light didn't come on until six this morning. I guess she must have been exhausted.

I reach back and rub the muscles in my neck. I drifted just once, for half an hour, when the clock hit four and it didn't look like she was going anywhere. It's never a good sleep, hidden under a black blanket in case anyone walks by and chooses to peer in, but it's all I needed. Besides, this backseat is probably cleaner than the hole I rented—the walls shedding their floral paper and dark corners hiding roaches. It's fine, I've barely been in it since I got to San Francisco. I went back last night only to shower, jerk off to thoughts of her naked on her bed, and change clothes.

Even now, the sight of her fully dressed has my heart rate quickening. I need to push away the mental images of her still burning in the forefront of my mind and remind myself that she is a potential target.

A threat that I might need to eliminate.

Based on what I overheard of the girl's phone conversation, I assume she's heading back to the shop now, to clean before her afternoon appointment shows up. That gives me a few more hours inside her house, to search through the filing cabinet for clues on other properties, rented deposit boxes, anything that could be used as a hiding place.

Her taillights flash red just as the burner begins vibrating in my pocket.

I slink down in my seat, not wanting her to spot me when she pulls out. She'd remember my face, and that wouldn't be good. "What?" I don't hide my irritation from my voice. Bentley knows better than to call. It's against protocol.

"The house?"

"Negative, so far."

"What's taking you so long?"

I frown and don't answer.

"The girl?"

"I told you I'd call when I had an update." I slide down even farther, to a lying position as she passes.

"Then find a fucking update to give me *today*." He hangs up, leaving me both irritated and intrigued. This isn't like Bentley. He always cuts contact until I've completed my assignment. It's one of his requirements, to limit any dots from ever connecting him to my work, if I don't cover my tracks well enough. He's also never this impatient, trusting me to do my job swiftly and effectively.

It makes me wonder exactly what's on that video.

But I need to not think about Bentley or the pretty girl, and the private moment that I was privy to last night. I need to focus on simply finding this video and completing my job.

I quietly count to ten, then make my way back to the house, promising myself to stay the fuck away from her bedroom this time.

# NINE

# IVY

Dickhead.

I should have expected this. Ned always said these bikers operated on their own clock. They'll book an appointment and then stroll in three hours later, expecting you to drop everything for them. Ned said the first time he got fed up enough to tell one of them to fuck off because he had another appointment, he thought he was going to end up in a pine box by sundown. After that he learned to keep wide windows of time free around their bookings.

But it's now almost five, I have my machine ready and the back room prepped, and I'm pissed off enough to tell Bobby to take his blowtorch and shove it up his ass. I don't need it anymore, anyway. But I *do* need the big brute to move that chair out to the trash. I've finally accepted that no amount of independence and stubbornness is going to do it for me.

I also haven't eaten. It's a good excuse to visit Fez at the pizzeria, anyway, seeing that I woke up this morning to half a dozen texts from him. I hope he didn't wait too long for me last night.

Of course, the minute I have the handwritten BACK IN TEN sign ready and am walking down the long hall to tape it to the front window, knuckles rap against the door.

"You're two hours late!" I holler, rolling the shade up, preparing my best scathing glare for Bobby. It's not his giant frame I find looming outside, though.

It's that guy from yesterday.

We simply stare at each other through the grimy glass for a moment: me, in surprise; him, something unreadable, his eyes hidden behind dark sunglasses. He's swapped his black T-shirt for navy today, to go along with the jeans. Simple, clean, unremarkable. And yet very appealing on him.

"Is it Thursday yet?" There isn't so much as a hint of a joke in his voice. I can't tell if he's serious.

"You're persistent."

"Yes."

"Persistence annoys me."

Finally, a slight smile touches his lips, and I instantly find myself fighting the urge to match it. He slides his sunglasses off his face, meeting my eyes with that cool, indifferent gaze. "And what doesn't annoy you?"

"Not much, honestly."

Another staring match. As intense as the weight of his gaze is, it's not nearly as uncomfortable as it was yesterday, now that I'm no longer wary of his intentions.

I should be difficult and tell him to come back in a few days. The thing is, I don't want to be difficult. I want to be very easy for him right now, because I've been thinking about him more than is wise since yesterday. Especially since last night. If just a sketched picture and thoughts of him could get me off so quickly and easily, I wonder what the real man could do to me.

Not that I would ever flip my hair or giggle at his jokes or do anything else to make my interest obvious.

I unlock the door and pull it open, stepping back to give him room. "The guy I was supposed to be working on hasn't shown up, so I guess you're in luck, because I'm all ready to ink and I need skin to work on." I let my gaze drift over his arms, honed with muscles and free of any markings, before moving over to his chest and stomach. Wondering if the rest of him is this perfect. Wondering exactly which part of him I'll get to touch.

"You look more rested today," he murmurs, a secretive smile

touching his eyes. As if he can read my mind, as if he knows that he helped put me to sleep last night.

I don't answer, pushing the door closed. I lock it once again with a sly smile. As far as I'm concerned, if Bobby shows up now, no one's here.

"You've done a lot here since yesterday." His piercing eyes survey the interior, stalling over the six full trash bags sitting in one corner and the four boxes of "Ned things" that I'm not sure what to do with yet, but I can't bring myself to throw out.

"I'm having it painted at the end of the week, so I don't really have a choice." The painter showed up here at nine this morning for a quote, and I, still groggy from too much sleep, agreed to a Friday start, not really thinking about how much I'd need to get done by then.

But I *am* thankful that I wasn't too out of it to pack a change of clothes for the afternoon, knowing that I'd be covered in dust and dirt by now. I smooth my off-the-shoulder army-green shirt down over ripped detail black leggings.

"I see you've taken care of the chair." He turns, but not before I see the smug smile touch his lips.

"I haven't had time," I lie, eying his arms again, hopeful. I'm not going to ask for help outright. If he's smart, he'll have figured that out about me by now.

It looks like the hot stranger has brains to go with his brawn.

He steps past me without a word, the scent of fresh soap catching my nose and stirring my hormones. Grabbing the chair by its wide arms, he heaves the entire thing from its resting place, uncovering a square of pristine honey-colored hardwood. My chest swells ever so slightly when I catch a nostalgic glimpse of what Black Rabbit's floor must have looked like on the day Ned opened its doors for the first time.

"Is the Dumpster in the back?" he grunts under the weight of the chair, the strain in his muscles visible from beneath his shirt. He doesn't wait for my answer, heading down the hall, stopping at the back door to both unlock it and, I suspect, to give his arms and back a break.

I trail him, dragging two bags of trash along the ground behind me, all the way out to the Dumpster. He flips the lid open.

"I'm guessing it's too heavy to lift ov . . ." My words drift as he hoists the entire chair up and over his shoulders to topple it into the bin, the sound of metal ricocheting off the inside deafening.

". . . or not." My breath catches. I couldn't move that thing even an inch and he just had it over his head. How is he that strong? He *does* have broad shoulders. I study his hands as he wipes them across his jeans. Large, masculine hands that look like they've done their share of manual labor. An angry scar runs along his right thumb, faded by years.

"What are you staring at?"

"Your scar," I admit. I wonder how he got it, and if it bothers him, but I don't ask. "I've covered a lot of scars for clients."

"I don't need it covered," he says. "Scars give you—"

"Character," I finish in unison with him. "I don't mind them, either. They make people more interesting."

He closes the distance and pulls the bags from my grasp, his fingers grazing mine, and tosses them into the Dumpster. "Anything else that you need carried out here?" His words are slightly breathless, and a light sheen of sweat coats his forehead. At least it wasn't *too* easy for him. While I hate it when someone makes me feel small and weak and incapable, actually witnessing that made me feel something else. Something thrilling.

"I think I can handle the rest."

"Okay." He flips the lid closed. Looping his hand beneath the front of his T-shirt, he pulls it up to wipe the sweat from his forehead, giving me a glimpse of his chest and stomach, both of which are padded by an impressive layer of muscle. "So . . . should we get started?"

A flicker of light dances in his eyes, and I know that that was intentional. He could have used his arm, or his hand. Hell, he wasn't even *that* sweaty.

"Yeah, sure." I try to sound nonchalant, but for the first time since Ned died, I actually feel the urge to sit down in front of my machine. Even if it's for the wrong reasons. I don't care what this guy wants, or where. I'll do it. But that's not the most professional way to broach the topic with a new client. One whose name I don't even know.

I reach out. "My name is Ivy."

He pauses for a long moment, staring at my hand before taking it in his, his skin rough and warm and powerful. "Sebastian."

"And what exactly were you thinking of having done, Sebastian?" *Please let it involve taking your shirt off. Better yet, your pants.*

"A piece, right here." He runs long fingers over the left side of his torso, from below his armpit to his hip.

*Jackpot.* I stifle my smile. "That's a big area." Does he realize how long that will take? How much that will take out of him, and me?

"Yeah. It is."

"That's going to take hours."

His eyes flicker over me lightning fast. "All night, maybe."

He's flirting with me. I can't read him at all, but I caught that.

My heart skips a beat as I get lost in his face. I've had a few clients turned flings. I try to keep things separate, but sometimes it's hard. There's a heightened level of intimacy that comes with this job that is impossible to replicate. These men come to me, vulnerable and full of trust from the moment they climb into my chair. I have all the control, and it can be intoxicating, having an attractive guy lie there and watch me with anticipative eyes, allowing me to mark him with something that bonds us for eternity—or until he files for divorce in a tattoo removal process. Though, I've had no divorces yet, from what I know. If anything, they search me out on the Internet when they want more. I have my own web page set up, with my portfolio and where I'm working at any moment in time. One guy from Portland actually vacationed in Ireland last summer, just so I could finish his sleeve for him.

"Do you have a sketch already?"

He reaches into his back pocket, his T-shirt pulling tight against the ridges of his chest, retrieving a sheet of paper that he unfolds and hands to me. I study the grim reaper on the page, the gown heavy and black, the scythe oversized. A little morbid, but I've seen worse. I recognize it as a popular sketch. I'm not a fan of popular sketches. If you're going to mark your body, why not make it original? It disappoints me a little that he wouldn't feel the same. But I guess that's why he's coming to me, so I can set him straight. He just doesn't know it yet.

"Are you a virgin?" I like asking hot guys that question out of the blue and seeing how they react.

He blinks. "Excuse me?"

"Have you had any other work done?"

"Oh." The slightest exhale sails from his lips, but I notice it. "Yeah. I have."

My eyes roll over his form again, wondering where it could be. "Okay. Well, Sebastian . . . We should go inside and talk about this some more. This is about seven hours of work, and doing it in one sitting is hard, but I don't think we have any other choice. Ideally I'd outline it all and then begin the detail a month or so later, once it's healed. But I doubt I'll be around in a month."

"When are you leaving?"

I glance over my shoulder at the back of Black Rabbit, as dingy out here as it is inside. "As soon as this place is out of my hair."

"You don't like San Francisco?"

"I love it," I answer too quickly. "*Loved* it. But there's nothing here for me now."

His gaze drifts over to the dented, dirty back door. "Was this place yours?"

"No. It was my uncle's shop."

"The one who was murdered in this chair I just pitched for you?"

I grimace at the callous way he says it, but I wasn't any less callous when I said it yesterday, I guess. Of course he's not going to forget something like that. "Yeah. He was more my father than my own father is. And now he's gone, and I can't stand being here so I'm leaving." Wanting to get off the subject, I add, "And you'll have to pay in cash."

"Was it a robbery?"

"I have no fucking idea," I snap, but then temper my tone. He's a client, after all. "The cops think it might be, but it doesn't make sense. I mean, you've seen inside. There wasn't much to steal. A grand from the register and a VCR? Seriously. No need to tie someone up and torture, then kill him." I clear my throat several times, trying to get the knot out.

"Junkies do stupid things," Sebastian offers.

"These guys weren't junkies. They had balaclavas and gloves, and silencers. And freshly polished boots."

He frowns. "And the police have no leads?"

"Nope, nothing other than the one guy's name, which I gave them—Mario. Some midwesterner with the thickest accent I've ever heard."

His foot kicks a few loose stones as he closes the distance, his strength somehow radiating off him, that penetrating gaze distracting my thoughts. "I'm sorry that you lost your uncle in such a horrible, tragic way."

I drop my eyes to the gravel between us and swallow back the tears that threaten again. "Thanks."

Fingers grasp my chin and lift my face up to meet his again. "Will working on me help distract you from all that?"

"Yes." *Too breathless, Ivy. God, way too needy and breathless.*

A small smile curls his lips. "Then I'm ready whenever you are."

I swallow and take a step back, my heart hammering against my chest.

"There you are!"

*For fuck's sake . . .*

There's Bobby, ambling down the alley between Black Rabbit and the Happy Nails mani-pedi mill next door. He looks from me to Sebastian, and back to me.

"I've been waiting out front!" he says accusingly.

"Yeah." I throw a hand haphazardly at the Dumpster, the energy firing between Sebastian and me deflating like a needle stuck in a balloon. "He was just helping me pitch the chair."

Bobby frowns, holding up the long rectangular kit in his grip. "I told ya I'd bring a torch. I just had to wait until the guys were done with it."

"Turns out I didn't need one. Just a six-point wrench and some muscle." I smirk, impressed with myself both for remembering the tool Sebastian mentioned and for finding a way around needing this biker.

"Huh." Bobby doesn't look as impressed. "Well, I brought it. I've got a few hours now, so let's go and get this finished." He holds his arm out.

"Unfortunately she's booked for tonight." Sebastian steps forward, that eerie calmness settling onto him again.

Bobby steps forward as well, straightening his back to his full height, his girth dwarfing Sebastian. "Yeah, with me."

"You're two hours late. You'll have to reschedule." Sebastian's perfectly still and limber, seemingly unbothered.

Sebastian is fucking crazy.

And if he gets pummeled into the ground—or worse—I'm going to feel responsible, and I have enough guilt to carry on these narrow shoulders of mine right now. He may be able to launch a steel chair over his head, but going toe-to-toe with a guy like Bobby, who I'm sure doesn't fight fair, is only going to mangle that face I like looking at. He doesn't know who he's up against here.

I force myself in between the two men, placing a hand on Sebastian's stomach—the hard ridges beneath his shirt were begging for my attention. "Your design is going to take a lot more time than I have tonight, anyway. Come back tomorrow and I'll start it for you."

I don't think he heard me. He's not moving, not even acknowledging the contact.

"Hey!" I snap. That works, pulling his gaze down to me, to my hand still on him. "Can you come back tomorrow?" Will he be working? What does he do? Is he from around here?

"Yeah. Fine. See you tomorrow." He steps away, leaving my fingers hanging in the air as he strolls around us and down the alley, as if he doesn't have a care in the world.

"Ballsy fuck," Bobby mutters, eying his back with disdain.

*Hot, ballsy fuck.* Who could be stretched out in my chair right now, if we'd gotten behind locked doors one minute sooner. "Come on, Bobby." I sigh, taking in the bulky mass in front of me. I'm guessing his gut will be well on its way to a trip over his belt within two years.

Not exactly the same.

Definitely not something I'll be thinking about alone in my bed tonight.

■ ■ ■

"You all right?" Bobby squints, peering down at me through deceptively pretty baby blue eyes.

"Fine," I force out, wiping the last of the ointment over his arm and then tossing the paper towel into the trash. "We're done here."

He frowns. "Aren't you even going to show it to me, to make sure I like it?"

"There's a full-length mirror right there." Two feet over from where he's sitting, the lazy ass. I start pulling apart my machine as he eases himself out of the chair and wanders over. He turns his body and twists his arm to get a good look at the underside, where I've incorporated red and blue into the zombie princess's cape just like he asked, to represent the American flag. Ironically, this one-percenter is also patriotic to the country whose laws he regularly breaks. "Happy?"

"Yeah." He eyes me warily. "It looks great."

"Good. You owe me six hundred."

His eyebrows spike and he starts to laugh. "Are you kidding me?"

"Two hours at three hundred per. The last I checked, that equals six hundred. I can bring you a calculator if you want."

He shoots me a flat glare. "Three hundred is Ned's rate."

"It's also my rate when I'm finishing my dead uncle's work for you, when all I want to be doing is cleaning this place up and getting the hell out of here!" I'm yelling at him and I don't give a damn, because raising my voice is the only thing keeping the tears at bay.

It finally started sinking in today. Listening to the familiar buzz of my tattoo machine for two hours helped chip away at the shock that's dulled my senses up until now. *Ned's gone.* My uncle, who taught me everything I know about this industry, who took me under his wing the day I finished high school, who was my guinea pig when I was cutting my teeth on technique—judging skin depth, offsetting movement, gauging pain levels—who never once made me scrub a toilet during my apprenticeship, who inspired a passion that I expect will live with me until I'm too old to hold a needle steady, is dead.

And the person who did it—that psycho Mario—will probably get away with it.

My teeth have been gritted for two hours, my answers clipped as I listened to that buzz that brought with it no serenity, no joy. All it did was remind me about the last moments of Ned's life, when I couldn't do anything but cower in the back room.

"Okay, Ivy." He pulls his wallet out and pulls out a stack of bills. I don't want to know how he earns his money. I really don't care right now. "And here. You let me know if you need any help with anything else around here. It's a lot for one person to handle on their own." He hands me a business card: BOBBY AND BROTHERS TOWING AND AUTOMOTIVE.

"Thanks." I chew on the inside of my mouth as guilt chews on my insides, watching him lumber out the door. Because, once again, I've been a complete asshole to someone who doesn't really deserve it. "Hey, you'd tell me if you heard anything more about what happened to Ned, right?"

He turns to meet my eyes, an exaggerated frown turning his mouth down. "Nothin' on our end."

"'Kay. See ya."

I clean and pack everything up into my case as I do after every shift, wondering if Sebastian will still come by tomorrow. I'm hoping that he does, because I'm desperate to shake the unease I felt today. I need his canvas in order to do that. Maybe working on him will somehow be different.

I'm wired. There's no way I'm falling asleep anytime soon, and I can't just sit around in Ned's house with his ghost, so when my phone buzzes with a text from Fez, I jump on the chance to do my next favorite thing to inking skin.

Inking walls.

■ ■ ■

I have plenty of options. The owner of a building over on Forty-second and East Twelfth—who is coincidentally the owner of the sub shop down the street from Black Rabbit—has offered to pay me to paint a mural on his wall as part of the antigraffiti movement. Or, there's an already colorful cube van parked off Lombard that draws in artists like three-year-olds to a bowl of gumballs. Heck, I could even vandalize the inside of Black Rabbit, seeing as it's all being painted over on Friday.

But it's eleven at night and I don't feel like going the legal, good girl route. That's why I'm in the bowels of San Francisco—inside one of the many abandoned buildings in the Mission District—with a box of spray paint and my portable speaker. Two things, aside from my tattoo case, that I never go anywhere without. I really shouldn't be doing this. Ned warned me that the city has upped the punishment for vandalism to a misdemeanor. And I feel like I've outgrown that period of time when charges might pass as cool and excusable. At twenty-five, I'd just be a giant loser.

But it's quiet inside this remote and derelict office building and the windows are all boarded up. Frankly, I should be more concerned about the junkies and homeless that will no doubt filter through here than the cops. That's why I don't come to places like this alone.

"Ivy, tunes?" Weazy, a twenty-nine-year-old Mexican with a well-known passion for depicting jungle scenes, to the point that his work is almost as good as a fingerprint, sets up one of his battery-powered lights. We have four in total. Enough to light up one corner of this building while leaving many others dark and accessible to any creepers who may want to hide. And they do.

That should bother me but most of them are harmless, I'm in a group, and . . . fuck it. Ned's dead, Ian's gone, the few good friends I have are nowhere around, and I've never been the kind of girl to cry on someone's shoulder. This is the best way I have to work through my grief.

I crank the volume and my pocket-sized cube speaker pumps out a deep, rhythmic song. "It's my playlist tonight, just in case you were wondering." I hang out with these guys once every couple of weeks. They're pretty cool. Other than Fez, none of them hit on me. I'm pretty sure Weazy is convinced I'm a lesbian. Whatever makes them leave me alone.

"As long as it's slammin', I'm down!" Fez hollers, swinging around the chain that connects his wallet to his jeans, his cargo pants staying on his scrawny hips by the grace of a belt.

"Seriously, Fez. Stop talking." I can't listen to that all night. If it wasn't dangerous to put earplugs in around here, I would.

He waves his middle finger at me in response, but he takes no offense. He's used to being told to shut up by Ned, every time he came in to deliver a pizza.

The ball in the bottom of the can rattles with my shake, as I size up the wall before me. It's already been marred by taggers. Talentless fools with a can of paint. Nothing I can't cover, though, and I will, even if it takes me all night.

"Who wants?" A guy I only know as Joker waves a bottle of Don Q in the air, his beady eyes settling on me first.

"Rum. Gross. Not me."

The others flock to it, but I pull out my flask of whiskey instead, taking a small swig of it before I climb to the top of the three-step ladder. Not too much. Just enough to ease the tension out of my limbs.

With a spray can in my hand, I'm already feeling better.

# TEN

# SEBASTIAN

I have an obsession with time that I can't readily cater to here, in my dark, dusty corner of this dump, the stench of urine and vomit permeating the stale air. Any flicker of light from my phone or my watch will go noticed, if not by the group of four graffiti artists in my line of sight, then by the many crackheads and vagrants that hide out like rats in rafters.

Watching with interest. Or, perhaps, for opportunity.

I'm really no different.

The last time I checked, it was two in the morning. Hours must have passed since, but Ivy doesn't seem ready to leave yet. She must be a nocturnal creature, like me.

*Ivy.*

I'm no longer thinking of her generically. She's no longer simply "the girl" in my thoughts.

Worse, I gave her my real name. Why the fuck did I give her my real name? I never do that and yet, in a split-second decision, I convinced myself that I wanted to. That it was harmless, because she's not guilty of anything, and I'm not going to hurt her.

At least, I don't want to hurt her.

I *do* need her to trust me, though. I found nothing of any interest in the dead shop owner's files. No property holdings, no safety-deposit boxes, nothing. Which means I have no choice but to get my answers out of her, one way or another.

Either Ivy's a fantastic liar or she doesn't know a thing about this videotape, or her uncle's blackmail attempt. She's just a twenty-five-year-old tattoo artist with a prickly exterior, who lost her father figure and is trying to move on.

It will take creativity now, to question her about the existence of this videotape without her realizing it. To find out where her uncle may have hidden it. It will take time. I guess it's good that I've had this grim reaper tattoo in mind for the better part of five years.

The day I received my official discharge letter from the U.S. Navy, Bentley pulled up next to my parents' San Francisco house where I was staying and told me to get in the car. I had no idea what I was going to do with my life, or what he would be proposing. He had left the navy a year prior, and took his skills, his reputation, and his family money, and founded Alliance. It was still very much in its infancy stage then, but he had big ideas and even bigger connections, which were already landing him major security contracts in Afghanistan, the exact place we had been battling suicide attacks and ambushes while we toured together.

I hoped that he would hire me to go back, to continue putting my skills to use. To prove myself.

But he had other plans for me. I was someone he trusted like no other, someone he would pay well. Someone he needed to execute assignments that are never documented, that no one "officially" talks about, and that the world would never have any proof actually existed.

I would become a reaper of sorts, delivering an end to those who needed it.

Without medals, without fanfare, but with quiet honor.

Getting this tattoo buys me seven hours with Ivy. And if that's not enough, I'll have to buy myself more time in other ways. Maybe that's what drove me to bait her earlier, lifting my shirt to my forehead to wipe the sweat off my brow. A childhood of Krav Maga and boxing lessons, two years of intensive SEAL training, and almost eight years of daily conditioning have honed my body into what most women want.

I already know that she finds me attractive because of last night's phone conversation with her friend, but if she noticed my not-so-subtle move, she didn't let on. Her ability to school her expression, to feign indifference is impressive. Or maybe this idiot, with his spiky black-and-blue hair and pants hanging halfway off his bony ass, and holes in his ears where the metal rings have stretched his flesh out—maybe that's what breaks her out of her hard shell.

I had hoped to find that out tonight, instead of lurking here in the shadows. But that fucking biker showed up. She didn't want to work on him, she wanted me. I could tell. And she was protecting me by stepping in. Worried about me going up against a soft, slow man on a motorcycle. Probably assumed I didn't recognize the insignia, because why would I? Why would I familiarize myself with the gang the police are focusing their efforts on in her uncle's murder?

I could have had that guy in the Dumpster with the rest of the trash in under ten seconds. If Ivy wasn't standing right there, I might have. But I had to step away instead, because taking him on would have caused a scene, and I need to be a ghost. So I climbed back into my car and waited on the street for hours, until I saw her little Honda whip around the corner and head home.

Now I'm back to tailing her, learning about her. I haven't learned much, though, other than that she hovers on the abrasive side with everyone—not just me—and her body doesn't stop swaying when there's music playing.

And she's not just some miscreant tagger, marring city streets with spray paint.

She's one hell of a talented artist.

She also surrounds herself with half-wits. These guys . . . I shake my head. I'm guessing at least one of the three—probably the one with the shaved head whom they call Joker and who moves like a street brawler—has a criminal record. I don't think she intentionally seeks them out. They just have common interests. Biker gangs that love to get tattoos at her uncle's shop, local petty criminals she hangs out with when she's spraying walls. Who the hell knows why Bentley said she associated with the IRA. There's likely another coincidental connection.

The more I learn about her, the more I'm convinced that she has no idea what kind of trouble her uncle was caught up in and that she's just a young and edgy tattoo artist who simply doesn't want to settle down.

As I refocus my attention on her, I realize that perhaps that's only what I want her to be.

She's shed the light jean jacket she wore over here, revealing an oversize white tank top that's thrown over a second, tighter black one. It's a casual I-don't-care look. But with her skintight black pants and her boots, it's sexy as hell. All the more so because I've already had a good long look at what's hidden beneath. She shouldn't be dressed like that out here. I wouldn't trust the guys she's with, let alone the junkies in the shadows.

She's not at all concerned, though. If she were, she'd be glancing over her shoulder frequently. But she's in her own little world under the glow of the lanterns, working on a disturbingly accurate portrayal of the man in the inset of the newspaper article. Her uncle, a person she clearly loved very much. Her twiggy little arms, tense with effort, work tirelessly with sweeps of blues and purple shadows, until she's managed to capture finer details of his eyes, nose, and mouth.

She climbs down from the stepladder and backs up, simply standing there. She's admiring her work. Or maybe just thinking about him, about her grief. Reaching down into the shadows, her hand comes back with a small pink object. She unscrews the top and brings it to her lips to takes a swig. Booze.

"Dat's da bomb! Like a boss, yo!" The fucking moron with blue hair and pants barely holding on to his skinny thighs walks over with his idiotic limplike swagger to stand next to her, slinging his arm over her shoulder. Why does she associate with him?

It's moments like these—seeing guys like this—that I wish the American government took a page out of other countries' rule books and forced every eighteen-year-old male into the military to work this level of stupid out of him.

Of course, I don't really believe that because most of these men—boys—couldn't face a day of war. It would break them, just like it broke the strongest of us.

"Fez . . ." She turns to glare at him. "You sound like a douche bag. You realize that, right?"

"Whatchu sayin'? Everyone loves the Fez!" He actually sounds offended. Good.

"Not everyone."

"Then how come I got over five hundred thousand followers on my channel?"

"Because their brains haven't fully formed yet." She swats his arm off her and steps away. "And don't touch me unless I tell you that you can."

I smile. But I'm also on alert now, wondering how he's going to react to such a low blow to his ego. Wondering how I'm going to handle just sitting here and watching it happen, because I can't spring out of the shadows to save her.

He simply scratches the back of his head. Maybe he's used to this level of abuse from her. Maybe he likes it. "That's a good one of Ned. He would have loved that," he offers, suddenly switching to standard English.

A pause and then, "Thanks." Her voice softens instantly.

"I guess you're cuttin' it now?"

She drags the ladder over to the mostly blank canvas of wall beside him. "I'm just getting started." Her lithe body climbs the steps to the top, to stretch on the tiptoes of her Doc Martens, reaching as far as she can with seemingly no concern about falling.

With a sigh of relief, I settle back against the wall with arms folded over my chest, curious to see what she's going to come up with now. People so rarely surprise me anymore, but I have a feeling she might.

The latest song ends and a new one begins, with a stronger, more mesmerizing beat. While she needs to keep her hips and feet still for balance, her free hand begins waving and dipping with the rhythm as her other hand lays waste to the wall with large sweeps of black paint. It's another face, I can tell. Apparently she has a thing for drawing faces, if this and her sketchbook at home are any indication.

"Hey. You got a light?" A raspy whisper calls out from my left, about ten feet away, where the guy has sat quietly for the past hour.

"No."

He shuffles over, closer, until the pungent smell of him has my nostrils flaring. "How about a twenty, then?"

I don't answer. While my patience can be infinite for a specific task, it's almost nonexistent for late-night junkies trying to accost someone minding his own business.

"Come on, man!"

I should have expected this. They don't like it when you ignore them.

It's unlikely our voices will carry over the music, unless this junkie gets more irate, which is possible. Ivy can't be so oblivious to expect that they are the only ones here, but if she discovers me, there's no way to explain why I am, too.

"I just need a fix and I'll be good. Just help me out with—"

His voice cuts out as soon as my fist delivers an uppercut under his jaw. I grab hold of his filthy body to ease it down carefully. He should be out for a while.

Hoping that earns me some peace, I continue watching Ivy work, until the face begins to take shape. A man, with black hair and a long, slender nose and square jaw. It's hard to tell what color his eyes are from this distance, and the poor lighting, but I can tell they're dark. It's not until she begins spraying the outline of a short, sculpted beard that I realize who the man is.

She's painting me.

My face, on the wall of this dilapidated, condemned building.

It shouldn't please me, and yet it does.

I smile. I've gotten inside her head without even trying.

■ ■ ■

I've been trained to resist the urges of sleep, to push myself longer and further than a normal human being. I've survived on no more than four hours of rest per night for weeks at a time. Many nights, I rely on Ambien to drift off. But I've been awake for nearly two days now, aside from that short catnap in my car, and my eyes burn with exhaustion.

Still, I tail Ivy as she walks the length of Ocean Beach, her sketchbook tucked under an arm. The rising sun and quiet streets make it more difficult, but I manage to keep my presence unknown, because that's what I'm good at.

She heads toward the shoreline and settles herself onto a crop of stones, giving the surfer in the distance a moment of her attention. He's impressive enough to distract even me, navigating the treacherous swells of the outer sandbar with the expertise of a seasoned surfer. He'd have to be. These are some of the hardest waves to surf in the world, especially in prime season, which we're deep in the middle of.

Growing up in San Francisco, it's only natural that I know how to surf. Still, it's been eleven years since I rode these waves. Eight since I stood on a board in San Diego, near the base. At one time, some people called *me* an expert, too.

My experience with deep, frigid waters and sweeping currents certainly helped when it came to passing the intensive tests that are required to become a SEAL. Tests that only twenty percent of candidates ever pass. I blew through the basic physical requirements. In the intensive twenty-four-week-long BUD/S training program, I led my group for time in the physical conditioning and combat diving phases.

For a sport that I enjoyed so much, I'm surprised I've forgotten it so easily. I watch that surfer now with a small amount of envy, and promise myself that, when this assignment is over, I'll coast on a barrel wave again.

Ivy has dismissed the surfer already and is now flipping pages over in her sketchbook, her hair fluttering around her with the soft breeze. Her head's down and she has seemingly shut out everything around her. After a full night of spray-painting walls, I don't know how she has any desire to draw, but I guess that's why I'm not an artist. My creativity is limited to how I'm going to get past security gates and passcodes and barking dogs without being identified.

I simply lean against a lightpost and watch as she sketches from that rock for half an hour, as the sun rises farther in the sky and people in brightly colored latex outfits pass her, out for their morning jog—some alone, some in groups, some with dogs who veer off path with noses pointed toward her—until she closes her book, tucks it under her arm, and trudges through the sand toward her car.

Not until I've watched her drag her feet up the stairs of her home, her energy finally spent, do I leave her for my own rented bed.

■ ■ ■

"Yeah," I say into the receiver, my eyes shut against the beam of midmorning sunlight shining directly on me. The thin and tattered cotton curtain hanging over the window is pointless for both shade and decoration.

"What's the update?"

I sigh. "Negative for the house."

"You've searched everywhere?" Bentley pants into the receiver. I assume he's on his treadmill. The guy always loved going for a morning run.

"Top to bottom."

"Dammit," he mutters under his breath.

I reach over my head to pinch and tug at the lifted wallpaper seam until it begins to tear away, waiting for Bentley to say something. If he's going to annoy me by checking up daily like this, then he can be the one putting effort into the conversation. And if he pisses me off enough, I can just go back to Greece.

Except I'm not going to do that, because for some stupid reason, I already feel a vested interest in making sure that video is found and nothing happens to Ivy in the process. Because even though I don't have evidence for this, I have a gut feeling that she's completely innocent.

"What's your next move?"

"The shop. And her."

"Keep me informed. If nothing turns up today, I'll bring in help for you."

"What? No." My stomach tightens instantly. "You know I work alone."

"And you know that this tape needs to be found or we're all fucked!" he snaps. "This job of yours? Any future assignments? You can kiss it all good-bye." He pauses, and when he speaks again, his tone is more calm. "They'll be there to help turn over rocks."

"I thought you said you didn't want any more people involved?"

"I don't. These two are the idiots who helped make the mess, so now they're going to help clean it up."

The two guys who killed Royce and Ivy's uncle. Great.

"They'll stay out of your way with the girl. I agree, it's best you work on her alone."

The dial tone fills my ear and I realize that he's hung up on me. Tossing the phone onto the bed next to me, I simply lie there for a moment, listening to car doors slam and horns honk from down below. It's cool outside, but that doesn't translate in here, with the poor air circulation. The air duct on the wall across from me is meant for air-conditioning, but it's being used for nothing more than the hidden camera that I found in my preliminary search, expecting as much. I covered it with a piece of cardboard for privacy and left it at that. The scrawny forty-year-old male receptionist downstairs doesn't need to be jerking off to the sight of my unconscious naked body, but I'm not going to say shit about it, just like he's not going to say anything about the torn wallpaper.

I give my forehead a hard rub, an annoyed whisper of "Fuck . . ." slipping out of my mouth. Bringing those two guys in means that they could connect me to this. I'm usually far removed from Alliance and for good reason. This is a mistake on Bentley's part, but it's his call. He must be desperate.

I reach up and pull another chunk off. Something to kill time with while I wait to resume the search for this damning video confession.

And see Ivy.

# ELEVEN

IVY

I jump at the sound of knuckles hitting glass.

The shade is pulled down, so I can't be sure that it's him. And as much as I'd love to not care whether it is, I already know that if I go to the door and find anyone besides Sebastian standing there, I'm going to be royally disappointed.

We never agreed on a time yesterday, thanks to Bobby, something I realized when my eyes cracked open at noon. So I threw on some clothes and rushed to my car, telling myself that I was in a hurry only because I'd already wasted enough of the day sleeping and still had plenty to do at Black Rabbit.

Really, it's because I didn't want to miss Sebastian.

*If* he's coming back, that is. And I so desperately need him to, so I can prove to myself that my reaction to working on Bobby yesterday was an anomaly—an insidious after-effect of Ned's horrific death and nothing that will stop me from inking people permanently.

Forcing myself to walk at an extra-slow pace, so as not to appear overeager, I make my way to the door and peer out from behind the shade.

My heart skips a beat at the sight of Sebastian.

And I'm instantly disappointed in myself. I can't be having this kind of a reaction to a guy who lives in a city I'm about to leave. "Sebastian."

His intense gaze is hidden behind reflective aviators today. I can see myself in them. My bright, wide eyes. I'm not hiding my eagerness very well.

"Ivy." Even through the closed door, his voice is so deep, so even, so instantly soothing to me, that it sends a shiver down my back. No one should be able to elicit that kind of reaction by just saying my name.

I turn the dead bolt and open the door for him.

He steps past me, and suddenly Black Rabbit doesn't seem as eerie and lonely anymore. Just his presence swallows up some of the anxiety that's been hanging over me.

He inhales deeply. "You like that scent, don't you?"

I use the excuse of locking the door to turn my back on him and hide my reddened cheeks. There's nothing cheaper than a woman who wears too much perfume, and it doesn't matter how much she paid for the bottle. Or how much her friend paid for the bottle, in this case. Still half-asleep, I must have gone a little overboard with it before I left the house, if he's commenting on it now.

"We're doing this in the back room, I gather?" His sharp raptor gaze sizes up the shop in a very calculated way. I worked double time all afternoon, both to keep my idle hands and mind busy while I waited, and because the painters are coming first thing tomorrow morning. There's nothing much left here, except a few cardboard boxes and a thousand thumb tacks, where Ned had pinned up old newspaper clippings and pictures. I'm probably the least sentimental person on the planet when it comes to material things, and yet I can't bear to throw them out, so they're now neatly piled in a box. Maybe someday I'll put them in an album.

Or I'll get Dakota to put them in an album. She likes to scrapbook when she gets high.

Composing myself, I edge past him, reaching for the clipboard. "Unless you want to lie out here on the floor. You need to fill out this paperwork, and then I need a copy of your ID."

He stares at it. "What's this for?"

"It's a legal requirement. I can't put a needle to your skin until you've signed. You can fill it out while I finish getting the room ready." Ned was always strict about filling out the required paperwork. The threat of losing his license was enough to scare him and, while I was working here, to scare me into following his lead.

"Right," he mutters. "I forgot about that." I lead him into the back room, watching quietly as his gaze scans the black walls—covered in dusty square outlines where Ned's portfolio of the weirdest tattoos that he'd ever done used to hang—then the cases of ink that I haven't decided whether to take home for my own use or sell with the store, and the leather table, laid out flat and covered in plastic wrap, my tools and supplies set on the tray beside it. "The room looks ready to me."

It's been ready for him for over two hours. What I need to do is get *me* ready. "So you said this isn't your first time?"

The corner of his mouth curls. Setting the clipboard down on top of a box, he reaches over his head and peels off his T-shirt to reveal a canvas of skin and hard muscles and a few scars, along with a sizable tattoo covering his left shoulder.

All nerves temporarily forgotten, I automatically step forward to study its quality and design. "Where'd you get this?"

"San Diego."

"When?" It looks to be a few years old, at least. And well done, which is good. He probably did his research on that artist, like he did with me. It tells me he's no idiot.

"Awhile ago."

I roll my eyes. Not the most talkative guy when it comes to personal questions, I guess. "What is this? A . . ." The helicopter covers the ball of his shoulder. Five men in black dangle from ropes below it. This has to be military, and I'm guessing it has meaning for him. "Were you in the army?"

Cool eyes peer down at me, but he doesn't answer.

I take that as yes, he was, and no, he doesn't want to talk about it. It doesn't really matter to me, but it helps me understand him a little more. His quiet, somewhat rigid demeanor, his lack of re-action, his readiness to help me, willingness to go toe-to-toe with a biker. He's a soldier—or was—minus the brush cut and "ma'am" at the end of every sentence. Or maybe that was just the Texan Marine I picked up one night in San Diego.

"So, about your design . . ."

He reaches into his back pocket and slips out the folded piece of paper, handing it to me again. I can't help but frown with disdain. Instead of taking it, I grab the sheet I tore out from my sketchbook, waiting on a side table. "I was thinking something like this would look better on you."

He stares at the sketch I pulled together while watching the waves come in off Ocean Beach this morning, after I'd emptied my soul and mind onto a shitty old brick wall in the Mission District. It's a risky design and one he may not want on his body. I know that even as I mentally cross my fingers and hope that he'll say yes, because I really don't want to ruin his beautiful torso with something as generic and common as what he has suggested.

He stares at the sketch for so long that I start to fidget and backpedal. "You don't have to go with this. I just thought—"

"It's incredible." He shifts his gaze to me, and a flicker of warmth burns in those cold irises of his. "When did you do this?"

I stifle the grin that wants to slip out. *He thinks it's incredible.* "This morning. I had some time to kill."

He looks at me like he knows something I don't. "I want this one."

I swallow, the intensity of his gaze and his presence seeming to suck all the air out of the room. "And the size. You want it . . ."

"I'm sure you have an opinion." He watches me intently.

I rarely give a damn about anyone or what they do with their lives, but I *always* have an opinion when it comes to body art. And this one, especially, I want to be flawless. "I think we should start it here"—I reach up to tap his skin, my fingertip just a curl away from a solid pectoral muscle—"and end down here, with the bottom of the scythe cutting into your bone right here." My other hand slides across the base of his waist, at that delicious spot where his abdominal muscles meet his pelvic bone, forming the one side of a V that disappears below his belt.

My hand is trembling.

My fucking hand—the hand of a tattoo artist about to leave a giant, permanent marking on this perfect canvas—is trembling.

And he must be able to see it. If I were him, I'd throw my shirt on and head out that door and never look back.

His fingers, the skin hot and dry and ridged with history, seize mine, squeezing them under his thumb. My hand looks childish next to his.

I open my mouth, ready to fire off excuses for the shakiness—need for caffeine, though the remnants of a Starbucks Venti is sitting on a box next to us; too cold, though the AC is shut off and it's suddenly stifling in here—when he says, "How about a little farther back, like here?" He shifts my hand an inch over.

"That will work, too." He releases my hand, and I exhale with relief. "This is going to take seven hours in black, more if you want color. That would put us at"—I glance at my phone—"ten tonight. Are you sure you can handle it? It takes a lot out of people, and the rib cage is especially sensitive."

"I can handle it. Can *you* handle it?"

I snort. "Yeah, I can handle it."

"I figured you could." He nods toward the front. "Then go and make that transfer so we can get started."

Normally I'd bristle, having someone tell me what to do. But right now getting away from him and his bare chest and the masculinity that radiates from him sounds like a smart plan. So I bolt to the front of the shop, both elated that he's going with my design and uncomfortable with how easily he's been able to slide under my skin, with nothing more than a look.

The computer is the only thing I haven't packed up, and that's solely because I knew I'd need to make a transfer for Sebastian. After tonight, I'll have to move it to the house, just in case these painters are stupid enough to take a coffee break and leave the place wide open and unattended. This isn't the kind of area you can do that in without coming back to find yourself cleaned out.

Letting the scanner warm up, I study my design with a smile.

She's lethal but sexy, quiet but strong.

I'd like to think that she's a little bit like me.

# TWELVE

# SEBASTIAN

She's doing her best to hide that she's attracted to me. If I hadn't just witnessed her hand shaking as it grazed my hip, and the slight flush of her cheeks when she realized it, I might not have believed it. She's good at hiding her emotions.

Just like I am.

I smile. Aren't the two of us a pair.

I peek around the corner to see her back to me, her left boot tapping to the beat of the music as she studies her sketch. Now I know what she was doing on the beach this morning. It's impressive that she could work so quickly, after no sleep, and produce such an exquisite piece of artwork. As foreboding as the sketch is, I can see elements of her surroundings in it—the reaper's cloak curling at the ends like crashing waves, the crows dipping and diving from above like the seagulls had.

That she would actually have the nerve to redesign my tattoo—with a female reaper, no less—surprised me.

Ivy has surprised me twice, actually. The first time was the uncanny resemblance to me that she sketched out on the wall with nothing more than two brief encounters. I should be concerned that my face—and therefore evidence of my presence in San Francisco—exists.

But I don't have time to be surprised or concerned right now. I have only a few minutes to search this room. All the boxes are sealed with original package tape. I can't very well tear into those before she gets back. That leaves me with the six rectangular ceiling tiles above me that I can search now. Hopping onto the leather table that I'll be spending a long time on tonight from the sounds of it, I pop the first tile off its frame and ease it down. Using the flashlight on my phone, I stand tall enough to see into the space above and scan the interior. The walls are interior structures and not load-bearing, so there's nothing to obstruct my view far beyond just this room, other than the darkness, and plenty of wires, cobwebs, rodent droppings.

No videotape.

I pivot around, searching as far as the light carries. There's nothing.

"What are you doing?"

*Fuck.* I should have expected that. She's a damn ninja, moving so quietly. I should have remembered that from the other day, at her house. "I heard something running through here," I say, my voice calm and unconcerned about getting caught. The sound of an innocent man, just trying to be of help.

"So you figured you'd dismantle the ceiling and, what . . . catch it?" she mocks. Not so much as a suspicious inflection in her voice, at least.

"You said you were selling, didn't you?" I finally look down, to find her small face peering up at me. "The last thing you want to be doing is trying to sell a place infested with rats."

"Rats?" She pauses, her demeanor suddenly shifting. "Did you see something up there?"

"No. Why?"

"It's just . . ." She folds her arms over her chest, hugging herself tight, reminding me that she's hiding a curvy little body under that loose T-shirt. ". . . They have those beady eyes and long tails . . ." She glares at the ceiling as if one's going to suddenly drop down on her head.

The girl who will crawl through gaps in boards and spend an entire night spray painting by lantern, with every kind of junkie and vermin—*including* rats—within a hundred-yard radius of her, is now freaked out.

"What?" she snaps, scowling at me, and I realize that I'm staring at her. "I just really hate rats. That's normal."

Reaching down for the ceiling tile, I replace it in its frame and hop down to the floor, a slight sting shooting through my leg. The bullet wound hasn't completely healed yet. "No rat. Maybe I was just hearing things."

By the frown on her face, that doesn't seem to appease her new concern.

"Do you want me to check the rest of the place?" I offer, selfishly. I can search for the videotape more efficiently if I'm supposed to be looking for something to begin with.

She hesitates, that stubborn, independent streak of hers keeping her from asking for more help. Finally, her disgust for rodents in the workplace must win out. "Maybe after I'm done with your design."

I nod. That works. "How do you want me?"

She gives her head a subtle but noticeable shake, before clueing in. "Lying on your side, with your arm over your head, for the work. But I need to put your transfer on you first, so go stand over there." She points to the other side of the table, where there's more room and a full-length mirror propped up against the wall, and then busies herself with the music playlist on her phone, syncing it with the same little portable speaker she had out last night. When she ties her hair back into a ponytail, I notice the flush in her ears.

I smile to myself. That's what she does. Ducks to hide her emotions when she can't control them, when she's most vulnerable. I'm sure that knowledge will come in handy later.

I shift over to take in my reflection as a slow, rhythmic song begins playing. "Are you trying to put me to sleep on your table?" The cushion on that bench looks soft enough, but I doubt it would be after that many hours. Then again, I've fallen asleep in much worse conditions than this.

"If you can sleep through a needle on your ribs, I'll be impressed."

"And what does impressing you get me?"

She exhales softly but doesn't answer. I watch her reflection in the mirror as she turns and walks toward me, gloves on and spray bottle in hand. She slows to a pause, her pinched gaze on my back.

# THIRTEEN

# IVY

The scars are scattered across his back, from shoulder to kidney area. They make me flinch.

They make me think he isn't just a soldier who survived boot camp and wore a uniform.

They make me think that he was hurt very badly.

They make me think that he's seen a lot worse than I ever have.

I clear my throat, pushing those sad thoughts aside. "Okay, the end will reach down to where your belt sits. It'd be better if you pushed your jeans down a few inches."

"Are you asking me to take off my pants, Ivy?"

There it is again. The words are flirtatious but his tone is entirely neutral. Almost sterile. But I can see his eyes in the mirror. They're on me, sharp and perceptive and anticipating.

Waiting for my reaction.

"After seven hours under my needle, we'll practically be married. You may as well unbuckle now," I answer, gritting my teeth to keep from smiling like a fool who's excited at the prospect of Sebastian flirting with me.

With one deft hand, he unfastens his belt and jeans. They slide a few inches to reveal the elastic band of Jockey boxer briefs. I doubt this guy owns even one overhyped name-brand item of clothing. He seems too practical.

A quick glance in the mirror shows me more of that line of

dark hair running down from his navel and the prominent bulge below. It's good to know that he didn't lose any vital parts in whatever war he was a part of.

"Is that good?"

"It'll do. Come here."

I take his hand and settle it on my shoulder, so it's out of the way when I mist his body with green soap. I expect him to flinch from the cool temperature like everyone does, but his face remains even. It's like he doesn't even notice. He simply watches me. Grabbing a paper towel, I quickly wipe off the excess, silently admiring the ridges carved into his stomach, which he's clearly worked so hard on. I squeeze several globs of the gel needed for the transfer to adhere to his side and begin running my fingers over the full length of his side, gently smoothing and massaging it in, my breathing quickening with each dip and rise of his body, especially as I reach the sharp cut between his abdomen and hip. Wishing for the moment that I didn't have to wear gloves. That I didn't need the excuse of a tattoo machine to touch him like this.

I've turned into a hormonal fourteen-year-old. I hated being fourteen when I *was* fourteen. Now . . . it's dangerous. I have no issues with acting on my desires. Like the desire to slide my hand into the front of his briefs right now.

Thank God no one can read minds around here.

"Okay, take a deep breath and let it go . . ." I watch his chest rise and fall. "Now relax and stand normally. And hold still." The warning is unnecessary. Sebastian is a natural statue beside me as I position his design on his body and carefully peel away the paper, leaving my creation behind.

I smile. "So, what do you think?"

"Fierce. Stunning. Captivating."

"You're not even . . ." I sigh, feeling my cheeks flare under his scrutiny. He can't see the design; he's too busying staring at me, and he's not even covert about it. I nod toward the full-length mirror on the wall opposite us. "Take a look for yourself."

He turns away from me and strolls over to peer at his reflection again, making no effort to grip his jeans, letting them slide down more, until I can see the round humps of what I'm sure is a hard, perfect ass.

I have to clear my throat again to gain composure. "Move around a bit. You know, twist your body, lift your arm . . . make sure you like the way it looks from all angles."

He does, leaning over and arching his arm, giving me a harsh view of those scars as they stretch under the halogen track lights. Abruptly, he turns and my eyes automatically drop to that V and the waistband and the bulge hiding beneath the thin navy-blue cotton before I can help myself.

"It's good." His voice pulls my gaze up to his face and the hidden smile.

He caught me. Thankfully he has the grace not to say anything.

He climbs onto the table and stretches out on his side. "Like this?"

"Almost. Can you slide over to the middle? I'm going to need room to sit up on the table." Normally, I'd stand over or sit next to a client, but seven hours of leaning will wreck my back.

He adjusts without a word, giving me just enough room to perch one ass cheek and nudge myself up next to him.

I take a deep breath, peering at the half-naked man lying before me and the tattoo machine gripped in my hand. I'm a jumble of nerves right now. I'm afraid that the second I put this needle to Sebastian's skin, I'm going to feel the same revulsion I felt last night working on Bobby. I'm certainly feeling an attraction to Sebastian that's becoming hard to ignore, a desperate need for intimacy and diversion, even if it's only temporary. But there's something else amid the skittishness I feel, something steadier that's pulling me to him. I think I just feel safer when he's around.

This tattoo is a lot to take on, and clearly I'm not myself, the way I'm acting today, all needy. Maybe I shouldn't be doing this right now.

Sebastian suddenly rolls onto his back to stare up at me. "Are you sure you can handle seven hours of this?" he asks, as if reading my mind.

It's like he knew those words would flip that switch inside me. It's one thing for me to doubt myself internally. It's entirely different for someone else to voice that same sentiment.

I press the pedal and a buzzing sound pushes the music into the background. He rolls back without another word. His raised arm isn't out of the way so I push against it, reveling in the shape and size of his triceps for a brief moment.

And then I begin to mark Sebastian.

Everyone reacts to that first stroke of the needle differently. Some people flinch, some grit their teeth, some close their eyes. Sometimes it's not what I can see but instead what I can feel, as tension tightens their muscles, and deep breaths swell their chests.

With Sebastian, there is nothing. And in a sensitive spot like this, to have absolutely no reaction is just not normal.

"How is that?" I ask anyway.

"Fine." And it *is* fine, based on the even timbre of his voice. I guess the thick layer of muscle is more protection than even I expected.

I begin on the outline of the reaper's head, the side of my palm ever so gently resting against him as I work, his body heat warming my skin even through the latex.

This is where my clients usually begin talking. They're excited, they're nervous, it's a bit awkward to have a stranger touching their flesh and they want to get comfortable . . . there are plenty of reasons for them to strike up a conversation. It always starts with small talk—the basics about the person, the all-too-common "What's the weirdest tattoo request you've ever had?"

Depending on how detailed the piece is and where I'm doing it, at some point the conversation usually veers into personal territory. Their dysfunctional relationships, failed marriages, their lifelong battle with weight, the loss of a child that has inspired their ink work, spirits of deceased family members sending them signs from beyond the grave.

People divulge all kinds of things that I never asked to hear, that I'd rather not hear, and that they never planned on telling

me. It makes me feel like a bartender at some seedy desert bar in
nowhere-Nevada. But I keep quiet and go along with anything
they want to talk about, because that's part of the job. Ned's Rule
Number Two: These people are letting you permanently mark
their bodies, so shut up and smile and let them cry about their pet
gerbil that they accidentally stepped on when they were two years
old if that's what they want to talk about. While I avoid small talk
outside the shop, I've become something of a connoisseur when a
client is in my chair. I've had to.

But Sebastian hasn't said a word in ten minutes. I'm beginning
to think he could go seven hours in complete silence.

I can't do the same, or I'll end up thinking about Ned and the
night he died, and then this tattoo could go horrifically wrong.

"So, tell me a little bit about yourself."

"What do you want to know?" It's like he was waiting for my
question.

*Everything*, I realize. I just don't want to have to ask. At some
point I'm going to bring up the whole military thing again, because
that's interesting, but seeing as he quickly shut the door on that
conversation before, it's probably not the best place to start now.
"Do you live in San Francisco?"

"Yes."

"Whereabouts?" I realize that I forgot to get the personal
information clipboard back from him. I was too distracted by . . .
well, *him*. And the idea of rats in here. I'm not even sure that he
filled it out yet.

"Potrero Hill."

"Huh." I search for something to say as I wipe excess ink off his
skin with a paper towel. All I can come up with is, "Very residential."

He doesn't answer.

"Did you grow up around here?"

"Yes."

I give him a few moments to elaborate, until I realize that he's
not going to. Great. He's clearly not into small talk. "Well, this is
going to be a really long night," I mutter under my breath.

That earns his smile. I'm pulling teeth to get him to talk and he's *amused*.

"Which part of San Francisco did you grow up in?" he finally asks, flipping the question on me.

"Who says I grew up here?"

"Did you grow up somewhere else?" He throws this out with a hint of a challenge in his voice.

"Richmond. Until I was fourteen."

"Huh . . . very Asian." He's mocking me for my earlier "residential" comment, I can tell.

"Well, I know this will come as a huge shock to you but I *am* part Chinese."

"So I've noticed."

And I'm back to trying to read that calm, even, unreadable tone.

"What do you do for a living, Sebastian?"

There's a long pause, and I assume he won't be answering that question. I heave an annoyed sigh.

Earning another smirk from him.

He's going to drive me insane.

"I'm in security," he finally says.

Security? "What . . . like a mall cop?" I say, and I regret my condescending tone the second it comes out of my mouth, because what if he *is* a mall cop? God, I hope not. While I don't really care what a guy does, just picturing Sebastian in one of those ill-fitting uniforms and hovering around a teenybopper chain store, watching for twelve-year-old shoplifters, has somehow knocked him down a notch or three in attractiveness for me.

*Please don't be a mall cop.*

"No. I'm not a mall cop." He chuckles, forcing my needle away from his skin until he settles down. He has a nice laugh. And nice straight white teeth, I see, watching him from this angle. When his laughter dies down and my needle touches his skin again, he admits, "I'm a bodyguard."

I have to pull away again, to process. "Really . . ." That is *way* more interesting—and appealing—than a mall cop. "I've never met a real bodyguard before. That sounds dangerous."

"It can be."

"Who do you protect?"

"People who need bodyguards."

I wipe away the excess ink just a touch harder than I probably should. "Are you always so evasive?"

"Are you always so inquisitive?"

"Only when I'm doing someone a huge favor." I bite my bottom lip to keep from tacking on an extra-acidic remark about his shitty communication skills.

He sighs. "For politicians, for celebrities, for civilians facing safety concerns. Pretty much anyone who needs a shield."

"That's . . . commendable." And brave. "I guess it's a natural career coming out of the army?"

"I guess," he says quietly.

It's all beginning to make sense to me now. No wonder Sebastian is so in shape, so strong. No wonder his movements seem so fluid and measured. No wonder, when he stepped into Black Rabbit for the first time, I felt his looming presence taking control of the entire room. Though I couldn't have articulated it at the time, I sensed right away that he could protect me from anything.

"So, are you working now?" His schedule seems flexible, if he's shown up here three days in a row, ready to spend seven hours under my needle on any one of them.

"I'm taking a break," he says simply.

"A bodyguard on vacation?"

He smirks. "We need vacations, too."

"I guess. But why'd you stay in town, then? I think I'd be on a beach the second I had a chance."

He smiles. "Maybe next week. I really needed to get this tattoo before you ran off."

"Sure you did," I mock, but I also smile. "Where are you going to go?"

"Greece."

"Why there? You have family there?"

"Nope."

"So you're just going to pick up and go to Greece?"

"Pretty much."

I grin. Finally, something that Sebastian and I have in common.

# FOURTEEN

# SEBASTIAN

HOUR TWO

The ink on my shoulder was done by a small shop in San Diego nine years ago. It took four and a half hours to complete. I didn't feel nearly as vulnerable with the artist—a scrawny middle-aged hipster named Marcus—as I do now, under Ivy's skilled hands, with her leaning over me, her gloved fingers touching my skin, that intoxicating perfume wafting around my nostrils in seductive waves.

I have no choice but to lie to her about my work—for obvious reasons. She bought the cover instantly. I wasn't sure that she would.

"How are you doing? Still good? Need a five-minute break?" she asks, a hint of concern in her voice.

She was trying to figure me out earlier. A guy who doesn't even flinch when he feels the sting from that needle like a knife carving into his flesh. Odd to her, I'm sure. But she saw the shrapnel scars on my back. It doesn't take a genius to figure out that they were serious, that they would have hurt far more than any tattoo.

"Keep going." We passed the one-hour mark quickly enough, even with my ambiguous answers and her annoyed sighs. But we still have six more hours, and I need to steer this conversation away from the places we've traveled—between the two of us I think we've covered every continent except Antarctica—and start pumping her for any information that might be useful to me in finding this tape.

"So what made you want to become a tattoo artist?"

"I love doing it," she answers simply, wiping away excess ink.

I'm careful not to move my body when I turn my head to peer up at her face. She knows I'm watching her, but she seems intent on avoiding my eyes. "Who's being evasive now?"

Her lips press into a tight line, like she's trying not to smile. And suddenly I wish I wasn't having this piece done on my side. I wish I'd picked my chest for its location, so I could lie on my back and stare up at her the entire time.

Because I meant what I said: Ivy *is* fierce, stunning, and captivating.

"I love to draw," she finally says. "I've been drawing on every surface I could reach since I was able to grip a crayon in my hand. Paper, walls, cars, you name it, my parents will tell you I marked it." A wistful look flickers past her eyes. "And my uncle. He's what got me into this career of drawing on bodies."

"The uncle who owned this shop?"

She swallows hard. "Yeah, him."

"Tell me about him."

She frowns. "Why?" There's a hint of suspicion in there.

I need to tread carefully. "Because sometimes it helps to talk about loved ones you've lost to a complete stranger." Even though that's not why I'm asking, it's still true. I watch her as she seems to think about that, still working away on the outline.

Only when she breaks to clean the ink do her dark brown eyes flicker to mine. "Have you lost any loved ones?"

She's already figured out that I was in some sort of armed forces. The army, she assumes. I haven't corrected her because I need to be cautious. With only a few thousand active SEALs at any given time, it wouldn't be impossible for someone to connect dots that lead to me.

But I also can't blow her off now. She finally seems to be relaxing around me, revealing more about herself. "One to a sniper bullet, and two to a roadside bomb. I watched all three of them die."

She settles a gentle, knowing gaze on me. "I saw my uncle, just after they shot him and ran out the door," she says softly. "But he was already gone."

Yeah, I pretty much figured that. "It's hard to get that image out of your head, isn't it?"

She averts her gaze to my side, but I catch the small nod.

"So tell me about your uncle," I prod. "It will help, I promise."

She sighs. "I'm not really sure what to say. No one's ever actually asked me that question before. I mean, you either knew him or you didn't. You either liked him or you didn't. But how to actually describe a guy like Ned?" She chews the inside of her mouth, until a slight smile pushes through. "He was a real fucking asshole."

I wasn't expecting that answer, and I can't help it. I burst out laughing. Luckily Ivy pulls away a second before my entire body starts shaking. "You can't move!" she yells, but she's laughing along with me, and smiling. Trying so hard not to smile, by pulling her bottom lip into her teeth.

"Then don't be funny."

"I'm not. He really *was* an asshole." She shakes her head. "But man, did I love him."

"Was that a part of his eulogy?"

She snorts. Reaching over, she pushes my head back to its resting place, where I can no longer stare at her. "He always had a soft spot for me. I'd come in here with my cousin when I was as young as six and watch him work on people. Sometimes I'd just sketch in a corner quietly. He never sent me away. I thought he was the coolest, most badass adult ever."

I'm trying to picture a six-year-old version of this woman and I'm struggling. However she looked, I can't imagine this place would have been suitable for her. "Your parents didn't care?"

"Oh, they cared. They *hated* me being here, but there wasn't much they could do. My aunt Jun would watch me after school while my parents worked. But she also had a part-time job, and when she was working, I had to go somewhere. My parents didn't have enough money to send me and my brothers to day care. I was the oldest and therefore easiest to unload on someone else, so I came here. I pretty much fended for myself growing up."

No wonder she's so independent.

"By the time I turned fourteen and they realized that I actually *wanted* to come here, they packed us all up and moved us to Oregon."

This is good. She's opening up, and it seems to be comfortable for her. Oddly, talking to her is easy for me, too. Definitely more pleasant than my typical interrogations. "So they moved your entire family away just to get away from your uncle?"

"I guess that's what it boils down to, yeah." I can hear the displeasure over that in her tone.

The needle runs over a particularly sensitive spot and I inhale through the pain. "Sounds like they must have had reasons."

"I don't know about reasons. Fears, yeah. My dad was raised by quiet Chinese immigrants; my mom comes from an affluent family of accountants in Spain. They've always had strong opinions about Ned's clientele."

"Are any of those opinions warranted?"

"Well . . ." Ivy has shifted her body to focus on the midsection of the tattoo. I can just barely catch the way her lips twist with hesitation in the mirror.

"The guy yesterday, in the back. The biker who wanted his arm done. I'd say that your parents' opinions of him might be warranted." All this talk of parents makes me think of mine, something I never do when I'm on an assignment. They're no more than a fifteen-minute drive from here.

She smirks. "So you knew who he was when you tried to provoke a fight."

"Just like you knew who he was when you stepped between us." Her tiny body, her delicate fingers, pressing into my stomach. The girl doesn't back down, even when she's afraid.

In the mirror's reflection, I see her smile. "I guess it would make sense that you recognize those kind of people, given what you do for a living."

"It would. And I wasn't provoking anything."

"Sure you weren't." She pauses to adjust something on her machine. "But I guess it's all about who you associate with, right? My uncle Ned, he was just trying to run his business and didn't really give a shit about what anyone did as long as they didn't bring it into the shop. But he's been painted with an ugly brush by my parents. And now the cops are only too eager to somehow pin the blame for what happened to him right back *on* him. Whoever did this is going to get away with killing two innocent men. Or at least one. I didn't know the other guy."

Her expression, her voice, the way her shoulders seem to sag with the weight of that reality—she really believes that her uncle was needlessly murdered, probably collateral damage in a burglary gone wrong. And if she believes that, then there's no way she knows anything about the blackmail scheme.

"What's wrong?"

I frown. "What do you mean?"

"Your whole body just . . . relaxed. Not that it wasn't unusually relaxed before, but I felt it shift."

*Because now I know that I don't have to kill you.* I smile. "Yeah, I guess it did."

# FIFTEEN

# IVY

"Why are you selling the shop if you love this job so much?"

So much for "small talk," though there hasn't been much in the first two hours as it is. Sebastian is finally opening up to conversation, but the questions are pointed, the topics hard-hitting. And every time he turns his head to watch me with that penetrating gaze of his, I feel compelled to answer him.

"Because my cousin can't run it. He lives abroad and he has a lot of commitments over there." I keep my eyes on my work. I'm more than halfway through the outline already. Another hour and I should be ready to begin filling in.

It's going to look incredible.

"Then why don't you run it? Too many other commitments as well?"

"No. I don't have any, actually."

"Why not?"

"What do you mean, why not?" I frown. "I don't know why not. I guess I've avoided having them up until now."

"All commitments?"

"As much as possible."

"Why?"

"You already asked me that," I mutter.

He pauses, seems to ponder that. "I thought all women wanted commitment."

I chuckle at the generalization. For someone who must rely on good intuition on a daily basis, he's still *such* a guy. "Maybe all the women *you* associate with. I guess I'm not like the kind of women you're used to."

He cranes his head to see my face. "And what kind of women am I used to?" There's amusement in his voice now.

I reach over and shove his face back down. "Oklahoma State beauty pageant winners? Cocktail waitresses with boob jobs? I don't know. Why don't you enlighten me?"

"Why?"

"Morbid curiosity."

He opens his mouth and I think he's actually going to answer. "Why do you avoid commitment?"

I guess Sebastian will not be sharing his preferences in females today. Maybe that's for the best, because I don't want to hear about the future stay-at-home, childrearing, Pinterest mommies he regularly screws. "Because I've always liked to be able to pick up and go whenever I want. I like living out of a suitcase and not answering to anyone. I love doing my own thing and being my own person." It helps that he's not looking at me right now. It's kind of like being in a confessional, when you're telling all your sins to the mysterious voice behind the curtain.

Although I'm committing another sin while saying these words. I'm lying. I actually *was* enjoying staying in one place. It was nice having four walls and a door that felt like they belonged to me. And I didn't have to sacrifice doing my own thing and being my own person to have that.

"What about your family?"

"What about them?" He asks like he knows my family.

"They're okay with your lifestyle?"

"The way I see it, they have their own lives to lead however they want. They don't get to lead mine for me, too. It doesn't work like that."

"That's a good answer. I like it."

I smile. His validation feels good.

"But what about when you get married and have kids?"

I start to laugh. "Do you always get this personal with people you don't know?"

"Only the ones who tell me to unzip my pants."

I duck away to get a fresh paper towel from the roll and hide my smile. Sebastian is witty, and witty people excite me. And he's really beginning to open up, probably because I am, too. It's easier for me to do here, while I'm working. I'm in my element.

So, do I answer truthfully? Will answering truthfully crush any chance I have of getting his pants all the way off him tonight?

I'm beginning to see why Amber says I think like a guy.

Fair enough, but I don't want to lie like one just to get laid.

"I don't have a maternal bone in my body, and I have yet to meet a man who can hold my interest for more than a night." He's dissecting me with his gaze. I roll my eyes. "Why are you asking?"

"I'm trying to figure you out."

*"Why?"*

His mouth twitches. "Because I find you fascinating."

"Fascinating, like an exotic animal at the zoo fascinating?"

"No. Not like that at all." His gaze dips a little, to my baggy shirt that leaves everything to the imagination. Working in a place like this, it's smarter to keep at least somewhat covered up. I want business because of my talent, not my boobs. Plus, it creeps me out to have guys like Bobby ogling me.

But a guy like Sebastian . . .

This back room has suddenly grown hot. I thought that talking would make these hours manageable. I'm not so sure now. "Get back on your side," I demand.

His eyes linger on me for another moment before reassuming his position with a smile, allowing me to finish tracing the outline of my design on his body while reading too much into his words. "You're obviously capable of obligating yourself when you want to."

"Why do you say that?"

I pause to run my gloved fingertip over the man that hangs on his shoulder blade. "Don't all you guys live for God and country and family?" I haven't pushed with questions about his time serving overseas, though I'm dying to. I could easily slap a quid pro quo on him for his earlier interrogation about my choice to become a tattoo artist. I'll bide my time, though, and slip in casual questions and comments to help me figure him out.

He doesn't answer. I take it as a sign that that topic is still not okay.

"How old are you?" Something I'd know if I had him fill out his paperwork.

"Twenty-eight. Why?"

"Just trying to figure you out," I say, throwing his words back at him.

I see no ring, no tanned outline of a ring that's been taken off. Does he have kids? Does he want kids? Has my not wanting kids already turned him off?

And why the fuck am I even thinking about any of this? Ned's death has obviously screwed with me more than I realized, making me think about my future more than I ever have before. I'm basically a homeowner, and I didn't ask for that. I could be running this shop, and I didn't ask for that either. And now I have to make decisions, and I'm afraid that they'll be the wrong ones. That little voice in the back of my head is warning me that if I walk away from Black Rabbit, I will have regrets.

"I'm not a soldier anymore," Sebastian says, cutting into my thoughts. "Now I'm a lot like you."

Like me? I frown. "In what way?"

"I don't want to bring children into this world. I've seen too much violence to be able to sleep at night." There's tension beneath my fingertips, something I haven't felt from him until now. But it slips away just as easily, as if he's aware of it and can choose to control it. "And I have yet to find a woman who holds my interest for more than a few hours."

Most women would balk at hearing that.

I smile. "Until now, of course."

He doesn't answer. But he's smiling, too.

■ ■ ■

"What do your parents think of your chosen profession?"

"They think I'm going to be broke and homeless in my forties, that I can't possibly have a lifelong career doing this. So I guess that means they don't approve."

"And what about the tattoos and the shaved head and streaks of blue?"

"You say that like it's a bad thing. I thought I was *fierce, stunning, captivating*," I tease, though inside there's a hint of panic. What if he was just leading me on before?

"You *are* all those things. You're also not my daughter."

*Thank God for that.* "Fair point," I mutter under my breath.

"What made you come back to San Francisco?"

"I got tired of floating, and going back to Oregon just wasn't for me." My arm is settled against his stomach, and the feel of my bare skin against his is intoxicating. And, seriously . . . I think it'd be impossible for any guy to be turned on right now, but it looks like he could be, or else he must just have an impressive—

"Are you almost done with the outline?"

"Just about," I say, too breathless, flushing as if I just got caught. "Why? You need a break already?" That Sebastian hasn't asked to stretch or take a moment to pee up until now may be a new record for my clients.

"Keep going."

# SIXTEEN

# SEBASTIAN

She's switched positions to fill in the bottom part of the design, her ass cheek perched on the table and her thigh pressed against my back as she faces my lower half. It's the perfect angle for her to size up my junk, and she thinks I don't know she's doing it.

The mirror across from me, which gives me a good angle of her face, doesn't lie.

"How're you doing?" she murmurs.

"I'm good."

"Seriously, you're the most unaffected person I've ever worked on."

"I have a high pain threshold." "Unaffected" is probably not the right word for what I feel, with her draped over my body. Luckily I don't enjoy pain, so getting a hard-on right now is just about impossible.

"Are you sure you're not just a cyborg?" she jokes. I love her humor, and the way she delivers it—deadpan.

"Are you saying I don't have feelings? That hurts." This pain is laughable compared to the bullet in my thigh.

"Or maybe you're just playing tough and trying to impress me, Army Boy."

"Navy Boy, if you want to get specific. Those army guys are wimps." It's the first shred of real information I've offered her about my past life and I shouldn't have done it. This room, this chair, spending hours motionless, completely at her mercy . . . I haven't spent this much time with one person in years. It's messing with my head.

"Did you serve overseas?" she asks quietly, as if she knows she's treading in unwelcome territory.

"Two tours in Afghanistan."

She slides off the table. "Roll back this way. It's easier for me to fill this with you lying on your back." Her hand guides me and then slides onto my hip, pushing the elastic band of my briefs down and holding it there. The needle digs into my sensitive flesh. "Did you have to kill anyone?" she asks, and the question sounds so jarring, even though I knew it was coming.

"Yes."

"How many?"

"Too many." I close my eyes, like I still have to sometimes when I let myself really consider that question. It's easier now that I'm out, when Bentley hands me a specific target and gives me an order. I know it's a verdict that isn't being reached lightly because Bentley doesn't treat casualties carelessly. Back when I was a SEAL and trudging through enemy territory with my team, guns trained, and adrenaline propelling my limbs forward, I never knew exactly where the danger would come from, and in what form. We were forced to make split-second decisions or risk death all the time. Self-preservation is a powerful and sometimes blinding need.

It was so easy to make a mistake.

"Why did you choose the reaper?"

The harbinger of death.

"Why do you think I chose it?"

# SEVENTEEN

# IVY

I'd like to think that all people put great weight into the designs they mark their bodies with. That they choose something symbolic, that represents their passions, their personality, their struggles. I think Sebastian reached deep within himself when deciding on this design. Given the brief glimpse into his past that he just allowed me, I'm beginning to wonder exactly how dark it is in there.

The second the question left my lips, the tension in his body rippled beneath my fingertips. I hit a nerve. That's never my goal, and it's why I've always stuck to small talk and ambiguous yes and no answers when conversation gets too personal.

I pause for a second to wipe the ink away. There's no way to answer his question without making it sound like I think he's fucked-up.

"I'm starving. I'm gonna order pizza. You want some?"

"I could eat." As if on cue, his stomach growls obnoxiously in my ear, making me smile. "And you need a rest, too."

"I didn't say that."

"That's because you're stubborn."

I smile. "I'll have it delivered to our back door in fifteen minutes. I know the guy working tonight." If I'm going to tolerate Fez, I can at least get something out of the deal. "What do you want on it?"

"Don't care. Just no tomatoes of any kind."

"No tomatoes of any kind?" I frown, pulling away from my work to look over my shoulder at his face. "You do know what pizza is, right?"

He lifts his head to look at me.

"You're joking."

"I'm joking," he confirms with a playful smirk.

I climb off the table and, peeling off one glove, hit Fez's number in my contacts list. Just like that, we've veered back into more comfortable territory. We're also back to flirting.

■ ■ ■

The moment I open the back door and see Fez's face, I regret ordering pizza from Pasquale's.

"Yo, yo, yo! Here's da za!" He holds up a medium-size pizza that can usually feed me for three days, but I'm guessing Sebastian has a much bigger appetite than I do.

I hand him a twenty. "Thanks, Fez. Keep the change."

I'm hoping he takes the hint.

Fez never takes the hint. "So . . . you chillin' tonight?"

"Doing a friend's ink. We're just taking a quick break to eat before we get back into it. We have another few hours or so to go."

"Damn! You savage! A'right. Well, ima hang in here, then." He attempts to step in but I block him.

"Sorry. This isn't the kind of night for hanging out." I can only imagine what Sebastian would think of Fez.

He snorts, like I made a joke, but when I don't move, he finally clues in. "Serio?"

I heave a sigh of exasperation. "Fez! You're thirty-five! Stop trying to talk like a fifteen-year-old half-wit. You don't sound cool. You sound like an idiot!"

He frowns. "You be trippin', gurl."

"Fuck. I give up," I mutter, shaking my head at him. There's just no point having this conversation.

"Is that dinner?" Sebastian asks, suddenly behind me. I didn't hear him coming. He's as stealthy as I am.

"Yeah. Here." I shove the box into his hands.

Fez's left brow pops as he eyes the shirtless, pants-undone Sebastian. "Oh. I see how you playin'."

I roll my eyes. "Fez, I'm serious. This is a friend, and I'm *very clearly* working on his tattoo. I've gotta get back to filling him in. Thank you for delivering." I wait for him to step off the threshold before I shut the door.

"What was his problem?" Sebastian asks.

"You, likely . . ." I mutter, plucking the box from Sebastian's hands because he's not moving fast enough and I truly am starving. I toss it on the desk and rip off a slice, watching the cheese threads stretch and dangle and snap until it's free.

"Please tell me you've never fucked him."

"Even suggesting that is an insult." I savor my first bite. Fez's parents really do make the best pizza in Outer Mission.

"Thank God," he mutters, stepping into my personal space to collect his own slice. "What's that for?" He nods toward the thirteen-inch monitor.

"Nothing, now. The feed from the video camera out front used to be wired into this and a VHS player for surveillance. But the two guys that came in busted the camera and then took the player. So, it's useless now."

"A VHS player . . . I don't think I've seen one of those since grade school."

"I know, right? Ned was stuck in the eighties as far as technology goes. He hated anything to do with computers. He was probably the most New-Age-tech-illiterate person I've ever met. That computer out front? He had no Internet connection until I set it up. It still has Microsoft Office 2000." I shake my head and laugh. "He just got a smartphone three months ago, because I made him. And he had no idea how to use it. Those assholes stole that, too."

Sebastian frowns but says nothing. He hits the Power button and the same gray static that I saw that night fills the screen now. I turn away, the sight of it pulling me back to that night.

*Why is it even still in here?*

*In fact . . .*

I throw my pizza down on the cardboard box and, giving my hands a half-ass attempt at a clean with a napkin, rope my arms around the monitor and begin dragging it off the desk.

"Here, let me—"

"I've got it," I snap. It's not heavy, but it's awkward.

Sebastian says nothing more, simply leaning down to yank the plug out of the wall. He trails behind me as I make my way toward the back door, reaching over my head to push it open because he knows I can't, but I won't ask him for help.

"Don't let it close or we'll be locked out," I warn him as I head toward the Dumpster.

I hate this Dumpster. It's not made with small people in mind, and I have to climb onto cinder blocks just to be able to flip the lid open. But before I can do that, Sebastian is there, still shirtless, with his pants unbuttoned and his rib cage a mess of smeared ink and raw skin, holding the lid open.

Waiting soundlessly for me to hoist the monitor over my head and into the bin with a loud crash.

"Thanks," I mumble, and even though I don't want to be happy that Sebastian was here to help and that I needed him . . . I am, and I did.

He trails me back into Black Rabbit, kicking up the doorstop to shut and lock the door behind him.

■ ■ ■

The last spot of unmarked flesh is filled. I take my time with a cloth, gently wiping the ink away. Even after seven hours, my hand on the verge of cramping, I'm thoroughly enjoying the process of cleaning Sebastian's body.

He doesn't move, doesn't say a word, as I spread ointment over the entire piece. Not until I've done all that I can, do I lean back to admire my work. It was beautiful in the sketchbook. On the Sebastian canvas, though . . .

He's watching my face.

"You're done."

He rolls off the table and stands in front of that full-length mirror again, to evaluate my work. This is the only time where my nerves override my outward confidence. When my work is finished and there's no going back, and my client will either without doubt love or painfully regret his decision, regret putting all his trust in me. "What do you think?"

He simply stands there, staring at it, and I can't see his face. So I grit my teeth and wait.

Finally he turns and comes back, stepping well within my personal space. He seems to be getting comfortable there. "I think you're even better than you say you are."

I feel the smile of relief stretch across my lips. "Better than badass?"

He smirks. "Better than badass." His voice drops an octave, to a softer, almost concerned timbre. He reaches for my hand, taking it in his. "How's your hand? Sore?"

It's such an affectionate, tender gesture, and on the heels of such an intense experience with him. It's too much, suddenly. I panic and pull away. "Sore. But I'll survive." Grabbing the plastic wrap, I command, "Arms up."

He obeys, folding and resting both hands on his head casually, and watching me through that penetrating gaze as I wrap the plastic around his entire torso. "Keep this on for the night. I'll give you an aftercare kit that should cover you for a day or two, but you'll need to hit CVS to stock up." I go through the aftercare steps with him. I could recite them in my sleep.

"And your shoulder? It must be sore." Again, he takes the initiative, reaching out to massage the ball of my right shoulder, a boundary he wouldn't have crossed before my work on him. This happens more often than not to me, when I make a connection with clients. Their tattoo is done, they're relieved and enthralled and grateful to me. I call it the "post-ink high." Sometimes I experience it, too.

Right now is one of those times, and his touch feels good—too good. Enough that I'd gladly stretch out on this table and let him tend to my entire body.

I shake off the thoughts. "Are you even listening to me? This is a major open wound on your body right now. If you don't follow this, step-by-step, you will get a serious infection, and you don't want this infected, trust me." I like to use strong phrases, like "open wound" and "you will," especially when I'm talking to men, who seem to have a hard time following instructions. I've only ever had one of my clients end up with an infection—a guy with questionable hygiene habits to begin with. He showed up at the shop where I was working a week later, wondering if the pus draining from his arm was normal.

Sebastian smirks and recites back to me everything I just said, word for word.

"Okay, Rain Man. So you *were* listening," I mumble, though I'm impressed. "You're good to go."

He fastens his pants and buckles his belt, and disappointment stirs in me. Not that I expected something to happen, right here right now, after I've etched half his torso with ink. I'm just not exactly ready to say good-bye to him yet.

He reaches over to grab his T-shirt. "What do I owe you?" he asks, sliding a clipped wad of money from his back pocket. He begins flipping out hundreds.

"Seven hours at two hundred per hour." I'm not going to charge him double, even if he is willing—and prepared, based on the money I'm seeing—to pay it.

He holds out the cash, watching me chew my lip as I stare at it. Suddenly I feel guilty for taking it. Working on him was the most fun I've had in a while. But business is business and he's just another customer passing through. For all I know, he was flirting with me for a discount. Plus, I need the money. Still, I stall over his hand. "Thanks. And thanks for your help yesterday. I couldn't have—"

"Wanna grab a drink?"

# EIGHTEEN

# SEBASTIAN

Seven hours of casual probing and I've gotten nothing out of her that I didn't already know or guess. And nothing at all that gives me a clue about where this videotape could still be hiding.

But after seven hours of her hands on me and her scent around me and her breath skating against me, I'm having a hard time giving a shit about anything that's on this tape.

It's been so long since I've actually tried to seduce a woman, I don't even know if I'm capable of it anymore. Even when I was a newly minted SEAL and my teammates and I would head to the local bars, I wasn't much into chasing skirts and placing bets on whom I'd bring home, and how many drinks it would take to get her there. Maybe it's because I never had to put much effort into getting someone to come home with me; or maybe it's because I knew it wouldn't last past the night.

My ex-fiancée, Sharon, was the first woman to grab my attention. I met her at a friend's BBQ on a Sunday afternoon. No booze involved. She was feisty, opinionated, and beautiful.

And I thought she was for me.

Maybe she was, but it turns out I wasn't the one for her because she kept trying to change me, right up until two weeks before the wedding, while I was between tours. I guess she realized she *couldn't* change me, and the things she didn't like—my desire for solitude, my reclusive nature, my "shitty" communication skills, my reluctance to have children—were amplified after all that I had seen and done abroad.

I haven't had to make an effort since then. All it's ever taken is my wallet.

But Ivy's done the tattoo and I'm supposed to go home, and I both can't and don't want to.

"A drink? *Now?* I mean, tonight?" She frowns, her eyes shifting from my bandaged side to the clock. "Aren't you exhausted? And sore?"

"Nothing a few stiff drinks won't fix." I know she drinks, because she had that flask last night. I also know she probably has no plans to go to sleep anytime soon, given her nocturnal habits.

And I know she's not ready to leave me yet either because . . . I can just feel it.

She bites her lip in thought. "Okay, fine. But I need to clean up here. And you"—she holds up the clipboard that I haven't looked at since she handed it to me seven hours ago—"were supposed to fill this out. It's a regulatory requirement."

"And charging me tax is a government requirement, but you're not doing that, are you?" My ID says Gregory White from San Diego. I don't want to have to explain why I introduced myself as Sebastian. I don't want anything documented about my time with her, period.

She twists her lips and tosses it aside. "If you die of a staph infection, I'll deny ever having met you."

"I think that's best."

She smirks, rifling through her purse to pull out and hand me a business card. "Meet me here in an hour. Give it to the bouncer and he'll let you through the line with no questions. I'll be upstairs in the VIP section."

*Daredevil.* "A club?" Deafening music, disorienting lights, a thick crowd of people that I can't tell apart. Tension slides into my back. "I don't dance."

She begins taking apart her tattoo machine, her back to me. "Then you can watch me, because I feel like dancing tonight and this is where I'll be."

After seven hours of a different, friendly, more vulnerable side of Ivy, she's reasserting her cool, indifferent side, and every vibe radiating from her right now tells me that if I want to continue tonight, it's on her terms. Fuck. She just better not be trying to ditch me as part of that display of power. "I have no problem waiting around for you. I can search for that rat." And anything else that the cops may have missed.

She shudders. "There's no rat. I've been listening for it. You may as well go. I need to clean this up and then run home to shower and change." She glances over her bare shoulder at me. "And you're *not* coming home to watch me do that."

*I've already seen you do so much more than just shower.*

"Even though we're practically married now?" I've been saving her earlier words for the right moment.

She lifts an eyebrow but says nothing.

I could step up my game right here, right now. Rub her shoulders again, take her hand again . . . kiss her. Maybe we could avoid the club altogether. I consider this as I watch her methodically wipe down the components of her tattoo gun and fit them into the foam inset of her carrying case. I'm guessing she cares for her equipment like a mother would care for her child.

No. This is on her terms and she bristles easily. I can't come on too strong. Not yet. "I'll see you in an hour, then."

"Yes, at twenty-three hundred hours, Navy Boy," she mocks as I head out the back door.

■ ■ ■

Ivy stalks past the lengthy line without a care, a siren amid a sea of commoners in her royal-blue and black dress and clunky platform boots, her jet-black hair hanging like a smooth and shiny curtain around her face. She looks like a small child next to the towering bouncer who has to stoop to hear her, even with her added four inches. They share a few words and then he laughs and waves her in, the thick band of ink circling his biceps proudly displayed. I'm assuming either she did it or her uncle did. I'm betting that all her associations are somehow tied to her profession.

I watch all of this from an alleyway across the street, hidden by shadow, the effects of Ivy's needle beginning to burn my ribs. But nothing I can't handle, nothing that will stop me.

Now that she's inside, I stride forward, card in hand. Just as she promised, it's a simple wave to the bouncer and he's unfastening the rope.

The music rattles in my brain as I push through a red velvet curtain, my senses on overdrive. I've been trained to block out unimportant distractions and to focus on the important—the target I need to take out, the code exchange I need to catch. But eighteen months of listening to bombs blowing up buildings, gunfire raining down on insurgents, and the screams of anguish when human beings don't die instantly from their injuries doesn't simply vanish when you get on that plane for home. That shit tends to follow you wherever you go and manifests itself in everyday life—cars backfiring, people shouting, plates shattering—pulling you back thousands of miles and years in the past in a single heartbeat. Places like this . . . they're my nightmare.

Forcing that all down, I quickly zero in on the closest set of stairs. I take them up, two at a time, passing several waitresses dressed in sparkly short dresses and garter belts, navigating the dark and the steep steps in their gold heels while they balance cigar trays in their hands.

In my jeans and T-shirt, I'm sorely underdressed, but so is everyone else. Everyone except Ivy, maybe.

My tension eases up a bit when I reach the VIP section on the second floor and see that there's actually space between bodies, and a soft breeze coming from the fans above. And two exits by conventional means—stairs—plus six more by necessity—the windows lining the walls. A large opening in the center, lined by a glass rail, allows people a view to the main dance floor below and the chance to drop a beer bottle onto someone's head.

Ivy is impossible to miss. She's the woman standing at the rail, drink in hand, observing the mass of gyrating bodies below like a queen. An ice queen, who dismisses the line of lackluster candidates for her attention with nothing more than a glare when they attempt to strike up a conversation about her tattoos. I know I should go in and save her from them, but instead I watch from my corner for fifteen minutes as she deftly rejects them two . . . three . . . four times, sneering at one who has the audacity to touch her arm.

I smile, feeling triumphant, because she hasn't rejected me. Yet.

Her eyes are glued to the crowd below, as if she's not waiting for anyone. But I notice the two covert glances at her phone as well as the single glance at the stairwell closest to the front entrance, which I took to get up here. She's almost finished her drink, and by the irritated drum of her fingertips against the glass rail, I know that she's about to ditch me, even though she made a point of making it sound like she had plans to come here anyway.

It's time to move in.

Her body, already tense, goes rigid as my hands find her hips from behind. I use the loud music as an excuse to lean in and get my mouth nice and close to her ear. "Anything interesting from up here?"

She relaxes against me for a moment, but then snaps, "I thought soldiers knew how to tell time."

"I'm not a soldier anymore." Not the kind that she thinks I am, anyway.

She turns to peer into my eyes, her face inches from mine. "Did they kick you out for tardiness?"

It's an innocent dig, but it drills me right where it hurts all the same. "No, not for that." That would have been more palatable than how I got discharged.

She eyes me, curious to know more but not about to ask—that's what I like about her, she can tell when I'm not willing to talk about something and she doesn't prod.

"Actually, I'm never late. I was standing right over there for the last fifteen minutes, watching you get hit on." I point to my hiding spot.

Her brow spikes. "You like watching me?"

I chuckle. *You have no idea how much.* "I guess I do."

She tips her glass back to finish her drink, the ice shards rattling in her glass. "Jameson and Coke, when the waitress comes back around." She twists out of my grasp and shoves the empty glass into my chest, holding it there until I take it.

Then she begins walking away.

I reach out and seize her wrist with my free hand, faster than she expected, I think, and pull her back against me. I could hold her against me all night if I wanted to. "Where are you going?"

"You said you like watching me. So you can stand here and watch." She slithers out of my grasp and carves a path through a group of bodies to an open area. She doesn't care that she's alone, as she begins to sway to the beat, in her own world. While I have no interest in dancing, watching her is more than enough to get my blood flowing, the pulse of the strobe lights that I normally hate making her simple movements more electric, more sexual.

*I'm here to find incriminating evidence against Alliance,* I remind myself. It's so easy to forget that when I'm watching this creature, but I can't let myself forget. I already expect Bentley's call in the morning, and if I don't have something to give him, those fuckups are going to come in and wreck any chance I have with Ivy. When they don't find the video in the house—because they won't; I was thorough—what's next? Will Bentley at some point decide that I'm not getting anywhere with Ivy and it's their turn with her?

I don't trust guys who are motivated by self-preservation. They'll do anything to cover their asses. And I'm guessing in this case, "anything" could result in one of those low-key, coincidental deaths Bentley mentioned.

She's lucky she has me here, then. Even though she has no clue.

I'm not the only one who's interested in Ivy. A quick glance around this VIP area finds men and women alike sharing curious glances as she sways with perfect rhythm, her movements sleek yet graceful. There is something about this woman—a dangerous, unapproachable quality that I find alluring.

Two schmucks to my left elbow each other, each goading the

other on. I wonder which poor sucker is going to make a move. It's a meat market in here, and this crowd of late-twenties and up has come for one reason, and one reason only.

To get fucked tonight, either by booze or bodies. Or both.

I'm not judging. As I watch her hips move, I know I'll gladly take the latter.

I sense the waitress approach a second before her shouts catch my ear. "Can I get you a drink?"

"Jameson and Coke, and a straight Coke." I never drink in these types of situations. It dulls the senses, which are already severely challenged in here.

"Anything else?" She bumps my biceps with her tray and she winks, her long eyelashes fluttering. I take quick inventory of what's on offer—rows of cigars and cigarettes, which is amusing given you can't smoke them in here; and a selection of Trojans in various varieties. I already know that I won't need those if I go back to Ivy's. She has a decent stash waiting. "Not for now. Thanks."

The waitress disappears with a nod, and when she arrives moments later to deliver our order and settle up, Ivy magically reappears. "Thanks." Her dark eyes settle on me as she sucks back her drink in a few gulps, leaving nothing but a pile of ice chips.

"Thirsty?"

"Very." She eyes my glass. "What are you drinking?"

"Rum and Coke," I lie, because I think she's the type of woman to take my drink right out of my hand and devour it just to prove a point—that she can, and I'll let her, because I want to fuck her tonight, and she knows it.

And she'd be right.

But then she'd also know that I'm not drinking alcohol, even though I got her out under the guise that I was going to get drunk tonight.

Her face pinches up. "I hate rum."

*I know.* That's the beauty of doing my own recon. All those trivial, seemingly useless bits of information can come in handy.

"Then I guess it's a good thing this drink isn't yours," I say through a smile and a sip.

She hands me her empty glass and then struts back to her spot, the little game she's playing with me becoming all the more obvious.

That's fine. I'll play, happily. As long as she doesn't stoop to pitting me against any of these assholes in here, because I don't do well in those kinds of situations and, frankly, I'd be extremely disappointed in her.

Just in case, I do a quick scan of my "competition"—most of them Silicon Valley–type geeks, smart entrepreneurs who will probably make a ton of money and will use that to land themselves a hot wife.

The hairs on the back of my neck suddenly spike.

Someone's watching me. I'm surprised my senses picked up on that, with all the distractions in here.

It's not Ivy.

It's not the horny cougars to my left.

It's the guy to my right, whom I noticed standing on the other side earlier. He has shifted closer now. I keep sipping my drink, using the reflection in a mirror on a nearby wall to watch him alternate his attention between Ivy and me.

Wondering who I am, if we're together, if she's working for me maybe . . .

My gut says it's all that and something else.

He's military, even though there's nothing about his outward appearance that would label him as that to an unsuspecting person. His dark cropped hair is gelled back, his black pants and black button-down and suit jacket stylish. Plenty of room to hide a piece under there, if he wanted to. Then again, my Beretta's strapped to my ankle. It's not hard to hide anything anywhere if you want.

But I know he's military because of the way he moves, how he blends into the background.

And his shiny black boots. Even in the poor lighting, the gleam from the polish is impossible to miss, and it triggers something that

Ivy said. Something that could be a complete coincidence, and yet I can't ignore. Listening to my gut has saved my ass more times than I can count.

I continue my covert appraisal of the guy through four more painful songs, while Ivy dances and pretends to ignore me. Aside from the occasional typing into his phone, he does nothing but watch both of us. And the more he does that, the more I know this isn't just someone looking to pick up a hot chick for the night.

This has to be one of Bentley's Alliance guys.

Why the fuck is he here?

He has a drink in hand, so he'll need to use the restroom soon. He's a guy, it's inevitable. Hell, I already need to piss, too. I could follow him in, corner him, get him to talk. It'll be loud and crowded in . . .

"What's going on with you?"

I start, surprised. At some point, I stopped watching Ivy completely and she snuck up on me. No one should be able to sneak up on me. This is why I hate clubs. I'm not at my best in here.

I push aside thoughts of the guy for now and focus on her, on the thin sheen of sweat that makes her cheeks glow and the swell of her breasts—pushed up in a top made to look like a corset—glisten. "Nothing. Why?"

"You looked like a fucking statue just now. It was weird."

"I'm sorry. Something distracted me. I'm fine." But I'm not fine, because that guy is still there watching, and I've reached my sanity maximum of strobe lights and head-splitting music.

She follows my gaze, though she's not noticing the mirrors, with the reflection of him. She's zeroing in on two college blondes with shorts that barely cover their asses, and her eyes narrow.

"That's not what distracted me," I scold.

"How do you even know what—"

I loop my arm around her tiny waist and pull her into my good side, holding her tight. "Can we please get out of here?"

Fire dances in her eyes as she glares up at me. "Maybe I still feel like dancing."

"Then you can dance all you want at home." For me.

She smirks, opens her mouth to answer, but decides better of it. She flags down the waitress passing by instead. "How much for the Cohibas?"

"Twenty each," the waitress answers with a grin.

I feel a hand slip into my back pocket, but I don't panic because I already know it's Ivy, fishing out two twenties. "I'll take two."

My brow spikes, watching the exchange with amusement. "Who are those for?"

"One's for me."

"And the other?"

She tucks them into her cleavage, the ends sticking out. Making my mouth water. "I haven't decided yet." The way she's staring at me now, I can't tell whether she wants to undress me or slap me. Her words, though, are clear. She's still undecided about what—if anything—to do with her attraction to me.

I'd like her to decide sooner rather than later, because I'm leaving here and she's not staying without me.

I watch patiently as she makes a point of pulling money out of her small purse and putting it back into my wallet, enough to cover the cigars and the drink I bought her. Figures. She's too independent to actually let me pay for them.

When she makes a move for Gregory White from San Diego's driver's license, though, I snap my wallet out of her hand and slide it back into my pocket.

The last thing I want to do is expose my weakness to her, but I need to leave. I lean in close to her, reveling in her perfume. "Listen, I really need to get out of here. The strobe lights and flashes . . ." A perfectly timed parade of servers with bottles prance by, waving sparklers in the air to announce their delivery. ". . . Sometimes they remind me of shit from the past."

I can't be sure that she'll even understand what I mean. Or care. But there's an instant flicker of recognition; I can see it in her demeanor. She doesn't say a word. Slipping her hand in mine, she begins leading me to the stairs.

Thank God.

"I drove," I call out.

She glances up over her shoulder, a step below me. "Good, because you're taking me home." She doesn't have to spell it out, I can see her meaning in her eyes.

We exit the front door with a nod to the bouncer and a smile on my face.

"Which way is your car?"

I place my hand on the small of her back and she has no choice but to let me lead, though she doesn't tense or scowl. She doesn't seem to mind at all.

As we round the end of the building to the street parking behind, I casually check the entrance.

The guy with the black blazer and black dress pants and polished black boots is standing on the sidewalk.

Watching us.

# NINETEEN

# IVY

I prefer short flings.

Not because I'm a slut—I detest that word; it's so disparaging, and who the hell is anyone to judge anyone else's sexual preferences?—but because there aren't any expectations beyond, hopefully, a good time. There is no opportunity to hurt anyone's feelings. I don't know him, he doesn't know me. It's just pure physical attraction.

Like what I've been feeling with Sebastian all day.

I want to take him home. I want to take his clothes off and mother his wounds—my artwork—with a gentle, experienced hand. And then I want to fuck him. I decided that somewhere between tucking the cigars into my cleavage and him revealing a vulnerable side that he was hiding so well, until he wasn't.

But to be honest, I'm not entirely sure that this is simply physical attraction anymore. Had I had sex with him on the dirty floor of Black Rabbit two minutes after he walked in the first time, or even yesterday, then it would have been. But after spending seven hours with him and his body today, I feel connected to Sebastian, for reasons that go beyond his looks.

So maybe this is going to be a huge mistake.

Maybe Sebastian is going to be the one who messes with my head.

Maybe I should call it quits right now.

"Make a left turn up here," I instruct, a split second before his finger hits the signal, as if he already knew where he was going. Just like he begins to slow his obscenely clean car as we approach my driveway. "Pull in behind that Honda there. Please." I bought the used silver Civic for five grand cash a few weeks after I moved here. It's been reliable so far, if not exactly sexy.

He turns in. And cuts the engine.

"Quite presumptuous of you," I say.

He rests his elbow on the console and turns to give me a look as flat and unreadable as the one I've perfected. "Is it?"

It's not at all. I think it's inevitable, really. There's no way in hell I'm calling it quits. *That* decision I would definitely regret.

Flutters explode in my stomach. This guy is not good for my cool, unflinching mask. Soon, I'm going to be giggling like a fucking Valley Girl. "How's your side?" There *is* that giant open wound to think about in all this.

"A little sore." His gaze skates over my mouth. "Nothing hindering."

"I guess I could take a look at it for you. Show you how to clean it properly."

"That's what I was thinking." I watch his hand as it reaches out for me. His fingers dip into my top to pull the cigars out, the edge of his thumbnail skating against the inside of my breast. "And then we could smoke these."

I shrug. "Maybe."

I duck out of the car before he can see my excited smile, slamming the door shut behind me, thinking I'm going to get ahead of him and up the stairs, so he'll have to trail. But he's somehow already out and waiting for me by the time I get around. "Do you do everything so fast?"

Amusement sparkles in his dark eyes. "When it matters, yes." He steps closer, pushing my hips into him with one hand on my back. He cups the back of my head with his other hand. "And when it matters," he says as his breath skates across my lips, "no."

And then his mouth is on mine, firm and demanding and arrogant, because he already knew I wanted it. He ropes a fist around my hair and pulls my head back to get a better angle of my neck. He takes it, and when I feel the edge of his teeth scrape against the underside of my jaw, I know that we may end up doing this right in front of Ned's house.

"Inside," I whisper, pushing against his chest. I charge up the steps while fumbling for my keys in my purse. Not because of the whiskeys I pounded back—I sweated those out on the dance floor—but because I'm suddenly very nervous about being with Sebastian. About *pleasing* Sebastian.

I finally find my keys. I pull them out, then drop them—twice—each time earning a loud clank and a groan from behind me as I bend over to retrieve them, my extremely short dress not made for modesty at that angle. This is the longest, most graceless trip up a set of stairs in my life. If I wasn't so anxious to get inside, I'd be mortified. Finally, I get a good grasp of the ring, climbing the last few steps.

It turns out I don't need my keys.

"What the . . ." I come to a dead stop in front of the iron gate with the visibly mangled lock. The door sits open a crack.

Sebastian grabs my arms and shifts me back behind him before slipping through, the tension suddenly radiating off him palpable. When we find that the front door sits ajar as well, he smoothly reaches back and hands me his keys. "Take my car and drive down the street. Lock the doors," he whispers calmly, without looking behind him. Then he disappears through the front door.

Leaving me standing there, debating whether I should actually listen to him or not.

# TWENTY

# SEBASTIAN

This is not a coincidence.

Ivy's home has been trashed, the flat-screen smashed instead of taken, the heating vents ripped from the walls, drawers pulled out and overturned, the couch torn apart and emptied.

Someone was searching for something.

I slide my piece out of my boot and flick off the safety. Standing in the living room, I simply breathe and listen. For creaks, for windows sliding, for anything that might indicate the person is still here.

Or people. Because what I see here suggests more than one person.

Whoever it was, we missed them by only minutes. I can still smell their sweat in the air. I'm now sure that the guy at the club tailed her all the way there from here and was tasked with being on lookout while whoever he is working with ransacked her place.

Was this on Bentley's orders?

My adrenaline courses through my veins as I slink from room to room, expecting that someone might be waiting in a closet or behind a curtain.

They've been through the entire house.

I check my watch. It's only twelve thirty. Ivy would have left to meet me just before eleven. That gave them less than two hours to do this much damage.

Sirens sound in the distance. They could be for anyone, but I know they're not.

Ivy must have called the cops. *Fuck*.

This entire house will be canvassed for prints. I quickly dart into Ivy's room, intent on wiping down the perfume bottle—the one thing I touched without a glove in this house—only to find the glass smashed, the alluring scent now too potent as it seeps into the carpet.

Careful not to touch the walls, I run down the stairs, bending over to slide my Beretta back into my boot when I reach the bottom.

When I stand, I find Ivy in the living room, aluminum baseball bat gripped in her small, talented hands, ready to take a swing. Watching me.

"The house is empty, but they were upstairs."

She twists her mouth, glancing down at my boot—wondering, I'm sure, why I'm carrying a gun when I'm "off duty"—but she doesn't ask about that. "I called the cops."

"I can hear that. You also didn't take my car, like I asked you to." I should have known she wouldn't listen.

She relaxes her arms, tossing the bat to the floor. "I'll need their report to file any insurance claims," she says, ignoring my chastising. She gazes around the main floor, her attention not really grabbing onto anything for more than a second. "Why would someone do this? There's nothing of value to steal in here."

I know exactly why, but I can't tell her.

I shouldn't be here. I should leave right now.

I close the distance and rope an arm around her as the screams of sirens approach.

■ ■ ■

Ivy flips through her sketchbook, the sheets half torn from the spiral spine and dangling. "Seriously? Even my sketchbook?" She whips it across the dash of my car in a fit of rage, blinking repeatedly to stave off the tears that coat her eyes.

I pull up to the curb in front of a simple green California bungalow in the Haight, an artsy neighborhood that my mom used to like to drive through on hot summer days, to look at the brightly painted Victorian houses. My parents actually aren't far from this quiet side street, no more than a ten-minute drive.

Reaching over, I silently retrieve the book from my dashboard and shift the pages as best I can to fit within the cardboard cover. A man's profile fills the page in front of me.

"The police sketch artist did a shitty job. I've been trying to get it right," she mumbles. "Haven't, yet."

*Probably a good thing.* I don't want to give Bentley's guys any more reason to consider her a risk.

I say nothing, continuing to tidy the pages. The last one before a stack of blanks is a sketch of me. A highly accurate depiction, which I can't say I'd want ever handed to law enforcement.

When she sees me studying it, she reaches over and yanks the book out of my hand. "I like to draw people I meet," she explains simply, holding her ruined sketches close to her chest, her arms roped around the book. If she's blushing, it's too dark to tell.

But I know she's shaken up by the entire experience tonight, whether she'll admit it or not.

The cops let her collect a few overnight things before sending us out so they can finish their evidence collection. I lean over to grab the handles of her duffel bag in my backseat, taking in the scent of her as I get close. She doesn't make a move, and I'm not about to try anything on her now. "Whose place did you say this is?" I ask.

She glances toward the house, where a porch light is now on. "My friend Dakota, from Oregon."

"Okay, well, you'll be safe here. I'm sure of it." I know because I watched my mirrors for a tail the entire drive over.

Silence hangs inside my car for a few long breaths. "How's your side?"

"Don't even feel it," I lie. It's not too bad, but it's definitely noticeable.

"You'll need to take the wrap off soon." She pauses. "If you come inside, I could do that for you."

I glance at the shadow watching from the window. "You've already woken your friend up in the middle of the night. You don't think she'll mind you bringing a stranger in with you?"

"Dakota?" She snorts. "She'll love it. She invites strangers over all the time."

"That doesn't sound safe," I joke. It'd be so easy to say yes, but I have things I need to deal with. "I'll be fine. But thanks."

She chews the inside of her mouth, but she doesn't say anything. She's probably wondering why I didn't offer to bring her back to my place for the rest of the night. I considered it, because I'd rather not let her out of my sight after what happened, but I don't think even someone as open-minded as Ivy can look past the motel with hourly rates and hookers hanging off the streets outside. "Thanks for sticking around and helping me deal with the cops," she finally says. "And driving me here."

As far as the police know, Gregory White accompanied Ivy home from the club. Luckily she wasn't around when I was giving them that information. They'll run it through, I'm sure, and they'll find the dummy profile that Bentley had set up—a thirty-one-year-old truck driver—as a precaution. And hopefully, that's where that'll end.

"When you want to go and get your car, give me a call and I'll take you."

She slips her duffel bag out of my grasp. "That's not necessary." The cool, I-don't-need-help-from-anyone Ivy is slipping back.

"Yeah, it is. You heard the cops. These people ransacked your place. Given your uncle was killed two weeks ago, it's suspicious. I don't want you going to that shop again without me, either."

Rare amusement dancing in her eyes. "Is this you going all badass bodyguard on me?"

I smirk. "Something like that."

"Well, don't think I'm gonna pay you. I have no money for protection."

"I seem to remember handing you fourteen hundred bucks today."

"I don't know what you're talking about." She gives me a sly smile, but then all amusement fades from her face. "Do you always carry a gun, even when you're not working?"

I figured that would come up, eventually. "Yeah." I hesitate but ask, "Does it bother you?"

She shakes her head and then dismisses the topic entirely. "Well, I'm going to the shop at nine in the morning to let the painters in. That's"—she glances at the clock—"only five hours away." She looks from the house back to me. I can't tell if she's just pointing out the obvious or fishing for me to stay. I don't even think it's about getting laid anymore. By the way she seemed to gravitate to my side for the past few hours, dealing with the cops, I think she just feels safer having me around. And that is why I'd love to say yes to her right now.

Pulling out my burner phone—idiot move but it's the only phone I have on me—I demand, "Give me your number."

She recites her number and then pushes open the door and climbs out.

I briefly consider grabbing her arm, pulling her back in to taste the last of the whiskey and Coke in her mouth, but I resist because I know where that'll lead and I do need to go. "Get some sleep. I'll come back in the morning," I call out, watching her saunter up to the house with her duffel bag slung over her shoulder. The door opens and a pretty woman with long dark hair and tan skin appears in nothing but a nightshirt. She's smiling wide, like she's not at all bothered by the late arrival.

I wait until the door is closed, send her a quick generic "sleep well" text so she has my number, and then pull away.

■   ■   ■

Bentley answers the phone with a gruff, "Yeah?"

"You sent those fuckers into her house!"

There's a pause and then I hear rustling on the other end, followed by a muffled, "It's not even five in the morning, John. Who's calling?"

"It's okay. It's work."

"What phone is that? That's not your iPhone, is it?"

"Go back to sleep, Tuuli." He heaves a sigh. Footfalls sound, and I can picture him trudging down the long hall to his office. Not until a door shuts does he speak again. "I warned you, didn't I?"

"You said tomorrow, and you didn't say anything about going into her house."

"I changed my mind and had them go in to do a final sweep tonight. Figured we had to be sure."

"That wasn't a sweep, John. They ransacked it."

"So the police will file a report and she'll claim insurance. Not a big deal."

I grit my teeth against the urge to yell. "You also said they'd stay away from me. One of those assholes was ten feet away from me tonight. He followed her to the club."

"Did he approach you?"

"No, but—"

"Then he followed orders and there's nothing to discuss here, so stand down!" Bentley doesn't like being questioned, and he's not used to it coming from me.

"Don't you think turning over a recently murdered man's house will raise suspicions?"

"Maybe, but no one will have anything to go on and it'll die down soon enough. It's worth it, if it means finding that tape."

"And did they?" I already know the answer, because I *already searched the fucking house!*

A long pause. "No."

"Keep them away from me. *And* her. If she has the tape, she doesn't know."

"How do you—"

"Because I'm good at what I do. I can read people, and I know that she had no fucking clue why anyone would want to bust into her place tonight. If she were hiding a tape that got her uncle killed, she'd be freaking out and running. And now the cops have turned their attention to her, and they're already starting to ask questions that tie back to her uncle."

A quiet "shit" slips out of Bentley's mouth.

Seriously, what did he think was going to happen when he told those guys to tail us? They'd already acted beyond the scope of his orders before. *Stupid amateur move, Bentley.*

"Just . . ." He sighs. "Keep an eye on her. You're right. We don't want her turning up dead right now."

"Or ever."

"Right."

"And your guys?"

"They'll stay away from you." He's awful quick to say that.

"If I see them again—"

"Just find that fucking video and everyone will be happy and safe," Bentley snaps.

The phone line goes dead. I toss it aside and stretch out on my bed. The center caves under my weight, but I barely give it any thought, my mind reeling over tonight's developments, which veered in a much less enjoyable direction than they were supposed to.

As long as that videotape is out there, Ivy's not safe, that much is clear. Tonight, Bentley's other guys trashed her house for no good reason. I already searched that place top to bottom and told Bentley as much. He must be under a lot of stress here, to undermine me like that, to not trust me after bringing me here explicitly because I'm the only one he trusts. He's not thinking rationally. Which means that tomorrow . . . who's to stop him from telling these guys to go straight to Ivy?

They're not getting their hands on her. I won't allow that.

I need to find this goddamn tape.

■   ■   ■

The willow tree that my mom planted when I was fourteen is gone, replaced by a generic young maple. I wonder if the willow died. There's no way my mom decided to cut it down—she loved it and all its messy tendrils.

Everything else about the house is exactly the same, except the new windows. The stucco is the same pale yellow, the front door the same stark white that my dad paints every spring to erase the scuffs. The property is still manicured to perfection.

I haven't laid eyes on my family's home in five years, and now I sit parked across the street, with a coffee in hand, a necessity after only two hours of sleep. Something compelled me to take the long way around and see my parents' home this morning. Maybe to see them.

It's seven twenty-five and the daily newspaper still rests on the stoop. I expect the door to open any moment, and for Captain George Riker to step out and collect his morning reading. He'll sit at the kitchen table with a glass of orange juice and read it from cover to cover, even if it takes him all morning.

Unless, maybe, he's changed. Maybe enough years have passed after retiring from a thirty-year career in the navy that he's learned to relax a bit. Maybe he doesn't polish his shoes every day and make my mom iron his golf shirts. Maybe he doesn't still get together with his guys on Tuesday nights for poker.

Maybe he wouldn't look at his son through the eyes of a disappointed father.

At exactly eight a.m., the door creaks open and my father steps out in his pressed golf shirt and pressed khaki shorts, his hair still cropped short but nearly all white now. He was thirty-five and halfway done with his career before he met my mother. I inhale sharply, both wistfulness and resigned sadness swelling inside my chest at the sight of him. I used to idolize him, standing tall and proud in his uniform.

He takes a leisurely glance around the neighborhood, waves at Mr. Shaw two doors over, who's watering his flowers, and then stoops to collect the paper on the welcome mat and disappears inside.

No . . . He's still the same hard-nosed man.

Before I can think too much about it, I crank the engine and pull away, determined to find that damning video evidence today.

# TWENTY-ONE

# IVY

I snort into my coffee mug, my eyes still glued to the single text Sebastian sent me last night. I responded, "You too," but he never answered. "Are you kidding? He's not coming back."

"Of course he is," Dakota says in that mellow, singsong voice of hers. She's the same from the moment she wakes up until the moment she goes to bed. If I didn't like her so much, I'd find it highly irritating. "Here. Have a breakfast bar. I just baked them." She holds a plate of squares out in front of me.

I eye them warily from my wicker chair. Pistachios, sunflower seeds, raisins . . . they *look* safe.

"Oh, relax." She rolls her eyes. "I made them for the people at the shelter."

I smirk, helping myself to one. Dakota's unconventional, but even *she* wouldn't drug homeless people with hash.

My gaze shifts around her rustic greenhouse, an attachment that runs along the back of the home she rents. It's a simple frame of wooden timbers and hard plastic above and glass windows that make the sides and back. Beneath my feet are flagstones. And all around are plants. Vibrant purple orchids and blooming cacti, lemon trees with fat, yellow fruits hanging from them, even though I don't think lemons are in season right now. Dozens of colorful planters rest on the floor and on tiered shelves. Giant trees form a canopy in the corners, vines climbing up the walls. It's a secluded jungle in the heart of San Francisco, decorated with Christmas lights and countless chimes dangling from the beams of the ceiling.

And off to the side, hidden by innocent, floppy tropical green leaves, is her little marijuana grow-op.

"It's really nice in here. Peaceful," I offer.

"Isn't it?" She beams, her almond-shaped eyes rolling over the space in wonder as she tightens her afghan to her shoulders and curls up in the wicker chair opposite me with her own coffee. Dakota has always been a natural beauty—she has Native American roots, with thick black hair that she keeps long, dark olive skin, and slender but supple curves to prove it. She wears very little makeup, if any, and in all the years I've known her I don't think I've seen a single pimple mar her complexion. "So, what do you have planned for today?"

"Well . . ." I sigh. "I have to let the painters into the shop and call the insurance company about the house."

"After all that you've been through, now this." She offers me a sympathetic smile. "Is it beginning to sink in yet?"

I nod, avoiding an answer with another sip of coffee.

Helping herself to a square, she offers, "You can stay for as long as you need to. You know I don't mind. And I'd rather you did. That area your house is in isn't the safest. *Clearly*. I don't like that you're alone over there."

I wasn't alone. Not last night. Had those jerks not ransacked my house, I would probably be tangled up in the sheets with Sebastian right now. "Thanks. I may take you up on that." That house isn't fit for living in at the moment, anyway, even if I did want to stay there. "I'm going to get my things, and my car." I glance at my phone. It's eight fifteen. Sebastian will be here soon. *If* he's coming.

He's not coming.

"So, how did you meet this guy, anyway?"

Leave it to Dakota to change topics from grieving my murdered uncle to the guy I picked up with one sentence. "Someone referred him. He showed up three days ago, wanting a piece done on his rib cage." I chuckle, remembering the afternoon, how angry

I was. "I turned him down at first, but then he helped me with a rusted bolt, and I felt guilty."

"Hmm . . . So you gave him what he wanted?" There's the mischievous twinkle in her eye that I saw that first day I met her back in Sisters. I was a high school sophomore and she was a junior, and both of us were skipping class to enjoy a sunny fall day on the grassy hill behind the school with our sketchbooks.

I smirk. "I did his ink for him, yeah. It took seven hours."

She casually asks through a sip of coffee, "His design or yours?" The look on my face makes her laugh. "Have you ever actually finished someone else's design without modifying it?"

I shrug. "It's called creative license. Anyone going under my needle is warned. Even that hummingbird you sketched for Alex has a few Ivy-inspired adjustments."

A normal person might get annoyed hearing that. Not Dakota. She sighs. "I miss Alex. She's such a kind, strong soul."

"I know. So do I." Dakota is actually the reason I met our friend Alex. She sent her to the Bend shop that I was working in at the time, sketch in hand, bright ocher eyes filled with nervousness and excitement. She's also now practically married to the only boy I've ever loved, Amber's brother.

But I'll never admit that to any of them.

The shrill of my phone's ring disturbs our morning peace. Normally I wouldn't even bother looking at it, but the ringtone tells me that Ian got my text about the house.

"Sorry. Gotta get this." I answer with, "Good times, yo." I sound like Fez.

"Jesus, Ivy."

I love the way he says "Jesus," in his weird Irish-American blended accent. "I know, right? Fucking crazy."

"Are you okay?"

"Yeah, I'm fine. Luckily I wasn't alone when I got home."

There's a moment of pause; I can almost hear Ian rolling his eyes. He's the kind of guy who dates girls before sleeping with them, and he doesn't date girls unless he can carry on an in-depth conversation about politics with them, using words like "banal" and "hegemony."

So he doesn't date a lot.

"How bad is it?"

"It's totally wrecked. It's gonna cost thousands to fix."

He heaves a sigh. "I'm going to start looking for a flight back."

*Yes! Come back and help me deal with this!* I scream inside my head. "No, I'll handle it. You have school and shit." Commitments that I don't have. "I'll give the insurance company a call as soon as I get to the house this morning."

Ian heaves a second sigh. "That's part of the problem . . ."

I can already tell by his tone that I'm not going to like this.

"I was going through some of Ned's unopened mail. His homeowner's insurance lapsed two months ago. I called them to see about getting it renewed, and they said it's not that simple, seeing as he's deceased. I'm sorry that I forgot to mention it to you earlier."

My stomach pinches with anxiety. "What does that mean?"

"That we don't have insurance to cover the damages."

"Oh my God." I stare blankly at Dakota as she watches. "We're fucked!"

"No, we're not. It just means that we'll take a hit on the sale price."

"A huge, enormous hit, Ian. You don't realize how bad it is." I blow a strand of hair out of my eyes. "I guess I better go get my broom and start cleaning."

"Okay. I'm coming back."

"No. Don't. There's nowhere for you to stay anyway."

"He can stay here," Dakota mouths.

"No he can't," I mouth back. He can't throw away his PhD for this.

"Send me some pictures, will ya?"

"Sure," I lie. Maybe I shouldn't have told him in the first place.

"And call that detective we talked to. Make sure he knows about this. I don't trust those police departments to talk to each other."

"Do you really think there's a connection?"

"Honestly, with Ned . . . yeah. Listen, I gotta run to my next class. Let me know if you need something, Ivy. Please."

I hang up with my cousin and toss the phone to the table, troubled by what this "connection" may be.

"So, you did his seven-hour tattoo, and then . . ." Dakota prods, pulling us back to the topic of Sebastian.

I sigh. Sebastian *is* a more pleasant topic, and I can't tackle the insurance problem right now. "And then he asked me out for a drink. I told him to meet me in the VIP lounge of Daredevils. I went home to shower and change." That was at around ten thirty. Were they already in the house when I was there? Hiding in the closet, watching me change? No, they broke down the door, so they couldn't have been. Still, just the thought sends chills down my spine and I hug my blanket tighter to me. "We were at the club for a little over an hour and then he drove me home. I didn't know that someone had broken in until we were at my front door. He ran in to check things out and I called the cops."

Sebastian ran to check things out with a gun in his hand. A gun that he had tucked in his boot at the bar, and possibly all day while I worked on him. It startled me to see him with it. But I really don't know anything about him, other than that he was a soldier and now he's a bodyguard.

"Thank God he was there with you." That's what I love most about Dakota. It's pretty obvious to anyone who knows me—and people who don't—why I was bringing Sebastian, a guy I'd just met, home with me. But there isn't a judgmental bone in Dakota's body. It could be her spiritual inclinations, or her relaxed nature, but she has always been like that. And she's always lived life with the expectation that no one should judge her, either. People do, because people are critical assholes, by and large—but the thing is, she doesn't care, and she's enjoyed life more because of it.

"Yeah. He was there with me last night. I'm not dumb enough to be counting on him to be there today, though," I mutter.

My words end with a doorbell and Dakota's know-it-all smile.

"Shit. He's early." I look down at myself, still in my boxers and tank top, my teeth not even brushed. "I need ten minutes. Can you stall him?"

She nods eagerly.

Okay, maybe unleashing Dakota on Sebastian at eight fifteen isn't the best idea. He may still run. "But don't start talking about all that weird aura stuff. You'll freak him out. He's . . . different. Very reserved." I dart past her and toward the spare room that I slept in last night, slamming the door shut behind me. I don't have a lot of choice in clothes—I can't wear the corset dress I had on last night. All I managed to grab in the chaos were leggings and . . . I rifle through my bag and realize that I didn't grab a shirt. I don't have a shirt to wear.

I heave an annoyed sigh at myself. I'll have to borrow something of Dakota's.

She's at least six inches taller than me, so this should be interesting.

I pass through the joint bathroom that connects the two bedrooms and walk directly into her closet. She wears a lot of maxi dresses that would drag around my feet, and likely not stay up to begin with, so my options are limited. Very limited. I manage to root out a rose-pink shirt—just about the last color I'd ever choose to wear in my life. It fits well enough, though its cropped length leaves nothing to the imagination thanks to my leggings.

Maybe Sebastian's imagination needs help anyway.

I shift into the bathroom to do a quick makeover. Dakota's bathroom is old and cramped, with original tile and poor lighting. I'd never rent this place but I know why she does. It's charming and quirky, just like her.

And I've left her out there with Sebastian.

I throw on daytime makeup and run a brush through my hair. The sides are beginning to grow in. I haven't decided if I want to shave them again or grow my hair out. Or just lop all my hair off. For now, I leave it down and brush the morning nastiness from my mouth.

When I reemerge, I can hear Dakota's voice carrying from the greenhouse. I round the bend to find her holding up Sebastian's T-shirt—charcoal gray, today—as she examines his work. ". . . Yes, the crows circling around her head, that very much signifies the sudden loss of her uncle, and the guilt that haunts her."

I don't know where she comes up with this shit. She didn't even smoke a joint this morning.

"Hey!" I exclaim too loudly. Sebastian peers over his shoulder, his arm raised in the air to accommodate Dakota's intrusion. He has a strange look on his face—part amusement, part annoyance, part unreadable. When his gaze drifts over my outfit, his expression warms a little.

And it warms my body along with it. It's impossible for me not to react to this man's attention. We were *so close* to ending up in my bed last night. As if falling asleep hasn't been impossible already, add a break-in and complete trashing of the house, and I'm not entirely certain that I was ever fully unconscious last night.

Leaving me plenty of time to think about Sebastian.

He looks like he got about as much sleep as I did, his eyes tarnished with heavy circles. That he still showed up here to help me speaks volumes. It must be in his protective nature. Or he's still hoping to get laid.

Maybe I'm too cynical.

Regardless, I wonder how long I have him for today, before he leaves.

I direct my focus to Dakota, though I can still feel Sebastian's eyes on me. "I borrowed your shirt, just until I can get my clothes out of Ned's. Hope that's okay."

Dakota merely winks, and I know it has nothing to do with borrowing her clothes.

"This is really nice work, Ivy. You should be so proud of yourself."

As awkward as this is, I should probably check on Sebastian's tattoo. "Did you follow my instructions?" I ask, moving in closer to inspect the swollen lines and pink skin around it. As expected only twelve hours later. But I can tell that he's already washed off the ointment and coated it with fresh moisturizer.

"It took a while," he says, lowering his arm. "We should probably get going so we get to your shop for nine, right?"

Dakota and I now seem to be ogling him without shame. I clear my throat. "Yeah. I don't want the painters taking off."

Dakota, who still has his shirt hiked up and bunched in her fist, lets it fall. She pats him on the shoulder. "Grab the spare key hanging by the door on your way out."

I assume that instruction was for me, but who knows with her? "Will you be here later?"

"I'm heading into work soon, but I'll be back before dinner." Dakota opened a little store five minutes away, basically replicating the same one that her aunt owned in Sisters, which sold an eclectic collection of art and jewelry made of recycled and natural materials. As far as I can tell, it's doing quite well, but that would make sense given this is California, and everyone's about the environment and art.

"Oh, don't let me forget, I want you to look at a design I did. I'm thinking of having you do one here." She trails her fingertip down the top of her right shoulder.

I've done all of Dakota's work, save for her first. "All right. I'll make sure to bring my kit with me when I come back tonight." To Sebastian, I ask, "Ready?"

He nods, taking quick steps to get in front of me and out the door, as if he's eager to get away from Dakota as fast as possible.

"I thought you said you knew how to tell time?"

"I said I'm never late."

"Thirty minutes early is almost as bad as being late."

"That shirt looks nice on you," he responds, ignoring my selfish complaint completely.

"Then enjoy it, because it'll be the last time you see me in anything that resembles bubble gum," I grumble, opening his passenger-side door. "Can you drop me off at my house after so I can get out of it?"

"Yeah. But I'll be coming with you. You're not going in there alone."

"Is that so?" I roll my eyes, but I can't ignore the small thrill that zips through my body. God, I think I'm attracted to this dominating side of him, and I *hate* it when guys try to tell me what to do. But when Sebastian does it, I don't mind. It makes me feel safe. Maybe that's because, for the first time in my life, I truly am not safe. "Do you think the burglary might not have been random?"

With his hand on the ignition, he pauses. "Can you think of any reason why someone might want to break into your dead uncle's house?"

"No." Same answer I gave to the cops last night. "But there *must* be a reason."

"Did he say anything to you recently, about coming into money or needing money?"

"You think this was about money?"

"Everything's about money," he says under his breath.

I sigh. "Ned liked to gamble but . . ." I tell Sebastian about the hundred thousand against the building and his empty accounts. "Do you think that's what it's about?"

"Could be. Or something he knew about that he shouldn't. Did he say anything about any of his clients lately? Maybe someone told him something that they shouldn't have?"

I frown. "No. Nothing he mentioned to me, at least. I told you, he wasn't exactly the warmest guy. I have a hard time imagining someone spilling their deep, dark secrets to him."

After a long pause, Sebastian offers, "Well, then it could be nothing." His face is unreadable. "People in the neighborhood would have heard about your uncle's death, and unfortunately that means that thieves would assume the house is an easy target."

I study his face. "But you don't actually believe that, do you?"

"Why wouldn't I?"

"Because they tore the place to shreds and smashed the flatscreen—the only thing worth stealing in there."

He sighs, his gaze drifting out the window. "Could have been jacked up on drugs. Could have been pissed off that there was nothing there to take. Whatever the reason, you're not stepping foot in that house without me again for now. Understood?"

"*For now?* What does that mean?"

He slides the key into the ignition and cranks the engine, but doesn't answer.

I guess the bodyguard who showed his protective head last night is here to stay. "I don't need a bodyguard."

"No one said you did."

"I'm serious. I'm not paying you to do this. I can't afford it."

He snorts. "I never asked you to."

*Then why are you still here?* "Don't you have things you need to do? People to see?" Maybe that's the issue. Maybe he has nobody else to fill his time with. Maybe he's a complete loner, married to his job, with no friends or family. I really don't know him at all.

He turns to level me with a look. "Do you *want* me to have something else to do today?"

I hesitate, before admitting casually, "Well, not *necessarily*, but—"

"Then shut up and stop trying to get rid of me." He pulls out of Dakota's driveway.

I press my lips together to keep from smiling.

. . .

"I would reco white. A nice, crisp one, like . . ." Fausto, a thirty-something-year-old guy with slicked black hair hiding beneath a baseball cap and a heavy New York accent, pulls out a deck of paint colors, fanning them out on the dirty floor in front of me. ". . . Ghost or Ice."

"White for Black Rabbit?" I don't bother to hide the skepticism in my voice. I spin slowly around, taking in the main room. Without all the clutter to hide the dinginess, this place looks atrocious at best. As a customer, I'd take one look in here and turn around, with thoughts of hep C screaming inside my head. Fair enough.

But *white?*

"As a starting off point, yeah. You can weave in some bold colors—a nice jammy red over on that wall there, an indigo or peacock blue over here. Maybe hammered-bronze ceiling tiles. Tons of possibilities. I'll help you make your shop stand out."

"We're selling this place," I'm quick to say.

He shrugs. "All right. Fine. Then leave it as a blank canvas for whoever comes in, because everyone has their own spin. Just get rid of this black. The grunge look is dead. People want a nice, clean environment."

I chew my lip in thought. I'm always so sure of colors and design when it comes to my sketchbook and a skin canvas, but for some reason I can't see past Ned's version of his shop. He'd be rolling in his grave over this.

"But, hey, if you don't want to listen to someone who actually knows what he's talking about, then, sure, we can go with your plan and you guys can lose a boatload of money," Fausto adds.

He's a cocky bastard.

He sounds just like me, when I'm convincing someone that my design is better than whatever they have in mind.

I turn to Sebastian, who stands with his arms folded over his chest. The other painter already stripped the window of its shade in order to prepare all the work surfaces—filling holes, patching cracks—so the front of the store is wide open and bare. He looks every bit the guard that he said I didn't need, surveying the street. I'm starting to think he was lying to me.

"What do you think, Sebastian?"

He turns at his name, his eyebrow pops up from behind dark sunglasses. He has no idea what I'm talking about. He's barely paid two seconds of attention to me since we stepped in here. The flirtatious guy from last night, who had his hands on me at every chance, has disappeared, replaced with this cool, detached replica of the first day we met.

"I was going to have him paint everything black again but he said—"

"Go with Ice." He turns back to watch the street again.

I smirk. He's probably *always* listening, and watching, even when I don't know it.

I heave a sigh. "All right, Fausto. I'm going to trust you on this." What do I care? Ned is dead and repainting it black isn't going to bring him back. Stripping it of all character and personality might give some closure.

Fausto claps his hands together. "*Buono!* I'll get this mixed. Jimmy will stay and prep."

I dangle the spare key on a finger and then toss it to his waiting hands. "How long do you think this will take?"

"Depending on how many coats it takes to cover the black . . ." His face twists into an exaggerated frown with his thought, reminding me of Ned. "With two more of my guys to help, give us three days and we should be done."

"All right. You have my number if anything comes up." I glance at Sebastian. "Ready to go, driver?"

He nods, not acknowledging my dig with so much as an eyebrow spike, now focused on Fausto. "If anyone shows up here and starts asking questions or is poking around, I want you to take down a physical description and call Ivy immediately."

Fausto snorts. "What the hell do I look like? I'm the painter, not your fucking secretary."

Sebastian slides his glasses off and takes several steps forward, peering down at the short Italian man. There's a shift in the air. I can feel his dominance radiating; he somehow seems taller, stronger, his presence more ominous. I think I'm going to have to dive in between them. Sebastian can't go breaking my painter's arms. "This is important. I would appreciate the help." His tone is always on the clipped side. Now, though, it's laced with a threat.

"Yeah. Okay. Either me or Jimmy will relay to Ivy if something comes up," Fausto mumbles, adjusting his baseball cap several times as he takes a step back.

I slip a hand around Sebastian's arm and tug his arm. "*Ready?*"

He slides his glasses back over his eyes. With a hand on the small of my back, he leads me out without another word to the guys.

"What was that?"

"That was your painter being smart." He opens the passenger-side door for me, his eyes veering to the left and right. Everywhere but to me.

I sigh and climb in.

■ ■ ■

The broom handle clatters loudly against the tile floor and I gasp at the sudden noise.

Sebastian simply props it up in the corner again without a word. I've been jumpy since the moment we climbed the steps out front, and I've done a terrible job of hiding it.

I *hate* that the assholes who did this have made me nervous to simply be in this house.

Shaking it off, I right the wooden end table in the living room and focus on the silver lining. "At least this makes cleaning the house out and getting it ready to sell easier for me." Pretty much everything—right down to the Raisin Bran and mac & cheese from the kitchen pantry—is now trash. I need to rent a Dumpster.

"What did the insurance company say?" Sebastian asks, leaning the smashed flat-screen TV against the wall, giving me a good view of his muscular backside.

"It said, 'We're sorry that your uncle didn't pay his premiums in time and have fun with this giant mess, suckers.'" After a moment, I look up to see Sebastian simply standing there, staring at me.

"What?" I snap, though I don't mean to.

He gives his head a quick shake and then calmly says, "You'll need new locks on these doors right away."

"Yeah, I'm aware of that." I sigh, tossing the broken lamp onto the torn-apart couch. "I guess I'm going to hire a locksmith."

"I can put new locks on for you."

"You're a bodyguard *and* a locksmith?"

He smirks, like there's some sort of inside joke. "No, but I know a lot about locks."

I'm not going to ask. Maybe it's something he picked up in the navy. Besides, refusing his help hasn't even crossed my mind today. Since stepping into this house in broad daylight, I've been nothing but quietly relieved that Sebastian didn't drop me off and leave, that he feels the need to stay with me, for whatever reason.

A loud, abrupt holler of "Hello?" from the doorway makes me jump again.

I curse and spin on my heels to see Detective Fields stepping over the threshold, sliding his sunglasses off his clean-shaven face to hook the arm in the front of his olive-green dress shirt, his gaze taking in the destruction.

"I take it you got my message." I left it this morning, on our way to meet the painters, just like Ian told me to. But honestly I assumed I wouldn't be hearing from him again.

"I did." He has an even, calm don't-mess-with-me way about him. Almost bored. I can't tell if he even likes his job. I haven't seen him smile much. Then again, most people say I don't smile much either, and I love my job.

"And?"

A piece of broken glass crunches under his shoe as he comes to stop a few feet from me, glancing at Sebastian, who keeps working away. "And I agree that it is *too* coincidental."

"Have you talked to the cops who were here last night?"

He nods slowly. He's an attractive enough guy, though ordinary looking. He's in his late thirties, with sandy brown hair, cut with four-inch clippers all the way around. Someone you'd expect to see in a picture with two kids, a wife, and a sweater-wearing dog. "I saw a copy of the preliminary report. They have no prints and no witnesses to work from yet, unfortunately."

"Great, so basically a dead end." Just like Ned's murder. Surprise, surprise. I'm beginning to feel firsthand how easy it is to get away with crime in this city.

"Not yet. They're thinking the culprits are probably either a bunch of vandals who like to destroy homes, or someone Ned owed money to, coming to search."

*Money.* Sebastian asked about Ned owing money.

Fields stretches on his tiptoes to study the hole in the wall where the vent cover was ripped off.

"I guess that would explain that, then."

"Did your uncle ever mention anything about owing money to Devil's Iron?" Fields asks, turning his attention back to me, in time to catch my frown.

"No. Why?" They're *still* after the biker gang for this?

"I have a source that says Ned was into it large with them."

"But . . ." I frown. Bobby told me there was nothing there. Unless the sneaky fuck was lying to me.

Fields gestures at the vents and the holes in the wall. "This, to me, looks like someone on the hunt for hidden cash in hopes of settling up a debt that otherwise won't get paid."

Because corpses don't pay.

"I'll send some guys over to feel them out," he offers.

"Thanks," I mutter, my anger boiling. Those assholes were supposed to be Ned's friends. Would they do something like this?

Fields heads out with a single nod toward Sebastian, leaving me stewing in silence. What did they expect? That there'd be wads of cash hidden in the walls? Maybe there was. If that's the case, then I guess I'm safe from a repeat visit. But if not . . .

I just want to get this over with and go back to Dakota's.

"There's a Home Depot not far from here. If I give you cash, can you—"

"Nope. You're not staying here alone," Sebastian replies quickly. He was silent during the detective's visit—although I'm sure he was listening to every word.

I really don't want to either, but there's just so much to do . . . "It's fine. The lock on the handle still works. Besides, who's going to come back a second time? There's nothing left to steal or break."

Sebastian stands, pulling off his work gloves, and levels me with a look.

I rest my arms over my chest. "Are you always this bossy and paranoid? Or do you know something I don't know, because if you do, maybe you should tell me so we don't spend all afternoon arguing. Look at what I have to deal with." I stretch my arms out at the mess. "It makes way more sense for you to grab the locks and me to keep collecting this shit so we can be done with this mess and I can go have a nap because I'm *so* damn tired of this nightmare," I ramble on.

In three quick strides he's over the pile of stuffing torn from the couch and on me, his fingers weaving into the back of my hair as he pulls my mouth to his.

The kiss is hard and fast, lasting just long enough to remind me of last night on the front steps before everything fell apart. "Shut up and get your purse," he whispers. He turns and strolls out the front door.

And I follow, quietly, my senses suddenly wide awake.

# TWENTY-TWO

# SEBASTIAN

What the fuck is happening?

I go from hunting down a videotape with a highly sensitive, incriminating, and libelous confession to picking out paint colors and shopping for locks with the woman who used to be a potential target.

And I'm enjoying it.

Then again, I let that same potential target permanently mark my body with her hands. And I fully plan on being inside her the first chance I get.

So, this situation was already all kinds of fucked-up, even before today.

"Okay. What do you think about this?" Ivy holds up a dead bolt. "Schlage. That's a good brand, right?"

"Not as easy to pick as some of the others."

She shoots a sideways glance but doesn't ask any questions, tossing it into the shopping cart, already filled with trash bags and new lightbulbs, to replace the ones that were smashed. Bentley's guys had no reason to go as far as smashing lightbulbs. "Then I think we're good, unless you need any other tools?"

"Nope." Her uncle's toolbox was well stocked, though its contents were scattered all over the garage floor.

"Okay, then. Cash register it is," she says through a sigh. She seems to be taking this all in stride, though by her jumpiness and the look of dismay on her face when we saw the interior of the house in daylight earlier, she's far from fine.

Ivy pushes the shopping cart down the aisle, not checking to see if I'm following.

I smile at her back. She changed out of that soft pink shirt the second we stepped into the house, switching it for a blood-red loose-fitting one that falls off one shoulder and covers that fantastic ass, and has the word FIERCE scrawled across the back.

How appropriate.

It's that ferocity that keeps reeling me in tighter.

But I'm glad she's also not arguing with me every step of the way anymore. She knows, or at least suspects, that what happened at Ned's house is not complete coincidence, even though I tried to distract her with lame theories about neighborhood vandals that she saw right through. And *I* know that if her uncle ever made any comments about Dylan Royce to her, she hasn't made any connections to any of this.

I can't decide if having Ivy think that the burglary is tied to a biker gang and her uncle's debts is a good idea. It's definitely a convenient cover story for Bentley's purposes. The detective's visit today did help answer some questions for me, though. Mainly, why Ned Marshall would try to blackmail Alliance for money. If he owes a biker gang like Devil's Iron, that might be reason enough.

But I want to throttle Bentley right now, because he's fucked her over large. That house is a wreck. It's thousands—easily—in repairs. *I should not do this. I should not offer* . . . "I'll help you patch the walls and fix the other damage." *Why the hell did I just promise her that?* I'm gone as soon as this assignment's over. I have no reason to stay.

She spins on her heels as she keeps walking, facing me.

"Unless you're going to refuse and tell me that you know how to patch holes and plaster walls, and you don't need any help," I add with a small smile. That's what she probably would have done just days ago. That's basically what she *did do* just days ago.

"Oh, so you've figured me out so quickly, have you?" Her gaze trails over my body. "You're a handyman, too?"

"I know a bit about home construction." It's been years since I held a hammer for something that doesn't involve scaring criminals into giving me answers, but there was a time when my dad and I would work together on our little family cabin near Lake Tahoe. I wonder if they still have it.

"Do you wear one of these?" She reaches over and pulls a tool belt off the shelf, letting it dangle from her index finger with a secretive smirk on her lips.

"If you want me to."

Her eyebrows spike in amusement. I'd pay to read what I'm sure are dirty thoughts going through her mind. I'm glad she still has those, despite the mess she's dealing with right now.

She tosses the belt back onto the shelf and continues down the aisle without another word about my offer. "I'll be back in a minute," she calls over her shoulder, leaving the cart and heading down the hall that leads to the restrooms.

I follow and veer left, into the men's room. A piss is a fantastic idea. I've had too many coffees to count, trying to stay awake after another near-sleepless night.

It's empty inside—these places usually are. I know because I spend a lot of time in public restrooms and it's rarely to relieve myself. They're private locations, perfect aids for insidious acts, like the extremist who ducked into a café restroom in Paris to fix the trigger wire on his vest of C4, intent on blowing himself up during the Bastille Day parade. Bentley had sent me after him to learn about his associations, but when I realized what he was about to do, that assignment ended with a bullet in his head at an angle to make it look like suicide. I even left my gun.

Surprisingly, the media gobbled it up, pegging it as a suicide bomber with a guilty conscience, who couldn't go through with it at the eleventh hour.

It was the only time I've ever defied Bentley's orders, but he commended me for it. I saved so many lives that day, and no one will ever know except Bentley and me.

But today I'm just a normal guy, taking a leak in the Home Depot urinal.

The door creaks open behind me as I'm washing my hands. It's just instinct for me to check my peripherals at all times when someone is entering my circumference.

The guy from the club is standing three feet away from me.

"You're Bentley's guy." He's not asking. He's making a statement, a stupid one, because you never walk into a public place and name names.

"Don't know what you're talking about." I move to leave the restroom but he grabs my forearm and squeezes tight.

"Then who the fuck are you?" His Chicago accent is thick.

Someone faster and better trained than this ex-Marine.

It takes a split second for me to turn the tables, twisting out of his grip. He's quick, though, and he takes a swing, catching the edge of my lip with his knuckle. I taste copper almost immediately.

I deliver a return hit across the jaw.

So much for being just a normal guy.

This can't be happening in the men's room of Home Depot, though. Any second, someone could come in, see what's developing, and call the cops. That wouldn't be good for me. Dragging him to the large handicap stall at the end, I shut the door before delivering a hard blow to his nose, feeling the bones and cartilage smash beneath my knuckles. "I think the right question is, Who the fuck are *you* and why are you tailing me? You were told to stay away from me." And *how* did he tail me? I was watching, the entire drive from Ivy's house. At one point I thought we had someone on us, but whoever it was turned off and I dismissed it. These guys must be in more than one car. I'm an idiot.

"Fuck . . ." He grits through the pain, holding a hand up to his nose as blood pours from both his nostrils. A serious burn mark mars the skin on the back of his hand.

"Come on . . . We're on the same team."

"I work alone." I may have felt a connection to him, given our common background, our shared ties, but he's pulling this kind of shit here?

"You work for Bentley, don't you?" he asks this time.

"Shut the fuck up about him. Why did you break protocol to come in here?"

"You're kidding me, right?" I cringe at his smile, his teeth coated in blood now. "The video with that bastard Royce blabbing about what happened *cannot* get out. The stuff he would have said . . . you get it, don't you? Some of the things we have to do to get a job done? Would you want everyone finding out about that?"

I'm fighting against the compassion I feel for this guy. He and I *are* the same in that sense. I have enough skeletons in my closet to fill a cemetery. I sure as hell wouldn't want them aired to the world for all to know.

For Ivy to know.

Fuck . . . if Ivy knew what I've done, why I'm even here, she'd want nothing more to do with me.

Would she?

The fact that I even care is concerning.

But there's something about his words that is distracting me more . . . Bentley said that the video is full of bullshit, lies.

This guy's making it sound like there's truth there.

"Civilians don't understand. Ricky and I will be scapegoats." The guy leans over to spit on the ground, leaving a gob of blood and saliva next to my feet. "She's got it. She has to have it hidden somewhere."

"If she does, I'll find it and return it to Bentley. But you need to leave. She'd probably make you from your voice alone."

"That's why I'm here. I don't wanna leave any loose ends. You've obviously got an in with her. She trusts you. Maybe you and me could tag-team to get her to give up the tape and then I'll—"

One smooth shot against his jaw cuts his words off, and his eyes roll back in his head. Just the idea of him going anywhere near Ivy makes me want to snap his thick neck and solve *my* loose end. It's too risky, though. My face is all over the store's camera feed. I wasn't prepared for this today.

And where is this other guy—Ricky—in all this? Waiting outside or . . .

*Shit*. Panic sets in.

I fish the guy's wallet out of his pocket and then settle him on the toilet, slumped against the wall. Plucking his piece from his coat pocket, I tuck it into the back of my jeans and slide under the bottom of the locked stall. A glance in the mirror shows a small cut and a trail of blood down my jaw. I quickly wash that off, along with my bloody hands, and then charge out of the men's restroom.

And directly into the women's.

Ivy's in front of the mirror, brushing something onto her eyelashes. Perfectly safe.

Her eyebrows spike, but otherwise she shows no outward sign of surprise. Not like the lady who's standing beside her, mouth gaping like a fish.

I nod to Ivy. "We should go."

"You missed me that much?"

"Something like that."

She throws the tube into her purse and stalks toward me, pausing as her dark gaze touches my mouth. "What happened to your lip?"

"Walked into a wall."

Her eyes narrow, and I know she's thinking of calling me on that bullshit. But all she says is, "That takes talent."

I ignore her sarcastic tone and rope an arm around her back, guiding her out of the restroom and toward the cash registers at the front, my eyes scanning every face that we pass.

While she's checking out, I pull out the wallet I lifted, flipping it open to the picture ID.

*Mario Scalero.*

I warned Bentley to keep them away, but in a way I'm glad they didn't listen. At least now I know that Scalero is a threat to Ivy, and I don't think finding that video is going to change that. Another reason for me to stick close to her.

■ ■ ■

Ivy tosses a second duffel bag on the front porch, waving a hand dismissively. "I can't deal with this mess for another second today. Are you almost done?"

I shut the door and test the key. The bolt fastens smoothly.

"Well, look at you."

I hand her the key. She smiles sheepishly. "Thanks for the help."

"You're welcome."

"So . . ." She hesitates over her words. "Dakota's making dinner tonight. I'm heading over there now. If you're hungry and you have nothing else to do, you're welcome to come. As a thank-you." She shrugs dismissively. "But if not, that's cool, too. No big deal. Just thought I'd offer."

She's chewing on her lip. She wants me to come, but I think she's afraid I'm going to turn her down, and I don't think her ego can handle being turned down right now. Under that tough exterior, I'm beginning to see extreme sensitivity.

I scoop up her bags and march down the stairs without giving her an answer, scanning the street for any new cars that weren't there when we arrived. There's nothing, thankfully. Scalero and the other guy have backed off for the time being; Scalero's likely preoccupied with the hospital and canceling his credit card, which, in hindsight, I wish I had used to pay for the locks, seeing as he helped bust them. But at least I used one to fill up my gas tank and buy lunch.

"Thanks. I'd love to come."

She presses her lips together to keep me from seeing how much that pleases her. "Just to warn you, though, she's a little bit out there."

"I noticed." The woman is stunning in a very natural way, but she had no qualms about lifting my shirt to see Ivy's work thirty seconds after introducing herself to me. I tolerated it for Ivy's sake. "How much of that weed in her greenhouse does she smoke?"

"So you noticed that, too," she murmurs with a wry smile. "I think she's always been a bit 'spiritual.'" She uses her fingers to air-quote that word. "Even before she started smoking. Speaking of weed, how are you with seaweed?"

I chuckle. "I'm not sure how to answer that."

"She likes to experiment with strange ingredients. Last time I had dinner at her place, she made this seaweed salad. It wasn't bad but . . ." She winces, then does a sideways glance of my body. "I doubt it'll sustain you. Tell you what," she says as she throws her purse onto the passenger seat. "Follow me to Safeway and I'll grab some burgers and things, just in case." She presses the button on her key fob to pop her trunk, but then frowns and slams it shut. "Oh, that's right. There's no room with all my other stuff in there."

*Other stuff?* This is all I saw her bring from the house. "What stuff?"

"Just that shitty old computer from the shop." She opens the door to her backseat and backs up so I can toss her duffel bags in. "I packed it up last night after you left. That and my kit . . . I bring it home with me every night, anyway, but thank God I left it in the car, or those assholes would have torn it apart. Oh my God." She shakes her head. "I would have gone homicidal if they had fucked up my kit. That's the only thing I own that I actually *really* care about."

Her words drift as their meaning begins to sink in.

Her kit.

She brings her kit everywhere with her.

But . . . I frown. No. I saw the inside of it yesterday. There wasn't any videotape in there. I would have noticed that.

"Hey."

I look down to find her already sitting in the driver's seat, seat belt on, engine cranked, staring at me. "Are you going to follow me?"

# TWENTY-THREE

# IVY

This was a terrible idea.

The cramped quarters, the quinoa and seaweed wraps; Jono, the homeless man Dakota invited over for dinner tonight.

All of it.

"This was a great idea! I'm so glad you're all here with me tonight." Dakota reaches out to squeeze my biceps with her left hand and Jono's hand with her right, grinning at Sebastian, who sits across the small round salvaged teak table from her. Jono smiles in return, I think—it's hard to tell because his face is covered by a beard that rivals Grizzly Adams's. It's a clean face, at least. Actually, he's one of the cleanest homeless people I've ever come across. I wouldn't have guessed that he had nowhere to live had he not enthusiastically announced it. Apparently he bathed at the public beach showers and changed into new clothes, donated by a friend today, all for this dinner. And he made a point of telling us about that, too.

"Sebastian, please, help yourself to more if you're hungry. I'm sure your appetite is impressive." Dakota throws a wink my way and I roll my eyes in return. She's not the most subtle with her sexual innuendos.

He nods his thanks between mouthfuls of the hamburger I threw on the grill for us the second I saw what was on the menu tonight, seemingly protective of the left side of his mouth, where it's slightly swollen. The fact that he stormed into the women's restroom with a bloody lip, giving me that lame-ass excuse about running into a wall, has me a bit wary, but I figure it's something I either don't need to know about or don't want to know about.

I'll ask again later, maybe.

*If* I have a chance. He hasn't said much of anything since we stepped inside the house, and I'm wondering if he regrets accepting this invitation. I wish I could read minds right now. Or at least his steely expression.

Jono doesn't need encouragement, though, reaching over to take another helping.

"So, when did you two meet?" I ask casually.

"Just today," he says, not bothering to wait until he's done chewing to speak. "I was getting breakfast at the shelter when this vision strolled through with those squares." He smiles at her. It doesn't take a genius to see that he's already madly lusting over her, as most guys do.

"Really. Just *today*." I glare at her. This isn't the first time I've sat at a dinner table with Dakota and one of her "friends," people who, I swear, she seeks out based on their peculiarity. There was the séance lady, the worm collector, the puppeteer. And that's just in the last two months. But never has she brought home a complete stranger.

As soon as I have a chance, I'm going to take Dakota by the arms and shake some sense into her. How much can she possibly know about this guy in ten hours? He could be a serial killer, and she invited him into her house! Is she planning on sleeping with him, too? With Dakota, you never know. And I don't judge but . . . *what the fuck, Dakota?*

Suddenly I'm happy that Sebastian's here. With a gun.

Sebastian must be thinking the same things that I am. "Have you lived in San Francisco all your life, Jono?"

He nods. "Born and bred. In the Bay City area, anyway. My parents still live out in Diablo. I visit them sometimes."

"Diablo . . ." I frown, remembering it simply for its name

when Ned was talking about it once. "I thought that was a wealthy neighborhood."

"It is," Sebastian mumbles, just before downing a sip from his bottle of Bud.

Jono snorts. "No one there is going hungry, that's for sure."

I look to Sebastian, who's watching Jono with mild curiosity now. "So that means . . ."

Jono takes a huge bite of his burger and then says something that sounds like, "My parents are rich."

I don't like to pry, and normally I don't care enough to, but this is just too sad. And weird. "So your wealthy parents disowned you and you live on the streets."

"Disowned?" He scoffs, like the idea is preposterous. "No. I left of my own free will when I was twenty. I've been on the streets for almost a year now."

"But you have a *roof* to sleep under." A beautiful roof, I'm sure.

"If I wanted to continue mankind's dependence on artificial happiness."

"Jono made the decision to turn away from the materialism and capitalism that feed today's greedy civilization and live a simpler life," Dakota explains, not a hint of irony or criticism in her tone. Jono, who is only twenty-one and therefore five years younger than her. "Isn't that fascinating?"

"So you're not *actually* homeless."

"Oh, I am," Jono says, his brow furrowing in earnest.

"No, you're a California bum. There's a difference." There's plenty of them, more the closer to San Diego that you go, where it's even warmer. They couch-surf at people's houses, surf and party all day, and feed themselves with food stamps. I can't say how often Ned bitched about those leeches. At least every time one of them wandered into the shop in flip-flops and his board tucked under his arm, definitely.

Sebastian clears his throat, hiding a small smile behind his burger, but says nothing.

"I'm exercising my right to live how I want to in my country.

Isn't that why America is so great?" He grins and nods at Dakota, waiting for her smile and nod. "See? She gets it. I don't need all those covetous belongings—the Mercedes, the designer clothes—and the pressure of the rat race that gets you nowhere."

"You mean nowhere like a job? To pay your bills?" I've never actually had a serious conversation with one of these bums before. Is this guy for real?

He shrugs. "I have no bills, and if I get a job, then I have to pay taxes. Why would I want to do that?"

"To earn your keep?" I know my voice is rising now, but I can't help it. I guess Ned rubbed off on me, because this guy's logic is making me insane.

"There's enough money to go around."

"But . . ." I feel my face crinkle up before I can control it. I open my mouth to say that that's the stupidest thing I've ever heard, but I find a burger shoved into it, thanks to Sebastian. He winks at me.

Jono turns his attention to him now. "Dude, you get me, right? The way this government expects us to serve its whims, buy into its bullshit, and fight its battles like little puppets and sheep, under the guise of freedom and honor, when it's all about greed and power."

This idiot just said that to a soldier. Oh, the irony is too much.

Thank God my mouth is full, to stop me from blurting out what Sebastian is—or was. I'd feel like a complete ass, because I make it a rule not to talk about anything shared while I work on people's ink. Kind of a body artist–patient privilege. Plus, I know that Sebastian doesn't like to talk about his time in the military.

Three heartbeats of silence hang over the table, where Sebastian's stony expression gives nothing away and Jono waits for him to respond, and Dakota watches with wide, curious eyes, and I wonder if I'm going to have to apologize for my friend killing her dinner guest.

"Oh, yeah, definitely," Sebastian finally says.

My eyebrows must be halfway up my forehead.

"We're all like little pawns in their master scheme. Millions and millions of little tiny puppets with strings attached to us"—

Jono starts miming the act of puppet master over his plate of food—"doing whatever they tell us and bullying us into paying for things we don't need or want. We end up working like dogs until we're old and gray so they can waste it on unnecessary things like . . ." He frowns, searching for an example.

"Military defense?" Sebastian offers.

"Yeah! Armies and ships and guns. See?" Jono bumps his arm with his fist. "You totally get it! You want to talk about wasting taxpayers' dollars. I was down on Coronado Island a few months ago—have you seen that place?"

Sebastian nods once.

"Man, the billions of dollars they spent on all those ships and submarines, when our own country's infrastructure is sorely lacking, for wars that don't even exist."

"What? What are you talking about, they don't exist? Do you not read any news?" I finally blurt out.

Jono waves away my words with a dismissive hand. "It's all propaganda. They tell us there's a war so they can justify spending our tax dollars on defense toys and all these highly trained soldiers. I read an article in the paper the other day about those . . . what are they called?" His eyes scrunch up in thought. "Yeah, those super-elite guys that they always send in. What are they called?"

"Navy SEALs," Sebastian says.

Jono snaps his fingers. "Yeah! Them. Do you know it costs a quarter of a million dollars to train each of those human weapons? And for what? So our government can say that we have these indestructible stealthy task forces, so don't mess with us?"

"Actually, it cost them half a million to train me," Sebastian says quietly, taking a long sip of beer, his eyes downcast. "And no one is indestructible."

I'm no longer paying attention to the idiot sitting across from me. Now I'm keenly focused on the stranger who sits beside me, and how much more I need to learn about him. Sebastian already said he was in the navy, but did he just admit to being a SEAL? Granted, everything I've learned about our military forces comes from Hollywood, but the one thing they've all portrayed is that those guys are some of the toughest, smartest, bravest of any soldiers out there.

They actually *are* weapons.

Jono hasn't clued in to the fact that he's insulting the man sitting next to him. "Half a million dollars!" He whistles. "And, really, what has that bought America? Not nearly enough, *I* say. Those guys are probably over there, drinking beer and playing Ping-Pong on taxpayers' hard-earned money. I'll take my lifestyle over slaving to pay for that any day."

Sebastian turns to size up the California bum with a hard look. I lean forward, itching to hear his response, to hear him drop a hammer down on this ideological asswipe.

"Ivy, where are your keys?" he says instead, his tone calm and low, unbothered.

It takes me a moment to process the question. "Hanging by the door." I frown. "Why?"

He wipes his mouth with his napkin. "You shouldn't leave computer equipment in a car overnight." He nods to Dakota. "Thank you for dinner. It was great. Excuse me." He pushes out of his seat and heads into the house.

Leaving me to glare at Jono, who seems either unconcerned or oblivious that he offended Sebastian. But at least he's watching me with wariness now, as I thumb the tines of my fork.

"Isn't it great to be able to live in a country where differing opinions are celebrated?" Dakota says with a slightly apologetic shrug.

"Right. It's just peachy," I mutter sarcastically. Eying the doorway into the house, wondering how long I should wait before going after Sebastian.

# TWENTY-FOUR

# SEBASTIAN

I admire the California bum. He gets to live in a fairy-tale world, where he is free to take what he has in front of him for granted, where he has the luxury of choice. And as long as there are "sheep and puppets" like me, working within the shadows to keep him in the dark about the kind of evil that exists in this world, he'll get to stay snug in his ideological fairy tale until he's old and gray.

Or until someone crushes his larynx, which is what I almost did five minutes ago. That would have been twice today that I lost control due to pure emotion. I had no choice but to dismiss myself. I figured it would be impolite as a dinner guest to kill another dinner guest.

And I have something much more important to do anyway.

I close Ivy's bedroom door and press my knee against it, to hold it shut. She's still in the greenhouse. Likely ready to lunge across the table and choke our dinner companion. She's not as concerned about being impolite. But I have a feeling it won't be long before she comes to check on me; I saw the look on her face as I stood to leave.

So I need to hurry.

Setting her tattoo kit down on the floor in front of me, I flip open the latches. Inside, it looks exactly the way I saw it yesterday, except now the machine pieces are all safely secured within the custom cutouts in the black foam.

There's only one possibility . . .

Holding my breath, I curl a finger around one corner of the foam insert and begin pulling it back. It's definitely removable.

I lift the entire foam panel—tools and all—up . . .

And feel the grin of satisfaction spread across my face and relief slide through my limbs.

There, secured to the roof of the case with two strips of silver duct tape, is an unmarked videotape.

I was right. Just like Beijing.

And now I have exactly what Bentley wants. Another successful assignment. As soon as I get this to him I'm free to leave.

The floor in the hallway suddenly creaks, giving me only a second's warning before someone twists the knob. "Sebastian?" I feel the door push against my knee.

Peeling the duct tape off will make too much noise. I'll have to get the video later. "Hold on a sec." I place the foam back into the case, but it isn't sliding in as easily as it came out. *Fuck.* I'll have to fix that as soon as I get a chance, too. As quietly as possible, I lock the latches and slide the case aside then open the door.

Ivy pokes her head in, her eyes narrowed with suspicion as they dart from me to the bed, where her bags of clothes sit. "What are you doing in here?"

I point down to the computer, tucked neatly into the corner next to the door. "Figured I'd stack it to get it out of your way."

"Oh." She frowns. "You didn't have to do that."

She still hasn't come to terms with letting me do things for her. "You're welcome."

She bites her lip, and then smiles sheepishly. "I mean . . . thanks." Stepping into her bedroom, she pushes the door shut. "I'm sorry about that, back there."

"It was fine. I usually eat alone, so this was a nice change," I say dismissively, ever aware of the kit and the videotape—my entire purpose for being in her life—sitting next to my feet.

When she looks at me with that curious frown pulling at her eyebrow, I know that I've admitted to something strange. Now she's probably wondering why I'm always eating alone. Why I don't have friends or family to eat with.

"Well, I wish you had blasted him." She eases herself onto the bed and begins untying the laces of her boots. "He would have deserved it. He was insulting you and every other person who's ever risked, or lost, his life. I'm sure having some bum tell you that there is no war, when you carry the scars to prove it exists, must make you angry."

There's really nowhere to go in this room besides the bed, so I lean back against the door as casually as possible. "It's not the first time I've heard it."

She frowns, kicking off one boot, then the other. "So, you weren't just 'in the navy.' You're this super-elite soldier."

I heave a sigh. It was a moment of weakness—and pride—that made me admit that. "Yeah, I guess so."

"Why don't you like talking about it?" She's not even looking at me when she asks that; she's focusing on her laces instead. It's so unlike her to seem shy, but so is asking personal questions. Up until now, she's had a keen sense for touchy subjects and veered away whenever she sensed she'd hit too close to home. So to see her sitting on this bed now, frowning with curiosity, averting her gaze with hesitation . . . I'm guessing it's a side of Ivy that most people don't get to see.

And I'm afraid it's a side of Ivy that actually cares.

I wish it was smart to let her care. I wish I knew how to let her get closer to me. "I just don't."

She purses her lips, her gaze lifting to meet mine. I see her vulnerability shuttering, her temperature cooling. The need to get to know me shrinking away.

"I promised Dakota I'd do her next piece for her tonight." She stands and stretches her slender arms around in the air, rolling her shoulders to loosen them. "And if I have to listen to that ass during it, I'm going to kill him. Accidentally, of course."

She's making a joke—I think—but all I hear is the part where she's going to need her kit. "You're doing it right *now*?" If she opens that case, she's going to see that it's not set right. Ivy's the type of person to notice that kind of thing. And be suspicious of it. Then she'll start adjusting the foam and if she adjusts the foam she could find the tape, and if she finds the tape, she'll watch the tape, and if she watches the tape . . . Bentley's words ring loud in my ear.

Whatever's on that tape, Ivy can't know about it. She needs to stay in the dark.

"Yeah. As soon as she's done smoking the joint she just lit. I want to get it over with. I'm tired."

"Then you should wait until tomorrow. Didn't you just spend seven hours on some asshole yesterday?"

She's walking toward me, her eyes on the case. "I'll be fine. Speaking of some asshole, you haven't done shit for your side all day, have you?" She glares at me with reproach as she leans down to reach for the handle.

My hand shoots under her arm, pulling her upright and to me. Thinking fast. "You're right, I haven't. Can you do it for me?"

"You're a big boy. You can manage it." She twists, trying to pull away from me.

I have no choice. I scoop her up by the armpits and carry her with ease to the adjoining bathroom.

"Don't fucking manhandle me!" she snaps, shoving against my stomach the second I put her down. When I don't even budge, she settles on shooting daggers at me with her eyes.

I say nothing as I span my arms across the width of the crammed space to slide both pocket doors closed. I reach over my head to yank my T-shirt off, then unbuckle my belt and jeans, and push them down an inch or two lower than I need to for the purposes of my tattoo.

Her eyes immediately drop to my chest and slip down, before she catches herself and averts her gaze.

But I don't miss the hitch in her breath.

"Fine," she snaps, spinning around to the sink to wash her hands. There's really only standing room for one in here, giving me every excuse to be in her personal space. "I didn't work on your body for seven hours so you can fuck up that piece of art. You can't forget. Three times a day, especially with it being so fresh."

I stare at her face in the mirror's reflection as she lectures me, resting my hands on top of my head as I tower over her. I like it when she scolds me.

With the tap running, she turns around and begins gently—more gently than anyone might believe her capable of—rubbing the soap over the entire area, peeling back the elastic band of my briefs to get at the bottom without a word. This is her MO—cool and calm, indifferent. Unfazed.

But I feel the way her hands linger a little longer than necessary against my skin.

I see the way her gaze keeps flickering toward my briefs, where I'm already hard.

When she has coated the area with moisturizer, rubbing it in so carefully, not uttering a word, she softly says, "I'm finished." She lifts her head to meet my gaze for a brief moment before shifting for the door, as if she's going to leave.

I'm much too fast for her, and my hand on her stomach, pulling her back against me, stops her. "No, I don't think you are." Only a small part of me, deep inside where my motives collide with human need, feels guilty for what I'm about to do.

I wait five long seconds for her to say something. To tell me to fuck off, to tell me no. But she says nothing, and she doesn't pull away, turning to stare at me through the mirror with a look that I can't begin to read but makes me hesitate all the same.

Maybe it's that the stakes are somehow higher now than they were yesterday.

Maybe it's that she's starting to care.

Maybe it's that *I'm* starting to care.

But I have to get that videotape out of here before she even knows that it exists.

And . . . I'm dying to have her.

I slip my free hand around her soft, slender neck, feeling her blood pulse beneath my fingertips as I pull her tiny body flush against mine, barely noticing the discomfort in my side. My other hand tugs at her oversize shirt, curling and lifting the material until it's above her waistline. She has such narrow hips, such slender thighs, all the more evident by these skintight elastic pants she wears. I can't even imagine her legs stretching wide enough to accommodate my body, but I guess I'll find out soon.

She watches me in the reflection with fire in her eyes as I slide my hand down the front of her pants, into her panties.

Into her.

I smile at how primed she is, and she matches it with a small, knowing smirk of her own, allowing me to explore her with my hand, much like I watched her do to herself only days ago. It's been so long since a woman has let me touch her like this purely because she wanted me to, not because I've bought her body for a few hours. Bentley's right—being with a whore isn't the same as being with someone like Ivy. Someone I chose for her beauty, her intelligence, her wit. Someone I care to please.

When she closes her eyes and sighs, I dip down to grab the edge of her earlobe with my teeth, wondering how long she'll take to come, and if I have it in me to wait patiently.

She doesn't let me find out.

Her talented little hands push her pants down her hips to her knees, wriggling out of them until they're in a pile on the floor beside us. Her shirt and bra come off next, all while my hand is still inside her, and now I have that perfect tight naked body in front of me.

"I hope you weren't looking for romance when you planned this maneuver of yours," she says with a pant, turning around and hoisting herself up onto the sink counter, her legs spread and back arched, staring at me with an intensity I've never seen before from her. She holds a condom up between two fingers—where she plucked that from, I didn't notice—waiting.

And my dick starts to throb. Fuck, this girl is something else. "Romance isn't really my thing," I murmur. I have my jeans and briefs down in two seconds, the condom slipped on in another five, my mouth on hers in eight.

And I'm inside her with one hard thrust.

She's so small and tight, and yet she takes me with flexibility I hadn't expected, her body flush with mine as she clings to me, one hand hooked around my neck and squeezing tight, the other between her legs, working away on herself with small strokes that nearly make me lose it.

Fucking on a bathroom counter has never been my first pick, but I'm not about to complain now, keeping my hand at her back to block the tap from slamming into her tailbone. She's let me hook her left leg beneath the knee and hike it up, both to get deeper and to keep her leg from rubbing against my tattoo. She matches each thrust, her breathing growing more ragged, her nails digging into flesh.

I loved watching her come the other night.

But actually bringing her to the brink?

It takes every ounce of control in me not to go with her when she does, her moans loud and unfiltered. Sounds I already want to hear again. The second I'm sure I feel the last muscle spasm inside her, I pull out and tear the condom off. Without having to say a word, she reaches out and pumps me until I let loose all over her smooth stomach and tits, a muffled "fuck" slipping out through my groans.

She sighs, lying languidly against the mirror and sink, her body limp and used and covered in sweat and cum. "Yeah."

I never stick around after. With whores, there's no point anyway. It just costs more. But with Ivy, I don't want to leave. I'd do this all night with her.

But I have a job to do first.

I reach for a facecloth from a shelf above and hand it to her. "I'll let you clean up," I offer, laying one last kiss on her swollen lips before ducking out of the bathroom, sliding the door shut.

I listen for it.

As soon as I hear the door lock latch, I dive for the case, keeping one ear on her movements inside. I made one hell of a mess on her intentionally. Now that I know where the tape is, I make quick work of the duct tape, peeling it all the way off to remove the video. I slide the video under the bed and focus on tucking the foam back into the kit exactly how it was to avoid any questions.

I finally get it right, just as the toilet flushes.

When Ivy steps out a few minutes later, fully dressed, I'm doing up my belt.

"So . . . Dakota's tat will probably take me about an hour and a half. You can watch if you want. But you don't have to. You can do whatever you want. Stay or go . . ."

Back to being indifferent. She's adorable when she's trying to act like she doesn't care, like we didn't just finish fucking in the bathroom five minutes ago. The truth is, I want to stay. I could be hard again in no time, just looking at her. We could do it in the bed this time, and I wouldn't get up and leave right away.

But I can't stay, not now. "Actually, I need to get going." I tug my shirt on. "I have some errands to run."

"Really?" She glances at the clock—it's almost nine—and then shakes her head. "'Kay. Well, it was nice hanging out." She lifts her kit. "And thanks for all the help around the shop and the house."

She thinks I'm ditching her now that I've gotten what I wanted.

The thing is, I *should* be ditching her, and it has nothing to do with fucking her and everything to do with the tape lying under the bed. Once Bentley has it my assignment is over. I could be back in Santorini by Sunday, and that's for the best, for everyone. As much as I've enjoyed these last few days with Ivy, my lifestyle is a solitary one; it doesn't yield to anyone else's needs or questions.

But handing that video over to Bentley is not going to resolve the potential issue of Scalero. Ivy is still a witness in a double murder that he committed. Will he simply leave her alone? From our conversation today, I'm guessing not.

I can't just leave her here, unprotected, waiting to be plucked off once he's given the chance.

Cupping the back of her neck with my hand, I lean down to steal a last deep kiss from her. "I'll pick you up at ten tomorrow."

"I can drive myself now that I have—"

"I'll pick you up. Ten a.m. Sharp. You still have a lot to clean up." I let my voice drop an octave and grow softer. "Let me help you."

She purses her lips. "Fine. The real estate agent is meeting me there at ten thirty."

She's already written me off as not coming back. I know there's no point trying to convince her otherwise, I'll just have to prove it to her. I let her go, ducking in to use the bathroom. When I step out, she's gone, and so is her case.

Sliding the tape out from beneath the bed, I crack open the window and stick it in the bush butting up against the house. There's no way I can hide something that bulky under my thin T-shirt.

Ivy's already setting up on the table in the living room when I come out, clearing the space and lining up the soap spray and gloves. She's meticulous about her space and her process. Music pumps through the tiny speaker next to her. The woman loves her music.

"See you tomorrow."

"Uh-huh." She shoots a quick smile over her shoulder at me, her freshly fucked glowing cheeks a thing of beauty. Telling me that she's not angry about the bang-and-run. Or at least I think that's what that is. Fuck, I don't know how to deal with this kind of shit. I can read a person's motives and evil intentions like they're painted on a wall, but this?

Dakota steps into the house, her limbs relaxed and eyelids slightly lazy, the smell of her recently enjoyed weed wafting toward me.

Something else I haven't done since my teenage years.

"Are you leaving already?" Dakota's lips curl in a pout, and she looks genuinely upset. She's an odd one, and I can't understand what attracts the two of them to each other. Dakota's acceptance of others, maybe. Because, as much as I like Ivy, you have to be a pretty open-minded person to understand—and tolerate—her.

I offer her a smile. "I am. Thank you for dinner."

Dakota peels off her light sweater, revealing several feminine tattoo designs already decorating her arms, back, and shoulders. "My pleasure. I'm making kimbap for dinner tomorrow. You'll love it."

She's not asking *if* I'll be back for dinner tomorrow. There's no doubt in her voice that I will be. And, if I'm honest, the idea sounds more appealing to me than it should. Even if she's making another seaweed dish. I've spent enough time in South Korea to recognize the name.

Ivy's head shoots up to glare at her, but Dakota ignores it, smiling broadly, first at me then at Jono, who wanders in from the patio, his eyes narrow slits. "Is this the design?" He lifts a sheet of paper, and Ivy's glare shifts to him, sharpening to razors. "You gonna do it freehand?"

"Yup," she replies curtly.

"Right on. Dakota's got a lot of trust in you. You must be really good." Rubbing his beard, he taps his shoulder and mumbles, "I've got this surfer emblem I've always wanted to—"

"I'm four-hundred-bucks-an-hour good," Ivy throws out, ending his attempts to mooch a free tattoo off her.

I leave chuckling, and with a glance around to make sure no one's watching, I swing past the window to retrieve the tape, a shadow of disappointment trailing me. Seaweed dinner, idiot company and all, that was . . . fun. I wish I could stay.

I wonder how long I can pretend to be this version of Sebastian and get away with it.

Would I even have to, with a girl like Ivy? If I opened up to her, told her what I *really* do—the kinds of contracts I take on for Bentley, the number of people I've killed in the name of saving many more lives—would she be able to accept that?

But then I'd have to come clean with why I'm here in the first place and I'd be fucking delusional if I thought she'd ever be okay with *that*.

I need to get this videotape into Bentley's hands, get a handle on Mario, help her clean up the mess in her house like I promised her I would, and move on. Let Ivy move on.

I crank the engine. But before I pull out, I weigh the tape that has Bentley and Scalero so rattled, that got Royce and Ivy's uncle killed, in my hand. What exactly did Royce accuse Scalero of doing in that tattoo shop? Even if it was a bunch of lies, the allegations were clearly serious, if Ivy's uncle thought he could get money out of Alliance for it.

And increasingly, I can't help but think that perhaps Royce was telling the truth.

I toss the thing onto the passenger seat. I don't do this. I don't ask questions. I trust Bentley and I do my job. But I've also learned not to question my gut, and none of my other assignments have left my gut feeling unsettled like this.

I'm ready to call Bentley and tell him I have the videotape and the assignment was successful, but I pause and stare at the tape for a moment longer. That will tell me if what Royce and Scalero and who knows who else did over there was worth the end goal.

If people really needed to die over this.

If it's worth Ivy spending the rest of her life with no answers, no closure to her uncle's death.

I'll know why I'm here, in San Francisco. It'll prove to me that what I do matters for the greater good.

A white corner of paper peeks out of the case. I shake the tape out, and a folded note tumbles out along with it. A man's scratched handwriting fills the page.

IVY–IF SOMETHING SHOULD HAPPEN TO ME, SEND THIS VIDEO TO DORRIS MACLEAN AT NBC. PEOPLE NEED TO KNOW ABOUT THIS. AND DON'T TELL ANYONE YOU HAVE IT. ~N.

I need to look up this Dorris Maclean, but my guess is she's an investigative reporter. So at least Ivy's uncle had some idea that what he was doing might be risky. Which likely means that he was desperate for the cash he presumed this blackmail scheme was going to get him. He must have already been under threat from whomever he owed money to.

*People need to know about this.*

What exactly did Ned think people need to know about?

If I phone Bentley now, I have exactly an hour and a half—the time it will take to drive to his Napa home—to produce the tape before he grows suspicious.

And then answers to any questions will be lost to me.

I stare long and hard at the tape.

• • •

I can't believe they still sell these fucking things, but thank God they do.

I push the tape into the machine and cross my fingers that the cables the department store sales guy said would work on this shitbox motel television actually do. At first, all I see is static and I curse the idiot for being wrong. But after jogging the wires a few times, the screen wobbles, then clears, and the inside of the tattoo shop appears.

At the bottom of the screen is a time stamp of 4:00 p.m., October 21 of this year. About three weeks ago now. A Willie Nelson wannabe—Ivy's uncle, from the pictures that I've seen—is hunched over a woman's arm with his tattoo gun, working away quietly.

I grin as Ivy saunters past the camera with her case in hand, her narrow hips swinging casually. "You want me to come by with dinner for you later, Ned?"

"Nah. I'll call Fez." He has a deep, guttural voice. Not the most friendly-sounding guy.

"I thought he drove you nuts."

"Ya see . . . Me and Fez, we have an understandin'." Now he glances over his shoulder at her, and I can just make out the crinkles around his eyes, telling me he's smiling at her. "He don't talk and I like 'im."

She laughs. "I wish I could figure out how to get him to do that for me."

"You gonna be home later tonight, girl?"

"At some point."

With a sigh and shake of his head, he mutters, "Stay out of trouble," as she pushes through the front door.

He continues working in silence. There's nothing valuable here, from what I can see, so I begin fast-forwarding through, watching the customer pay and leave, Ivy's uncle clean up his area and reset it, the pizza delivery guy to show up—I slow down for that, to see that the uncle's not lying; Fez says nothing but hello and goodbye and "That'll be six forty-two, sir." There's a good two-hour time lapse of Ned Marshall sitting in his desk chair with his feet up as the sun goes down outside. I'm beginning to wonder if this is the right tape after all.

Finally, the door pushes open and Dylan Royce marches through. I recognize him immediately from the newspaper clipping.

This is definitely what Bentley is after.

I slow the tape in time to see Ned reach out and shake his hand. "Royce! How's the arm?" he asks.

Royce holds out his arm to display the partially finished sleeve. Some parts are outlined, others are completely filled in. I'm guessing Ivy's uncle had been working on it over a few sessions. He and Royce had probably gotten pretty chummy.

I watch the screen as the two men go through the usual bullshit niceties and paperwork. It's nice to have audio. A lot of surveillance videos that I've watched don't have it. Then again, Bentley *did* say that it's the conversation he's after.

"Okay, we're all set." Ivy's uncle pulls out a transfer he must have prepared earlier. Royce pulls his shirt off to reveal a hardened body that's seen plenty of hours in the gym, and likely some war-inflicted injuries, from the small scars across his rib cage. He's a big guy, bigger than Scalero. But Scalero had a gun and I'm guessing he didn't waste time using it on his former comrade's head.

Royce settles into the chair that I just helped pitch the other day and positions his arm. I turn the volume up to catch their words, which are surprisingly clear for that retro surveillance system. He tips his head back, giving the camera a good angle of his eyes, glossed over. He's high, I'm guessing. Bentley did say he had a problem with both Vicodin and smoking pot. It would make sense that he'd do it before sitting under a needle for hours.

I sip away on my coffee—caffeine is one of my few vices, and a godsend at the moment, given how tired I am—and listen to them talk. All this Medal of Honor recipient seems to do is complain: about his asshole neighbor's annoying dog that he wants to poison because it keeps shitting on the sidewalk in front of his house; about his mother, who won't let up on him about his breakup with his cheating cunt of a girlfriend who was fucking some guy on the side while he was away. About the Marine Corps, and how he misses those years and wishes he had stayed, hadn't been swayed by the opportunity to make more money.

About the private military company where he worked until four months ago, and how they're a bunch of money-hungry dicks who should be bowing down to him for what he's done for them, but instead fired him for some lame-ass excuse about violating company policy with drug use.

The Vicodin is legit, he swears. To help manage the ongoing pain in his shoulder from a bullet wound that never healed properly. And it's the stress of that job that made him start smoking. Never touched the stuff before and then he goes into Afghanistan as contracted arms for Alliance and comes out needing a spliff every night just to fall asleep, and sometimes to get through the day, when he's especially anxious. That's another aftereffect of the job, he says. Severe anxiety. But if he violated company policy, why'd they also make him sign a gag order and give him a bunch of money to make sure he kept his mouth shut? And why'd all this happen a month after he put a formal complaint in about his coworkers?

They paid him off to keep quiet about things, but not nearly fucking enough, according to him.

"Alliance, you say?" Ned murmurs, his head down and focused on the new outline on Royce's forearm. "I think I heard of 'em."

"Probably." Royce tips his head back and closes his eyes, his voice nasally and annoying. "They were big in the news two months ago over a civilian shooting near Kandahar."

"Thought that war was over."

The expression that takes over Royce's face is one I recognize well. In his mind, he's drifting back into it. He can't help himself. It happens to the best of us. "As long as American troops are there, that war will never be over. And bad shit will keep happening to good people."

"I guess that's war, though, right?" I can't tell if Ned is actually interested in this conversation or just going through the motions because Royce is his customer.

Royce chuckles—a wicked, bitter sound. "Have you ever been in a war, Ned?"

"Nope. Glad to say I was too young for Nam."

"Well, let me tell you something about war. It can last forever, if there's enough money to keep it going. As long as war is profitable for companies like Alliance, they'll be there, front and center. You know our government gave Alliance a *billion* dollars in contracts to go over there?"

Ned lets out a low whistle.

"Exactly. They handed them that much money and sent them over to basically govern themselves. It's a privately owned company. No one knows what's going on inside because nothing's released. No one's checking on them. No one's telling them what they can and can't do. There's an actual legit immunity law that protects them. With that kind of money, they're above the law over there. Or at least they act like they are. They're a bunch of fucking mercenaries is what they are."

"What are they supposed to be doin'?"

"'Maintaining security.' Which means all kinds of things. Protecting American diplomats, training troops, guarding prisoners." He pauses, his voice growing softer. "Questioning insurgents.

That's what I was there to do."

Ned sits up for a moment, stretches his arms, twists his neck as if he has a kink, and then hunkers down over Royce's arm once again. "Sounds rough."

Royce takes a deep breath. "They were some of the longest, worst days of my life."

Silence hangs through the shop as Ned works to the subdued tune of Willie Nelson and Royce stares up at the ceiling, facing down his demons, I'm sure. I've been in his place.

"You heard of Adeeb Al-Naseer?" Royce suddenly asks.

"Probably. Can't keep those foreign names straight, though."

"He was the leader of the terrorist cell that bombed that office building in Seattle seven years back."

"Oh, yeah . . . I sure remember that one."

"I helped catch him, you know." Royce's eyes flicker to Ned's furrowed brow. "A battalion brought in a guy with cryptic messages written out on paper and taped to his body. They couldn't get him to talk, so they told us to have a go at him. See what he'd tell us." He hesitates. "So we did. And he talked, all right. By the time we were done with him, he told us everything we needed to know."

Ned pauses to peer up at his customer for a brief moment, before ducking back down. "What does *that* mean? What'd you do to him?"

"You name it. Slapped him around, electric shock, hung him from his wrists, grabbed his balls and gave them a good twist," the hand on Royce's free arm clenches. "Broke his leg, his arms . . ." He goes on, listing techniques that have been used more times than anyone cares to admit.

Some that I've used to get people to talk.

I've never enjoyed a second of it, never reveled in scaring another human being, of causing pain. But I've done all I had to in order to get the answers, and justice, that I needed. And I've felt the weight of it on my shoulders afterward.

I have no doubts that what Royce is admitting to doing right now is the cold, harsh truth.

And, by the disgusted look on his face, he didn't enjoy a second of it either.

"Jesus," Ned mutters. "What finally broke him?"

Royce hesitates, swallows. "The two guys I was working with went out and found the man's fourteen-year-old daughter and took turns raping her in front of him. That's what broke him," he says quietly.

Ned is silent.

"These two other former Marines that I was stationed there with, they were something else. I don't know where Alliance found them, but they should never have been hired. One of them, this guy Mario, he was seriously fucked in the head. He'd always be the first one in line to interrogate, to start smacking someone around. He loved to take on guard duties and go into the city. I think it was just so he could hold his gun to people's heads and make them piss their pants."

"Sounds like a real asshole," Ned murmurs.

"He's sadistic."

"Sounds like it." I can hear a distinct shift in Ned's voice, from indifference to at least mild concern.

Royce's jaw clenches. "That girl they raped? She wasn't the only one. One night I caught him and Ricky in an interrogation room with a fifteen-year-old girl who'd been brought in on suspicion of aiding in a terrorist plot. She died the next day. Found out later that she was completely innocent."

I hit Pause on the VCR as my stomach sinks. Bentley said that everything Royce was claiming was pure lies. But I've met Mario, and my ten-second gut read is that he's a nutcase, and someone I don't trust. He went against Bentley's orders just by approaching me, and he seems hell-bent on not being tied to any crime, either overseas or here. Plus, he basically admitted to what's on the tape as being true. And if that's the case . . .

Bentley didn't create Alliance to rape innocent young women. That isn't for the greater good.

Taking a deep breath, I let the tape keep playing.

"He get into trouble?" Ned asks.

Royce smiles, and it's not at all pleasant. "Who's gonna give him trouble?"

"You said this was a private company, right? Ain't the owner worried about employees doin' that kind of stuff?" Ned has obviously been listening—and understanding—far more than he's let on.

"John Bentley doesn't give a fuck what happens over there as long as the contracts keep coming in. That's why I got paid off and told to keep quiet."

My stomach clenches. That's got to be the bullshit Bentley was talking about. I know Bentley well enough to know that he would care about rape.

"Don't nobody say nothin'?"

"This is war. It's so easy to cover that kind of shit up, and all the other shit. And people there are scared. Say the wrong thing and you may find yourself with a bullet in your head. Enemy fire, of course."

"But you're back home now."

Royce pauses. "Nobody in America wants to hear about how a Medal of Honor recipient stood by and watched women get raped."

Ivy's uncle works away and listens, dropping a question here and there, as Royce spells out countless other horrific things he saw while working for Alliance, all the times that basic human rights were clearly violated by Mario and Ricky and other employees—not to protect American lives or interests, but for pure, sadistic enjoyment.

But what about Royce? Did he partake? Is he saying he was *always* just an innocent bystander?

Their conversation eventually shifts to menial things, and then nothing at all, and after four hours in the chair, Royce is passing over a wad of cash. "I'll wanna come in next week to finish this piece up here," he says, tapping the top of his shoulder. "Same time, same day?"

"Sounds good."

Ivy's uncle sits at his desk and stares at the door for a while, long after the guy has left. Processing everything Royce just admitted to, I'm sure. Clicking a key on the keyboard, he waits for his computer monitor to light up. Then he types something into Google. I can't see what it is, but when a website comes up that I know like the back of my hand—with a black background and a picture of founder and CEO John Bentley on the left-hand side—I know that the wheels have begun to churn in Ned's head.

He gets up to pull the metal screen across the entryway, locks the front door, and disappears down the hall, to the back where there is no surveillance.

And then the tape cuts out.

And I'm left staring at my reflection in the monitor.

Royce may have deserved to be punished for his part in all this, but he didn't deserve a bullet to his head to shut him up.

And Ned . . . well, he was a fucking fool to get involved, but he definitely didn't deserve to be killed over this either.

But Bentley was telling the truth about one thing: If this confession—from a Medal of Honor recipient, no less—gets into the hands of the American public, Alliance is finished.

The bigger question is: Do Bentley and Alliance deserve that end? Is this just a case of a contractor or two going rogue? How often is shit like this happening over there? How many of these guys, with God complexes, are doing inexcusable things to innocent human beings?

I'm about to hand over the only evidence that might ever spark an investigation into those questions.

Dammit.

I shouldn't have watched the tape. I can't simply unsee that, unknow that.

And yet Bentley's paying me to do a job.

I need to finish it.

■ ■ ■

The sun is just cresting over the horizon when Bentley meets me at the front door of his Napa villa. I wordlessly hand the tape to him and his shoulders sag with relief, while mine hum with tension.

"Where did you find it?"

"Her tattoo kit, which she brings everywhere. Her uncle taped it to the inside, under the foam." So obvious.

He snorts, shaking his head. "And she had no idea?"

"None."

He heaves a sigh. "As always, you're the most proficient man I know at getting the job done."

"I wouldn't have guessed you felt that way as of late." I don't hide the sarcasm.

He hangs his head and offers me a sheepish smile. "I'm sorry about that. It was a moment of panic, I suppose. I just finally squashed that civilian shooting issue, so having this to worry about was more than even I could handle."

*Because this will destroy everything you've worked hard to build.*

"I'll have the money wired to your offshore account in the next hour. You can go back to your Greek haven, and we can get back to regularly scheduled programming." He turns to head back inside.

"What about Scalero?"

Bentley stops. "What about him?"

"Is he going to cause any more issues?"

Bentley turns slowly, his face expressionless, impossible to read. "What issues?"

"He made contact yesterday in a restroom." I hold up his wallet as evidence. "Made some comments about her being a loose end that he needed to tie up." I watch Bentley closely, looking for a sign that tells me he already knew about this.

He holds my gaze. "He had strict instructions not to go near you or the girl."

"And yet he broke them."

"I'll deal with him."

"Like you dealt with him before?" If Royce's confessions to what he saw are true and Bentley knew about it, that means he brought me in here to help bury evidence that would put him and his company in the wrong, and rightfully so. Nothing about what I heard last night is what we stand for, why I do what I do. None of it is for the greater good of our country.

It's for the greater good of Bentley's pockets.

I'm struggling to believe that this could be true. That's not the man I went to war with. That's not the man whose life I fought to save.

That's not the man I've trusted all these years, when I've trusted no one else.

"If he comes near Ivy again, I'll assume it's to hurt her." I give him a knowing look. I shouldn't have to spell out what'll happen. I've never killed an American soldier before, but the more I learn about Mario Scalero and his partner in crime, the more I believe they need to be put down. And, for once, I don't feel the need to be ordered to make that happen.

Bentley raises an eyebrow. "Ivy?"

"She's not a threat."

"She's a witness."

"Who didn't witness enough to be a threat to them."

He presses his lips together and offers me a curt nod. "As long as it stays that way . . ." He holds out his hand. "Peace offering?"

I toss the wallet into it. I don't need it anymore. I've already memorized Scalero's driver's license info. I know exactly where he lives.

"How soon will you be on a plane?"

"Not sure yet." I pause, wondering if he's going to keep tabs on me. Wondering why he cares. "I may stay for a while. Visit my parents." The thought flickered briefly through my mind, but I haven't committed to the idea.

Sympathy passes over Bentley's face, but I see the distrust lurking there. He doesn't believe me. "Good, Sebastian. I think that's a great idea. You need to hold on to the people who are important, who keep you grounded. Let me know what you decide. And don't worry about Scalero. I'm sending them overseas again soon, on another contract that's about to come in, so they won't even be around to cause any issues for you, or for her. Now get some sleep; you look like shit. You know what to do."

Drop my piece into the bay and leave the car in a long-term parking lot for pickup. Yeah. I know the drill.

Just like that, my official purpose for being in San Francisco is over. I'm free to slip back into anonymity, to find a little slice of peaceful paradise and detach myself from human connection. To live simply and without feeling.

Normally, I rush to get the earliest flight out.

But for the first time, I don't feel the same urge to run.

# TWENTY-FIVE

# IVY

"How does it feel this morning?"

Dakota struts into the greenhouse in a gauzy tank top and turns her shoulder toward me, the fresh ink boldly displayed on her arm. "Perfect, as expected from my talented friend."

"Everyone's my friend when they want some ink," I mutter. I have tattooed almost every last one of my closest friends, and if I haven't inked them, then I've designed their work. Jesse Welles was the first person to ever take my design and actually put it on his body, back in my sophomore year of high school. I inked Dakota's design on Alex's shoulder. I've done six of Dakota's seven tattoos, which she designed herself, and I embellished because it's a compulsion. I even did Amber's Irish fling's tattoo—for free—just to keep him occupied one night last year, while I was in Dublin. The only good friend who won't let me near her skin is Amber.

"So you said it was four hundred an hour?"

I shoot her a flat look from my curled-up perch in the wicker chair, my oversize coffee mug in hand. "For the freeloading leech, yes. But you are not paying me a dime. If anyone owes anyone anything, I owe you."

She waves it off with a laugh. "People like that make life interesting, don't they? And you know me, the more the merrier. That room is yours for as long as you want it."

I can't believe I'm thinking this, but I could get used to rooming with Dakota, despite her questionable choice in dinner guests. And I know the offer will still stand even if she figures out that, while she was smoking a joint with her homeless friend, my bare ass was on her bathroom sink, next to her toothbrush, last night, when I was getting nailed by Sebastian. God, he was something else. Spending hours working on—and admiring—his body the day before did not prepare me for the nerves I would feel when he pulled those doors shut.

And then he took off, like a convict on the run.

"What are you and your Navy SEAL doing today?" Dakota asks, pushing the spout of a watering can into one of her plants. She must spend hours every day tending to her plants.

"*I* am going to start bagging all the trash in the house." I climb out of the chair. "And I'm sure that last night was the last time I'll ever see him." Saying that out loud gives me a small twinge of disappointment, but I'm no idiot. He got what he wanted, and it was off-the-charts amazing. Let's be honest—I got what I wanted last night, too.

The problem is, now I want more of it. I can't remember the last time I actually missed a man after he left. Jesse, maybe, but that was completely different. Jesse was a high school junior, I was a gangly sophomore, and that little fling of ours lasted only a couple of weeks before he broke it off for no good reason. And we never slept together during that time. Sometimes I think my hurt feelings were more about my own ego than my feelings for him, even though they were strong.

But Sebastian . . . I already crave the feel of his hands peeling away my clothes. I crave the way he so confidently took my body. I crave the sensation of his all-consuming presence.

For the short time that we were within the walls of that bathroom I didn't care about anything else. I focused on nothing but him.

And then he ran.

I'm not stupid enough to believe that he's going to ring this doorbell at ten a.m. today. In fact, I'm going to leave early.

"Hmm . . ." She frowns deeply, her eyes glued to the lemon tree.

"Hmm . . . what?"

She doesn't respond. That's not surprising, though. Dakota can be spacey at the best of times.

"Dakota!"

"He's very guarded, isn't he?"

"Understatement of the *millennium*." I grab a blueberry-and-God-knows-what-else muffin from the plate she brought out. Given that she bakes almost every day, I'm going to put on weight living here. That's probably a good thing, though.

"The aura that surrounds him is"—her face pinches up; *here we go*—"dark and troubled. He's not at peace with himself."

I'd love to dismiss what she says, but at the same time, I like getting someone else's take on this odd bodyguard who strolled into my shop and insinuated himself into my life. "He was a soldier. He saw terrible things that he probably can't forget." Just like I saw a terrible thing that I can't forget. "He served two tours in Afghanistan, and he's got some nasty scars. So I'm not surprised if you think his aura is troubled." I hear enough in the news about PTSD and other challenges for these soldiers who return. In fact, the common message seems to be that they never come back the same person they were when they left.

There's this ginger-haired guy, Ross, who hangs out a lot on the corner near Pasquale's sometimes. He was in the army. I don't know what he was like before the Iraq War, but I'm guessing he wasn't the angry drunk Fez occasionally gives free slices to now.

Sebastian's much more put together than Ross, though. Aloof, yes. Closed off, yes.

But he also seems to be operating with principle, and purpose.

Right now, that purpose is me. At least it was, until last night when I let him fuck me.

Am I regretting it? No, that's not what this is.

I'm just dreading the inevitable swift end.

"He carries a heavy burden on his shoulders," Dakota adds. "I think you'll be good for him. I can already see that he's been good for you."

I laugh. "Good for him? Dakota, we barely know each other. It's already over. Done."

"You'll give him the space he needs in order to open up to you," she says, as if I hadn't just spoken, "and he will, eventually. He just needs to know that he can trust you with his darkness." The heavy frown vanishes with a sudden, excited look. "Oh! And you should tell him how you feel about him. He'll want to hear that."

"Hi. Have we met?" I don't tell guys how I feel about them. I don't tell anyone how I feel about them.

She smiles. "Don't be so afraid, Ivy."

I need to get out of here. "Well, while he's deciding what to do with his darkness, I'm going to be cleaning up glass and couch stuffing so I can sell Ned's house before the bank forecloses. Actually, first"—I pull out Bobby's business card, my anger flaring—"I've got a bone to pick with someone."

"Have fun! I'll see you and Sebastian here for dinner around six?"

I roll my eyes but don't bother to deny Dakota her delusion, grabbing my purse and keys and heading out.

■ ■ ■

I'm guessing the two guys flanking Bobby are the brothers in Bobby and Brothers Towing and Automotive. Both are even bigger than he is.

I make a point of slamming my car door as I march toward the open garage doors.

"Ivy." Bobby saunters over, the chain hanging off his stained work pants clattering with each step. "What are you doin' here? Comin' to check on your ink?" He holds out his arm to show me the brilliant colors that I filled in. It's scabbing over nicely. "I drove by Black Rabbit yesterday." His face scrunches up. "Man, why *white*? Ned would lose his shit if he saw that. It looks—"

"You lied to me," I snap, cutting him off before he sends me into a panic over what's happening at the shop. Given the auto shop behind me—in a run-down area of Daly City, where trees are sparse and litter plenty—is a grimy mix of cobalt blue and construction orange, I shouldn't let his opinion sway me too much.

"Look at you, with your hands on your little hips." He chuckles, giving me a once-over, like I'm some cute little kid.

I have the urge to punch him in the face, but I restrain myself.

Pulling a rag out from his back pocket, he casually wipes the oil from his hands. "So, what're you goin' on about now?"

"When I asked you if Ned owed one of your guys money and you said no, you were lying right to my face, weren't you?"

A frown takes over his jovial expression as he glances over his shoulder at the other guys. "What have you heard?"

"That Ned had a sizable gambling debt with one of your guys."

His boots drag over the gravel as he gets closer. "And who told you that?" His eyes aren't nearly as soft, his face not nearly as friendly as it was a moment ago.

Maybe I shouldn't have charged in here like this. I straighten my back. "The cops."

He laughs. "Bullshit." I guess the idea that the cops know about Iron's internal affairs is crazy.

I hold his gaze until he realizes I'm not lying, and his grin falls off his face.

"Who told them?"

"You'll have to ask Detective Fields that."

He runs his tongue over his teeth. "Ned didn't owe *us* nothin'. Tell your detective he has a shitty source."

The meaning behind his words, his inflection, isn't lost on me. "Who did he owe, then?"

Bobby heaves a sigh, muttering something unintelligible to himself. "Ned was into it with a guy named Sullivan. He's not Iron. He's . . . an associate of ours, who sometimes joins our game nights."

"What kind of 'associate'?"

"A business one," he answers vaguely.

I fold my arms over my chest. "Guns?"

"No."

"Hookers?"

"No."

"Drugs?"

He falters. "No."

My stomach turns. So Ned owed money to a drug dealer. Hell, that's worse than owing one of these bikers. "How much?"

Bobby sighs. "Two hundred and fifty g's, originally. He paid up a hundred of that, but couldn't get any more from the bank."

My mouth drops open. "How the hell did Ned end up owing someone a quarter of a million dollars?"

"Poker. Your uncle had a bit of a gambling problem."

I scowl. "No he didn't."

"Yeah . . . he did," Bobby says, his voice firm. "For a few years now. Dad warned him about owing money to a guy like Sullivan, but he wouldn't listen. Fucking stubborn old man."

Ned had a gambling *problem*? Was it worse than he let on? Obviously yes, if he owed that kind of money. I rack my brain, trying to think of a particular Wednesday night over the past few months when he came home distraught from a poker night. The problem is, I was never home to see him come in. And by Thursday when I strolled into Black Rabbit at noon . . . well, Ned was always on the grouchy side to begin with. "And you didn't think it was important to tell the cops all this?"

Bobby snorts. "Nobody's tellin' the pigs shit. You know that, Ivy. Besides, why would it matter? Sullivan didn't take out Ned. What good would that do? He wouldn't get his money."

"Well, he obviously wasn't getting his money anyway. Ned had no money!"

"Not cash. But he had Black Rabbit." Bobby gives me a knowing look. "And Sullivan was after that."

*Oh my God.* Ned would have lost his mind if he had to hand over the shop. But now that Ned's gone . . . "This Sullivan guy trashed Ned's house the other night looking for cash, didn't he?"

Bobby's brow furrows. He looks genuinely surprised. "What?"

"Ned's house was torn apart two nights ago. Someone was looking for money. Or something."

"I don't know nothin' about that." Bobby heaves a sigh and reaches up to scratch his scraggly beard.

"What?" He knows more than he's telling me.

"It's nothing, really. It's just . . ."

"Spit it out, Bobby!"

"Okay! Okay." He glances over his shoulder at the guys again, who are focused on the car on the hoist. "Dad said that Ned came by the clubhouse to talk to him and Tiny."

Moe and Tiny are two fifty-something-year-old bikers who have been coming to Ned since he opened up. I remember sitting on Tiny's giant lap when I was just six, while Ned worked on his sleeve.

"Ned wanted their backup for a meet he had with someone in a few days' time."

I frown. "Backup? What does that mean, like *protection*?" Did he know he was in danger?

"Sounds like it, but Ned didn't tell them too much. Alls he said was that he had something to trade that was worth a lot of dough and he'd be able to pay Sullivan and get him off his back about the shop. He needed a couple guys with him, so he wasn't going to the exchange alone. He said he'd give them a five percent cut."

"What was he exchanging?"

"Don't know. Honest. But it sounds like Ned had something going on the side. And that's a lot of money for one deal . . ."

My stomach sinks. What the hell was Ned into? "When was this supposed to happen?"

Bobby's lips purse. "He came by to ask Tiny for help around noon. The exchange was supposed to happen four days from then. And then a few hours later, he was taken out."

"The same day!" I yell, making him flinch. "Are you serious?" This means it wasn't a random robbery at all. "You need to tell this to the cops!"

"Not gonna happen, darlin', so you can stop with the screaming. I don't like being yelled at."

"The hell I will!" Sure, it incriminates Ned, but maybe the police will make more of an effort to solve the case if they know there was a clear motive here. If these guys had just told the cops the truth in the beginning, then maybe more could have been done by now.

Behind me, I hear the sound of tires on gravel and a car coming to a stop, but I'm so overwhelmed by what Bobby just told me, I dismiss it—and everyone else—for the moment.

"You know what? I'm going to tell the cops myself then. And they're going to come here and question your ass about it until you tell them the truth."

"Good luck with that. Tiny and Moe will never admit a damn thing to the pigs. They'll deny everything I just told you." Bobby looks over my head. "What the hell is he doing here?"

I turn just in time to see Sebastian marching over, his eyes covered by his glasses but the stern jaw telling me he's anything but happy.

He showed up, just like he said he would.

He showed up and Dakota must have told him where I went, and he is oh-so-pissed with me right now.

But I can't ignore the tiny bubble of relief that he's here.

I push it away, though, because I need to deal with Bobby. "So, let me get this straight. Ned had something worth a lot of money to give to someone. He felt he needed backup with him during the exchange, and then he ends up dead. Now someone's *torn apart* our house—which we're trying to sell because we can't pay the mortgage and we have no insurance, by the way—because they were likely trying to find whatever he was handing over at this exchange, and you guys, who are supposed to be Ned's friends, won't do a thing to help me? Fucking bikers!"

All amusement has left Bobby's face. "Me telling you what I just did *is* helping you." He steps closer and looms over me, and I can't help but shrink back. "But don't you fucking dare come here and—"

It all happens so fast. One moment Bobby is hovering over me, the next he's flat on his back and Sebastian is standing above him. I see that his gun is tucked into the back of his jeans. As if he placed it there before getting out of the car, expecting something like this to happen.

The other two guys come running, their guts bouncing with each step. They're not coming to see if Bobby's okay; their focus is zeroed in on Sebastian, who doesn't seem at all concerned. I instinctively take a step back, because that's what you do out of self-preservation when six hundred pounds is charging your way.

Sebastian doesn't, though. He turns to face them square on, his stance relaxed. And when they finally reach him, fists in the air, it's like one of those horrifically choreographed fight scenes from older movies, where the bad guy swings and the good guy maneuvers out of the way with ease, making the bad guy lose his balance and tumble. That, coupled with a few lightning-quick swings and kicks, and both guys are lying in heaps next to Bobby; one's moaning and holding his jaw, while the other one is out cold.

"Jesus Christ!" A gruff voice yells from somewhere inside. A moment later, Moe—who is not much smaller than Bobby—comes around the corner. He must have been watching the entire thing from the office windows. "What the hell is goin' on out here?"

I step up and place a hand on Sebastian's hand, staying him, because the last thing I want him doing is beating up a fifty-something-year-old man. Even if he's betraying Ned by not helping the police.

"Just a disagreement, Moe."

"Yeah, well, I can see that." He glares at Sebastian and then takes in the three men, all conscious now. "About what?"

"About him talking to Ivy in a way I didn't appreciate," Sebastian says with complete calm.

"She fucking started it!" Bobby bellows, like a child.

Moe smirks. "You know, when you were five, you used to chase Ivy around Black Rabbit, trying to get her to kiss you?" He turns to look at me. "Didn't work then, and I assume it's not gonna work now. What's the matter, honey?"

"Someone trashed Ned's house two nights ago. They were looking for something."

Understanding flickers past Moe's eyes. "We're looking around. We're asking some questions. Be patient."

Ned always said that these guys don't work with the police, even when it has no impact on them, out of principle. But at least they haven't just forgotten about him. Unless Moe's lying to me right now.

"What about this debt that Ned has with Sullivan? Do I have to worry about some asshole trying to take Black Rabbit from me?"

Moe turns and spears his son with a stern look. I'm guessing he wasn't supposed to mention that. "It's taken care of."

I frown. "What does that mean?"

"It means that Sully ain't seein' another dime out of a gambling bet that didn't cost him none anyway and he's just gonna have to live with that. We made sure he gets it. Now leave it be!"

I bite my tongue from any snappy reply. Yelling at Bobby is one thing . . . "Thanks, Moe. Sorry about . . . this." I wave a hand at the three guys still sitting on their asses in the gravel.

"Yeah, well . . ." Moe glances at them and starts to chuckle.

"I gotta get back to Ned's house now. There's a month's worth of work there." I grab Sebastian's biceps and pull him back to his car before Bobby can get to his feet and take a run at him.

"You were supposed to stay at Dakota's until I came," Sebastian says evenly, though I hear the irritation hidden.

*You were supposed to stay last night!* "Ten o'clock didn't work for me," I say instead, calmly.

I attempt to move past him to my car but he grabs my arm, pulling me into him. I stand my ground, my heart racing. Daring him to say something confrontational about the fact that I disobeyed him. And struggling not to grin like an asshole with relief.

*Sebastian came back.*

His jaw clenches. "What did that guy tell you before I got here?"

"That Ned owed someone a lot of money and he was probably doing something stupid to earn it. I'm going to the house now." I glare at him, and catch myself staring at his handsome features for too long.

He releases my arm and I march to my car, my mind spinning with possibilities. My insides filled with rage.

*What did you get yourself into, Ned?*

■ ■ ■

"We can't put the house on the market like this," Becca announces, peering down her nose at the pile of trash I've already swept up. "I just . . . I won't do it."

"We'll get it cleaned up. I promise."

She sighs. "Absolutely no insurance?"

"Nope." I let the "p" pop in my mouth for emphasis. Becca—in her indigo pantsuit and white pearls and bleached blond hair pulled back in a professional bun—seems to know what she's talking about, but she has still managed to irritate me in the fifteen minutes that she's been here. I'm well aware of how bad this is, and yet she feels the need to keep telling me.

"When do you think it'll be ready for my photographer?"

"When I call you to tell you that it's ready." I honestly don't know how long it's going to take to fix this mess. Weeks, maybe. And I don't have weeks. The bills and mortgage payments on both the house and Black Rabbit need to be paid next week. Ian and I have pooled some money, but he has his own bills, and if I don't work, I can't make more money. And I can't work if I'm here every day trying to fix all this.

Becca turns to Sebastian, her drawn-on brows raised in question, as if he may have a more suitable answer for her.

"We'll see," is all he says.

Sebastian hasn't said a word to me since we parked outside the house and he snatched my house keys out of my hand. He led the way in through the front door and then disappeared, checking rooms and closets, climbing the steps, his giant frame somehow avoiding each creak, as if he already knows the house's quirks.

"Fine. Let me know." Dried macaroni crunches beneath her pumps as she picks her way along the floor and out the front door.

"She's something else," I mutter.

His eyes flicker to me but it's still radio silence. This isn't the passionate guy who took me in the bathroom last night. But it's also not the cold, protective bodyguard.

He's genuinely upset.

And now that he isn't wearing sunglasses anymore, I can see the dark circles lining his eyes. I don't think he slept last night. So where the hell did he go? Maybe he actually *did* have to leave.

I shove the last of the burgundy leather couch stuffing into a trash bag and knot the top. I've already filled two extra-large bags. Fez's cousin runs a trash pickup service—basically, an old beat-up cube van that will haul anything to the local transfer station for a fee—and he and Fez will be here in a couple of hours to take whatever I have ready to go for the cost of gas and dumping rates, plus some ink on his shoulder.

Wiping the layer of sweat from my brow with the bottom of my tank top, I take a moment to survey the place. Aside from the devastating mess, the dated walls and furniture, it's actually a nice house, with good bones. Ian's right—spending a bit of time and money here could be worth it. I could probably borrow enough to update the kitchen and bathroom, do some landscaping, replace the roof. All the kinds of things a responsible adult who had just inherited an old house would do.

If only I had a compelling reason to stay . . .

I shake my head. Who am I trying to fool? Sebastian is the sole reason I'm even entertaining the idea. Before Sebastian walked in, I was ready to pack my bags. Now he's got me thinking about home renovations.

I can't believe I've let a guy get under my skin, and so fast.

And I've been a complete asshole to him.

"I'm sorry," I finally offer, dragging my trash bag across the tile floor to toss it onto the front porch.

He picks up the broom that is lying on the floor and begins sweeping the loose macaroni into piles. "Don't do it again." His dark eyes flicker up to me as he adds, "Please."

I want to ask him why he cares, why he came back, why he

doesn't have anything better to do, anyone else to see. Why he'd stick around if I'm being so difficult.

Instead, I quietly pile the magazines and newspapers together and tie them for easy removal.

Because right now, I'm just happy he's here.

■ ■ ■

I groan, slumping against the doorframe to Ned's office. Every file on every customer that Ned has kept over the years—I'm sure he shredded the oldest ones, at least—was neatly organized in the row of cabinets.

Now, every file on every customer that Ned has kept over the years covers the floor. You can't even see the faded beige rug because of the paper.

"What do you want to do with all that?" Sebastian asks. I feel him standing close behind me.

"Shred it." I sigh. "Except for any customers I worked on while I was here, I guess. They can't take Ned's license away, but they can still take mine."

"And where are yours?"

"They should be in that pile over there, next to the upturned boxes. I just brought those in the other day." And the assholes dumped those, too.

"How will you know which ones are yours?"

Paper crunches beneath my boots as I step through the mess and stoop down to pick up a sheet, pointing out my name in Ned's scrawl on the top of the form. A twinge of sadness stirs in my stomach at the sight of it. "They'll all say my name like that, on the top."

Sebastian pulls it from my grasp and steps around me to take a seat in the office chair. He reaches down to grab a stack of papers. "Why don't you tackle your uncle's room? I can manage this."

I leave quietly, but not without a glance over my shoulder to see Sebastian eying me.

# TWENTY-SIX

# SEBASTIAN

I go for the latest records first, because I know that Ivy's clients will be in there.

And because I'm hoping that Royce has a file in here, too. I need his address.

I need to find out more about him.

Ivy's worked on a lot of customers in her seven months at the shop. I'm no longer wondering how she has a chunk of money saved. It's not on account of any criminal side jobs. She just works really hard, and at two hundred bucks an hour, she's earning a solid living for herself.

After twenty minutes of digging, I find the original paperwork Royce filled out. I fold it and tuck it into my back pocket just as Ivy passes by, tossing in two more box flats and several trash bags on her way. "You don't have to do this, you know. I wouldn't do it if I were you."

I level her with a look. I don't normally hold a grudge but I'm still pissed at her, even though she's apologized.

I can't help it. Bentley has the videotape now, so Alliance has no more use for Ivy, alive or otherwise. But Scalero, he has reason not to want her alive, a thought that's been pricking at my mind since I pulled out of Bentley's driveway this morning. An hour and a half later, that little prickle had grown into something more difficult to ignore.

And then I showed up at Dakota's to find Ivy's car gone.

I nearly came straight here, but I'm glad I went to the door first. Dakota told me she had left only ten minutes before, and where she was heading.

It's one thing to have Ivy believing that a biker gang is somehow behind all this.

It's an entirely different thing to have her confronting them about it. By the time I arrived at that auto shop, it was obvious Ivy and that big guy, Bobby, were well into it. The only other time I've had any direct experience with bikers in the past was in San Diego, and the shithead was waling on his woman outside a bar.

I wasn't going to stand back and watch that happen again.

Ivy ducks out without another word, leaving me to this nightmare.

I could easily make my excuses and leave now.

I grab a trash bag.

■ ■ ■

I've survived eighteen months of intensive SEAL training.

I've survived two tours in Afghanistan.

I've survived thirteen assignments for Bentley that no one will ever talk about, or know about.

I've been shot, stabbed, blown up, and beaten.

But it's the dozen paper cuts on my fingers that may finally break me.

"Fuck!" I curse as another page slices across my knuckle. I toss the bag aside and suck my knuckle to relieve the sting, just as Ivy speeds past. I expect a glance, a derisive snort, some mocking.

When she doesn't even lift her head, I know that something's wrong. She's been on edge all day. When I got to the auto shop, it was clear by the look in her eyes that she was happy to see me. That didn't stop her from punishing me for leaving so abruptly last night by giving me attitude. But this must be different.

Forgetting my personal woes, I make my way to her bedroom

to find her crouching over her dresser, trying to lift it back to its upright position.

"That's heavy. Let me help you with—"

"I'm fine!" she snaps, but her voice doesn't carry its normal sharpness. It's shaky and higher pitched. When I step closer, she hides her face behind a curtain of hair, turning away from me.

That's when I know.

She doesn't resist me when I scoop her up and settle onto the foam mattress—still basically intact—with her in my arms. She rests her head against my chest and my shirt grows damp with her tears, her entire little body shaking as she cries. But she barely makes a sound.

Ivy's hard shell has finally cracked.

# TWENTY-SEVEN

# IVY

I didn't cry the night of the robbery.

I didn't shed a single tear at the funeral.

And now I can't seem to stop.

I wasn't even doing anything particularly nostalgic. Tossing Ned's underwear and socks into a trash bag. Dumping his button-down shirts and jeans into a box for Goodwill. Deciding what to do with his white wedding day suit that he's kept all these years, insisting that he'd be buried in it when his time came, because the day he married Jun was the happiest day of his life, and he wanted to relive it for all eternity. His day came too early and forty pounds too heavy, unfortunately.

Then I started to think about how maybe none of this would have happened if he just hadn't been gambling, and how I can't believe I didn't know about this mess with him and that guy Sullivan trying to take Black Rabbit from him. It was happening right under my nose and I didn't have a clue, too busy poking fun at him for being old, while I lived in his house and ate his food and worked out of his shop.

And then the tears started to roll and wouldn't stop, no matter how furiously I wiped at them.

I hate letting anyone see me cry, but I don't have it in me—physically or emotionally—to push Sebastian away right now, and if I stop lying to myself for a minute, I'll admit that it feels good to have him just hold me.

It actually helps.

"Thanks," I mutter, wiping my cheeks. I pull away from my little nest against his chest and cringe, streaks of black mascara and eyeliner smeared all over the front of his white T-shirt. I can only imagine what my face looks like.

He doesn't even flinch, though, his jaw working against itself, taut. The short beard that's normally so well kept shows signs of disarray, like he didn't have time to trim and edge it today.

"You look like you didn't sleep last night," I say.

"I didn't. But I'll be fine."

What kind of errands would keep him up *all* night?

"Don't look so worried." He sighs and stretches his long legs out in front of him. We're practically sitting on the floor, him on my mattress; me, on him. The muscles in his arms are cording, probably after holding me in this position for so long.

I try to move, to relieve him of that, but he squeezes, trapping me.

"I don't want to talk about it," I warn him.

"Neither do I," he fires back with a smirk. "But do you feel a bit better now?"

I nod slowly, because I do.

He opens his mouth but hesitates. "I told you about those three good friends I lost in the war?"

"Yeah." The ones he watched die.

His Adam's apple bobs with a hard swallow. "It doesn't really sink in for a while. Weeks, sometimes months."

Is that what this is? Is it finally sinking in? I thought it already had, back in the shop the day I finished Bobby's tattoo. It would make sense, this utterly wretched sadness taking over. But then there's that news from Bobby today.

I fill Sebastian in on everything I learned before he got there. He simply listens, his thumb rubbing back and forth over my thigh casually. Affectionately.

"What do you think it means?" Can Sebastian hear the shake in my voice? The twinge of fear?

He sighs, pushing my hair off my face, his gaze drifting along my features. "I think it means your uncle got involved with people you want nothing to do with."

"I just wish I could remember something useful about that night. I keep hoping I'm just going to be hit with a detail that I somehow overlooked. Something that will help catch them."

"You can't put that pressure on yourself. You aren't responsible for what happened. It had nothing to do with you."

"But what if they come back? What if—"

He cuts my question off with a deep kiss, surprising me. With a slow roll, I suddenly find myself lying on the mattress, with Sebastian's arm crooked beneath my neck and his mouth on my neck, his scruff scratching my skin but in the most seductive way—half ticklish, half torturous.

"I won't let anything happen to you. Just listen to me next time." His voice is low and gravelly, much like last night. I can feel him growing hard against my thigh.

And I'm overcome with relief that he's not mad at me anymore. That I haven't completely screwed everything up with him today, being so mule-headed.

"Because you're a ninja?" My fingers tug at his soft T-shirt until it bunches in my hands.

I catch the smirk on his face as he lifts himself up enough to pull it over his head, uncovering that body I've come to love so much. "No, because I know how to keep people alive."

"Don't forget that I'm not paying you."

His smirk widens into a full smile, watching me as I slide my own shirt up over my head. "Don't worry, I haven't." He's already zoned in on the front clasp of my bra. He pushes the button and the material springs off.

He's resting on an elbow now, peering down at my bare upper half, his index finger trailing over my arm. "What do these mean?"

"A lot of things."

Dark eyes flash to me. "Like what?"

"Like . . ." Do I want to tell him? I've been asked that question by many people before, including Amber, and I've never given the complete truth to anyone.

He looms over me, waiting.

"Like that one there." I nod to the one he has his finger on—a classic weight scale with a tiny woman perched on one side, raised high while the empty side hangs low. "It means I'm nobody's burden. I can take care of myself."

A flicker of softness catches his eyes. "That's important to you, isn't it?"

"Yeah. And this one"—I tap the mask that Ian did for me last year in Ireland—"is *my* mask, that I like to wear to keep people from seeing how I'm feeling."

"And this one?" One by one, I describe each and every piece of ink on my arm. It's been a seven-year process beginning on my eighteenth birthday. Well planned out, each component my own design that I handed to a trusted artist—there are very few of them—to etch into my skin.

Each piece deeply personal to me.

"This one?" Sebastian's strong, large hands sweep over the beautiful woodland fairy that dances along my rib cage on my right side.

"That's Iridessa, my fairy godmother. Ned used to tell me that she'd watch over me while I was sleeping. For years, I believed him." That was one of my first pieces. Ned did it for me.

Sebastian's long fingers trail along the bramble of ivy and sharp thorns that runs along my pelvis. "And this?"

That anyone who wants past it is going to have to work for it and accept a few wounds. "What do you think it means?" I say instead.

His hand slides past it, down the front of my leggings and into my panties. "That it doesn't apply to me."

Completely unabashed by how wet I am right now, I close my eyes and turn toward Sebastian, finding a corner of that thick, strong neck of his to lay my mouth on, tasting just a hint of salt on his skin. I love the taste of Sebastian, I decide, as I fumble over his belt buckle and zipper, quickly unfastening them so I can wrap my fist around him.

I groan in protest when his hand suddenly disappears, but I soon realize it's only so he can pull my leggings down, over my hips and thighs. I help him, kicking my legs until they work their way down to my boots. They won't get past those.

"I'm stuck," I whisper.

"Are you?" He lifts his head to assess the situation, smiling a touch, before his gaze rakes over me and his hand lands between my legs once again.

I reach up to pull his face back to mine, but he's already on the move, leaving a wet, ticklish trail across my nipples and down the center of my body with his tongue and his scratchy beard, all the way down until my thighs are resting on his shoulders and his hot breath is skating over me. Torturing me.

I lift my pelvis until I feel his mouth against me. He's smiling, I can tell. I don't care if he knows how much I want this. I *am* needy right now.

And with the first swipe of his tongue, I know that this isn't going to take long at all.

The doorbell rings.

Sebastian pulls away.

"Ignore it," I growl, reaching to pull his face back down.

He complies, his hands squeezing my thighs tight. I weave my fingers around the back of his head, relaxing as he keeps going.

Until my phone begins to ring. It's Fez's ringtone. He's outside, with the truck.

I forgot about the truck.

"Dammit," I curse. "Stop. This isn't going to happen now." Fez is doing me a huge favor, but he's not the most patient guy out there. He'll leave.

Sebastian lays a few kisses on the insides of my thighs and then climbs off the bed, tucking that impressive dick that I pulled out back into his pants. "I'll be down . . . in a minute." He leaves me to get dressed and ducks into the bathroom. To pee, to wash me off his face, to jerk off. Probably all three.

And I want to be in there to help him.

Throwing my clothes on, I storm down the stairs and throw open the door, chanting to myself, "Fez is helping me, Fez is helping me, Fez is . . ." so I don't bite his head off the second I see him like the frustrated bitch I now am.

"Yo! I'm turning gray out here!" Fez exclaims.

"Sorry. Got caught up with something," I mumble.

"We're ready. Called up my homies, figured you could use the *halp*." True to his word, the cube van is parked outside and open. Joker and Weazy are tossing the trash bags already on the curb in.

"Seriously?" Suddenly, I can deal with Fez's weird obsession with slang. Three extra sets of hands and this place may be all cleaned up by tonight. "This is huge. I don't know what to say." I back up and let all three of them in.

"That face, though." Fez cringes at me and the black mascara that I'm sure is streaking across my cheeks. "Channeling your inner Cruella de Vil?"

"Shut up." He deserved it for that one.

Weazy and Joker step into the kitchen and let out a low whistle.

"It's better than it was," I say, reaching for another full trash bag to pass to them.

"Then it must have been a fucking wreck because damn . . . half the places in Mission look better than this," Joker says, scratching his shaved head.

"Well, then I guess I'm lucky to have you three to help me, right?" I toss the broom to Fez. "Here. You're good with one of these, right?" I give him a wink to soften the blow, as the guys start throwing jeers at him.

Sebastian's heavy footfalls down the stairs quiet them.

"Oh, I see how it is. 'Got caught up'?" Fez stares at me.

I just shrug. I don't need to answer to any of these guys. "Hey, guys, this is Sebastian. Sebastian, these are the guys. You already know Fez."

"The bro with the sick work, yeah." Fez reaches out with a fist and, to my surprise, Sebastian responds with one of his own. If Fez knew that the "bro with the sick work" was really an ex–Navy SEAL and bodyguard, he'd have a full-on man crush in under ten minutes. And then trail Sebastian around, driving him nuts.

"Dude, I thought she wasn't into dick?" I hear Weazy whisper to Joker from behind me.

"Seriously? She's just not into yours."

I shake my head at Sebastian, but he's smirking. Speaking of dick . . . I drop my gaze.

Yeah, I know what he was doing in the bathroom.

■ ■ ■

"What time is dinner?" Sebastian asks from the edge of my bed at Dakota's, kicking off his shoes.

"Dakota should be home in an hour." I dry my hands at the bathroom sink and peer over to get a good look at him. He looks like hell. "You need to sleep."

He rubs the back of his neck. "I'll be fine."

"Seriously, you were up all night, weren't you? You can lie down for an hour." I will, too, gladly. Beside him . . .

On top of him . . .

I guess we'll see. Maybe I should actually let him sleep.

He sighs, but he's smiling. "I was trained to stay awake for a lot longer than twenty-four hours."

"Oh, yeah?" I wander over to help him lift his T-shirt off his body. It's covered in drywall dust and dirt from hours of cleaning up. He could probably use a shower. Something else I'd like to try out with him, but maybe later. "What else were you trained to do?"

He eases back onto the bed, the springs creaking under his weight, to give me a good look at my work. It's healing nicely. "All kinds of things," he murmurs through a giant yawn.

I duck back into the bathroom to clean the smeared makeup off my face and brush my teeth, then decide that I really do need to hop into the shower to wash the day's grime from my skin, with or without him. Ideally, with him.

"Hey, did you want to . . ." My voice drifts off. Sebastian is stretched out on his back, his arm beneath his head, snoring softly.

After my shower, I tiptoe to the other side and ease onto the bed in my towel, expecting him to wake up with the dip of the mattress. I mean, he was a Navy SEAL. Don't they sleep light?

He doesn't so much as twitch; he's out cold, his normally taut jaw relaxed, his features almost boyish. So I simply lie there and watch him sleep for more than an hour as I fail at drifting off myself, until I hear the front door creak open and Dakota's welcoming hum.

I duck out to the living room and let Sebastian rest.

TWENTY-EIGHT

# SEBASTIAN

I wake with a start, my body jerking enough to shake the bed.

A soft moan beside me instantly brings me back to reality. I laid down in Ivy's bed. It was close to four in the afternoon. I was going to just grab an hour, at most.

I glance at the window. It's dark out now, the streetlight casting a dim light into the bedroom.

It's . . . Holy shit. I've been asleep for almost eleven hours? I can't remember the last time I slept this long without drugging myself with Ambien. And to not even stir when Ivy came around . . . No one's ever been able to step into a room without my waking up before.

"You're alive," Ivy mumbles, tucked under the covers, her eyes still closed, her jet-black hair fanning across the pillow. "You missed dinner. I thought you might have died in your sleep."

I can't help but smile. "And you willingly crawled into bed with a corpse?"

"Corpses are quiet, and I was tired."

"Did you even try to wake me?"

"Of course I did . . ." The words drag out in that tired, half-asleep way. "Then I stripped you down and took nude pictures of you with me, then with Dakota and with the bearded lady. Going to ask Fez to post them all over the Internet in the morning. You and Gerti are going to be famous."

I frown. She seems coherent but she's not making any sense. "Gerti?"

"The bearded lady from the circus. Dakota's dinner guest tonight."

"You're kidding, right?" She says it all so deadpan, I'm beginning to wonder.

She sighs. "Not about the beard."

I smile. But check my belt buckle all the same. "You're cute when you're half-asleep."

"Half-asleep and naked," she points out.

Just the thought of Ivy naked stirs my blood. Yesterday at the house, having to stop partway through was torture for me. By the looks she cast my way all afternoon, I left her just as frustrated. And then I fell asleep the moment we got here.

I reach under the bedsheet to find nothing but her warm flesh beneath. She rolls onto her back, letting the sheet fall away.

To entice me, I'm sure.

It works.

■ ■ ■

Ivy peers up at me through hazy, satisfied eyes. "I still can't believe you slept that long. You must have been a shitty SEAL."

"The worst." I place a kiss on her forehead, and another one on the tip of her nose. "I'm going to duck out now."

"Now? It's five in the morning."

"Do me a favor and stay put. I'll call you." When she doesn't agree, I press. "I mean it, Ivy."

"Fine," she grumbles, rolling away from me, curling into her sheet.

■ ■ ■

The doorbell makes a low buzzing sound when I press the button. I wait, and a few minutes later I hear the footfalls coming from the other side. Whoever it is, they walk on their heels.

The door to the small pink house flies open and a disheveled woman appears, midway through pulling a short pink silk robe over her rumpled boxers and a white tank top—no bra, her small tits sagging in different directions. A waft of incense floats out the door with her movements.

I guess eight-thirty in the morning is a little early to be paying house calls. "Hi, is Dylan around?" I ask.

She looks me up and down, tucking her yellow-blond hair behind an ear and then folding her arms self-consciously over her chest. "Who are you?"

"My name's John. I was in Afghanistan with him." I know enough about the Marine Corps to get by. I just hope she doesn't know enough to ask too many questions.

"How'd you get this address?" she asks, her eyes pinched with suspicion.

This must be the cheating girlfriend that Dylan was talking about in the video. She's not particularly friendly, but that could just be the situation. Either way, she may have useful information about her ex. "Dylan gave it to me awhile back. Told me to stop by when I was in town again. I tried emailing him but never got an answer, so I figured I'd just surprise him." I have no idea how long Royce was living here, but thanks to Bentley's recon, I do know that he wasn't living here when he died.

"I'm sorry to have to tell you this, but Dylan was shot and killed a couple weeks ago." Her voice wobbles. Bad breakup or not, she's obviously upset by it.

I slide my glasses off because that's the appropriate thing to do, though I'd rather keep my eyes hidden. "Seriously?" Luckily I can pull off a compelling cool, shocked reaction very easily. "What happened?"

She gives me the basic rundown—nothing that anyone who read the newspaper article wouldn't know about.

"Man, I'm just so . . . this is crazy."

"I know, right?" She swallows, blinks back the glossiness in her eyes. "I mean . . . we actually broke up a few weeks before that and then this happens. Shocking, isn't it?"

"Yeah. I hadn't talked to him in *at least* five months. Maybe longer. He was still over in Kabul with Alliance."

"Oh." She sneers. "Those assholes. They didn't even send flowers to his funeral. I know he wasn't working for them anymore, but—"

"He wasn't?"

She shakes her head. "They fired him."

"They *fired* him? He's earned a damn Medal of Honor! Why the hell would they do that?"

She shrugs. "Dylan changed a lot after he started working for those guys. You know how he was." She waves a hand my way. "He used to laugh and clown around. He was so happy and helpful. Just a genuinely good guy. But after he went back with them . . . he wasn't the same guy anymore. He was angry. He started doing drugs. Something there changed him."

I wish she had told me something different. That he was an abusive drunk, that he had always been a dick. Something that might suggest he was no better than Mario when it came to those poor girls, that he deserved the bullet.

"This is awful news."

"I know. I'm sorry to be the one to break it to you."

I pause. "I'd love to go see his mother and offer her my condolences. Would you happen to have her address?"

She studies my face—I twitch against the urge to reach up and touch my jaw; I shaved the beard off this morning, and it feels strange to be clean shaven after so many years under shadow. But if I'm going to be showing my face around San Francisco, digging for information, I need to make a small effort to camouflage my usual self.

A small smile touches her pale lips. She's pretty enough, in a boring, average way. Not an exotic Ivy way. "Sure. Hold on a sec." She disappears, leaving the door open a crack. I could slip in there now, end her life and stroll out, no one the wiser. It never ceases to amaze me how easily people trust strangers, how many simple mistakes they make that allow the wrong person into their homes, into their lives. Even Ivy, as street smart and suspicious as she is, has allowed me into her *bed*.

That's not to say she's oblivious, that she isn't quietly wondering about me.

Ivy didn't say much more about what the biker told her about her uncle, his gambling issues, and the sizable debt he accrued. I'm sure it's still percolating, but she won't show it. That's the way she operates. And that mind of hers, it's a sharp, dangerous thing because she's already figured out all on her own the gist of her uncle's fuckup: He had something he was trying to sell, and it got him killed.

"Here." Royce's ex-girlfriend hands me a Post-it note with an address in Sunset scribbled on it in blue pen. "If you don't mind, could you also pass this bag of Dylan's things along? Just a few things that he left behind."

I take the bag, silently thanking her. This will make my next stop easier. "And, again, I'm sorry for your loss." I feel her eyes on my back as I march down the steps and head down the street to where I parked.

■ ■ ■

Dylan's mom lives in a small bungalow in one of San Francisco's biggest neighborhoods. I used to hang out here a lot in my teenage years. It's close to the beach and lots of college kids rent out places. I woke up in more than one random bed around here, back in the day.

Now that I'm walking up the street, I'm rethinking the wisdom of speaking with these people. I've always followed the rule that I don't make contact unless absolutely necessary. That's how I remain an effective ghost.

But my need to know more about Royce overrides my common sense at this point.

I'm just about to turn from the sidewalk onto the path that leads to his mom's mint-green door when I hear a whimper coming from behind the fence that wraps around the side of the house. A small black snout pokes out.

I smile.

■  ■  ■

The woman's eyes widen as soon as she opens the door and sees the golden hairball—a Pekingese, or some version of it—squirming in my grip.

"Ma'am. She was running along the street. Her collar says that she belongs here."

Her hands go to her chest with shock. "But how did she get out of the backyard?" She looks from the dog—Fefe, from the tag—to her left, to the yard beyond the house. "I just let her out to do her business."

"The gate is open."

She frowns. "No. It can't be. I remember latching it last night. Unless . . ." I watch closely as the poor woman—in her late sixties, by the level of wrinkles around her jaw and eyes—doubts her memory. Deep bags hang beneath her eyes. The dazed eyes of a woman who just lost her son and hasn't wrapped her head around it yet.

Fefe finally twists her body enough that I can't hold on any longer without hurting her. So I bend down and gently herd her into the house.

"Oh, goodness. Thank you so much, young man. She could have been hit by a car," she says, silently accepting that maybe she did forget to latch it. I feel only slightly bad for deceiving her, but rescuing a dog is a surefire way to earn a senior citizen's instant trust.

"Are you by any chance Dylan Royce's mother?"

She pauses, frowns. "Yes."

"I was on my way here anyway. I wanted to offer my condolences. My name's John. Dylan was a friend of mine. I'm very sorry for your loss, ma'am."

Her eyes begin to water as her head bobs up and down in silent thanks. "It was terrible. He survived so many years in the war and then he was shot in a tattoo parlor, right here in his own city." She produces a tissue from a pocket and blows her nose. "Would you like to come in for coffee?"

That was even easier than I had expected.

■ ■ ■

"Here he is, receiving his medal." She taps on the picture of her son, shaking hands with the president. "I never saw his father more proud of Dylan than on that day. When he passed away six months later, it was as a happy man."

"I can understand why." An hour after sitting down to a pot of hot coffee, listening patiently as a devastated mother showcases his local hero medals, and his time as a volunteer firefighter, with letters from little girls and boys who thanked him for saving their kittens from trees and dogs from house fires; a picture of a baby he delivered on the side of the freeway. To top it all off, the highest medal that anyone can receive.

I'm now all but convinced that Royce was not the trouble-maker that Bentley painted him as. And if he was, it's probably because he didn't agree with what he was seeing over there.

And that is what got him killed.

And no one will ever know the truth, thanks to me.

I'm not sure what I expected to feel after I confirmed this hunch, but it's not this sickly pain in the pit of my stomach.

His mom sniffles. "As much as I hated what happened to Dylan and Jasmine, I was so happy to have him back home for a while, to help me with cutting the grass and taking out the trash, all those house things. Taking care of this house is a lot of work for just me."

I glance around at the small tidy house, in need of a good purge that I'm guessing won't happen until after she's gone. "Do you have any family in the area?"

She shakes her head. "My sister lives near Syracuse with her kids. They asked me to move there, but I can't handle the snow. So it's just me and Fefe now." At the sound of her name, the little dog runs up to paw at her thigh. Royce's mom leans over and scoops her up, giving the top of her head a kiss. "I can't thank you enough. Had I lost her, too, I don't know that I could handle it."

"My pleasure, ma'am. Glad I could help." This woman has helped—and burdened—me so much more.

"Isn't that right, Fefe? You should say thank you to this man." Royce's mother looks up at me and smiles. "She just loves company. The detective on the case has been over a few times and she's always at his ankles."

I fight to keep my face calm, curious. So Fields has been here? "Have they told you whether they have any leads?"

She shakes her head through a sip of coffee. "They don't seem to know anything. At first they said it was a robbery. Then they said it was likely a disagreement between the shop owner and someone. And then, just a few days ago, that Detective Fields started asking questions about Dylan's old job at that company."

"Alliance."

"Yes. Them."

"Are they thinking this is related to his old job?" This could just be routine questioning. This detective may just be doing his job thoroughly.

"They're looking at all possibilities, he told me." She shrugs. "He took my album, though. The one I made with all the pictures Dylan sent me over the years while on deployment. He promised he'd give it back to me when he's done. It's all I really have left of my son."

A sinking feeling hits my stomach. "Pictures of him with the Marines?"

"Yes." She smiles sadly. "He knew I loved getting pictures from him, seeing him safe and sound. Most times he'd just email them over, but I'd print them out and put them in this big square scrapbook. He kept doing it while he was at Alliance, though he wasn't sending nearly as many pictures by the end."

Which means there's a chance that Fields now has an album with pictures of both Mario and Ricky.

Fuck. If he puts two and two together, then Ivy's eyewitness testimony is all the more important.

And it makes her a threat to them.

And to Bentley.

It'll take Fields time, though, to do that. Unless a Mario is named in that album. Then it won't take much time at all. "I wonder if Dylan sent you a picture of us . . ."

Her face crinkles into a smile. "Oh, I don't know. I'll be sure to check the pictures more carefully when I get it back. I don't remember seeing any Johns in there, but of course, he rarely included names."

Okay. If Dylan's mom didn't identify them by name, then that may buy me some more time. I reach over to grab a pen. On the corner of the newspaper, I jot down my new cell number. "If you need some help, please give me a call."

"I'll call you when I get my album back. Thank you, John. That's so kind of you. All of you boys have been so good to me, coming by to visit."

"Family is important to all of us." I smile and feel like a complete hypocrite.

I say my good-byes and leave, my guilt over being involved with this cover-up growing with each step.

# TWENTY-NINE

# IVY

"Rough morning?" I ask, eying Sebastian's stony face from the passenger side. Considering he left my bed at five this morning after logging in eleven hours of sleep *and* getting laid—repeatedly—he should be outright chipper, not in this mercurial mood.

Which makes me wonder where he goes when he's not with me.

My distrustful side tells me he goes home to a girlfriend. Maybe they're on the outs, but still . . . that shit ain't cool. I push those thoughts out of my head, though. They're a sign of insecurity, which is the last thing I will let creep in.

"Have you ever had someone you trust completely betray you?" he asks softly. I don't think he meant to say that out loud, though, because when I turn to study him, he's clamped his mouth shut.

I can't help staring at his profile for a long moment. He shaved off his short beard, and he looks very different. Younger. No less handsome, though I can't decide which look I prefer.

"I don't think I've ever trusted someone completely." Except maybe Ned, and look where that got me, because I trusted him not to do something so stupid as to get himself shot.

"There's something for you on the backseat," Sebastian says, abruptly changing the topic.

I turn to find a small white Macy's bag sitting there. With a frown, I loop my finger around the string to grab it. Inside is a brand-new bottle of my favorite perfume.

"I figured you needed another one."

"Yeah. I did. But . . . how did you know which one?"

"I took the lid with me yesterday."

"Sneaky." I didn't notice. "So you really like it or is this a subtle hint?"

He smirks. "I really like it."

"Thanks." I guess I know what he was doing for part of this morning, at least. I tuck the gift into my purse. "When do you think you'll need to go back to work?"

"I'm taking some time off. A few more weeks, at least."

"So this isn't just a normal vacation?"

"Considering I'm about to spend another day cleaning up a ransacked house, I'd say that it's definitely not a normal vacation."

I reach over to pat his knee—affectionate gestures are not really my thing, but I desperately want to touch him—and offer, "I appreciate the help. Thank you."

He traps my hand beneath his before I have a chance to pull it back, curling his fingers between mine as he makes a turn into the neighborhood.

"You know, every time we turn down here now, I keep thinking that I hope whoever did this to the house found what they were looking for. I hope they never come back."

"If they do, then I guess it's good you have me here."

I roll my eyes. "I told you, you're not my bodyguard."

"So you say . . ." The tiny smirk curling his lips is adorable.

"I'm not paying you." I pause. "Unless you're taking sexual favors for payment."

His gaze veers off the street to settle on me for a moment. "I'm not opposed to that arrangement."

A bubble of nerves bursts in my stomach. He doesn't sound like he's planning on leaving me anytime soon.

The bubble is quashed the second we turn the corner to find three guys on Harleys parked outside the house.

I recognize the blond beard immediately. "What the hell is Bobby doing here?"

"Stay put," Sebastian says, throwing the car in Park. He slips his gun out from his boot and tucks it into the back of his pants.

I open the door and climb out, my adrenaline pumping. He sighs with exasperation, but he doesn't scold me. He knows better.

We meet behind Sebastian's car and walk together toward Bobby, who's climbed off his bike.

"Nice shiner," I say, nodding at the prominent black-and-purple bruise marring Bobby's left eye. Curtains in several windows of wary neighbors across the street shift. I wonder how long I've had bikers sitting outside Ned's house.

"What are you doing here?" Sebastian asks in an icy tone, his gaze shifting to size up the other guys—the two from yesterday. Another guy I've never seen before steps out from a pickup truck parked along the curb.

Four against one. I don't like these odds.

"We came to offer a hand." Bobby looks directly at me, ignoring Sebastian. "Ned was family to us, which means you're family, too. Carl over there," he points to the guy who got out of the truck, "does plaster. You need someone who knows what they're doing for that."

"Did Moe send you?"

Bobby's lip twitches just slightly. "Maybe."

I heave a sigh. I'm not in a position to tell them to go to hell, even though I'm still pissed at Bobby for leaving me in the dark about Ned's gambling situation. "Great. We can use all the help we can get." Spearing Sebastian with a warning glare and a whispered hiss of "Don't beat them up again" just loud enough that Bobby can hear it—for ego-bruising purposes—we head into the house.

# THIRTY

# SEBASTIAN

It's been a long time since I sat on a front porch with a cold beer, watching the sun set after hours of hard manual labor.

I forgot how good this feels.

Dean and Thomas—the guys I knocked out yesterday—are loading the last of the debris into the back of the truck. That's the third trip to the dump for them today. They've stayed out of my way for the most part. All of them have.

"So, if we come back here tomorrow, will you be here?" Bobby asks.

I roll my eyes through another sip. Dakota showed up about an hour ago with a twelve-pack of Coronas and some homemade muffins that Ivy interrogated her over before allowing her to hand them out. Bobby and his guys have been trailing her around like lost puppies after their owner, and she's happily let them, flicking her hair over her shoulder, showing off the tattoo Ivy just did for her.

"I guess you'll have to come back and help Ivy to find out, won't you?" Dakota laughs. It's such a soft, seductive laugh. I have to hand it to her—she knows how to manipulate men into getting what she wants, and right now that's helping her friend fix this house.

"Oh, we'll be here until this place is as good as new. Don't you worry." The dumbass is falling right into her trap.

"Good." Her sandals slide against the concrete steps as she makes her way down to sit beside me. "How's that beer?"

"Nice and cold. Thanks."

She smiles boldly at me. If it were anyone else, I'd say she was flirting, but I don't think that's the case with her. Glancing over her shoulder, she murmurs, "Who knew these bikers could be good for something besides causing trouble?"

"We should have the place fixed with a few days of solid work."

"I think Ivy should stay in San Francisco. Don't you?"

I blink at the sudden change in subject. "If she wants to, then yeah. It's a great city."

"She wants to. She just hasn't admitted it to herself yet. But I've never seen her this happy."

A sudden, angry holler of "Dammit, Bobby!" coming from inside makes me nearly spit out my mouthful of beer. "Is that so?" I ask with a wry smile. But inside, her words are resonating deep with me. I don't think *I've* been this happy in a long time either. Even with all the guilt and worry that's eating me up inside.

Dakota leans over to rub my biceps with her arm. "And she's perfect for you. I can just *feel* it. It's like"—she holds her hands in the air, her fingers rubbing together as if testing out an invisible fabric—"those first few warm days when the ice begins to melt. When you just know that the long, cold winter is over."

I have no fucking clue what she's getting at, but tension slips into my back with her choice of words. I know that's all it is—a word— and it's just coincidental, but it reminds me who I am. I'm not really this guy who follows a woman around, shares meals and beds, shops for locks and perfume. I'm only pretending to be him right now.

What if Ivy finds out?

"I'll leave dinner out for you two," Dakota says with a smile and a pat, climbing down the steps and heading to her car, a vintage yellow Volkswagen Bug. Exactly what I'd expect her to drive.

I sip the rest of my beer slowly as I watch first Dakota pull away, and then Carl in his pickup truck. Dean and Thomas follow minutes later, with silent but respectful waves to me that I match, the deep rumble of their Harley engines earning a few glances out of neighborhood windows.

It's when I tip my head back to finish my beer that I catch a glimpse of the figure sitting in the navy sedan down the street. I noticed the car there three hours ago, but it was empty. Or I thought it was.

Now it's very clearly not.

"Hey, you want another one?" Bobby asks from behind.

I would have said no. Now I reach up over my head and feel him shove the ice-cold can in it. Cracking it open, I force my eyes away from the car and the figure inside for just long enough to pretend I haven't noticed it.

Bobby hunkers down beside me, wiping the sweat from his brow with his forearm. "Jeez, that one has a temper on her."

"She has to compensate for her size somehow."

He bursts out in laughter, but then glances over his shoulder. "Don't let her hear you say that. You'll end up with your nuts in a sack on your pillow by morning."

I was always good at carrying on a conversation while scoping out enemy territory, but I'm struggling to do it now. Maybe I've been working alone too long. I just want Bobby to leave so I can figure out who the hell is in that car.

I'm pretty sure I already know.

"Where are you from?" he asks.

"Here."

"Yeah? Same. Went to school in Colma."

I sip on my beer instead of answering, letting the silence drag on.

"So, you and Ivy?"

Now I turn my attention to the burly blond guy next to me, to glare at him. "Are we really doing this, man?" I'm not going to sit on the steps and talk about whatever's happening between the two of us.

He shrugs and climbs the steps, disappearing back into the house.

"Thanks for the beer," I call out, taking the steps down two at a time. I walk to the end of the driveway and make a point of staring at the shadow in the car. Letting him know I see him.

The car pulls away from the curb and takes the first left turn. Too far away for me to catch the license plate.

*So this is how it's going to be, is it?*

I grit my teeth against the bubble of anger rising. Is this Bentley? Is it that fucking idiot Mario?

I reach into my pocket to pull my burner out, to call Bentley and blast him. But no . . . fuck it. I've warned them both.

I won't warn them again.

# IVY

"What do you know about this guy?" Bobby asks, peering out the window in Ned's living room. It has a perfect view of the front porch, and of Sebastian standing at the edge of the driveway, staring at something down the street that I can't see.

I fold my arms across my chest. "Enough." My body is aching from hours of stooping over and climbing stairs and lifting. I don't know how many times I had one of these guys trying to tell me to back off because something was too heavy for me, and me yelling at them that I'm fine.

I should have listened.

"Why?"

"Dude's weird."

"No he's not. He's just quiet. That's how I like my men. Not chatterboxes." I stare pointedly at Bobby. He hasn't shut up for more than five minutes all day.

"Where does he live?"

"In a house."

"Ivy . . ."

"He kicked your asses yesterday. Like I'm going to give you guys his home address."

Bobby scratches the back of his head. "Yeah, he did. What kind of guy needs to know how to do that?"

"He was in the navy. He served in Afghanistan," I finally offer, more because I want Bobby and the guys to show some respect for Sebastian.

Bobby nods slowly, as if that clears things up for him. "What does he do now?"

"He's a bodyguard."

"For what company?"

I shrug and scowl. "I don't know."

"I can ask around. What's his last name?"

"You're not asking around about him. Leave him alone."

Bobby looks at me in shock. "You don't even know the guy's last name, do you?"

"So what if I don't? I don't know *your* last name. Hell, I don't know what your dad's real name is!" I know it's not Moe, just like Tiny's real name isn't Tiny.

"Yeah, but you're not bangin' my dad or me."

I cringe at the suggestion.

"I'm just lookin' out for ya, is all. That's what Ned would want us to do. This guy just shows up out of the blue right after Ned dies, and now he's stuck on you like glue."

"He doesn't do things half-assed." I think it's all-or-nothing with a guy like him. Just like it's all-or-nothing with me.

"Yeah . . ." Bobby doesn't sound convinced. "Something about him doesn't sit right with me. You've always been a smart girl. Use your gut and get some answers about him. I don't trust him."

"Funny. He doesn't trust you either." Though Sebastian hasn't come out and said it, I see it in his eyes every time he looks at Bobby.

"Yeah . . . I figured as much. I'm takin' off now." He slings his jacket over his shoulder. "Same time tomorrow?"

I sigh, offering a grudging, "Thanks for the help."

"Thank my dad. He tore a strip off my hide yesterday for gettin' mad at ya."

I listen to Bobby's heavy footsteps pound down the steps, considering his words.

Sebastian is still a mystery, I'm aware of that. But is there something that I definitely *need* to know, and now?

Something he's not telling me?

The last thing I want to do is pry. He'll tell me more about himself when he's ready, just like Dakota said. As weird as she is, she has the uncanny ability of being right about these things.

"Hey, Ivy!" Sebastian's deep voice calls out and my entire being automatically responds, my heart skipping a beat, energy spiking, a thrill coursing through my limbs. All at the sound of his voice calling my name.

"Yeah?"

"Let's head out. I need to eat."

"Coming."

■ ■ ■

"Ned used to eat subs at least three times a week," I murmur through a mouthful. Not graceful, I know, but I'm starving.

"Hey, listen, would Dakota mind if I stay at your place for a few nights?" he asks, his eyes are on his rearview mirror more than the road ahead, as they have been since we left Ned's house.

"Not at all." I frown. "What's wrong with your place?"

"Plumbing issues."

I pick away quietly at the sandwich, not believing his answer but having no good reason to question it openly. Plus, that means Sebastian's guaranteed to be in my bed for the next few nights. Win-win.

The light ahead turns yellow. I'm expecting Sebastian to stop, because there's plenty of time. Instead he slams his foot on the gas and the engine roars as it kicks into high gear. I nearly choke on my mouthful of Dr Pepper as we sail through the intersection on a red light, earning blasts of angry horns as Sebastian swerves around a turning car.

Not until we've slowed down does he ask, "Are you okay?"

I turn to glare at him. "I'm fantastic."

His steely look breaks for just a second with a tiny smirk, but he doesn't say anything else.

■ ■ ■

I'm a deep sleeper. Once I'm out, I'm out for the night. But I'm not used to sharing a bed with anyone, or having anyone in my room while I sleep, period. I guess that's why I keep waking up through the night. I'm usually draped across Sebastian's body—an arm here, a leg there. This bed is only a double, and while I'm small, Sebastian takes up well over half, lying on his back.

But tonight, when my eyes crack open at three a.m., Sebastian isn't even lying beside me. He's settled in front of the window on the wooden chair that normally sits in the corner—a creaky, narrow antique that groans under the slightest weight—with one foot resting on the windowsill, an arm draped over his knee. His hard gaze is locked on the street beyond the billowy white eyelet lace curtain where he has pushed it aside.

I remain still and study him—his long muscular body, the faint streetlight streaming in highlighting the curves and hard edges. He's pulled on his briefs, much to my dismay, as I would have had a great view of *all* of him from this angle. As it is, I can still see my detailed work on his torso, which I find myself loving more and more each time he lets me tend to it.

"I know you're awake."

My heart jumps at the sound of his deep voice cutting into the silence, but then I smile. "How do you know?"

"Your breathing changed."

"You've been listening to me breathe? Why?"

"Because I like the sound of it. It's peaceful."

He hasn't turned from the window yet, so I continue my unabashed study of him. "How do you stay in such great shape?"

"I work out almost every day."

"You haven't the last couple of days."

"No." The corners of his mouth twitch. "I've been too busy."

I'm not sure if he's referring to the mess at the house, or the nights in this bed. I'll assume both.

My gaze wanders down. He has a runner's legs and I'm guessing he's fast. "What's that scar on your thigh?" I've noticed he protects his left leg whenever we're together, putting more weight on his right side. It looks like it might have been painful.

His hand slides over it, his jaw tensing a touch. He doesn't answer right away, and I don't push, simply watching him.

"Bullet wound."

Sebastian's been shot? I guess I shouldn't be surprised given his history and his career—and all the scars on him—but . . . I know skin and scarring, and that one is fresh.

The idea of Sebastian being shot recently ties my stomach up in knots.

"While you were working?" I assume so, given his job.

"Yes."

"Is your client okay?" Maybe not. Maybe this is why he's taking time off.

He nods, and I breathe a sigh of relief that I'm sure he can read. "Well, that's good." So maybe he took a bullet for the person. That would be commendable. I wonder when it happened and where. Was it in the news? I should pay more attention to the news.

"Does that happen a lot? You getting hurt?"

"Not a lot. Occasionally."

"Do you love your job?" He must. Why else would you do this?

"Yes and no."

I wait, watching him, hoping he'll elaborate.

"I'm really good at what I do."

"I imagine so." I've felt a thousand times safer since Sebastian stepped into my life, and he's not even my bodyguard. Officially, anyway. With the amount of sex we've been having, I may as well be claiming it as payment, all joking aside. Then again, I'm benefiting from it as much as he is.

"When do you not love it?"

His Adam's apple bobs with a hard swallow. "When I have to do things in order to protect innocent people. Things that a lot of people may not approve of. That may scare them."

I try to hide my frown but I fail. He's not looking at me, but I'm sure he saw it. He seems to see everything. *What kind of things would a bodyguard possibly do, besides fire back?* I bite back the question before it slips out, because my instincts tell me he'll tell me if he wants to, when he's ready. He's simply testing the waters with me right now, I gather. As in, *Would Ivy approve? Would Ivy be scared?*

I'm not afraid of Sebastian. The first day he strolled into the shop, I was. But since then, he's been this calm, quiet, reliable safety net for me. He operates with discipline and control and, my gut says, by a moral code. And somewhere in the mix of chaos, I think I've started developing real feelings for him.

*That* scares me more than anything he might have done.

But right now, I think he's waiting for some kind of answer from me. My breath shakes with a deep inhale. "Do you ever have a choice, doing whatever you've had to do?"

"No." His answer comes quickly, without hesitation. "Not if I want to save lives."

"Were you protecting someone who deserves to live?"

"Yes." Again, not a waver.

"Then I'm sure you've always done the right thing, even if it's not the easy thing."

His shoulders seem to sag with relief, as if he needed to hear that. I'm glad I said it, even as I'm quietly wondering what he's hiding. Bobby's warning from earlier resurfaces. He's not comfortable around Sebastian, that much is obvious. It could simply be because Sebastian leveled him and two of his guys without breaking a sweat.

But what if it's something else? I'm usually intuitive. Ned always said my mind was as sharp as an upturned tack lying on the floor, waiting for an unsuspecting foot.

What if my feelings for Sebastian are blinding my senses? Because, even with those thoughts swirling inside my head, all I see is a man I am beginning to care deeply about.

*I'm falling for you.*

He pries his eyes from the street to settle them on me, and my stomach clenches because I realize that I just spoke those words out loud. I wasn't supposed to. He's not supposed to know how I feel. *Dammit, Dakota!*

A conflict is at war in his eyes, and I silently try to guess exactly what he wants to say.

That he's leaving.

That this isn't going to work.

That he knows I care way more than I ever wanted to.

That he isn't falling for me.

He says nothing, though, and after a moment, his gaze drifts over my body, covered in a sheet. I feel it as surely as I feel his hands when they glide over my bare skin. I feel it in my chest, knowing that he's not going to get up and leave after my accidental admission. At least, not just yet.

"Is there something more interesting out there on the street than in here?" I don't know how he's capable of getting me worked up with just a look.

The chair creaks in relief as he stands. "Not at all." His thumbs slide under the waistband of his briefs as he peels them off and lets them fall, giving me a good eyeful before he climbs back into bed.

It almost distracts me enough that I miss the gun lying on the windowsill.

Almost.

I push that aside because I trust that Sebastian has a good reason for having his gun lying there, and it has nothing to do with hurting me, or anyone who might not deserve it.

His weight is almost too much as he fits himself between my thighs and guides my legs around his hips. I happily comply, my fingers weaving into the mess of hair on top of his head, savoring the feel of his jawline, covered in a thin layer of dark stubble, as his mouth skates across my neck. Needing him inside me right now, to comfort me in my uncomfortable, vulnerable state.

His breathing grows heavy and fast and eager against my ear.

I expect him to reach for a condom from the nightstand. But after several long moments of him simply pressing his body against me and building my anticipation and frustration, I slide a hand under his chin and push his face up to meet my questioning gaze.

"I'm sorry. I shouldn't have said that." *I've screwed everything up, haven't I?*

He smiles. "Yeah, you should have."

Relief swallows up this awful, vulnerable feeling inside me. I trail a finger over his bottom lip and he catches it with his mouth, kissing the tip gently, intimately.

And then he leans closer and begins kissing my mouth in the same way, not like he's kissed me before, with reckless abandon. Like he's trying to tell me something with each soft sweep of his tongue, with each gentle nudge of his nose against mine.

I try to match this unusual affection with my own. To tell him what I'm feeling right now without saying the words—that I'm crazy about him, strange, mysterious ways and all.

"You know I'd never do anything to hurt you, right?" he whispers against my mouth.

"Yeah." Why is he asking? What is he thinking?

He shifts his hips and sinks into me. He pauses to meet my gaze, waiting for me to object, I'm sure. Normally, I would. Hell, I'd buck a guy off me for assuming going bareback was okay, especially without asking.

Sebastian has never objected to putting on a condom before. He was always the one reaching for one, which made me feel good because it means it's common practice for him to use them.

But I can tell by the look in his eyes now that this wasn't a forgetful slip up in the heat of the moment.

He waits inside me, letting me decide what I want to do.

How safe I feel with him.

How much I trust him.

I curl my arms around his head and pull his mouth down. And push my hips into him.

He moans softly against my ear and then starts to move, the muscles in his body cording in such a beautiful way with each thrust, as they come harder and faster, and his pants grow louder, the bed creaking noisily with each one until the headboard is knocking on the wall behind us.

I don't care about that, though. All I can think about is that
Sebastian is about to orgasm inside me.

Just the thought of that brings me immediately to the edge.
His own groans follow closely behind, and I revel in the feel of
him pulsing inside me, my thighs squeezing his body involuntarily.

My chest swelling with warmth and adoration.

I've never trusted anyone this much.

Completely.

He rolls us over so that I'm lying on top of him, but he doesn't
pull out.

We fall asleep like that.

# THIRTY-TWO

# SEBASTIAN

The lemon falls from the branch with barely a touch of my fingers.

"I was thinking of making a lemon pie later today." Dakota strolls into the greenhouse behind me, coffee in hand. "Do you like lemon pie?"

"I do." I smile, counting out four more on the branches. "They remind me of Greece."

"What's in Greece?"

"A vacation." My villa, for another week. Sitting empty.

Dakota hums softly as she plucks the other ripe fruit from their branches and drops them into the hem of a billowy white shirt. Hums, just like she did half an hour ago, when I was taking a shower and she strolled into the bathroom to pee. I didn't think to lock the pocket door from her bedroom.

There really wasn't much I could do. This *is* her quirky little house with only one bathroom.

"Thanks for letting me stay here."

"Plumbing, right?" She says it like she knows I'm lying.

"Right."

The sound of Ivy's bare feet padding into the greenhouse turns my attention and, thankfully, ends that conversation. She's fresh from the shower, her long black hair combed poker straight. I've gathered that she's not much of a morning person, because I couldn't get her up with me, even with the lure of a shared shower.

She's a deep sleeper; I know because I listened to her breathing for hours last night, while I watched the street and played through various scenarios, and then again when she went back to sleep, and I played through our conversation. Her words bring me comfort, but they're just words, born of ignorance. She'd like to believe in me, that I only do good, with the best of intentions. Hell, I'd like to think that, too. And I did, up until this assignment. But the more time I have to dwell on it, the less settled I feel for having handed that video to Bentley.

The more I wonder if I've been lied to by the only man besides my father I trust unequivocally.

"Good morning, Ivy. The pot of coffee is almost brewed. I'll get you a cup." Dakota whispers something to her on her way by, earning Ivy's confused look, and then her sharp gaze on me.

I force the dark cloud from my thoughts. "She brings you coffee, too?" I lean down to steal a quick kiss from her lips as she closes the distance, tasting the mint from her toothpaste. She's already hidden her eyes behind dark makeup.

"And breakfast, sometimes. What were you two talking about out here?"

I shrug. "Lemons. And Greece."

"You sure?"

"Yeah." I frown. "Why? What'd she say?"

"That I'm a *very* lucky girl." She smirks, her fingers coiling around my belt buckle and giving me a tug closer to her. "That usually only means one thing with Dakota."

"Oh." I shake my head but grin. "Might have something to do with the clear shower curtain and her walking in on me."

Ivy groans, but her tiny smirk tells me she's not mad. "Get used to it, as long as you're staying here. She does it to me almost every day."

"That's . . . weird."

"That's Dakota." She hesitates. "As long as you don't pull the curtain open to invite her in, we won't have any issues."

I wrap my arms around her body. "Are you jealous?"

"No!" she throws back instantly, tension coursing down her back. I'm guessing being jealous would be as unappealing as being needy in Ivy's book.

Dakota's hot, I'll give her that, but I need more than just looks. "You don't have to worry about that."

Her hands run over my chest and down to my stomach as if memorizing the curves before her sharp, dark eyes peer up at me. "I've never let anyone do that before."

She doesn't have to spell it out. I smile. "I've never wanted to do that with anyone." That's the truth. I haven't come inside a woman since my ex-fiancée, and with her, it was more laziness than my own need. But with Ivy last night . . . I wanted to fill her with me. I wanted to mark her, in a way.

Just the idea had me rock hard.

I should have asked first, but . . .

Ivy inhales deeply and then releases. "Hopefully you'll get this plumbing issue fixed soon, and we can stay at your place once in a while."

She's watching my expression to see if she can read something from it. She still probably thinks I have a girlfriend hiding back home, even though I've told her that's not the case. "Yeah, hopefully." I checked out of the shit motel yesterday morning. I'm going to have to find a short-term rental somewhere, so we have some privacy while I'm here. Which could be a while, because I'm not going anywhere until I figure out exactly why that car was parked outside her uncle's house yesterday.

Ivy averts her gaze, but I sense the tension lifting. "So . . . lemons and Greece." She reaches up to touch the still-green one hanging.

"Yeah. Do you wanna go?" I blurt out.

Her eyes dart to my face. "Where? Greece?"

I nod.

"With you?"

I smile and nod again. The idea hit me last night. It'd get her far away from Scalero and this city and her uncle's death. She loves to travel, and she has no issues picking up and going. Would she go with me, though?

She looks to be considering it. But then she sighs, and I know the answer. "I wish I could. But my cousin's relying on me to get the house and the shop sorted out for selling. I can't just take off." Very quickly, she adds, "But I would, if things were different."

I accept her decline with a nod.

"Does that mean . . ." She frowns, hesitating. "Are you leaving? I remember you saying that you were going after I finished your tattoo."

"Do you want me to leave?" I already know she doesn't. I'm just wondering if she'll actually say it out loud.

She purses her lips and shakes her head no. Admitting that was a big step for her. Admitting that she's falling for me last night was an even bigger one.

I smile. "Then I'm not going anywhere."

Her shoulders sag with an exhale of relief. "Yeah, you are." She checks her phone. "To Black Rabbit, with me. I have to see what they've done to the place."

# THIRTY-THREE

# IVY

"How bad do you think it is?" I ask, watching the technicolor of buildings pass by.

"I'm sure it's fine."

I sigh. "I don't know." Fausto phoned me last night to say they would be finishing up this morning and that Black Rabbit—or, as he jokingly called it, "White Rabbit," much to my annoyance—would be ready. I'd love to hire him to paint Ned's house, too, but we don't have the money after I bought the materials to repair the walls.

Sebastian pulls up alongside the curb, where the same rabid rabbit that stared down at me when I was five stares down at me now. I can't imagine it not being there, but I guess that day will come.

"I'm just going to stick my head in and see what it looks like," I mumble, hopping out of his car. I step onto the sidewalk with my stomach churning. After what Bobby said about my paint color choice, I'm dreading this, and I don't necessarily want Sebastian witnessing my breakdown.

"Remember, this is for resale value, not immortalizing your uncle," Sebastian says, rounding the front of the car. Ignoring my request completely.

I shoot a glare at him, but he ignores that, too, slipping a hand onto the small of my back. He still has that cool, aloof bodyguard aura about him, but more and more he's taking any opportunity he can to touch me. I guess spending the last few days and nights together has helped inspire that. Whatever the reason, every time he's near, I find myself leaning into him, craving his touch.

Even now, when I can sense that something is still bothering him. I catch glimpses of it—a furrowed brow, a distant look. He's distracted. As distracted as a guy like Sebastian, who takes in everything, can be anyway.

The door to the shop is propped open. I hold my breath and step across the threshold. The shock of the glaring, cold white hits me around the same time as the paint odor. "Oh my God, what have I done?" I whisper under my breath, staring at the pristine walls.

Black Rabbit is officially gone. The only place I've ever truly thought of as home has vanished, buried under several coats of chalky white. I may as well tear the sign out front down now.

A painter is on his knees in the corner, brushing the thick baseboards with yet more white. It only makes the worn, honey-colored floors look dingier. I want to yell at him to stop ruining the place. I want to find Fausto and scream at him, tell him that he was wrong about this paint color, Ghost or Ice, it doesn't matter what.

Sebastian's soothing hand around the back of my neck, his thumb rubbing my skin back and forth, stays me.

Fausto rounds the corner from the back hallway, brush in hand, coveralls smeared.

"So? What do you—"

"I hate it." I can't keep the venom from my voice.

He snorts. "You're joking, right? This looks like a whole new place!"

"That's the problem."

He frowns at me, like he thinks I'm crazy. He doesn't understand.

No one understands. Everyone has already forgotten, moved on from Ned.

Everyone but me.

"When do you think you'll be finished?" Sebastian asks, taking over the conversation.

"By noon."

"Thank you. She'll be fine."

I'm both relieved and irritated with Sebastian for speaking on my behalf. He's wrong. I *will not* be fine. But I don't want to have to explain that to anyone.

With one last wary look at me, Fausto and the guy working on the baseboards disappear into the back.

"This kind of change was inevitable," Sebastian says.

I pull away from his hands and scan the space again. "Then why does it feel so wrong?"

We stand in the middle of the empty, lifeless room for a long moment, until finally he says, "Maybe painting it isn't the issue."

"Oh, I'm pretty sure it's the issue." I sneer at the empty white walls. Something about plain white walls drives me crazy. I need color and personality—art.

"Maybe *selling* this place is the issue. Are you sure that's a good idea?"

"Not you too," I grumble. Which reminds me, I need to talk to Ian again.

He chuckles. "You made the decision to sell and leave San Francisco when you were upset. You made it so you could run."

"You say that like you know me." He's right, though.

"But maybe that's not the right decision for you anymore," he goes on, ignoring my sarcasm. "Maybe, deep down, you want to stay here. Maybe you have a reason to stay now."

"What would that reason be?" Is this Sebastian's way of asking me not to leave San Francisco because *he's* here? Because if he is . . .

I desperately want that to be the reason.

I've known this guy for *days*, and yet I feel like I've been through so much with him. Is this what happens with his clients, too? Do they form hard-and-fast bonds with their bodyguard when he's shuttling them around, responsible for their well-being, protecting them from harm, spending long periods of time with them? That I've just been through a traumatic event only amplifies my dependence on him, I'm sure.

And it also probably doesn't help that I'm sleeping with him.

I sure as hell hope he doesn't usually do *that* with his clients, too.

I'm definitely guessing he doesn't ask them to go to Greece with him. That has to mean something.

Right?

This is not me. I don't form dependencies on people, especially guys.

And yet I can't push him away.

I sense Sebastian approaching me from behind, but I don't turn. His hands on my hips and the feel of his rough jaw against my cheek as he leans in make me shiver.

Settling his chin on top of my head, he murmurs, "It doesn't look bad. It's different, yeah. A bit cold . . ."

I snort. "It's so cold, it's icy. I guess that's why Fausto called it Ice. I hate it. It isn't me."

Sebastian hesitates, his body going slightly rigid against my back. "Then make it you. Add enough of Ivy to it to bring it back to life."

"And then what?"

"Then keep it. Run it." He spins me around to face him, tipping my chin up until I meet his gaze. "Stay here and make sure you really want this. You can always walk away later."

I don't think he's talking about Black Rabbit right now. "I don't know the first thing about actually running a shop, though."

"Do you know anyone who does?"

"My cousin." And Ian is all on board for keeping it open. "He has a place in Dublin."

"I'm sure he'll help you out. It can't be that hard." His eyes wander over the corners. "I can upgrade the security system for you. You need something better than a VCR."

"You know how to do that, too?"

He smirks. "I'm a man of many talents."

I take a deep breath and begin surveying the walls under a new light.

An Ivy light.

# THIRTY-FOUR

# SEBASTIAN

Did I do that to her today?

Did I convince her to stay in San Francisco because *I'm* here?

Because I don't fucking live here!

Technically, I don't live anywhere. Just a series of comfortable hideouts to choose from.

But standing in that shop and convincing Ivy to basically settle down made me wonder if maybe *I* could do the same. There's nothing stopping me. I have no commitments, nowhere I need to be. No one to be there with.

But here, in San Francisco, I could have her.

And she wants me. *She's falling for me.*

I don't have to tell her about what I've been doing for the past five years. No one besides Bentley knows, and he's not going to say a fucking word about any of it because he's tied to it as much as I am.

Though she's going to wonder why I'm not working after a while. Where all my money comes from. Maybe I could get a legitimate job as a bodyguard. Alliance hires them. It also hires people to train others—police, firefighters, military—in combat. I could do that, too. The money won't be as good, but what has all the money I've made gotten me so far?

Even as I convince myself of all this, that little voice in the back of my head keeps telling me that I'm a fucking moron if I think I can hide my past from her forever. That she'll have anything to do with me when she does find out.

"I'm getting out," Ivy says, peering up over her shoulder at me, her soaked black hair roped around her fist. Water streams over her body in rivulets, trailing between those perfect tits, down a taut belly, down thin but toned thighs. Her skin is coated in gooseflesh. I'm guessing on account of the cooling water. We've spent the entire hot-water tank fucking against the wall after a long day working on the house. I forgot both how difficult shower sex is and how much I actually enjoy showering with a woman, even if I spend most of it outside the stream of hot water.

"I'll be out in a minute," I promise, bending down to kiss her shoulder. She turns to me, meeting my lips with her own. I watch her duck out, wrapping a towel around her curves.

Staying here is the best thing for her, I tell myself. It's the easiest way for me to stay with her. If she takes off somewhere, I'm going to have a harder time explaining why I'm following her. And until I know that nothing can come of Detective Fields investigating Royce's former Alliance connections, I'm going to be following her everywhere, because I'll never forgive myself if something bad happens to her.

So that's it. The decision has been made.

I'm staying in San Francisco.

Maybe for good.

■ ■ ■

"The fucking guy actually knows what he's doin'."

I turn to find Bobby and Ivy standing side by side in the doorway, covered in plaster dust and watching me as I drill a support into the wall, readying it for the new chunk of drywall. This will be my seventeenth one, and there are plenty more. Ricky and whoever was in here with him while Scalero watched us at the club did a number on this house.

"I'm not just a pretty face." I wink at Ivy.

"No, you certainly are not." She chews the inside of her mouth as her eyes drift over my chest. I had to take my T-shirt off to keep from getting it dirty. It's my last clean one. I'm not going to lie—when Ivy picked my clothes up off the floor and tossed them into the wash this morning, I sighed. Not that I expect her to do my laundry.

But, hell, it's nice not to be alone.

Finally, she smiles, with heat in her gaze. "Do you like the tool belt?"

I look down at the leather pouch hanging from my hips that she threw into the shopping cart with a smirk when we went back to the store yesterday to buy drywall supplies. "It's come in handy."

"Yeah, I'll bet," Bobby mutters wryly, shooting Ivy with a look. "I see what's goin' on here. If you need me, I'll be fixin' the tile in the bathroom. Shirtless." He rubs his belly.

"No thanks," Ivy throws back, kicking the door shut with her boot.

I know that look well.

"We've still got a lot to do, Ivy," I tell her. She strolls toward me with purpose. "I could have all the holes filled by tonight if I keep going."

"Uh-huh." She stops in front of me, her head tilted back to keep eye contact.

"Didn't you tell your real estate agent that you'll have this ready to go on the market by next week?"

"I did." Her fingers search out my belt, unfastening it, a fierce look taking over her face as her hand slips down the front of my jeans. "You feel like you could use a break, though."

"Christ, you're greedy," I whisper, lifting her up to settle on the ledge of an odd-size window that's, thankfully, just the right height. "Neighbors are going to get a show if they look up here."

"It'll be a good one. Have you seen yourself right now?" She trails a finger along the light sheen of sweat down the center of my abs, and then sticks it in her mouth.

That's the end of my restraint. I grab her pants at the sides and peel them down over her hips, tugging at them until they're at her knees and I've got her legs pushed out of the way, gaining me access to her.

I'm just pushing into her when my burner phone rings.

That ring is like a bucket of cold water.

"Fuck," I hiss.

"Ignore it."

"I can't." I pull out, release her legs, and step back, pulling her down with me, sliding her pants back up. "I need to take this." Bentley will let it ring at least twenty times before hanging up.

"Why? Who is it?" Suspicion screams in her voice. She's still thinking I've got another life. I guess I do; it just doesn't involve other women.

"It's work."

"Oh." Some of the suspicion eases away.

"I'll meet you downstairs."

With reluctance, she walks away, closing the door behind me.

Just in case she's listening on the other side, I slide the window open, pop out the screen, and slip out onto that shitty old shed in the back that will afford me some privacy as I answer. "Yeah."

"Ice."

My stomach instantly tightens. This isn't just a check-in call. He has another assignment for me, and soon.

"I couldn't reach you last night."

"Dead battery," I answer without missing a beat. That's a lie. I turned it off, like I've been doing every night that I stay with Ivy. I'm not entirely sure how easy it is for his minions to track me down, but I know that if this phone rings and someone answers, he'll know where I'm staying. In the off chance that he hasn't already figured it out, there's no point making it too easy for him.

"I have a job for you," Bentley says, his voice as smooth as usual. Only I don't feel the same affection for it anymore, now that I can't hear it without a rush of distrust. "I need you to come and meet me—"

"No." Another assignment that involves me meeting directly with Bentley? *Hell* no.

There's a long pause. I've never refused an assignment before. But just the idea of leaving Ivy right now makes me want to puke.

"I think accepting is in your best interests."

What the fuck is that supposed to mean? How is sending me to China or Sudan, or somewhere else far away from Ivy, so Scalero can tie up his loose end, in my best interests? "I'm not leaving her." I'm not a SEAL anymore, and he can't order me around.

"What's this about?"

"The car that was sitting outside the house." He knows exactly where I am right now. There's no point pretending. "Was he on her, or on me?"

"Why would I have anyone on you?" Bentley's friendly tone is gone, but I don't buy his irritation for a second. Months drag between my assignments. He wants me gone now for a reason. He wants to erase this last question mark—Ivy—for a reason.

I don't answer him. This conversation has already gone on long enough.

"Don't forget who's had your back all these years, son."

"And don't forget who has done everything you've asked all these years with blind trust." He must hear the anger in my tone.

Silence hangs over the line.

Have I said too much?

"I need time." Time to reconcile my guilt over this last assignment, a guilt that seems to grow daily, as I get closer to Ivy. Time to make sure she's safe.

Time to get to know her.

Time to be sure that this is what I want. That she is what I want. Time to figure out how I'm going to lie to her for the rest of our lives.

"I don't think *you* understand what I'm—"

"I don't think you understand what *I'm* saying. I'm saying no. Send your mercenaries. I'm sure between the two of them, they won't fuck it up too badly." I hang up and shut the phone off.

Wondering exactly what refusing him will mean.

# THIRTY-FIVE

# IVY

I hadn't intended on eavesdropping. Honestly.

I left Ned's room and went to the office to collect the debris left after Sebastian patched all the holes. The window was open a crack, letting the cool air in.

The air that carried with it Sebastian's low voice.

At least I know he wasn't talking to a girlfriend, or a wife.

But who the hell was he talking to just now? Besides someone he said no to. He kept referring to "her."

Am *I* "her"?

And *mercenaries*?

Jesus Christ. Who the hell is Sebastian?

"You hungry?"

I gasp at the sound of his voice, my mind so preoccupied, I didn't notice him slip in. He's in the doorway, his T-shirt back on.

"Maybe in an hour?"

His gaze flickers to the cracked window and then returns to me, screaming with understanding. My heart starts pounding.

*He knows I overheard him.*

I wonder if this is what Dakota was talking about. His deep, dark secrets.

I wait for him to say something about it, to accuse me of something, to get angry and storm out. But he simply closes the distance and pulls me into his arms, leaning down until our foreheads press together, not saying a word.

"What are you doing?" I finally ask.

After another long moment, he simply says, "I'm staying."

■  ■  ■

I drop down to sit on the floor outside the bathroom, my back to the wall. Sebastian is still upstairs, filling the last of the holes, quietly brooding over something I don't understand. The pre-phone-call windowsill action is clearly not going to pick up where it left off, so I figured I'd let him brood alone.

I gingerly pick up a broken piece of tile from the box, examining it. "I don't know why they had to break the tile. Did they seriously think he hid money under there?"

"Watch those. They're sharp," Bobby warns, his ass sticking halfway out the bathroom as he kneels, setting the new flooring in. "Damn near hacked half my hand off pullin' them up."

"Thank God this bathroom is small." We went with cheap, generic tile and it still hurt when the bill rang up.

"You realize how much it would cost to have a professional in, right?" He peers over his shoulder at me, his brow coated with sweat and dust.

"I guess it's good that I know an amateur who can do it for free, then, isn't it?"

He chuckles, pushing himself off the ground to tower over me. "Ned would be laughin' his ass off at me right now."

A spark of sadness touches me with the mention of my uncle.

Bobby's expression softens. "The guys called. I gotta head out now. Got a tow."

I nod quietly.

"But I should be ready to grout here by tomorrow."

"'Kay." I hesitate. "Thanks, Bobby." For everything else that he is, he and the guys are saving my ass here.

"No problem," he says, peeling off his work gloves.

A shiver runs down my back as I'm hit with a flash of watching that guy Mario do exactly the same thing from my hiding spot under the desk. I was at the same eye level as I am now, and I remember focusing on the spot of fresh blood on his wrist. I was so horrified by it—by what it meant—that I dismissed everything else.

"Why you lookin' at me like that?" Bobby asks.

"A scar. He had a scar," I murmur, remembering it now. The skin was pink and puckered, like a burn mark. It stretched over his knuckles and covered the back of his hand.

When the cops questioned me, they pushed me to think about smaller details. Tattoos and piercings. Any other marks that would make someone stand out. I was so busy trying to push out the memory of Ned's blood on the guy's wrist that I pushed the scar out, too.

"Who did?"

"Mario. The guy who killed Ned."

Bobby frowns. "You just rememberin' that now?"

"Yeah. Weird, isn't it?" Fields told me to call him if I thought of anything else that might be useful. I figured that was the standard party line. I didn't expect to actually remember "anything else."

I don't know how helpful this will be, but . . .

I head into the kitchen to find my wallet and Fields's business card, along with my phone.

# THIRTY-SIX

# SEBASTIAN

"Keep the porn to a minimum. Dakota's streaming isn't unlimited," Ivy throws over her shoulder on her way out of the bedroom, her voice heavy with sarcasm.

"Like I'd even want that right now." I eye her ass as it sways in black pants. "Leggings" she called them when I sat here and watched her get dressed, completely spent after a long day working at the house, my mind churning after that disastrous call from Bentley. The one that Ivy ended up hearing anyway, despite my efforts. I played it back in my head at least a dozen times as I worked away, trying to recall every word I might have said. It couldn't have been too enlightening because she's still talking to me.

She still stripped down to nothing the minute we stepped into her room, covered in white dust and both needing showers.

She turns to eye me lying in her bed, her gaze drifting over the reaper along my side that she just tended to. It's scabbing over nicely now, and she seems impressed with the way it's healing. "I think I'm paid up for at least a week with your bodyguard services, right?"

"At least." I smirk. "I like your payment plan."

Her full lips stretch into a devious smile. "I think I do, too." Dakota's voice carries into the room. Another guest over for dinner. It's a revolving door around here. I wonder if this person will top the homeless Jono and the bearded Gerti, whom I never met. "I'm guessing dinner will be ready soon."

"I'll be out in fifteen," I promise her.

I wait until Ivy has rounded the corner before I type "Alliance" into Google's search engine on my iPad. A list of results fills the screen. They're the usual articles, most relating to the civilian shooting that government officials were investigating. They've been investigating for over four months, with witnesses from both sides giving different accounts. The civilians had guns; they didn't have guns. They fired first; the Alliance employees fired first. Just two months ago, officials finally concluded there was enough evidence to suggest that enemy bullets were fired, that the two civilians shot and killed may have had guns on them that were swept away by family members.

Alliance was not in violation of deadly-force rules.

When the verdict was first published, I felt only relief for Bentley. Relief that bullshit propaganda wasn't going to hurt him, or his cause, because it couldn't be true. Bentley would *never* support harsh and unfair violence against civilians. Now . . . my stomach turns.

Because the names of two of the Alliance contractors involved mean something to me now.

Mario Scalero and Richard Porter.

They probably did fire on unarmed civilians. They probably do deserve to be charged with murder. Just like they probably deserve to be charged with rape.

And yet they're going to get off for all of it.

I don't believe that any of what Royce admitted to Ned on that tape is bullshit propaganda. And now they're free to go back to a war-torn country to continue doing the kinds of things that Royce spoke up about and got himself killed for.

Worse, Bentley knows. He knows and yet he's sending them back in because Alliance just won another contract and Scalero is "effective" overseas.

I click on the news article posted just yesterday, showing a head shot of Bentley and a headline that reads, "Alliance Rewarded with Multimillion-Dollar Contract for Private Security Services in Ukraine."

Bentley must have been in negotiations for that one for some time. Had that video surfaced, I'm guessing that the government would have passed Alliance over for one of the many other companies in line. It wouldn't have taken too long for an investigative reporter to make the connection between the Mario and Ricky mentioned in Royce's tattoo shop confession. The confession of a Medal of Honor recipient who was murdered not long after the recording happened.

With an eyewitness who can place a man with a heavy Chicago accent by the name of Mario at the scene.

My stomach tightens. One way or another, that connection may still be made, with something as simple as a mother's scrapbook.

And the burn scar that the only witness to the murders just remembered.

*Fuck* . . . Why did she have to remember that?

It's only a matter of time before someone—Bentley or Scalero or even this Ricky Porter guy, whom I have yet to lay eyes on—feels that Ivy is too big a threat to be allowed to linger.

I toss my iPad to the side and close my eyes, struggling to suppress my panic.

■ ■ ■

I don't think I've ever been this unnerved at a dinner table.

We're in Dakota's greenhouse again. It was peaceful enough the other night, lit by dim lights, surrounded by a jungle of plants. I even liked the dozens of wind chimes dangling from above. Tonight, though, it all adds to the eeriness I'm feeling.

Dakota's psychic medium guest—she goes by Esmeralda, though I'm guessing that's her stage name—hasn't lifted her unsettling crystal-blue eyes from my face since dropping her plump ass into her seat across the table. It's not in a sexual way, either. She's not trying to attract me or seduce me.

She's trying to read me.

Or at least pretend that she can read me, because I know as

well as she does that she's a crook. None of that shit is real. No one can see the dead.

I've caught Ivy glaring at the woman through dinner several times. I'm guessing we share the same feelings about people like this. Right now, I'm wishing she'd stop biting that sharp tongue of hers and say something.

"So, Esme, any interesting readings lately?" Dakota asks, seemingly oblivious of the discomfort around her table as she slides a mouthful of scrambled tofu into her mouth.

I'm so uneasy under this woman's gaze that I don't even taste what's on my plate.

"Not as interesting as what I'm reading right now." Her eyes never lift from me.

Shivers run down my back.

This is bullshit. She can't see the dead bodies piled up around me. She can't.

The pain in my jaw tells me I need to stop clenching my teeth.

"So, what exactly is a psychic medium, Esmeralda?" Ivy asks in that dry, disbelieving tone that I love even more right now, skipping the tofu and going straight for the chicken she threw onto the grill for me.

"Oh, it's *so* much," Esmeralda answers in a soft, breathless voice. "You can be psychic and not a medium, but you can't be a medium and not a psychic."

"There's a difference?"

She smiles kindly at Ivy. As if she can see the same doubt pouring from her as it does from me. "A psychic reads your energy to understand your past, your present, and your future. Your friend Dakota has that intuitive ability."

"Yes. Auras," Ivy murmurs, her dark gaze flipping to Dakota, who simply winks.

"Yes, exactly. For example, I can see that you have been wandering for years but you've only just found an anchor. No . . ." She squints. "*Two* anchors. Or rather, one of your anchors has found you."

Ivy pauses, her fork in her mouth. I can see the tension in her jaw.

Esmeralda's eyes twinkle, as if she knows she's hit a mark. "That's a psychic. Now, a medium has the ability to read your *spirit* energy to see your past, present, and future."

"Sounds like the exact same thing to me." Ivy has regained her cool composure. "Do you charge double for that?"

Esmeralda reaches across the table to seize Ivy's small hand. "Someone from your past who has left you recently, who loves you, approves of these anchors, both the new and the old. Very much so."

Ivy's complexion goes from pinkish to deathly white in seconds as the blood drains from her face. I watch quietly to see how she'll react.

But she doesn't. She doesn't even pull her hand away. Her mind is too busy working through the woman's words, deciphering them. Making sense of them.

And I suddenly want to get the hell away from this woman.

That's of course when she turns her attention to me. "Now *you* are something else. Are you being chased?"

"No," I answer without missing a beat.

She frowns, as if disappointed in my answer. And not because she thinks she was wrong; because she knows she's right. "Yes . . . Yes, you are. Ghosts from your past that need to be faced. It wasn't your fault. You know that, and yet you haven't forgiven yourself for it yet, after all these years. She knows, as well. She has forgiven you. So have the others."

I shove a piece of chicken in my mouth to give myself an excuse not to answer, shooting her with a warning look. She gives me a slight nod in understanding and then purses her lips, signifying that she understands. That she won't push anymore.

But it's too late. Her words have already infiltrated my mind. I wouldn't have cared if she'd brought up the pile of human scum that I've dispatched on Bentley's orders. Those lives don't keep me up at night.

At least, they haven't before. Now that I doubt Bentley's motives, that's starting to change. I'm beginning to wonder if all my assignments have had more to do with money and less to do with saving lives. I push those worries aside, though, because if that's true, then I've become nothing more than an unwitting murderer.

But how the fuck does this woman know about my ghosts?

The small, round face that has lingered in my mind for almost six years. She would have been twelve now.

Dakota and Esmeralda chatter easily through the rest of dinner, while both Ivy and I stew in our own inner turmoil. I push my food around until Ivy stands and collects her plate—her food uneaten—and swipes mine out from under me. "We're heading out," she announces. "Thanks for dinner." With a heavy sigh, she adds, "It was nice meeting you."

Esmeralda beams, her gaze shifting between the two of us, settling on me once again. "You know what you need to do, Sebastian."

"Excuse me?" An eerie chill skitters down my back. Just hearing my name on her tongue bothers me.

She nods. "You *know*."

I want to grab the woman and shake her. What do I need to do? Punish Scalero for the crimes he's committed?

Punish Bentley for what he's allowed to happen?

Turn myself in for what I've done?

Tell Ivy everything?

"Okay, see you guys later!" Dakota waves and continues with her conversation.

I trail Ivy to the kitchen in a daze, where she scrapes the food off the plates and dumps them into the dishwasher, kicking the door shut on her way by.

She grabs my keys from the kitchen counter. "Come on."

"Where are we going?" She's clearly on a mission.

Chewing the inside of her cheek for a moment in thought, she finally answers, "To fix one of my anchors."

# THIRTY-SEVEN

# IVY

Fausto and his guys have cleaned up and left, leaving behind nothing but this cold, sterile white cave and the stench of fresh paint.

I drop the box at my feet. It's every last spray paint can I have. They clatter noisily against each other with the impact.

Sebastian's boots clomp against the ground as he wanders over to stand next to me, arms folded across his chest, staring at the wide white canvas in front of me. He hasn't said much since leaving Dakota's, appearing as disturbed by Esmeralda's intrusive words as I feel. Though I'm not sure for the same reasons.

How the fuck did she know about anchors? As soon as she said it, I knew exactly what she meant. She *had* to be talking about Sebastian, and this shop, because they're the only two things keeping me in San Francisco right now. One old—this shop—and one new, who found me. Sebastian found me.

And someone I lost recently, who loves me dearly . . .

*Ned.*

Would Ned approve of Sebastian? He didn't approve of most people, so I find that hard to believe. Then again, Sebastian's not like anyone I've ever met.

I want to race back there and shake Dakota until she admits that she fed that loony tune all my personal information before dinner, that they're just fucking with my head. But I know Dakota well enough to know that she'd never do that. She actually believes in that stuff.

And she's almost made me a believer. Almost.

So then, what do Esmeralda's words to Sebastian mean? By the set jaw and the stiff back and the way his eyes keep drifting elsewhere, she hit a raw nerve with him, too.

Who is the "she" Esmeralda referred to? Is Sebastian in love with her?

Suddenly, Sebastian turns to catch my gaze. I want to ask him what he blames himself for. I want to ask him about this ghost. I want to ask him all kinds of questions.

Instead, I reach for a can of black paint. With his eyes on my back, I close in on the longest wall in Black Rabbit, a solid mass of white with not a single window to break it up.

All it takes is a single swipe with my finger on the nozzle, the inky black marring the canvas in a long line, and I already feel better. "Ned would hate the white." I point to the expanse of blank wall behind me. "But this . . ." I exhale with a sense of relief. "He'd be all for this."

"You're going to need a lot more paint," Sebastian murmurs, a hint of a smile on his lips now.

He's right. I will. And capable hands.

Luckily I know where to get both.

I pull out my phone.

· · ·

"Why did you have all these extras lying around?" Joker asks, rubbing his bald head with one hand as he shoves a slice of pizza in his mouth. It's long since cold, but no one around here minds cold pizza.

"Because I'm da shit," Fez hollers, and I roll my eyes, sharing a look with Joker and Weazy. I don't say anything, though. Fez has earned his status as a decent friend to me. Within twenty minutes of my texting the guys to see if they'd be into helping me around here, they showed up with their entire supply of paint cans, and they've worked next to me all night.

I step back now and take in the long eastern wall in Black Rabbit, and the mesmerizing kaleidoscope of colors staring back at me. Some of the original paint remains. It's still there in the background, peeking out between the loops of letters, incorporated into the whites of eyes and the collars of shirts, but it's nowhere near as overbearing as it used to be.

Now the cold, sterile white complements my wild side nicely.

In the center, I've sketched another depiction of Ned, his devilish grin filling up the bottom half of his face, his braids resting on either shoulder. Weazy did one of his infamous jungle scenes, except the asshole added a barely dressed Asian girl swinging from a rope. The blue streak in her hair is telling.

The rest of the sketches are different scenes from San Francisco—the Golden Gate Bridge; a trolley speeding down one of the steep streets and into a pit of fire. That's Fez's addition.

We have so much still to do—I've decided I want to cover the ceiling, too—but the sun's coming up soon, we're out of paint, and everyone's tired.

"Hey, Ivy." Joker leans in next to me as I stoop to collect the empty cans. "Was that a gun I saw tucked into the back of your guy's jeans?"

"Yeah. Probably." I glance back over my shoulder at Sebastian, who stands like the soldier he once was by the propped-open door—we had to get some air in here; the fumes were getting to be too much. He's been stationed by that door without complaint all night, as if he knew how important it was for me to do this, scaring away any curious wanderer with a simple look. I guess he wanted his gun within reach, just in case.

Though, that doesn't explain why he had it lying on the windowsill last night.

I wander over to him, pressing myself up against his chest. He's so hard to read most times; right now, he's impossible. "What do you think?"

His strong arms rope around my body, pulling me in tight. "I think it's perfect."

"Does it say Ivy?"

He lays a gentle kiss on my forehead. "I said it was perfect, didn't I?"

Yeah, I'm beginning to think that Esmeralda was right.

Ned would like my new anchor.

■ ■ ■

"I look like a three-year-old who got into an art studio," I muse, scratching at the dried splotches of green and yellow paint that cover my skin, my clothes. They're probably in my hair, too.

Sebastian gives me a sideways look as we wade through the sand toward the crop of rocks. It's the very same pile at Ocean Beach that I sat at while designing his reaper. "No, you don't. Not at all."

His recently smooth jaw is already covered by a thick coat of stubble, and I can't help but reach up to scratch my fingers across it now. "You going to grow that back out?"

"You want me to?"

I shrug. "I'm good with it either way." *As long as I have you.*

He throws an arm around my shoulders, pulling me into him. Though that dark cloud that formed during dinner with Esmeralda last night still hovers, I've managed to get a few smiles out of him this morning.

"I come here sometimes, to think," I admit, settling onto my favorite perch, which gives me a perfect view of the surfers in the water.

"I can see why." His gaze narrows as he watches them, too. It's six forty, and the sun is just cresting over the horizon behind us. The circles under his eyes are probably as dark as mine, but if he's tired, he doesn't let on. "Do you feel better about the shop now?"

"Now that I've vandalized it, yeah," I chuckle.

Reaching down to pluck a perfectly intact seashell from between the rocks, he flips it between his fingers. "Now what?"

I shrug. "Now I call my cousin and tell him I want to keep it." I sigh. "It's what Ned would want. It's what I want." Oddly enough, saying the words out loud for the first time brings me a sense of peace.

"Because she was right, wasn't she? It's an anchor."

I glance up to see that distant worry in his eyes. Esmeralda's words are still lingering in his mind, too.

"One of them."

His chest lifts with a deep breath, and I'm hit with a wave of panic that something between us has changed since yesterday, that he's grown bored with me overnight. That he's decided he doesn't want to do this, after all.

I hate this insecurity swirling inside my head and my heart. I'm not used to feeling it; I've managed to avoid it all this time by not committing to people. And now, here I am, finally ready to commit, and I'm already losing my cool.

"She was right. About my ghost," he says quietly, his gaze holding to the ocean's water line.

I sigh with relief. This isn't about us at all. "What do you mean?"

He clears his throat, as if voicing the next words is going to be hard. "We used to go on these regular raids through Marjah, routing out insurgents. There were a lot. I can't tell you how many rounds of ammunition I fired in my time over there. Anyway, there was this one day on my second tour, we had a tip on someone and I was out with my team, hunting them down. We found ourselves driving into this long corridor in our Humvee. And there was this little girl running at us, with these big blue eyes and dark hair, and wearing a backpack. The Taliban were known for using children in these kinds of attacks. Where we were, with buildings on either side, we'd be leveled by an explosion. She was so little, six or seven. She was scared, I could see it in her eyes."

I'm trying to picture this but I'm struggling, partly because I don't want to. I've always rolled my eyes at Dakota when she talks about auras, but right now the very air around Sebastian has chilled. I'm shivering.

He heaves a sigh. "We yelled at her to stop, but she kept coming. I was the only one who had the clear line of sight. So I took it. She went quickly. We scouted the area for insurgents before we closed in to secure the backpack. There was a blanket, a bottle of water, and naan wrapped in cloth." I look over to see his profile, an image of sorrow, as his voice grows thick. "She wasn't coming to kill us. We found out later that she had no home, no parents. She was running to us for help."

My chest begins to throb. "But . . . that wasn't your fault." Even as I say it, I understand that wouldn't mean anything to the man who pulled the trigger. To a man with Sebastian's discipline and code of honor. Something like that must have destroyed him.

He says nothing, peering down at his boots.

"So what happened?"

"It got swept under the rug as a wartime casualty and everybody moved on." He pauses. Everybody but him, I'm guessing. "The next time a kid darted out from behind a car at our outfit, I froze. Even when my commanding officer yelled the order to fire, even when I saw the IED in his hand, I couldn't pull the trigger. He lobbed it at the Humvee in front of us and blew them up."

"The one your friends were in?"

"They were all my friends," Sebastian explains quietly. "But, yeah. That's the one."

This story is getting worse and worse.

Sebastian has an army of ghosts trailing him.

I reach over to take his hand and squeeze it. He turns my fingers in his palm, lightly tracing the splotches of color with his free hand.

"I took some shrapnel to the back. Kirkpatrick, my commander at the time and a fucking dick wad, wrote me up for insubordination. When I filed my papers to leave the navy, I ended up with an 'Other than Honorable' discharge."

"What does that mean?"

His lips twist in a bitter smile. "It depends who you ask. For someone like you, who doesn't know anything about the navy, it doesn't mean much at all. For someone like my father, who retired as a highly decorated navy captain, it's almost as bad as if I were some street thug, murdering innocent human beings." He pauses. "It means that it can be hard to get a job, and a lot of veteran benefits don't apply to me, even with my years of service."

"But you did get a job."

His lips twist in thought. "Yeah. Through a friend."

"Well, then . . . screw that less than honorable discharge, because you're doing what you're good at anyway. Right?"

He studies the sand for a moment. "Right."

No wonder he doesn't like talking about the navy. I wouldn't either if those memories were tied to it. And it sounds like he doesn't have anyone in his corner, now that he's trying to move on. "Are you and your parents close?"

"Not really." He hesitates. "But I haven't made much of an effort, to be honest. I haven't made an effort with anyone."

"Where are they now?"

"Still in Potrero Hill."

I frown. "Don't you live in Potrero, too?"

A slight frown touches his forehead. "Right."

So they're probably *minutes* away from each other? While I'm not necessarily one to push family bonding, after watching Ian miss out on making amends with his father, I don't want to see it happen again. "Thanksgiving is in a couple of days. Maybe it's time to make an effort?"

"Maybe."

Silence hangs over us as we both watch the waves crash in.

I finally reach up to smooth my hand over his back in a soothing way. Wanting to take some of his agony away, to make him feel less alone. "So . . . I guess creepy Esmeralda was right about a lot of things."

"Fuck, was she ever creepy," he mutters, and we share a laugh. Sebastian pauses to toss the seashell into the water. "These anchors she talked about . . ." He shoots a sideways glance my way.

"What about them?"

"Well, they sound like they involve some commitments, and I remember Ivy Lee telling me that she didn't make commitments."

"I did say that, didn't I?"

"Has that changed?"

It's endearing, watching Sebastian—a man who's normally so controlled and in charge—hesitantly probe in a way that he wouldn't have before.

How has he not figured out that *everything* has changed for me, and it's all because of him?

I answer by throwing a leg over his thighs to straddle him, my back to the ocean. Because I'd rather be looking at this man anyway. "Maybe."

His eyes scan my face, settling on my lips, and I expect that he's going to lean in and kiss me. But he suddenly scoops me up in his arms and trudges easily through the thick mounds of sand toward his car. I squeal like the kind of girls I mock.

"We should get home. Get some sleep." His deep voice hums through my body, because I know we won't be going to sleep immediately.

"When is your plumbing going to be fixed?" I'm desperate to see Sebastian's home. To be surrounded by his things. To invade his life like he's invaded mine.

"Don't know yet. Soon."

I groan. "Are you sure you don't have a wife there?" That would be just my fucking luck. I hate that I asked, but it's beginning to drive me nuts.

"Yes, I'm sure."

"Girlfriend?"

"None."

"Boyfriend?"

He chuckles. "Trust me, after last night's dinner, I'd rather be bringing you to my place than risk meeting another one of Dakota's friends." We reach the car and he sets me down, opening the door for me.

I climb in and watch him as he rounds the front, his raptor gaze scanning our surroundings.

■ ■ ■

When Sebastian told me we were going to his parents' for Thanksgiving dinner, I remember being happy that he actually listened to me, and that this was a big step for him. I completely dismissed the reality that Sebastian's parents would be meeting me.

And, most likely, judging me.

Normally I wouldn't give a damn. But these are *Sebastian's* parents.

I give a damn.

"So, on a scale of one to ten, how much do they hate tattooed women?" I ask, taking in the perfectly manicured little house before us, the American flag drifting ever so slightly in the cool fall breeze.

Sebastian's eyes float over me from head to toe, settling on the black turtleneck I chose for today's meeting. The temperatures allow for it, thank God; it's only about fifty degrees out. "You look great."

"Right. And you're sure we shouldn't have brought flowers or something?" Showing up at someone's house for Thanksgiving dinner empty-handed feels like the wrong thing to do, even though I really have no experience in this sort of thing. Aside from meeting Jesse's father—albeit years later, when he nearly arrested me—I've never actually met a guy's parents.

"You're nervous?"

"No," I lie, smoothing my long hair down around my face to cover where I recently shaved the sides. They were getting too long and mangy.

"Well, don't worry. It'll be fine." He sets his jaw, like he doesn't really believe that.

He curls his fingers through mine, and then presses the doorbell. Moments later, footfalls sound on the other side and the door cracks open, and a small woman with a blond bob appears.

She gives her head a shake. "Sebastian?"

"Hey, Mom."

She looks dazed for a moment. "Why didn't you . . ." Her words drift off as she glances from him to me, to our clasped hands, to him again. And then she heaves a sigh and smiles. "Come in, please."

I smile in return, though internally I'm frowning. Something's off here. Did he not tell them that he was bringing a guest? I will kill him, if that's the case.

We trail her inside, getting past the door so she can close it. The delicious smell of turkey wafts through the house and I inhale, savoring the scent. It's an American tradition that my family never really picked up. Suddenly I feel like I've been missing out for twenty-five years.

"Mom, this is Ivy. Ivy, this is my mother, Mona." He hasn't let go of my hand yet.

I stick my free hand out. "It's nice to meet you."

"Right, yes." She nods absently, taking it. "Come in. Come in."

No. This goes beyond me.

A deep older, male voice sounds from somewhere in the house. "Is that those lawn care people again? They don't know how to take no for an answer!"

"Uh . . . no," Mona answers, a slight wobble to her voice. "It's your son."

Silence.

My hand grows clammy in Sebastian's. He's sweating. When I peer up at him, he offers me a brief, tight smile.

A chair creaks, and then, moments later, a graying man in tan slacks and a button-down shirt appears. He's tall, like Sebastian, only much more slender. The same shocked expression sits on his face that appeared on his wife's moments ago. "Sebastian."

Sebastian releases my hand to offer his. "Sir." He's so serious, I half expect him to salute his own father.

After a long pause, and a nervous glance between the two from Mona, Sebastian's dad takes it.

Sebastian turns to me. "This is Ivy Lee. Ivy, this is Captain George Riker."

*Riker.* So that's Sebastian's last name.

"Just George is fine." His dad's piercing gaze shifts to mine, and I can feel the scrutiny as he holds out a hand.

"It's so nice to meet you." I sound like a parrot, but it's the only thing I can think of. This is beyond awkward.

Mona and George share a glance and a subtle nod.

"So . . . umm . . . I have a large turkey in the oven. You know how your father likes leftovers." Mona wrings her hands.

"That sounds great, Mom."

Again, another sigh, then a smile. "Okay. Great. Well . . ." She gestures toward the living room. "Make yourselves at home. Not much has changed. I'll be back in a few moments."

We follow George into the living-dining room. It reminds me a lot of Ned's house in its layout, except it's immaculate and tastefully decorated, with couch cushions that match curtains, and an area rug that looks like it has never been stepped on. The dining room on the other side is big enough for six people. Two formal places are set.

And the oddness makes sense now.

I turn to glare at Sebastian. *They didn't know we were coming!* Did we just crash Thanksgiving dinner?

He simply shrugs and gestures to the love seat. But when Mona rushes in with plates and cutlery, I head that way instead. "Here. Let me help you with that." I reach out and take the plates from her.

"Thank you, dear."

I can't say the last time anyone has ever called me "dear."

From behind me, I hear George say something about a cigar on the back veranda. The two of them step through the sliding door, shutting it behind them.

Leaving me alone with his mother.

"If I had known that Sebastian would be surprising us like this, I would have had things ready beforehand," she rambles on, fussing with the spacing of the knife and fork. "I'll just have to throw some more potatoes and carrots in . . ."

"I'll help you. And . . . I'm sorry. I didn't know. I'll strangle him later for you."

She chuckles, glancing out the window at her son, at his profile. "He looks so much older." Shaking her head, she murmurs more to herself, "I guess that shouldn't be a surprise after five years, but still . . ."

The butter knife slips from my hand and clatters against the china.

# THIRTY-EIGHT

# SEBASTIAN

Not until the first ring of smoke sails out of his mouth and into the cool late November breeze does he speak. "So? . . . How are things?"

I look at the cigar in my hand and smile, thinking about the ones Ivy bought and tucked into her top. We never did smoke those. "Fine."

"Work?" He peers out over the chestnut tree, a few prickly shells still hanging from limbs. The ones that littered the grass have long since been picked up and disposed of.

Dad knows what I do. Well, not *exactly* what I do, but he's smart enough to put two and two together and not ask questions. He despises Alliance and companies like Alliance that profit from war, taking money that should be put toward funding the troops. That means he despises men like Bentley, living in their Napa vineyards, reaping the rewards.

He was watching from the window the day that Bentley pulled up in his car and took me for a long, enlightening drive. He was watching when Bentley dropped me off and shook hands with me, and handed me an envelope full of cash and my first false ID.

And when he asked me what it was all about, and I told him that I couldn't give him details but that I'd be doing good work, he warned me not to go down this path. He warned me that I'd get burned. Then he turned his back on me.

He would have come around, eventually, I think.

But I was a fucking mess back then. Lost, angry, and unable to handle that perpetual disapproving gaze of his. So I packed my bags and left the next day, and haven't been back since.

I figured that was best for everyone.

"Did Mom get the birthday card?" I ask, leaving his question unanswered. Her birthday was six weeks ago. I always send one, just to let her know I'm thinking of her, and that I'm okay. It never eases the guilt.

"She did." His cheeks lift in a tight smile. "She's always happy when those arrive."

Silence hangs over the backyard as we both puff away at our cigars. I used to love sitting on the porch floor and watching him smoke them with one navy buddy or another while they went off about the government and what they should be doing, and what they weren't doing.

I check inside the house to see Ivy and my mom in the kitchen, their backs to me. Ivy's peeling something, from the looks of it. I probably shouldn't have left the two of them in there alone, but there's not much my mother can tell her that Ivy doesn't already know, and there's no way my dad told my mom anything about Bentley.

It's always been that way between the two of them. My mom, happy and oblivious in her world of gardening and catering to my father's every need. They're straight out of the 1950s as far as their marriage goes, and both are content with that.

"Where'd you meet her?"

"Here. In San Francisco."

He nods, his mouth opening to say something, but hesitating. Captain George Riker forms opinions of people quickly. I'm sure he's already formed an opinion of Ivy, and that's without seeing all her tattoos.

A feature he would definitely not appreciate as I do.

"She seems nice," is all he says. "How long have you been in town?"

"Not long." I can't bring myself to admit to having been here for a couple of weeks already.

His jaw tenses, like he's figured that out already. "Staying?"

"I wasn't planning on it but . . ." I glance back at Ivy again. "Yeah. I'm pretty sure I am."

Astute eyes settle on me. "Does she know?"

I shake my head.

He takes another long puff of his cigar. "You gonna tell her?"

"I'm not sure I'll have a choice but to."

His eyes narrow. "How so?"

I hesitate. "She's tied to an assignment that I shouldn't have been brought in for. I don't think I can keep it from her forever." The guilt will eat me up more than it already has.

"He's got you doing something wrong, doesn't he?"

"Something to cover his ass, yeah."

My dad nods, like he expected this all along. And he did. This is exactly the kind of thing he warned me about.

He's always loved being right. But right now, I see only worry. "You're going to do the right thing. Right?"

I puff quietly on my cigar, not sure how to answer that.

If only it were that easy.

■ ■ ■

"It was so nice to meet you, Ivy." My mom's eyes light up as she shakes Ivy's hand, and I know she approves. Honestly, I wasn't sure if she would. Ivy's nothing like the girls Mona Riker always tried to steer me toward growing up. She's the opposite of Sharon in every single way, and Mom was heartbroken when Sharon called off the wedding.

Maybe she's just so happy that I'm here, that she doesn't care who I bring home. Either way, I'm happy that tonight ended peacefully.

"So . . ." My mom's gaze shifts to me and I see her fighting off tears.

"We'll be back to visit very soon," Ivy says for me, in a voice that tells me she means it, and a sharp look that tells me I'm going to get an earful from her later.

"Okay." After a moment of hesitation, my mom ropes her arms around my neck and squeezes me tight. "I hope so," she whispers, making my chest tighten with guilt and regret.

My dad gives me a single nod, his arms settled over my mom's shoulders.

I feel their eyes on our backs the entire way to the car. Ivy must as well. "Your mother is incredibly nice," she murmurs, slipping her fingers through mine affectionately.

I smile. "She is."

"My own mother isn't even that nice to me."

"You're exaggerating."

"I'm not. Just you wait . . ."

I open the door for her to climb into the passenger seat, and then I come around to the driver's side.

A sharp pinch on my triceps has me wincing in pain.

"*Five* years? You live in the same city and you haven't visited that poor sweet woman in five years?" Ivy barks. "When you said you weren't close, I thought you meant you did the occasional drive-by, half-assed attempts at calling. But they haven't seen or heard from you in five years!"

I knew that was going to come out somehow.

I can only offer, "I know."

"She doesn't care about your less than honorable discharge, Sebastian. All she cares about is that her son is happy and safe."

"I send her birthday cards," I mumble, earning her sharp glare.

"A card." Her tone is flat but her glare is scathing. "That doesn't even begin to count."

I didn't think Ivy of all people would get so fired up over this. "What? How often do you see your parents?"

She sputters for a moment.

"Thought so."

"I call them once a month. I email regularly. We *correspond*. I get my regular parental dose of 'you're fucking your life up' from them. And if I actually lived in the same city, I would visit. But I've never iced them out like you have. So what's your excuse?"

I heave a sigh as I pull out. It's time for some truth. "I haven't been living in San Francisco for the past five years." Truth in small doses is the best way with Ivy, I think.

She falters. "Where have you been?"

"Around."

"For work?"

"Yeah." That's not a lie.

"When exactly did you move back?"

"I'm in the process of it right now."

Her head falls back against the headrest. "So . . . there are no plumbing issues."

"Depends on if you consider the cracked, leaking toilet in my shitty motel room a problem. I checked out of there a few days ago."

She's still trying to make sense of this; I can see it on her face. "Why'd you lie to me, then?"

"Because I was afraid you wouldn't give me the time of day if you thought I was just passing through."

"But you're not. Passing through, I mean. Right?"

I reach over and weave my fingers through her hand. "No. I'm not. Definitely not, now."

# THIRTY-NINE

# IVY

I watch Sebastian's long lashes flicker as he sleeps.

He finally lay down about an hour ago, after I woke up to find him sitting by the window again. Who knows how long he was there tonight.

Is he like this all the time? Or just for now?

The more I get to know him, the less I know about him, I'm realizing. He's complicated. I sensed that from the moment I first met him. Dakota sensed it. This supposed "darkness." But it's more than just his ghosts—the little girl, his friends, his time in the war.

There's definitely more.

Is Bobby right?

This stranger shows up at the shop one day, apparently on vacation, willing to pay just about anything to get a tattoo from me. He keeps coming back until I finally agree. And, except for a few hours apart while he "runs errands," he has basically refused to leave my side since. Not that I'm complaining. Not once have I felt overwhelmed, or suffocated. I love having him around.

But aside from meeting his parents and what happened during the war, I know *nothing* about him. I don't know where he actually lives because he lied about that. He's never mentioned any friends. The one work phone call he received was him refusing to actually go to work and talking about mercenaries.

Was that a joke?

Nothing about his tone of voice that day would suggest it.

Everything that he's said suggests he's a loner. He shut his own parents out for five years. He's back in San Francisco now; why, I have no idea, but he came with one small duffel bag that holds five T-shirts and two pairs of jeans. He comes out of a Home Depot restroom with a split lip that was *not* caused by walking into a wall because an ex–Navy SEAL who can take down three grown men without breaking a sweat is incapable of walking into walls. He sits by my window at night with his gun ready, waiting for something to happen, and his late-night confessions included doing things that he's afraid I might not approve of.

*Who are you, really, Sebastian?*

Besides the stranger who strolled in and seized my heart?

# FORTY

# SEBASTIAN

"She probably thinks she's alone."

Ivy lies on her back next to me, staring up at the bedroom ceiling. "Both of our cars are parked outside."

"Well, then . . . maybe this is payback. We haven't exactly been quiet either." I woke up to the sound of the front door closing about twenty minutes ago. Two voices—one, Dakota's, and one, a male voice—carried through the small house, on their way to her bedroom.

Ivy woke up when the moaning began and the headboard knocking started.

"That's something *I* would do. Dakota isn't spiteful enough." She groans. "When are you finding a place?"

"Maybe we can look later today, after we get all the paint supplies. Carl should be done with the plastering soon."

She smiles, pleased. "Okay."

Dakota's moans have reached their peak and, coupled with some deep grunts and groans, sound like the two have come to the end of the performance.

"I'm betting it's the California Bum." Ivy pulls herself out of bed. "We need to get out of here before they emerge. I'll vomit if I witness that."

"Ten minutes?"

Ivy turns to see my hard-on and scowls. "Not a chance."

I shrug. It's hard for any guy to listen to that and *not* be affected. I watch with an arm tucked under my head as she pulls on fresh clothes, covering up her body. "Hurry up and get dressed!" she hisses, tossing a T-shirt and briefs that land on my face. I pull them off with a grin to see her sliding the pocket door open.

At the same time that the pocket door from Dakota's room slides open, and a very sweaty, very naked Bobby fills the doorway.

■ ■ ■

"You knew that was him all along, didn't you!" she accuses.

I don't say anything as I drive, because she's right. I did recognize Bobby's gruff voice. I just didn't know how to bring it up without Ivy losing her mind, like she is right now.

"God, why him? She's a beautiful woman who could have anyone she wants, and yet . . . *him*!"

"Why do you care? You know she has . . . *eclectic* tastes."

She sinks into the car seat. And frowns. "I don't know. I guess . . . I guess I still blame those guys for what happened to Ned. They shouldn't have let him gamble."

"Ned was a grown man who made his own decisions." *And they have nothing to do with what happened to him.*

"I know. I just . . ." She shudders.

I can't help it, I start to laugh.

"Oh, you think this is funny?"

I can't stop laughing, even as I pull into the driveway behind Carl's pickup truck. Carl is on the front porch, having a smoke, the phone pressed to his ear, a wide grin on his face. I'm guessing that's Bobby on the other end, warning him to stay on Ivy's good side because she's already pissed off.

I climb the steps behind her.

"How's it going in there?"

Carl has managed to wipe the smile off but there's still amusement there. He's a decent enough guy. Less rough looking than the others, with short, dark curly hair and a clean-shaven face. "Almost done. Another day to dry and sand again. Plastering is tricky."

"And then it'll be ready for you to paint and clean?" Carl's already said he's "not painting any goddamn walls," but the way Ivy delivers it, you'd think she's seriously expecting it.

He holds his hands up. "Not doing it! Especially not with those fucking pigs coming around."

She frowns. "Cops were here again?"

He pulls a card from his shirt pocket, holding it like he's going to catch leprosy from the paper. "Came by an hour ago, looking for you."

She digs her phone out of her purse. "Crap, I didn't hear it." She looks back at me. "It's Fields. I wonder what that's about?" She hits Dial and holds the phone to her ear.

My body breaks out in a cold sweat as I listen to her conversation, easily filling in the side that I can't hear.

# FORTY-ONE

# IVY

The silence in the car is deafening as Sebastian pulls up to the curb at the precinct.

"You're not coming in with me?"

Sebastian bows his head to peer out the passenger-side window, his eyes hidden behind glasses. "You'll be safe in there."

"Well, yeah. I'm not worried about that." I'm going to be looking at pictures of criminals. They want me to identify Ned's killers. "What kind of errands do you *suddenly* have?" Only an hour ago, we were going to be shopping for paint supplies and an apartment.

"Shit I need to do." His face has taken on that stony expression that I really don't like, not right now anyway.

I glare at him.

"Don't suddenly turn into one of those women, Ivy. Please."

"What . . . One of *those* . . ." I feel like he just sucker-punched me. "I'm not 'one of those women.' I will never be 'one of those women.'" I have *never* questioned him about anything until now. Even when I desperately want to know what's going on. And the fact that I desperately want to know makes me pissed off at myself, and him. "Maybe you could stop being so fucking mysterious!" I snap, yanking on the handle to get the hell out of the car before he sees the tears beginning to well.

A viselike grip latches onto my wrist and pulls me back in. "You'll be fine. They may not even have anything concrete." He sounds about as convincing as he did when he was telling me that drugged-out junkies might have trashed Ned's house.

I don't get this guy sometimes.

He leans in and plants a quick but hard kiss on my mouth, and the feel of his stubble against my skin makes some of my anger melt. "Call me when you're done and I'll be here to pick you up."

"Yup." I slip out of the car and make my way to the precinct doors. Not until I'm inside and turning around to check the street do I see him pull away, the tires squealing.

Leaving me confused and sad.

And already missing him, as I go in to face this alone.

Something I've been comfortable with all my life.

Until now.

# FORTY-TWO

# SEBASTIAN

She's terrified. I could feel it in the shake of her hands, hear it in the pitch of her voice, see it in her eyes. And I just left her to deal with that alone.

I feel like a complete asshole.

But what she doesn't realize is that I'm just as scared, because everything is going to move at lightning speed from here on in, and if I misstep just once . . .

I'm guessing that Detective Fields found something in Royce's mother's scrapbook. I'm guessing it connects at least Scalero, if not Ricky as well. And I'm guessing whoever Bentley has on the inside will be calling him as soon as the APB is released for his contractors' arrests.

This could all just be my paranoia, but my gut tells me it's not. That this is the loose end—the threat—that they were afraid of.

I stare at the burner phone resting beside me. Itching to hit Dial, to confront Bentley. To ask him when exactly he sold his honor and morality for cash. And why he thought he could use me to help him do it. But that would be the dumbest thing I could do right now, because then I'd be tipping him off and giving those fuck wits a head start.

If I had only myself to think about, I'd do it, and I'd enjoy it. Let them come to me.

But now there's also Ivy to think about, and I can't risk this falling on her.

Which means I need to play my cards right.

And fast.

Rolling down the window, I toss out the battery, then the burner phone, watching the pieces get crushed under the wheels of a truck.

■ ■ ■

Gravel kicks up behind my tires as I speed into the lot. I can just make out Bobby's hulking figure in the office as he shifts around a filing cabinet.

I reconsider this plan of mine. Can I really trust the likes of these guys?

Yeah, I think I can. And I don't have a choice. I know that Fez and the other two don't have the brains or strength to go head-to-head with Ivy. But this two-hundred-and-fifty-pound biker . . . well, he at least has the strength and I don't doubt he has the know-how, one way or another.

And from what I've seen, these guys are honorable enough when it comes to Ivy.

The buzzer goes off as I push through the door. Bobby glances up. "You better not be here to give me any grief about earlier."

"I don't give a shit about that." If Dakota wants to nail this guy, have at it.

"What do you want, then?"

"Is that how you treat all your customers?"

"You need somethin' towed? 'Cause I've missed plenty of work over here on account of helping with Ned's house."

"And you're about to miss some more."

Suspicion fills his face. "Who says?"

I sigh. Threatening him into helping isn't going to get me anywhere. "I need your help with Ivy until I get back."

Tossing the paperwork on the desk, he settles his arms across his chest. "Back from where?"

"Doesn't matter."

His eyes narrow.

I know he's always been suspicious of me. Now I'm going to give him more reason to be. "It has to do with what happened to Ned."

"I knew there was something off about you." His lips twist with disdain. "You a pig?"

I chuckle. "No."

He rounds the desk, his arms dropped and looking ready to grab hold of me. "Did you have something to do with Ned being put down? Because if you did—"

"No. But I know who did."

He seems to consider that. "You better not be lookin' to cash in on whatever it was he was into."

"No, I want nothing to do with that. I want to make sure these guys get what they deserve."

His tongue presses on the inside of his mouth as he considers this. It's language he knows well, I suspect. "Me and my guys would be more than willin' to help—"

"I work alone." I hesitate. "But thanks anyway."

He purses his lips and then nods. "What exactly do I need to do?"

I sigh. "Something Ivy's probably not gonna agree to so easily." I hand him a new burner phone.

"Fuck . . . You're gonna owe me." He shakes his head. "That one's something else when she's mad."

# FORTY-THREE

# IVY

"Yeah. That's the scar."

"You sure?" Detective Fields hovers over my shoulder, his musky cologne the only appealing thing in this place. I was on edge the moment I stepped into the precinct, part of me anxious to turn around and run out, the other part excited to finally nail someone to the wall for what they did to Ned.

"I'm positive." Now that it's come back to me, I remember it well. I even drew a sketch of it that I hold up next to the computer monitor. The guy's hand is blown up and, though pixelated, I can still see the shape of it clearly.

"They're identical," he agrees. "That's . . . crazy how accurate that is."

"Are we done here?" I don't know what I expected, but it wasn't this long-drawn-out process to get to this place. Still, I feel lighter than when I stepped in here. I was afraid that Sebastian was right, and nothing would come of this. That Ned's killers are long gone.

"For now. We'll put APBs out on these guys and bring them in for a lineup. You'll need to come back in to positively ID them."

"You have my number." I collect my purse and stand to leave. "How'd you find them, anyway?"

Fields thumps a handful of folders against his desk to tidy the papers tucked inside. "While I had some of my guys looking into our main angle with the bikers, I thought I'd check out some less likely ones. Just to close the loop. That's what I like to do. So I started looking into Dylan Royce as the potential prime target instead of your uncle. He was an ex-Marine with an impressive record and the know-how to defend himself. I figured whoever took him out had to know what they were doing, gun or not. Made me think that they knew each other, so I started digging into his Marine Corps buddies."

"These two guys were Marines?" An unsettling feeling begins to stir within me. There has been an unusual influx of military guys in my life lately. One in particular.

"Ex. Now they're working for a private security company."

A private security company.

Like Sebastian.

"I've already told you more than I should. Keep it to yourself, okay?" He leads me down the hall, toward the main entrance, files tucked under his arm. "How are repairs going at your house, anyway?"

"Almost ready for paint," I answer, though I'm not really listening anymore, my mind racing. *You're not stupid, Ivy.*

*Sebastian walking into your shop wasn't a coincidence, Ivy.*

I don't want to listen to my conscience, but I can't seem to drown it out anymore, either.

*Be smart, Ivy. He's not really a bodyguard, is he . . .*

Fields's voice finally overpowers my dark worries. ". . . I know this is a bit of a shock to your system. Do you have someone picking you up?"

"My . . ." What is he? ". . . Friend. You know him."

He scans the case folder still tucked under his arm. "Gregory. Or Greg? Yeah."

*What?* "No. Sebastian."

He frowns. "Then, no. Don't know him. I only met the guy at the house the night of the robbery. Anyway, let me know if you need anything, and keep your phone close to you because I'm going to call as soon as we've picked up these guys," he throws over his shoulder, already on his way back to work.

He leaves me standing inside the front doors.

Sebastian gave the cops a fake name. Or is Sebastian the fake name?

No, his parents called him Sebastian.

I shake my head. I think I've reached my limit with that guy for today. The last thing I want to do is see him right now. Let him run his errands. He can come find me and explain shit when he's done. And if he doesn't want to explain?

I'm done.

Even as I tell myself that, I know I'm lying. All he has to do is tell me the truth and I'll accept it, I'm sure of it.

But I *am* going to make him work for it. At least a bit.

I push through the glass doors, intent on defying Sebastian and hailing a cab to Black Rabbit. I'm almost at the sidewalk before I see Bobby's hairy face. My feet falter. "What are you doing here?" Besides Sebastian, he's the last person I want to talk to right now, given how I saw—and heard—way too much of him only hours ago.

"I need you to come with me."

"What?" I snort. "I'm not going anywhere with you."

He heaves a sigh, like he was expecting this. "Your guy asked me to come get you."

Okay, now I know he's full of shit. "No, he didn't. He doesn't trust you."

"Well, I guess he trusts me enough right now."

I grab my phone and quickly hit Dial on Sebastian's number. It goes to automated voice mail. I can't even leave a message. It's been turned off.

What the hell is going on? Sebastian expected me to call when I was finished so he could pick me up, so why is his phone now off? Did these guys do something to him? Did they finally get even for him embarrassing them so badly?

Bobby's heavy boots scrape against the concrete as he closes the distance. All calm, like he's approaching a wild animal, and an edge of unease settles in. I glance around. A few people mill about.

There are security cameras in front of the precinct, pointing down this way. Are they too far?

"Don't make this hard, Ivy." Bobby reaches out and grabs my puny biceps. I can't break free.

He opens the door to the pickup truck. Carl's behind the wheel.

"I'm going to scream." This is an obvious abduction. Why is no one doing anything?

Bobby's hand slaps over my mouth in answer, and then his large arm ropes around me, pinning my arms down. I squirm and kick, and sink my teeth into his fingers, but it's to no avail. In no time I'm lifted and stuffed into the middle of the truck. Bobby slams the door shut, and the truck is roaring to life and heading down the street.

"Did you have to bite me? Fuck!" Bobby yells. "I'm bleeding!"

I open my mouth to let out an ear-piercing scream, when a familiar gruff voice from behind steals my breath.

"Ivy, Jesus! We're not going to hurt you!" Moe sits in the extended cab. He reaches over the seat to cuff Bobby in the head. "What the hell did you say to her?"

"Nothin'! I told you she was gonna be a pain in the ass." To me, he demands, "Gimme your phone."

"No."

He snatches my purse out of my hand and roots around until he's found it. Rolling down the window, he tosses it out.

"Why the hell did you do that?" I yell.

"So no one can find you."

My stomach does a complete flip.

"Oh, relax. Here." He opens a basic flip phone and, pressing Redial, hands it to me.

Sebastian answers on the third ring.

"What is going on?" I can hear an engine in the background. He must be on the road.

"You're with Bobby? Everything okay?"

I look at Bobby's hand, at the marks sunk into his fingers. The sensation of biting into his soft flesh is still fresh on my teeth, making my mouth water in disgust. "Yes."

"Did you ID the guys?"

Do I want to tell him that? Do I trust him? I don't know.

"Ivy," he barks. "It's important that I know. Did you ID them?"

"Yes. They were two ex-Marines that knew Ned's client." How the hell is Ned involved with this? Was he just in the wrong place at the wrong time? Did his gambling debt have anything to do with this after all? There are still far too many unanswered questions.

But I'm focused on one in particular for now. "Who's Gregory White?"

"An alias." He didn't even hesitate.

"Why do you have an alias?"

"I'll explain later. Stay with Bobby. He'll take care of you."

"Fine. But when this is over, you're telling me everything, and I'm not asking."

"Okay, Ivy." There's resignation in his voice.

The phone goes dead. I close it and hand it back to Bobby, who is shooting daggers at me, a ball of tissue in his fist. "Ned always said you were as fucking stubborn as a mule."

■ ■ ■

"Stop sulking."

I eye the giant metal warehouselike building ahead and the chain-link fence surrounding the property. The rows of motorcycles along the far side mark this place for what it is. "Seriously?" It took almost an hour to get to their clubhouse, in a remote neighborhood south of San Francisco. They haven't told me a goddamn thing. Bobby swears he doesn't know anything.

I think he's a big fat fucking liar.

"It's safe here. Fences, security . . ." Bobby says, pointing out the cameras in the corners.

"To keep the bad guys in?"

He chuckles, like that's so funny.

A woman's giggle carries across the parking lot. Probably a

hooker. Ned said these guys throw some wild parties. Though tonight it seems pretty quiet.

I spot my kit in Carl's hand and dive to snatch it out of his grip. "Why do you have this?"

"It was at Dakota's. I swung by to pick it up," Bobby answers with a smile.

"Why?" I already know exactly why.

Moe steps in behind me, settling a hand on my back. I bristle and speed up to walk ahead of him. "Oh, don't be like that with me, girl. Slow down!"

I don't, pushing my way through the solid front doors. The inside of their clubhouse is much more lively than the outside. I count eighteen members sitting around in the makeshift living room/bar, some looking every bit the stereotypical biker with their leather vests and beards, others looking like normal young guys in faded T-shirts and ripped jeans. Open beer bottles are scattered throughout, and the buzz of a radio playing old rock carries through the air. Three scantily clad women float around, cackling at whatever the men are saying.

A few at a time, heads turn at our entrance, and I feel them sizing me up. I don't recognize any of them, but Ned did say this club had over two hundred members.

I wonder how many of them are truly "just bikers." They can't *all* be into the kinds of things that Bobby, Moe, and the others have their hands in.

"How long am I stuck here for?" I ask Moe. I've cycled through panic and anger and have settled into exhaustion. I just want to go home.

"Until Bobby hears otherwise," Moe murmurs, leaving us to chat with the other guys.

"And until then, he promised me you'd do a shoulder piece I was thinking about gettin' done, seeing as he owes me for this and we have time to kill."

"You want me to give you a tattoo now?" I grit my teeth in a smile that can't be pleasant. "*Sure*, I'll do that for you."

Doubt flickers over his face. "Maybe we'll wait until you've cooled off a bit."

"Probably a good idea." Taking a deep breath, I march farther into the clubhouse, putting on my best tough-girl gaze, even though inside I'm feeling anything but.

# FORTY-FOUR

# SEBASTIAN

"How long ago did the APBs go out?" I speed past a slow driver.

"A good hour," Bobby says.

I knew these guys would have someone in the SFPD in their pockets. "She's safe?"

"Yep. Mad as a snake, but nothing we can't handle," Bobby promises. "What are you up to?"

"This and that."

"Right. Well, if you can get 'this and that' done before she bites me again, that'd be great."

Despite everything, I smile. "Thanks, man." It's been a long time since I've relied on anyone but myself, and here I am relying on a bunch of criminals. "Just . . . take care of her." I hang up and toss the phone into the console in time to pull up to my parents' house.

And take a deep breath. I had a feeling I'd be visiting again, sooner rather than later.

My dad answers the door with a frown. "Twice in two days."

"I know." I lock eyes with him, swallowing my fear that he'll say he won't help me. Besides Ivy, he's the only one I trust. "I need your help and I don't have a lot of time to explain."

He looks over his shoulder and then steps out, shutting the door behind him.

I pull a phone and a slip of paper out of my pocket. "There is a sensitive video on this phone that I want you to have a copy of.

Don't watch it. And on the paper is the information for a safe-ty-deposit box in Zurich. It has you marked as next of kin, should anything ever happen to me." I hand it to him. "I need you to make sure these two things are safe. And use the contents, if something happens to me."

His frown turns to understanding. "I don't want to know what this is about, do I?" His voice has taken on that stern, no-nonsense tone that has given me both comfort and fear all my life.

I shake my head. "Not unless you don't hear back from me."

He nods and, with a moment's hesitation, adds, "Be safe."

"I will be," I promise, though I can't be sure that my next stop won't guarantee a bullet in my head.

■ ■ ■

"You found me." Bentley fingers a vine, empty of fruit and ready for winter's slumber. "I didn't expect you here so soon."

"Your wife gave me directions." With a smile and a bat of her eyelashes, all while the cold metal of my gun pressed against my back and I considered using her as leverage.

Bentley doesn't seem at all concerned by my presence. He doesn't seem intent on anything but the grapes, and the western skies, where the sun is slow to set. "There's something therapeutic about this place after it's been harvested. Have you ever seen grape-vines in the winter?"

"No. Not that I've noticed, anyway."

"Well, I guess they're like any plant. They look dead, incapable of ever coming back to life. Of ever producing anything again. And yet they do, year after year, as long as you protect their roots."

It seems like such a casual conversation. If I weren't on edge, I might enjoy it.

But I don't have time to waste here. "Why'd you lie to me?"

He pauses, a dried leaf against his palm. "What was I going to tell you? That I lost control of some of my operatives? That the last boy scout was going to sink Alliance because of it?" He sounds defeated.

"So you did know what was going on over there. What Scalero was doing."

His silence answers me.

"When did it become about money, John? Don't you have enough of that?"

"It's not about the money!" he fires back, his anger flaring. Finally. But he tempers it just as quickly. "You know as well as I do what happens to human instincts when they've succumbed to that world over there. To that kind of life."

"No, not everyone loses themselves like *that.*" We all lose something, but basic decency . . . no. Not most of us, anyway. I'd love to say that *all* the stories of soldiers going off course are wrong, but that would be a lie.

Some people would say that *I* went off course long ago.

"If you knew what was going on, why didn't you stop it?"

He sighs. "I didn't know until it was too late."

"Bullshit."

Weary eyes settle on me. Bentley looks like he's aged years since I saw him last. "Believe what you want, but it's true. Alliance has grown beyond anything I ever expected," he admits. "It's beyond anything I want. I've been in talks with investors for over a year now. People who want to buy me out and take over. They have all kinds of ideas for running internal affairs and managing people. They'll be good for the company's future. Talks stalled for a while during the investigation into the civilian shooting in Kandahar, but they're back on now, and people are ready to sign. Had that videotape surfaced, everything would have fallen apart."

"So it *is* about the money."

"To the investors, it's *all* about the money. If they can't get contracts, there's no point buying Alliance. They want the expertise and connections I've established. The good parts. There are a lot of good parts, still, Sebastian. *You* are a good part."

"I'm not a part of Alliance."

He smiles. "No, you're not. You could be, though."

He's trying to offer me an olive branch. I don't want it. "You used me. Lied right to my face. You and I, we don't do that to each other."

"You would never have agreed to this assignment otherwise. I needed that videotape and you're the best at what you do. You always have been. Even now, when I'm guessing you're about to fuck me over." Bentley reaches into his pocket and I immediately move to grab my gun. He pulls out a loose cigarette and lighter, his hands raised as if to prove his innocence. "So, what's your plan here, exactly?"

"You know about the APBs on Scalero and Porter."

He nods, the end of his cigarette burning brighter with his inhale.

"Your guys are about to get nailed for murder, with a witness."

"With no line of sight on the actual murder."

"So you're saying you don't consider her to be a threat?"

He exhales, smoke sailing out his nostrils and into the crisp air. "I didn't say that."

"I didn't think so."

His lips purse. "I never thought a woman would be the death of our friendship."

"She isn't. But you lying to me is." I'm not used to being in this position with Bentley—the one in control of the situation. That's what I feel like I finally have here—control of this fucking disastrous situation. "Are they after her yet?" Now would be the ideal time to make Ivy disappear, before she's able to listen to Scalero's deep midwestern accent or see the burn scar covering the back of his hand, or study Porter's profile, and confirm on a recorded lineup that, yes, these are the two men who killed a Medal of Honor veteran and her uncle. Once that official statement is made, getting rid of her won't help them any.

"No."

"You're lying."

"How would that look, the witness turning up dead hours after an APB goes out? Give me some credit." He pauses to take another drag. "They're in a secure location for the moment."

"They need to answer for what they've done, Bentley. Tell me you know that."

"I do. That's why I called you the other day, but you refused to take the assignment and hung up on me."

Scalero and Porter were my next assignment? "You mean I was going to be tasked with getting rid of those two so your ass is covered completely?" I chuckle, though none of this is funny. He must take me for an idiot.

He turns to meet my eyes, his hard and gray. "And what exactly is your plan, then, coming here? Is it any different?"

When I don't answer—because getting rid of those two is exactly my plan—he continues. "Despite what you think, I don't want anything to happen to you. I wouldn't be standing here today if it weren't for you. And you and I have saved tens of thousands of lives together. Maybe more. What I have built here? Fuck the media. Alliance is a powerful organization that does incredible things. Yes, I make a lot of money because of it. Yes, there are . . . hiccups . . . Bad seeds, like those two. But I won't let them tear down my legacy to this country. I need Scalero and Porter dealt with before they can hurt anyone else. I wish I'd figured that out sooner. Save everyone a headache."

"They do need to go. But they also need to answer for what they've done."

I reach for my phone and Bentley's eyes widen in a flash of panic. Holding the screen out for him, I press Play on the video. Royce's voice breaks into the quiet peace of the vineyard, and understanding fills Bentley's eyes.

"I made copies of the video. Several. You'll never track them all down before they're released, I can promise you that." In this case, I'm bluffing. My dad has the only copy, and I'm sure he went straight to the bank to secure it in his safety-deposit box. "So if you're lying to me and they're out there looking for Ivy, you might want to stop them now."

He doesn't make a move for his phone. "What exactly do you want from me?"

"You're going to tell me where Mario Scalero and Ricky Porter are right now."

"There's no need for the theatrics." He gestures to the ended video. "We want the same thing."

I don't think he understands, exactly. But he will.

"Give me their location, and I'll do the right thing."

He sighs. "And then?"

"And then I'm going to walk away, and this arrangement of ours is over." I can't do this and live a normal life. "You're going to forget about me, you're going to forget about Ivy, and everyone wins."

"It's not that simple, Sebastian."

"It is. Because if you don't, and if for some reason something should happen to either Ivy or me, then everything I've done for you over the past five years will fall into big hands. Names, dates, locations, purposes. *Everything.*" While I may not have listened to my father's warning when Bentley first invited me to work for him, I did hear it. And it ate at me, an insipid voice that grew louder and louder, until I couldn't completely ignore it. And so I began documenting critical details, figuring that if something ever happened to me, my father could see firsthand that I was doing good, that his disappointing son was making a difference, was saving lives. Maybe he would finally approve of me.

Never did I think I'd be using that information as leverage against Bentley, and yet here I am, doing exactly that.

Bentley's eyes narrow. He thinks I've betrayed him. He's right, but I don't really have a choice.

"As long as nothing happens to either of us, that information will never see the light of day," I promise.

"How can I believe—"

"Because unlike you, I can be trusted."

Bentley chews the inside of his mouth. He's always been good at knowing when he's cornered, with no way out. It rarely happens. "I'm not going to walk away from this unscathed, am I?"

"No. But you'll walk away because you finally did the right thing." I meet his gaze. "Where are they?"

He grits his teeth.

# FORTY-FIVE

# IVY

"This isn't exactly like the picture!"

"No, it's better." I start pulling apart my tattoo machine to clean it.

"She's right," Ren, a twentysomething-year-old blond guy with a giant smile and a bad habit of flirting with anything female, says, winking at me.

Bobby studies the rottweiler riding a bike in the mirror, then glares at me.

I stop what I'm doing to fold my arms over my chest and stand my ground. "Am I wrong?"

"No," he grudgingly admits.

"Well, then." I glance at the clock on the wall. Two a.m. "How much longer?"

He shrugs. "There's a bed in the back that you can use for the night."

With crusted semen from God only knows how many of these guys? "I'm fine." I've seen two guys stroll out from the dark, dingy hall that leads to the unknown part of the clubhouse since I've been here.

The same stupid, sated grin on their faces, the same hooker on their arms.

"Okay. Ain't gonna fight with you."

"Finally . . ." I mutter, earning his snort.

"Oh, look who it is . . . perfect timing." He reaches into his pocket and pulls out the flip phone. I dive for it, but he's too tall, twisting out of the way to answer. "Yup . . . yup . . . all good."

I drill into Bobby's face with my impatient glare, making him uncomfortable enough to finally mutter, "Jesus, talk to her. She's drivin' me nuts." He thrusts the phone into my waiting hands.

As annoyed and confused as I am right now, I also miss Sebastian. I've gone from being with the man all day, every day, to being locked up in a smelly biker clubhouse with vague, random phone calls and no information to sustain me.

"Hey."

"Hi." Sebastian's voice is low and soft, as if he's trying to keep quiet. I can't hear anything in the background. "Are they treating you well?"

"Yeah, fine. Where are you?" *What are you doing? Is it one of those things that people won't approve of?*

Silence answers me.

"Will I approve of this?"

After a long moment. "Yes. At least, I hope so." I hear the sorrow in his voice, the worry.

"Just tell me I won't be held hostage by these bikers for much longer."

Bobby grumbles something unintelligible behind me.

"I've gotta go. I just needed to hear your voice."

"You're safe, right?" Will he end up with another bullet in his leg? Or worse?

"See you soon, Ivy."

The phone goes dead, leaving me with an odd, inexplicable sense of dread.

I try to slide the phone into my pocket, but Bobby snatches it out of my hand. He settles onto his stool and takes a swig of his beer, nodding at my drink. "Now that you're done working on me, I'll let you have a drink."

"Let me?" I roll my eyes. "Whiskey, neat."

The middle-aged Mexican playing bartender pours me a shot

of Wild Turkey—I cringe, but he merely shrugs and says that's all they've got—and I slam it back, earning Bobby's laugh. "You know, you're your uncle's niece, that's for sure. I can see why Ned was so happy to have you around." He heaves a sigh. "He used to sit in that very seat after a game. Just for one or two, though."

"He never was a big drinker." I haven't felt that painful ball in my throat for some time now, but it flares up at the mention of Ned. Probably because I don't have Sebastian to distract me. "Why did Sebastian send you to get me?" Why would Sebastian want me locked up here, behind walls and chain-metal fence and security? It's obviously to keep me safe, but from whom?

"He had something he needed to do."

*"Bobby."*

He avoids answering by taking another swig of his beer.

"You've basically kidnapped me. I think you could at least tell me why."

"Can't. Promised your guy."

"So you're more loyal to him than to me?"

"No, I was loyal to Ned. That's why I'm doin' this." He purses his lips, as if he just said more than he wanted.

"So this is about Ned." I pause, as puzzle pieces begin clicking into place. I still don't have any answer, really. But I think I've figured out one. "Sebastian knows who killed Ned, doesn't he?"

After a moment, Bobby offers only a nod and then a shrug. "Told you there was something off about him."

"Yes, you did." And I dismissed it because I was too busy falling hard for the guy. It's odd, but Bobby's confirmation is somehow anticlimactic for me. I think my subconscious had already accepted it along with everything else about Sebastian that I can't explain.

I tap the counter with my empty shot glass, waiting for another round, as I run through all kinds of questions in my head. Did Sebastian know *before* he met me, or did he find out at some point after? Who does he work for? Why the hell did he let me tattoo half his torso with my design?

320    K.A. TUCKER

But more worrying to me than anything else right now . . .
Does he really care about me, or has this all been some big scam?

Because that will crush me.

All these thoughts are going on under the mask of calm that
I've mastered as I throw back my drink.

Bobby watches me warily, as if he expects me to suddenly
explode.

"What?" I ask, and I realize my voice is way too steady.

"I figured you'd take that news a little harder."

I divert the subject away from me and my feelings. "If you
think there's something wrong with him, then why are you helping
him?"

Bobby considers that for a long moment. "Because I don't
think he means you any harm."

And yet he'll probably break my heart into a million tiny
pieces.

"Look, you two can hash all that out when you see him again. I
don't get involved in this shit. If you want uncomplicated, come sit
on my lap. Otherwise, drink, ink, sleep . . . or shut up."

Exactly the kind of answer I'd expect from a guy like Bobby. I
wave my empty shot glass at the guy behind the bar, who promptly
fills it again.

"To Ned," Bobby says.

I clink my glass against his. "To Ned."

# FORTY-SIX

# SEBASTIAN

The dilapidated trailer shows no signs of life—no lights, no sound. Apparently this is Ricky's uncle's property. Ricky dropped a trailer on it last year. He likes to come out here for weekends and shoot targets.

It took just over four hours for me to get to this middle-of-nowhere location, just outside Reno, Nevada. If I couldn't see the nose of an old Chevy pickup tucked behind the trailer, I'd think Bentley had sent me here on a wild-goose chase to get me away from San Francisco and Ivy. Had I not already secured her safety, I would have dragged him here with me just to be sure.

As it is, this could be a trap.

I move quietly and slowly in the dark until I find a sizable rock to hide behind. From there, I settle in, using night-vision binoculars that I swiped from Bentley's stash.

And I wait. For four hours, ignoring the cold, surrounded by nothing but desert and rocks and the high-pitched barks of coyotes circling their kill, until I'm sure that no one is on alert, waiting for me.

And then I move in, slithering beneath the truck and behind the tires to lie in wait.

The sky is beginning to lighten when I finally hear movement inside the trailer. Footfalls. Someone rolling out of bed.

My heart begins to race as it always does, as adrenaline kicks in, hoping that everything goes according to plan. It's so easy for these things to derail, especially when there's more than one person involved.

Moments later, the door swings open with a loud creak and bang. I'm careful to hide behind the wheel as I watch Mario step out, his nose still puffy and slightly discolored. His gaze drifts over the wide expanse of land. Someone else would think he's simply taking in the terrain, but I know better.

He rounds the corner with a stretch and then pulls his sweatpants down to take his morning piss, his back to me.

That's when I roll out, gun aimed, silencer on.

And close the distance silently, like I've been trained to do so well.

He deserves this. For all those girls he raped.

And to keep Ivy safe.

He deserves it because otherwise he's going to get away with it. And maybe do it again.

I wait until he turns around, until our eyes lock, but it's not long enough for him to react.

And just like that, in seconds, half of my problem is gone, and Ned's killer has been punished.

Ricky, still asleep in his bed, is a quick finish, too.

That's usually what my job is—hours, even days of preparation, seconds of execution.

And then I get to the real work, setting the stage for the cops.

# FORTY-SEVEN

# IVY

"Why couldn't we take the truck again?"

"Carl needed it," Bobby yells over his shoulder.

I glower at the back of his head as his Harley turns down Dakota's street. I'd like to punch him in the ribs, but I want to make it home alive, so I keep my hands where they are, with my kit sandwiched between the two of us. I refused to leave it behind. "What exactly did Sebastian say?" I'm still pissed that Bobby didn't wake me up when the phone rang. He says he tried, and I snarled at him and burrowed farther into the grimy leather couch in response, but I think he's bullshitting me. He also let me sleep in—something I only do after shooting half a bottle of cheap whiskey to keep my idle mind distracted.

"That he'd meet you at home."

My stomach does a nervous flip. I still have no idea what I'm going to say to him when I see him.

That I know he's been lying to me about everything?

Turns out I don't have to figure it out just yet. There is no navy Acura in the driveway. Bobby pulls in behind my car and I hop off the back of his bike, glad to have two boots on the ground. Dakota waits in the doorway with a smile and a coffee for me.

I think it's for me, only Bobby is trailing me in and she's smiling at him, too.

He's a sucker if he thinks that's going anywhere. "You owe me a new phone, by the way."

"Take it up with your guy," he grumbles, already dismissing me, his attention glued to my friend in her loose, flowing dress.

I roll my eyes. "Has Sebastian been around?"

Dakota shakes her head. "No. Sorry."

I grab a glass of water and Advil and duck into my room, glad for the privacy, something I haven't had since yesterday morning. Locking the bathroom doors, I take an extra-long shower, until I'm sure that I've missed whatever live show might be going on next door.

And then I curl up in my bed and wait for Sebastian to come home to me.

# FORTY-EIGHT

# SEBASTIAN

She looks so small, so fragile, so beautiful, her black hair splayed across the white pillows like streaks of paint, the evening's light soft across her sleeping body, wrapped in a blue towel.

I want to savor this peace—her peace—for a while longer, because I honestly don't know how Ivy's going to react to the truth. I'd like to think she'll take it in stride, like she's taken everything so far. But I have to prepare myself for the reality that she may be done with me after this.

And the idea of that scares the hell out of me.

So I simply stand there and watch her sleep, until she must sense me because her eyes flutter open and she sits up with a start.

My stomach twists into knots.

"Sebastian." She reaches out with a hand, beckoning me. "You're okay."

"I am." *For now.*

Her eyes rove over me and then freeze and jump to meet mine, as if silently reprimanding herself for her thoughts. I feel the sudden switch in temperature, as she goes from concern to anger and hurt. It's damn near icy, and it makes me shiver. "You're not a bodyguard, are you?"

"No."

"And you didn't just happen to hear about my work from your friend Mike, did you?"

I sigh. "No."

She grits her teeth. "And you know who killed my uncle."

She's pretty much figured everything out on her own as it is. At least that will make this slightly easier. I won't feel like I'm slapping her across the face as I deliver each truth to replace my lies.

"I told you not to make me ask."

I reconciled myself to telling her everything on the long drive here. If this is ever going to work, she needs to know. And if she doesn't want anything to do with me after she knows . . .

My stomach clenches at the thought.

I take a seat on the edge of the bed, but I don't dare reach out to touch her. "That day I walked into your shop for the first time?"

"Yeah," she says with wariness.

"I was there for a videotape." I meet her gaze. "And maybe to kill you."

# FORTY-NINE

# IVY

I've never felt so many different emotions for one person over the course of an evening.

It quickly began with the overwhelming urge to vomit, as Sebastian described, in great detail, how he followed me, studied me and, after searching Ned's house top to bottom for this video, decided to befriend me.

I flew straight for my case, tearing out the foam inset to run my fingers over the interior. Feeling the sticky residue left by the duct tape that Sebastian says held that damned video in place.

I can't believe Ned would put it there for me to find.

I can't believe Ned tried to blackmail someone to get out of his financial hole.

He got himself killed because of it.

He almost got *me* killed because of it, although I still can't believe he ever thought it would come to this point.

I don't know what to do with this reality yet. I can't ever tell Ian. He'll go back to hating his father all over again, and I don't want him to feel that way toward Ned.

And then Sebastian went on to explain how his assignment was done, but how he didn't want to leave, both because he wasn't sure that I would be safe and because he just didn't want to leave me. Because he had grown attached to me. I fought against the swell in my chest. I'm still fighting against it, because it's not right.

It *can't* be right.

At least all his strange, guarded behavior now makes sense.

Turns out I *did* need a bodyguard.

Only Sebastian isn't a bodyguard.

"So, what exactly do you call yourself?"

"I don't call myself anything." His deep, cool voice fills the darkness in the room. "I just do my job."

I peer down at those hands. Hands that have been all over my body *so* many times. Hands that have made me so happy.

Hands that have ended lives, and not just as a soldier at war.

As a calculated hunter.

"And that job is to kill people?"

"Sometimes. Yes." I feel his eyes on my face. They've been there this entire conversation, weighing my every reaction, my every word. "Only when it's necessary. And only when killing them saves lives."

"Why kill Ned, then?"

He hesitates. "I didn't kill your uncle, Ivy."

"But you know who did. You knew all along and you lied to me."

"It was safer for you not to know."

Because the guy was following us. I shudder. At the club. At the store, the day Sebastian "walked into a wall" and cut his lip. In Ned's house. No wonder Sebastian was sitting by the window with a gun. No wonder his gaze was always on everything around us. No wonder he wouldn't let me out of his sight.

My throat grows thick with a sizable knot. "And now?"

"Now . . . they got what they deserved. Both for what they did to Royce and your uncle, and for the things they've done to others. They won't be a problem for you."

I turn to look at him. "Did you . . ." I let my voice drift. Do I even want to know? Is knowing this safe for me, given who he is, what he is? "Don't answer that." Maybe they did deserve it. I don't even know how to begin wrapping my head around that.

The only thing I'm sure of right now is that when Sebastian

strolled into Black Rabbit and settled that deep, dark gaze on me, he knew that there was a chance he'd have to kill me.

And he still charmed me with his smile and his looks. Made me care about him.

How can I possibly ever forgive that? How can I trust him again?

I can't.

My eyes start burning. "I need you to leave."

"Ivy, I—"

"Get out." I pull my covers tight around me, hoping for comfort that I know I won't get.

Easing off the bed, Sebastian moves for the door. "Everything I've told you tonight—"

"Don't tell a soul or you'll have to kill me, right? Something along those lines?" My voice is hollow.

Sadness fills his eyes as he stares long and hard at me. "That'll never happen." He slips out quietly.

I manage to hold the tears until the door clicks shut.

■ ■ ■

"Why don't you just call him?" Dakota says through a sip of coffee.

"Because I don't want to."

"Liar."

"I don't have a phone."

"Use mine."

"I don't have his number."

His number is in the phone that's smashed on a San Francisco street somewhere. That's probably a good thing right now. It's been five days since I sent him away, and I miss him. I shouldn't miss him. I should hate him. I should be terrified of him. But I'm not, because I've only ever felt safer with him.

I sigh. "Everything's fucked-up right now."

"Really? That's not how I see it. Your house is fixed and ready to be painted. You're going to stay in San Francisco and run your own tattoo shop. You have an amazing roommate who adores you, and you have a gorgeous, nice guy who's crazy about you." She grins. "Sounds pretty perfect to me."

"I think you've forgotten a few details . . ." I haven't divulged anything about Sebastian to her. I'm no idiot. That kind of information goes to my grave. Hopefully it's a long time before I find my way into it.

Either way, Dakota knows that something monumentally bad has happened over the last few days. She's wiped away enough of my tears to figure that out.

"Not the important ones."

I spear her with a glare while I munch on one of her baked squares, secretly hoping it's loaded with hash so I can shed this melancholy for a few hours. I've become the girl I can't stand, and I couldn't be bothered to do anything to change that.

I'm brokenhearted over a guy and yet completely miserable without him.

"Hey, D! Where do you keep the sweetener?" Bobby hollers from the kitchen.

I groan, my head falling back. *"Why him?"*

She giggles. "Why not?" To him she says, "The cupboard next to the fridge."

"You realize he's a criminal, right?"

She winks. "I like to walk on the wild side sometimes."

*"Sometimes?"* Dakota *is* the wild side.

She reaches over and pats my knee. "Cheer up. I don't like seeing you so despondent. It's concerning."

"I'm just very . . . confused and conflicted. I don't know how I'm supposed to feel."

She purses her lips. "Forget about how you're *supposed* to feel and focus on how you *do* feel."

I feel . . . like I want to see Sebastian again, so badly. "But what if how I do feel is wrong? What if it's a bad idea?"

"Does it hurt anybody?"

I frown. "Well, no. I don't think so." Except maybe me, and my heart.

She shrugs. "Then I don't see how it's wrong, or a bad idea. Besides, you're not usually the type of girl to worry about those kinds of things. Why start now?"

Bobby saunters into the greenhouse in nothing but jeans.

I avert my gaze with a sigh. "This house is getting way too small, too fast."

"You sure didn't seem to mind when you had your guy here."

I climb out of my seat, both to free it up for him and to get dressed for a day of painting at the house, so we can get it on the market. And then I have to decide what I want to do about Black Rabbit.

And here I thought I had decided already . . .

"Yeah, well." I slap his protruding belly. "The view was slightly different."

"D likes this view."

"That's right, I do," she says with a playful voice.

"As much as the view of Sebastian in the shower, D?" I throw over my shoulder.

"What the hell were you doin' in the shower with him!" Bobby says, his voice suddenly full of irritation.

"It was nothing," Dakota says in a placating voice. "Ivy's just trying to get under your skin. She's good at that."

The doorbell rings, and I'm distracted from listening to Bobby's irate answer.

Detective Fields and two officers are standing on the doorstep. He heaves a visible sigh of relief. To the cops, he nods, and one of them radios in to dispatch, something about the witness being located. "I've been trying to call you."

"I lost my phone."

He hesitates. "I have an update on your uncle's case. Can I come in?"

"No!" Bobby yells, his footfalls hard and fast as he storms up behind me to barricade the door. "It's a nice day out. You should talk right here." He gives me a knowing look, and I immediately get his meaning.

Dakota's little grow-op.

"It *is* a nice day." I grab Dakota's sweater off a hook and pull it on to ward off the cold, and step onto the curb, shutting the door behind me. "What's up?"

Fields frowns at me—I think he assumes I'm the one sleeping with Bobby—but he doesn't push it. "The two men who we suspect of involvement in your uncle's murder were found yesterday in Nevada. Dead."

I take a deep, shaky breath. *No, I guess they won't be a problem for me anymore.* "How?" That sounds like the right next question to ask. Plus, I want to know how Sebastian did it. Was it quick and clean? Cruel and morbid? Will it make any difference to me?

"The investigators over there are suggesting that it's murder-suicide, cut-and-dried. We'll know more after the autopsy reports, though."

I close my eyes. Quick and clean, at least. Like I'd expect from Sebastian. Do I care? Do I feel bad for them?

I think back to that night, to the fear they inflicted on me, to the pain they inflicted on my uncle. To the fact that they shot two people—would have shot me, too, had they known I was there—all to cover their asses for other horrible, unspeakable crimes they committed. Sebastian didn't give me too many details, but he gave me enough.

I don't feel bad that they're dead.

Does that make me evil?

"So . . . what does that mean for my uncle's case?" I ask, pushing that worry aside.

"Well, that's the thing. There was some evidence found along with the bodies. A phone with a video of your uncle and the other victim, Dylan Royce. It's"—he frowns—"of interest to a lot of important people. There are likely answers to motive in it, but it's going to take some time to figure that out."

I'm guessing that's the very video that Sebastian was here to recover. He did say he was going to make sure the truth came out.

That none of this should ever have happened. That he wanted to make things right.

Did he plant it?

"Okay. Well, thanks for letting me know."

I watch Fields and the cops leave in two cars. Curtains rustle and doors close as curious neighbors go back to their daily grind, the excitement over for the meantime. With a sigh, I turn to go inside, when I spot the black Ford F-150 pickup parked just down the street. A single figure sits behind the wheel.

My heart skips a few beats.

Before I can talk myself out of it, I march toward it.

FIFTY

# SEBASTIAN

I sit up straight as she approaches my truck, her arms hugging her body to ward off the chill. She comes around the passenger side and throws the door open.

Our eyes meet, and I have no idea what to expect.

Is she going to tell me to go to hell for good?

That I'm about to go to jail because she set that detective after me?

"Recent upgrade?" Her gaze skates over the interior of my new truck. She's not wearing any makeup. She looks like she hasn't slept. I know I haven't. For days.

"Something like that."

She climbs in, needing the step to make it. "Could you have found something bigger?"

I clench my fists to keep from reaching out and grabbing her, pulling her close to me. "I was actually looking at a Hummer. But decided against it." I'm out of a job, so even though I have enough money to last me awhile, it won't last forever. As it is, this is a rental. I'm not ready to commit just yet.

I crank the engine. She plays with the knobs until some heat starts pumping out. "It suits you more than that Acura."

I finally left that in the covered garage where I was supposed to weeks ago, but not before having it thoroughly detailed and wiping down my prints. The Beretta is still in my boot. I'm not ready to ditch that.

A long, uncomfortable silence fills the truck, and I brace myself for the moment that she moves to leave.

"Aren't you going to ask me what I told the cops?" she asks.

"No."

"I didn't tell them anything."

*I know.* I've known all along that I can trust her. She may hate me now, but I know I can still trust her. Except, I don't think she hates me. Her mask is on, but she's never been able to veil her eyes well.

"Can I show you something?" Will she trust me to take her somewhere?

After a long moment, she simply nods.

■ ■ ■

"A little to the left."

I put my shoulders into the new chair, shimmying it over a few inches. It weighs a good fifty pounds more than the last one. I know because I loaded it into my truck last night after visiting three wholesale stores for the top-of-the-line client chair—according to the sales guy—complete with hydraulic lifts and a full recline option.

"A little more."

I follow her instructions.

"Hmm . . . no. That's not right. Maybe back to the right."

"You're kidding me, right?" Ivy's perched comfortably in her chair, legs propped on the new front desk and crossed at her ankles, her slippers tapping the surface. I'm not used to seeing her in anything but boots, but I guess she wasn't planning on going anywhere besides the front porch when the detective rang the bell.

She flips through a magazine, feigning indifference. "Yeah, I am. I just wanted to make you sweat a little."

There's the attitude I've missed so much. "You like making me sweat?"

She tries to hide the smirk by adjusting her chair farther away from me, to face the brand-new monitor.

"So? What do you think?"

Her eyes roam the space—the newly hung mirrors to the new, black window shades, to the security system that I had wired, to the floors that I sanded down and varnished in a warm honey finish, with the help of Fez and Bobby.

Black Rabbit is basically ready for business.

"I think your ease with breaking into places makes me very uncomfortable."

"Besides that."

She tosses the magazine to the desk. "Why'd you do all this for me?" There's a hint of vulnerability in her voice now.

"Because I don't want you to leave San Francisco."

She snorts. "You don't even live here."

"I will. If you're staying."

"And if I'm not?"

"Then I guess I'm not." I wander over to lean against the desk, lifting her legs at the ankles and settling her feet on my lap. "I want everything to go back to the way it was before."

"It can't go back to that."

"I know. But we can go to something better." No more lies.

We simply stare at each other. We've gotten good at doing that, of communicating without words. Like, right now, I'm hoping she understands how sorry I am that she went through this, how I did everything I could to protect her, how I can't stand the idea that this is the end of us.

She nods toward the monitor. "What do you think about these for the waiting area?"

I smile. She'll probably never be one to talk openly about her feelings, but that's okay. We seem to manage just fine without words.

I check out the screen, stealing a feel of her calf as I run my hand up along her leg. She doesn't pull away. "What are they?"

"What do you mean 'what are they'? They're chairs."

I snort, taking in the abstract orange plastic shape. "Those aren't chairs."

"Yes. They are. See? Chairs." She taps the screen.

"Hmm . . ." I switch positions, releasing her legs and coming up behind her, crouching to rest my chin on her shoulder, breathing in the scent of her, watching her chest rise with a deep inhale, as I look at the screen. "Still don't look like chairs."

"Well, they are."

I tap on the exorbitant price next to them. "You want to spend that on something that ninety percent of your clients won't use because they won't be able to identify?"

"Carry on with your grunt work, then, man servant," she mutters, waving an annoyed hand toward the chair. But when I make to move, that hand lands on the back of my head, pulling my mouth to hers. Her fingers weave into my hair as our faces mash together in a deep kiss that could easily mean good-bye.

She breaks away abruptly to peer up at me. "This doesn't mean I've forgiven you."

"I know."

Her breath skates across my face in a deep sigh.

And then she's kissing me again.

# SEBASTIAN

TWO MONTHS LATER

We step through the door and she inhales deeply. "Mmmm . . . sawdust." Her eyes wander over the interior of the house, about halfway between her uncle's—now sold—and Dakota's.

The real estate agent handed me the keys twenty-four hours ago.

"It needs some work. A new kitchen . . ."

She opens the door to the main-floor bathroom. I gutted it this morning while she was working.

"A new bathroom . . ."

She peers over her shoulder at me, her typical cool, coy smirk on display. "Plumbing issues. How ironic."

I smile at the dig. "The bathroom upstairs works, if you need it."

She makes her way into the kitchen, her hand running along the smooth marble countertop, her gaze on the cheap, white melamine cupboards. "It's nice." A mischievous glint catches her gaze. "A bit . . . boring."

"Are you calling me boring?" I stretch my navy T-shirt out with my hands. My "uniform," as Ivy mocks. "Even with this?" I peel it off to reveal her handiwork, now fully healed.

Fire lights in her eyes, like I knew it would.

I rope my arms loosely around her waist. "You can help me with the design, then. You're better at that sort of thing."

"That's right, I am. You're just the brute strength." Her hands slide over my biceps and her gaze wander the space again. "So I guess this means you're officially staying in San Francisco?" Dark, almond-shaped eyes land on mine, pleading quietly.

"I'm not going anywhere." I bought the house outright, sinking a good chunk of my savings into it.

That makes her smile. "How long do you think it'll take before you can move in?"

"Before *we* can move in?" We're already living together at Dakota's, and I know Ivy's dying to get out of there. Dakota's moved on from Bobby to a strange meditation guru who smokes as much weed as Dakota does. You can't have a morning coffee in the greenhouse without getting high off fumes. "Depends on work." I started with a security company two weeks ago, a connection through my father, a fellow navy officer who runs a company focused mainly on advanced training of troops and police officers. It took a few interviews to land the job, and a good heart-to-heart about exactly what happened in Afghanistan to earn me my less than honorable discharge.

I haven't heard from Bentley since that day in his vineyard, and I don't expect to know anything besides what I see on the news. Two weeks after Scalero and Porter died, Bentley sold Alliance to investors for enough money to keep him comfortable until the day he dies. But not too peacefully.

It seems the video found at the "murder-suicide" site of Alliance contractors Mario Scalero and Richard Porter has found its way to the investigative journalist Dorris Maclean after all, care of an anonymous video file mailed to her desk. It may never amount to anything, given the two men Royce accused are dead, but it's made for one hell of a news story.

While it doesn't bring Ned back, it made Ivy feel like he didn't go down without a fight. And I'll do anything to ease her pain over her uncle's death.

Ivy has handled the truth about my past better than I ever expected. There are some more specific details that she doesn't need to know and doesn't want to know. The hows and whos she doesn't want to hear about.

But the whys help her understand. And, on the odd occasion, late at night, when I find myself wanting to talk and needing her reassurances, she's always willing to listen.

She's never afraid.

And she's always there to ease my conscience.

"Let me show you the rest of the place." I grab her by the hips and hoist her tiny body over my shoulder with no effort.

"You know I hate being manhandled," she mutters, but she doesn't fight me when I carry her straight to the master bedroom. "You're painting this, right?" She cringes at the stark, cold white.

"Any color you want."

She nods, her wheels spinning as she wanders around the bright space, the south wall full of windows, stopping in front of the closet. She runs her fingers along the slats. "Just like at Ned's house," she murmurs.

I know exactly what she's thinking about.

I had no intention of ever telling her about that day. But one night, after hours of intensive interrogation involving harsh sexual manipulation, I finally admitted to spying on her.

I got the cold shoulder for two days.

"I think I like this house." She steps into the closet and closes the door.

And clears her throat, as if she's waiting.

*Fuck . . .*

I hang my head and smile.

"You're still not forgiven . . ." she reminds me with her trademark icy tone.

I think I actually am. She just enjoys the leverage she has far too much.

Oddly enough, so do I.

With a deep sigh, I unbuckle my belt.

# ACKNOWLEDGMENTS

Oh, Ivy. What a challenge you proved to be. You are who you are, not because you're broken or damaged or scarred. You're just you, and it was difficult finding the right match for you. I think I found him, though, in an equally complex character.

*Surviving Ice* concludes the planned books for this series, one that I am proud to have written. I strive to make each book unique, and each story line make sense for the character. The raw, sometimes dodgy elements of this story feel right for Ivy.

While this story is a work of fiction, the challenges that come with employing private security companies during war is very real. If you're unfamiliar, you should take some time to google news stories surrounding them, especially during the war on Iraq. Many of my plots are inspired by real-life news stories. *Surviving Ice* is another such one.

Thank you to my readers, for picking up this book, and every other book I've written. Whether you buy a print copy at your local bookstore, or order it online, or borrow it from your local library/sister/friend/mother, you are helping to give me the opportunity to write books.

Thank you to the bloggers who continue sharing my book releases within their world.

Thank you to my publicist, KP—for being patient with me,

and protecting me from a lot of the everyday things I couldn't deal with while writing TWO books at the same time, under tight deadlines.

Thank you to my agent, Stacey Donaghy—for sitting in Pickle Barrel and hashing out the plot of this book over a plate of bacon and waffles. Even though I had to make some major modifications to our plot ideas and Stan Donaghy the thug just didn't fit into the plot anymore, those breakfast dates are half the fun of writing books.

Thank you to my editor, Sarah Cantin— for your superhuman patience. You helped me save this book when it passed "lost" and kept going down a scary path.

To my publisher, Judith Curr, and the team at Atria Books: Suzanne Donahue, Ariele Fredman, Tory Lowy, Kimberly Goldstein, and Alysha Bullock—for another beautiful series, complete!

To my family—I promise I will never write two books at the same time ever again.